Field of Schemes

A LLOYD KEATON MYSTERY

FIELD OF SCHEMES

JOHN BILLHEIMER

FIVE STAR
A part of Gale, Cengage Learning

Detroit • New York • San Francisco • New Haven, Conn • Waterville, Maine • London

Five Star™ Publishing, a part of Gale, Cengage Learning.

This novel is a work of fiction. Names, characters, places and incidents are either the product of the author's imagination, or, if real, used fictitiously.

LIBRARY OF CONGRESS CATALOGING-IN-PUBLICATION DATA

Billheimer, John W.
Field of schemes : a Lloyd Keaton mystery / John Billheimer. — 1st ed.
p. cm.
ISBN 978-1-4328-2617-8 (hardcover) — ISBN 1-4328-2617-4 (hardcover) 1. Sportswriters—Fiction. 2. Doping in sports—Fiction. 3. Baseball—Fiction. I. Title.
PS3552.I452F54 2012
813'.54—dc23 2012015256

First Edition. First Printing: September 2012.
Published in conjunction with Tekno Books and Ed Gorman.
Find us on Facebook– https://www.facebook.com/FiveStarCengage
Visit our website– http://www.gale.cengage.com/fivestar/
Contact Five Star™ Publishing at FiveStar@cengage.com

Printed in Mexico
1 2 3 4 5 6 7 16 15 14 13 12

In memory of J. B. Moore and David Oke, whose friendship, humor, talent, and love of baseball are missed by all who knew them.

ACKNOWLEDGMENTS

Every work of fiction reflects some matters of fact. As always, I am indebted to a number of people who helped me get a few facts straight. These include Denis and Gail Boyer Hayes of the firm Hayes, Hayes, and Hayes for legal advice; Bob and Dale Lewis for pharmaceutical details; and Dr. Howard Sussman for insights into pathology and the history of amphetamine use. Any blame for misstatements in these matters belongs to the author.

In the interests of sharing the blame, I once again wish to acknowledge the contributions of the Wednesday Night Wine Tasting and Literary Society, whose members help to keep me upbeat, upstanding, and up-to-date. The West Coast contingent of this quasi-elite group includes Sheila Scobba Banning, Mark Coggins, and Ann Hillesland.

And I would be remiss if I failed to acknowledge an East Coast stringer, Sheila York, whose sharp editorial eye and good sense have saved me from embarrassment on more than one occasion.

"When you have a responsible job, you've got to accept the responsibility."

—Birdie Tebbetts, manager of the Cleveland Indians, 1963

Chapter One: The Great American Piss-Time

KEATON'S KORNER

The Menckenburg Mammoths, nine and one over their last ten starts, have turned a dreadful opening into an impressive May. Second-baseman Austin Reed is leading the International League in hitting, and Sam Tancredi, who was zip-for-April, is burning up the league this month and looks a lot like the Slamming Sammy who was in the running for A.L. Rookie of the Year before he was suspended two years ago for doping. Let's just hope the Tribe doesn't call him back to the majors before the Mammoths' AAA season ends.

It was one of those hot, sticky May days in central Ohio when everyone but baseball fans prayed for rain. Lloyd Keaton tilted his battered Panama hat back on his head and fanned himself with his scorecard. He sat a few rows beneath the press box of the Menckenburg Mammoths home ballpark, close enough to home plate to smell the grass and hear the infield chatter. He couldn't imagine any place he'd rather be.

Or anybody he'd rather be with. Keaton's son Davy sat on his right, intent on the game, pounding his fist into his glove to acknowledge every Mammoth hit. Davy had brought a friend from his high school team with him, and the two boys insisted on leaving Keaton's seats in the air-conditioned, glass-enclosed press box to sit in the sweltering air in the hope of catching a foul ball. Keaton didn't object, since he remembered coaxing his own father, a sportswriter as well, to leave the press box in Cleveland's old Municipal Stadium to find seats more likely to attract foul balls.

Keaton's father claimed that any boy who grew up in the United States could not help but absorb enough basic knowledge to be a sportswriter. The trick was to watch a familiar game play itself out day after day and make it seem new. Keaton could always find something he'd never seen before to hold his interest and fill his newspaper column. If it wasn't the score, then it might be a particular play, an individual effort, or the people watching the game.

Both boys had been boisterous in the early innings, but as the game settled into a scoreless pitching duel, Davy squirmed quietly in his hard plastic seat while his high school teammate, Hulk Anderson, a massive first baseman who looked big enough to play for the Mammoths, toned down his steady chatter with the umpires and players.

The boys' responses mirrored those of the other fans in the stands. Keaton saw it all the time. Give a crowd a high-scoring game and the fans come alive, cheering every pitch and erupting over every home-team hit. But give those same fans a tight pitchers' duel and the noise volume is reduced to a nervous murmur with scattered shouts from isolated, recognizable voices. Anxiety builds with the knowledge that the game could turn on a fielding error, a single misplaced pitch, or a lucky hit.

Austin Reed, the Mammoths' promising young second baseman, led off the bottom of the seventh with a double, bringing the fans to life with cheers and a cacophony of cowbells. Reed took third on an infield out, and the crowd clapped and stomped as Sammy Tancredi, the Menckenburg clean-up hitter, stepped into the batter's box.

"Let's go, Sammy," Hulk shouted. "Show Cleveland they got

to call you back up to the majors."

Tancredi swung hard at a fastball and nicked it just enough to send it skimming over the screen behind home plate toward the press box. Keaton flinched and backed away from the rocketing ball, but both boys stood and thrust their gloves into its path. Hulk, who had the longer arms and the larger glove, plucked the ball out of the air and held it aloft for the crowd to see, then high-fived the fans in neighboring seats and shouted, "This is my day! Five dollars says Sammy gets a hit!"

The bet begged to be covered, Keaton thought. The right-hander on the mound for the opposing Bisons had already struck out Tancredi twice, and the slugger's average against right-handers was a hundred points lower than against lefties. But Keaton didn't leap forward to take the offered bet. For one thing, he wouldn't take advantage of a kid. More importantly, his membership in Gamblers Anonymous had taught him that he couldn't afford to wager even a small amount of money. Ever. No matter how sure the bet appeared to be. Betting sure things had already cost him a job, his home, and his marriage.

Keaton saw his son glance at him briefly and wondered if Davy was thinking the same thing, if he was worried his father might rise to the bait. But then Davy turned to Hulk and said, "I'll take that bet."

So Davy was more worried about his own betting decisions than mine, Keaton thought. At least the boy had the sense to recognize good odds when they were offered to him, even if taking them meant betting against his hometown team.

"You're on," Hulk said, and the two boys bumped fists. After Tancredi took the next pitch for a called strike two, Davy pounded his glove and said, "All right. Get ready to part with your cash."

"He's still got one strike left. Only takes one to hit it," Hulk said as the pitcher bent over and peered in to get the catcher's sign.

"Change-up on the outside corner," Keaton said. "That's what's coming. That's how they struck him out last time."

"Won't he remember that?" Davy asked.

Keaton shook his head. "Tancredi's not the kind of hitter that processes that kind of data."

The pitcher checked Reed on third and delivered the ball to the plate, a change-up on the outside corner.

Fooled by the pitch, Tancredi tried to check his swing and sent a slow dribbler down the first-base line. The first baseman was playing too deep to field the ball, and by the time the pitcher got to it, Reed was sliding across home plate with the game's first run.

When Tancredi beat the pitcher's throw to first by a half step, Hulk pumped his fist in the air and shouted, "That's it. That's it. What did I tell you?"

Davy shrugged and passed a five-dollar bill over to Anderson. "It was worth it just to see the Mammoths score." As the bill changed hands, Keaton saw that there were only two singles left in his son's wallet.

The Mammoths held their one-to-nothing lead into the ninth inning, when the Bisons came up for their last chance at bat.

"Just three more outs to get," Davy said.

Keaton watched the Mammoths' dugout. "They won't be easy. Bait MacFarland is bringing in Bumper Jones to pitch."

"So? What's the matter with that?" Davy said. "Bumper's our closer."

"He's erratic, and the pitcher he's replacing gives up one less run a game and has been doing just fine. MacFarland's a paint-by-the-numbers manager. He's got a one-run lead in the ninth inning, so he brings in his closer, even if sticking with his starter would give him a better chance of winning."

Jones, a burly former major leaguer hoping for one more shot at the big time, finished his warm-up tosses and glared in at his catcher. The Bisons' lead-off hitter connected solidly with his first pitch and smashed a screaming line drive that Austin Reed, playing second, speared diving to his left.

"Don't be so hard on Jones, Dad," Davy said. "He just got the first man out."

"With a little help from his friends," Keaton said.

"That's what his friends are out there for."

The next Bison singled solidly to left field. Rattled, Jones hit the following batter, putting runners on first and second with just one out.

A smattering of boos floated from the stands, then faded as the Bisons' clean-up hitter scuffed his spikes in the batter's box and took a short practice swing that ended with the barrel of his bat pointing at Bumper Jones.

Jones missed the plate badly with his first pitch, and then hung a curve ball that the Bison hitter lashed on the ground past the pitcher's mound. The hit looked as if it was headed for center field to tie the score when Austin Reed dove to his right, made a backhanded grab, skidded on his stomach, and flipped the ball from his glove to the waiting shortstop, who pivoted off second and relayed the ball to first to complete a game-ending double play.

The boys leapt to their feet, whistling and clapping. Then Hulk held up the ball he'd caught and said, "Let's go get this autographed."

As Hulk started down the aisle toward the field, bucking the flow of fans headed for the exits, Keaton took his son's arm and stuffed a five-dollar bill into his shirt pocket.

"What's that for?" Davy asked.

"To make up for the five you lost. You were smart to take that bet. You'd expect to win it eight times out of ten."

"But I only got one chance at it."

"The lesson there is never to bet more than you can afford to lose. No matter how good the odds are."

Davy transferred the five to his wallet. "I guess you should know."

"Damned right I know. Look what happened on the field today. We hit a lucky dribbler and won. They hit three balls hard in the ninth inning and lost."

Davy returned his wallet to his hip pocket. "Well, thanks for backstopping me."

Keaton patted his son's shoulder. "My pleasure. Now let's go backstop Hulk. Maybe we can help him get that ball autographed."

They made their way down the stadium steps to the low wall that separated the box seats from the Mammoths' dugout. Hulk and several younger kids waved and shouted at Sammy Tancredi, who was wrapping up an on-field interview with the WBNS play-by-play announcer.

Tancredi ignored the autograph seekers gathered at the wall and disappeared into the dugout. Hulk spat onto the field as Keaton and Davy arrived. "Did you see that? Tancredi just blew me off."

"Don't worry about it," Keaton said. "WBNS is interviewing Austin Reed now. It'll be easy to get his autograph, and he's the one who really won the game."

When Reed finished his interview, Keaton waved and shouted, "Austin. Over here, Austin."

The second baseman smiled and ambled over. "Hi, Mr. Keaton."

Keaton put his arm around his son. "Austin, I'd like you to meet my boy Davy and one of his high school teammates. They've got a ball they'd like you to autograph."

"Sure thing." The second baseman scribbled his signature on

the ball and said, “You boys are teammates, huh? What positions do you play?”

“I’ll be a shortstop next year,” Davy said.

Reed handed the ball back to Hulk. “With those muscles, you must be a first baseman.”

Hulk smiled and nodded. “Thanks for the autograph.”

“That was some stop that ended the game,” Davy said. “Where’d you learn to make that flip from your glove?”

“Just takes practice. It’s pretty easy to learn.” Reed nodded at the low wall beside the dugout. “Come on over. Bring your gloves. I’ll show you.”

“You’re kidding,” Davy said.

“No. Come on over.”

The two boys clambered over the wall, then stopped short when a voice bellowed from the dugout, “What the hell’s going on here?”

Bait MacFarland’s head cleared the dugout shelter.

The two boys froze with sheepish looks on their faces, but Reed just smiled and said, “Wanted to get in a little infield practice, chief.”

“You know we don’t allow civilians on the field.” MacFarland jerked his thumb toward the dugout steps. “Get your tail inside here, Reed. You’re the only one left that hasn’t contributed your share to today’s drug test. No piss, no play.”

Reed picked up his glove, shook hands with Davy and Hulk, and trotted off the field.

The two boys looked uncertainly at Keaton, who waved them over. “Come on guys. Maybe Reed will have time some other day.”

MacFarland turned. “Oh, hey, Lloyd. Didn’t see you there. These your boys?”

“My boy Davy and his friend Hulk. They were hoping to get Tancredi’s autograph.”

MacFarland shrugged. "Best chance is to wait at the players' exit. Afraid I can't let them into the clubhouse today. The league's fussy about visitors when they've sprung a random drug test."

The boys climbed back over the low wall into the stands. "That was great, Dad," Davy said. "Thanks for getting us into the game. Hope we didn't get you or Austin Reed into any trouble."

Keaton smiled and waved at the center field scoreboard. "That big sign over the scoreboard says *Herald.* The newspaper put a lot of money into this ballpark. It'll take more than you guys to get me into trouble. And Reed's batting three forty, so MacFarland's not likely to come down too hard on him."

"He didn't seem too worried about his drug test," Hulk said.

"No reason he should be," Keaton said. "Far as I know, the only drug he's on is adrenalin. None of the Mammoths have turned up positive since the league started testing."

Keaton escorted the boys to the players' exit, where Davy and Hulk played catch while they waited for Tancredi. After a half-hour, every Mammoth but Tancredi had come through the door. "Maybe we missed him," Davy said.

"I don't see how," Keaton said. "I'll go see what's keeping him." He showed his press pass to the guard and was halfway down the long corridor leading to the Mammoths' dressing area when he heard a high-pitched voice say, "They better not detect it, you hear?"

"Sammy, I heard you the first three times. And keep your voice down. You don't know who might be listening."

Keaton stopped in his tracks. He had no trouble recognizing both voices. The high-pitched whine belonged to Sammy Tancredi, while the softer drawl was that of the trainer, Dale Loren.

"Hell, we're the only ones left. I waited around to make sure." Tancredi lowered the volume of his voice slightly, but not the pitch, which carried easily to Keaton. "Bastards just turned up. Without no warning or nothing."

"That's why they call it a random test."

"But you're sure my piss will pass."

"If you've been working out, they won't find anything unusual."

"Because you can be fucking sure, if they find anything, I'm not going down alone."

"Is that some sort of threat?"

"It's a by-God promise. That's what it is. If I go down, I'm taking you with me."

"Let me ask you this. If you test clean and the Indians call you up, are you going to take me along?"

"What kind of a question is that? You know I don't have no say over your promotion."

"If you're not going to take me up with you, why should I have to go down with you?" Loren's voice betrayed his exasperation.

"Because you're the one gave me that shit."

"Keep your voice down. I'm keeping you away from the crooks that set you up before. They're the ones that got you caught."

"Caught me with a surprise test. Just like this one today."

"Nobody singled you out. They sampled everybody on the team."

"Even that stiff Cory? Hell, he's hitting so far below the Mendoza line, they'd need a gallon sample to find any testosterone at all."

"They're paying him to field, not to hit."

"Well, those fuckers might have tested everybody, but they're after me, doncha think? I'm the one with a history. And I'm the one that's tearing up triple-A."

"Nobody's out to get you. The Redbirds' trainer told me they all got checked last week."

"The Redbirds? Hell, they're in last place. Only drug anyone's likely to find there is Prozac."

"Maybe you could use a little of that yourself."

"The fuck's that supposed to mean?"

"Means you could stand to calm down a little. You're going to pass the test."

"By God, you best pray that I do."

A locker clanged shut. Tancredi would soon be heading toward Keaton and the players' exit. The reporter backtracked toward the exit so he could pretend he was just coming in.

Tancredi's approaching footsteps echoed down the corridor and the outfielder turned the corner, stopping when he saw Keaton. "What the fuck are you doing here?"

"Came to interview the man who got the game-winning hit."

"Well, you can forget it. I'm on my way out. Besides, I got nothing to say to you. Not after what you wrote this morning."

"I thought you'd be pleased."

"You said you hoped I wouldn't get called up."

"I said we needed you here in Menckenburg."

"Well I sure as shit don't need you."

Tancredi passed Keaton without looking back and pushed his way through the swinging exit doors. Keaton watched him go, then followed the corridor past the empty training room, turned a corner, and found Dale Loren sitting on a bench. The locker room smelled of liniment, stale sweat, and damp towels. Loren was twisting a dry towel between his fists as if he wanted to wring the fuzz out of it.

Keaton jerked his thumb toward the exit corridor. "Just ran into Sammy Tancredi. You could cram that boy's brains into a gnat's navel and still have room for his charm."

Loren looped the towel around his neck. "That's a pretty good line. Ever consider being a writer?"

"The line actually came from my dad. And I think he got it from some old radio comedian."

"Your dad was quite a reporter."

Keaton stared down at Loren, a former pitcher who had kept his athletic build into middle age. "So tell me about the steroid tests."

Loren bowed his head and gripped the ends of the towel around his neck as if it were a life preserver. "What do you think you heard?"

"Enough. I'm not surprised that jerkoff is using steroids. I am surprised that you'd give them to him."

"He'd do anything to make it back to the bigs. I understand that. I've been there."

"Bullshit. He blew his own shot when they caught him doping. You had yours blown for you when that Neanderthal manager MacFarland overworked your arm."

Loren rubbed his left shoulder. "They doped me up with cortisone."

"Cortisone's legal. Those other steroids aren't."

Loren shrugged. "They're all performance-enhancing drugs."

"That argument gets us nowhere." Keaton pointed his index finger at Loren. "If Tancredi's caught, he's in for a long suspension. But you'll never work again."

"He won't be caught."

"What makes you think he'll survive the Great American Piss-time? You got some new designer drug that can't be detected?"

"You might say that."

Keaton shook his head. "For God's sake, Loren. It might work for a little while. But they'll find a test to detect it. That's the way the game goes. And you're risking a lot more than that asshole Tancredi. You could wind up in jail."

"You going to write it up?"

"Any reason I shouldn't?"

"Not much of a story if Tancredi tests clean."

"You're pretty sure he will. That could be my story right there."

Loren wiped his forehead with one end of his towel. "Suppose I tell you why I'm sure. Can you keep it off the record?"

"You know I can't do that."

"For a little while, at least. I've got a hunch you might want to."

"I've always figured you for a pretty straight guy." Keaton took his pen from behind his ear, examined it, and put it in his pocket. "I'll sit on whatever you tell me for a couple of days. More if your hunch is right and you convince me you're not breaking any laws."

Loren stood up and reached deep into the top shelf of his locker. "Join me in my laboratory." He took out a shoebox, removed the lid, and showed Keaton the contents: a jar of cold cream, a tube of suntan lotion, two lemons, and two small cosmetic jars with no labels.

Loren shook the box and the lemons rolled toward Keaton. "Here's what I've been mixing for Tancredi. Three parts cold cream, one part number sixty sunscreen, and the juice of one lemon. For bite. No pain, no gain."

"You're kidding me, right?"

"No, I'm kidding Tancredi."

"But he's been burning up the league."

"Half of hitting is confidence. The cream gives him that. And I've got him on some pretty rigorous weight training."

"Why?"

"Because he had lousy work habits when he got here. And I tell him to make sure he works out in public so nobody will suspect those biceps come from a jar."

"But they don't."

"I know that. Now you know that. But Slamming Sammy doesn't know that."

Keaton unscrewed the cap on the jar of cold cream, pinched a gob between his thumb and forefinger, sniffed it, and rubbed it on the back of his wrist. "You're right. This stuff isn't likely to show up in a urine test."

"Not unless he dips his dick in it before he supplies the sample."

Chapter Two: Cards for Cash

KEATON'S KORNER

News you won't get anywhere else: The Mammoths tested clean for steroids last week. In fact, random tests on every AAA team the past month produced no evidence of illegal drug use in any locker room. Maybe it's time for Representative Bloodworth and his congressional committee to stop posturing as guardians of baseball's sanctity and pay some attention to the more pressing problems of this country.

The newsroom was quiet. Most of the day shift wouldn't show up for an hour or so, and Keaton wanted to get an early start on his next column. He brewed a cup of tea and settled into his cubicle. Ever since he'd overheard Loren talking with Tancredi about steroids, his thoughts kept circling back to the Mammoths' trainer. He wanted to believe Loren, but the cold-cream story seemed preposterous on several levels. Still, as Loren had predicted, Tancredi had tested clean.

Keaton logged onto his computer and opened the folder where he kept his notes for column ideas and drafts in progress. There were two files on Dale Loren in the folder. One contained notes on what Keaton had heard and seen in the locker room a week ago. He hoped he wouldn't have to write a story about Loren and real or imagined steroids, but he had to be prepared. Whether or not Loren was telling the truth, it would make a hell of a story.

The other file on Loren contained details of his brief career as a pitcher, his mishandling by the Indians, and the way he'd rebuilt his career as a trainer. There was enough material there for a column, especially if he could get Loren to talk about it. And it would be good background if the steroid story eventually broke.

Keaton glanced through his notes. Then, as he always did when starting the first draft of a column, he unlocked the wide file drawer in his desk and hauled out an ancient Remington typewriter. He set it next to his computer, scooted his chair over, and rolled in two sheets of paper.

He started to type: "Once upon a time, Dale Loren was the most promising pitcher in the Indians' farm system."

"Hold it down over there. Some of us are trying to work in the twenty-first century." Meredith Atkins's red hair and green eyes appeared over the edge of the cubicle. Since she wasn't tall enough to see over the edge without help, she knelt on her desk for her frequent jousts with Keaton.

"If your generation can send text messages while driving, the clatter of my typewriter shouldn't be much of a distraction."

Meri made a sour face. "My God, that's disgusting."

"It's my grandfather's typewriter. I channel him for inspiration when I'm starting a new column."

"Not the typewriter. I'm talking about that hat."

Keaton's battered Panama hat hung on a standing hat rack so that the inner band, blotched with dark stains from years of use, was visible. Folded strips of newspaper, damp with sweat, had been tucked under the band to make it fit Keaton's head.

"That hat was my father's. You've seen it before."

"I've never seen the inside of it. Thank God." She pointed at the straw boater hanging next to the soiled Panama. "Is that other hat packed with moldy newspaper too?"

“No. that was my grandfather’s. His head was even bigger than Dad’s. No amount of newspaper padding would make it fit me.”

“I’ve seen pictures of your grandfather in that straw boater. Back in 1919 when he blew the whistle on the Black Sox. So heads have been shrinking in your family from generation to generation. Somehow I’m not surprised.”

“Jobs have been shrinking too,” Keaton said. “Back when Dad and Granddad were writing, people still got most of their news from newspapers. What with competition from radio, the Internet, TV, and ESPN, by the time folks get their morning *Herald,* the game’s old news.”

“That’s why Eddie’s got me working on my blog. Got to keep up with the times.” Meri shook her head. “Your whole cubicle’s an outdated disaster area. Have you considered upgrading it to a homeless shelter? And that movie poster could get you sued for sexual harassment. I don’t know whether to report you to noise monitors, the sanitation department, or the PC police.”

The poster in question showed Grace Kelly in a negligee, threatened from behind by a strangler in *Dial M for Murder.*

“The poster is an homage to Alfred Hitchcock. And you’ve got no cause to feel superior. That bicycling poster on your wall isn’t exactly PG rated.”

“My poster is an homage to sweaty hunks in spandex with bulging biceps and sinewy calf muscles. It speaks to my commitment to expand the range of this newspaper beyond its traditional coverage of sports with balls.”

“If those spandex outfits were any tighter, your bicyclists would clearly qualify as sports with balls.”

Meri rolled her eyes and disappeared back into her cubicle.

Keaton resumed typing.

“You’re a dinosaur, Keaton.”

"So sue me."

"You don't have anything worth taking."

He laughed. He didn't resent her comment. She had no idea how little he owned, or how close he'd come to total ruin. The management of the *Plain Dealer* had let him go with a little dignity. She thought he'd been downsized out of Cleveland. She also thought he was eccentric. And out of touch.

He enjoyed sparring with her. She was smart, quick, and knew most sports better than writers twice her age.

Meri was quiet for a short time. Then she said, "Your column this morning didn't suck."

"Thank you."

"But get a new hat, for God's sake."

City editor Eddie Oliver, a wiry, balding sixty-year-old wearing red suspenders, strolled into Keaton's cubicle. "That Remington's clatter carried all the way to my office. What are you working on?"

"I thought I had something last week, but I don't know now. If it pans out, I want to be ready."

"Need to talk about it?"

"Not yet."

"Tell me it's not about steroids."

Keaton leaned back in his chair. "What do you have against my steroid stories?"

"Been getting a lot of comments from readers. Some people think you're going too easy on the juicers and too hard on Congressman Bloodworth."

"Could some of those people be sitting in the publisher's office?"

"Wherever they are, they're not alone. Look, take Bonds. Most folks think his records are tainted."

"Most folks never tried to turn on a big-league fastball."

Oliver pointed his pipe stem at Keaton. "Come on, Lloyd, he

cheated and you know it."

"Everybody pulls out Bonds as an example. But okay, let's take Bonds. Again. Even if he did use steroids, baseball had nothing in its rules against steroid use when he set the single-season record. So I don't know how you can call it cheating."

"It gave him an unfair edge. Same with McGwire, Sosa, and all those other big names."

"Wait a minute. Wait a minute. Not *all* the other big names. There was no testing, so you don't know who was juicing. Maybe the pitchers were. Some of them have even admitted it. So maybe some of the edge evened out. But players started getting tested well over five years ago. Over five years, Eddie. Don't you think it's about time Bloodworth found another place to get his headlines?"

"Well, players are still getting caught."

"Damned few. Nobody at all in the International League last year."

"So long as there are a few, people think maybe the rest of them are using. They just aren't getting caught."

"I'll grant you baseball was way too slow in getting its act together. Blame the commissioner. Blame the players' union. But don't blame the players."

"But baseball never would have gotten its act together if it weren't for Congress and politicians like Bloodworth."

Keaton shrugged. "I won't argue that. But Bloodworth started grandstanding years after baseball had finally cleaned up its act. It's a nice safe soap box for him. He's the guardian of public morals. Of course he's too busy with his committee to, maybe, look into corruption in government. Or address issues that actually affect the daily lives of his constituents. He wants to pass a *law,* for God's sake, telling baseball it has to cancel the records of anyone who admits to steroid use. Even those people who set records before steroids were banned. I just want to keep reminding him that—in case he doesn't have anything better to do—he might want to read the Constitution. Especially the part that forbids Congress to pass ex post facto laws. He's a hack and an idiot."

"Best to leave politics to the editorial page."

"Judging by my emails, most of our readers agree with me."

"And those who don't are writing to me."

"This is advertiser bullshit."

"This isn't Cleveland. And it sure as hell isn't New York. I'm not going to fight with you. You've had your say on Bloodworth. Leave it at that. If something new happens, you can take another shot at him. For now, move on." Eddie turned and walked away.

Meri Atkins's voice broke the silence. "Now *that* sucked."

"Welcome to journalism, kid."

"Here's something for you, in case your typewriter's news alerts aren't working." She popped her head up over the wall again. "ESPN's reporting the Indians are about to call up Sammy Tancredi. This afternoon may be your last chance to see him in a Mammoths uniform."

Keaton watched from the press box as Sammy Tancredi rocketed pre-game batting practice pitches into the left-field bleachers with a smooth, unhurried swing. He certainly swung the bat as if he were on something. But except for his massive forearms, there were no other signs of steroid use: no acne, no hair loss, and no wild swings in his consistently sullen mood.

Tancredi kept up his batting-practice show when the afternoon game started, hitting home runs in his first two trips to the plate. His heroics helped to give the Mammoths a six-to-one lead by the fifth inning, and the crowd was boisterous. In the center field bleachers, Grace Hanson, who billed herself as the Mammoths' oldest fan, rattled her cowbell and former mayor Tony DiCenzo answered with his ooga horn from the stands behind home plate. The two serenaded the crowd with their "dueling banjos" act between innings and any time a Mammoth reached base, which was happening more and more often.

To the left of home plate, a row of box seats had been cleared to make spaces accessible to fans using wheelchairs. Through the early innings, Keaton had checked the row sporadically for his friend David Bowers. After the fourth, he'd given up. Now he saw Bowers wheel himself into his reserved slot.

He'd known David Bowers for twenty-five years. They'd been together at Notre Dame, where Bowers had overcome a drive-by shooting that left him crippled for life to parlay an Economics Ph.D. from Georgetown and an early retirement from the Treasury Department into a part-time consulting practice. And a discreet bookmaking operation.

Seeing his friend wheel into the park, Keaton stood, closed his laptop, and headed for the nearest concession stand. He bought a coke and a hot dog, showed his press pass to an usher, and walked down a concrete ramp to the accessible section. "Not like you to miss the early innings," he said as he approached Bowers.

Bowers smiled. "Had to meet with another contractor."

"That house ever going to be finished?"

"Not in our lifetimes. What brings you down here with the hoi polloi?"

"Hoi polloi, hell. You've got an unobstructed view close to the action with nobody sitting beside you to jostle your drink or tell you how he'd run the club."

"You come to fill that void?"

Keaton took a bite of his hot dog. "You read my column. You already know how I'd run the Mammoths."

"I read this morning's column. Glad to see somebody finally taking on those showboating congressmen. Your dad and granddad would be proud."

On the field, the first Redbird hitter in the sixth inning walked. Keaton and Bowers had barely registered the walk in their scorebooks when the next hitter lifted a long fly to right field. Sammy Tancredi was slow to pick up the ball's flight, hesitated, then took two quick steps forward before he realized the ball was carrying over his head. He broke back, waving his glove as if he were trying to flag a departing bus, but the ball bounced off the webbing and rolled to the wall. Sammy ran down the ball and airmailed a throw that cleared both the cut-off man and the catcher as the runner on first scored and the batter sailed into third base standing up.

The home crowd suddenly became quiet. Grace Hanson rang her cowbell once, but the ex-mayor didn't answer with his ooga horn. Bowers shook his head and returned his scorecard to his lap. "That's gonna be it for Clifton."

"Won't last the inning," Keaton agreed.

Clifton had a reputation for coming apart like a quartered watermelon whenever his teammates made mistakes behind him. True to form, he lost track of home plate. With each successive "ball" call, a fan two rows down who deemed himself to be on a first-name basis with the umpire bellowed, "Where was that one, Bruce?" The umpire ignored the heckler and kept calling balls until the bases were loaded. The Redbirds' first baseman then unloaded them immediately with a grand slam home run to tie the score.

Mammoth manager Bait MacFarland slouched to the mound, took the ball from Clifton, and gave him a farewell pat on the butt. The crowd rewarded the pitcher with a smattering of applause as he left the mound, but he kept his head down and didn't acknowledge it. As he crossed the first-base line, though, he cast an angry glance toward right field and Sammy Tancredi.

"If a guy only knew when the team was going to screw up

behind him, he could make a fortune," Bowers said. "Sure as sunset."

"Speaking of sure things, I see our buddy Bradshaw is umpiring behind the plate tonight in Pittsburgh."

"With that kid they call Wild Thing pitching for the Pirates."

Keaton nodded. "Against Oke and the Mets."

"Kid doesn't stand a chance. Bradshaw will eat him alive. The only strike calls he'll get will be ones the Mets swing at and miss."

"Hardly seems fair."

Bowers ran both hands over the rims of his chair's wheels. "Who was it said, 'All of life is six-to-five against?' "

"Damon Runyon, I think. Pirates will be facing tougher odds than that tonight."

"You're not thinking of laying money on it?"

Keaton raised his hands, palms out. "Not a chance. I'm still clean. White as the driven snow."

"Just don't let it turn to slush." Bowers turned his wheelchair and looked directly up at Keaton. "I won't take your money. And I don't want to hear you've been dealing with my competition."

"I'm clean, I told you. How many times do you think I want to screw up my life? You'll still take my baseball cards, though?"

Bowers smiled. "That's different. That's legal tender I can accept."

"Put me down for A-Rod and a Pujols. On the Mets."

Bowers penciled a notation in the corner of his scorecard. "A real plunger."

"Oh, yeah. I'm out to break you."

On the field, the Mammoths' reliever gave up a bloop hit, a walk, and a solid single that put the Redbirds up by a run.

The crowd was dead silent, except for the fan two rows down who kept up his one-way conversation with the home-plate umpire, yelling, "You happy now, Bruce? You happy?"

Keaton finished his hot dog and balled up the wrapper. "This is turning into a real contest. I better get back to my laptop. I'll catch up with you tomorrow to gloat over my winnings."

The Redbirds held the Mammoths scoreless for the rest of the game, so that their sixth-inning outburst provided their victory margin. In the locker room after the game, Bait MacFarland confirmed the ESPN announcement that the Indians had called Sammy Tancredi up to their parent club.

Keaton and two younger reporters, stringers for wire services, interviewed Tancredi about his call-up. It was a scene that replayed itself at least a half-dozen times each season. If the promoted player was at all popular, the team would crowd around to congratulate him and critique his answers. In the case of Tancredi, manager MacFarland and trainer Dale Loren were the only spectators.

From the first question, it was clear Tancredi would put his own spin on the commencement exercise. Where most call-ups said they "just wanted to help the Indians wherever and however they could," Sammy made it clear the Tribe was lucky to get him. "Fourth outfielder, hell. I'll be starting in no time."

Keaton lounged against a locker while the two younger reporters shared a wooden bench and stared up at Sammy as he thrust his arms into a Hawaiian shirt. The first stringer asked, "How do you feel about playing next to Roy Lave in the Indians outfield?"

Sammy thrust out his lower lip as if he considered the question either argumentative or beneath him. Finally, he said, "Better you should ask Roy Lave how he feels about playing next to me."

"How does it feel to be leaving Menckenburg?" the second stringer asked.

Sammy appeared to give the question some thought as he

began buttoning his shirt. "I kind of feel sorry for MacFarland and the boys. They'll have a tough time holding onto first place once I'm gone."

Keaton put a foot up on the bench in front of him and rested his elbow on his knee. "Sammy, what happened with that fly ball in the sixth inning?"

Sammy looked at Keaton as if the reporter had just raised the requirements for graduation beyond his reach. "Lost it in the sun."

The two seated reporters scribbled in their notebooks.

"Last time I checked," Keaton said, "the sun was at your back, shining over your right shoulder. Been that way most of the season. Last season too."

"Shows you never played right field here. Or anywhere else, most likely. Sun reflects off the glass in the press box. Get lots of glare there."

Before anyone could ask another question, Tancredi held up his hand. "That's enough, you guys. I got to get packed to catch up with the Tribe in Oakland. It's been real."

When the reporters had left, Dale Loren watched as Tancredi ambled down the row of lockers to stop in front of him. Glancing over both shoulders to make sure no one could overhear, he whispered, "Gonna need some stuff for my trip."

"Like what?" Loren asked. "Sunglasses?"

"What you talkin' about? I got sunglasses." Tancredi tapped the glasses clipped to his shirt pocket. "You know what I need. Lots of that magic cream. Enough to last me to the end of the season."

"When are you leaving?"

"Tomorrow morning. Early. I'll drive by here. You have it ready."

Loren shook his head. "Sammy. It's not like there's an all-night steroid station where I can fill up my tank."

"Well, get what you can. Anything I don't take with me, you can send later." Sammy turned and walked away.

Loren felt a slight twinge in his ruined pitching arm as he watched Tancredi depart. There was a twenty-four-hour Kroger store two blocks from his house. He'd pick up a dozen lemons and some sunblock there, mix enough goop to last Sammy a couple of months, and then shut down his manufacturing operation. He looked forward to putting the silly charade behind him.

The trainer was buttoning his shirt when he saw Ants Anthony, a lanky black pitcher, peeking at him around the end locker. In his second year of pro ball, Anthony had a wide assortment of breaking pitches, and the consensus was that he'd make the majors as soon as he learned to control them effectively.

"All clear," Anthony announced as he came toward Loren, followed by Bumper Jones, a burly reliever who had spent two years in the majors and was trying to get back.

Anthony moved as if his arms and legs had never been properly introduced, a condition that produced a herky-jerk delivery when he was on the mound. His out-of-sync movements usually made Loren smile, but this evening the trainer felt a pang of apprehension.

The two pitchers nodded and stationed themselves on either side of Loren like mismatched bookends.

After a short silence, Jones spoke. "We want what you been givin' Tancredi."

The bookends began to feel like the jaws of a vice. "Who says I've been giving anything but Band-Aids and aspirin to Tancredi?"

"He does. When the team's piss tested clean, he bragged on how you were supplying him with muscle cream."

Loren felt a flash of anger. "Bragged to who?"

"Just me and Ants here. We was in a bar in Buffalo. He was kind of drunk."

At least Tancredi hadn't blabbed to the whole team, Loren thought. Not yet, anyhow. "Guys, look. They'll eventually get tests that will detect what I gave Tancredi."

"Listen," Jones said, "if it works now, I need it now. It's my ticket back to the bigs."

Loren turned to the less imposing bookend. "Ants, you're not a power pitcher. What makes you think steroids will do you any good at all?"

Anthony moved his left arm up and down, snapping his fingers to a beat only he could hear. "Man, you give me a couple of miles per hour on my fastball and my breaking stuff looks all that more better."

"It's really not a good idea, guys," Loren said. "You'll be hurting yourselves down the road."

"I don't get me some help," Anthony said, "I ain't going to get very far down that road."

Loren took a deep breath and exhaled slowly. "Anybody finds out, my job is on the line."

"You already done it for Sammy." Jones folded his arms across his ample chest. "I hear that congress committee is offering rewards for information on stuff like that."

Anthony held up both hands, palms out, as if he were a third-base coach signaling a runner to stop. "Come on now, Bumper. No need for threats here. Man's just a cog like the rest of us."

"What are we playing here? Good reliever, bad reliever?" Loren stood, and both the pitchers took a step backward. "If I get you some, you can't tell anyone. Anyone."

"Course not. We'd be telling on ourselves," Anthony said.

"And you've got to agree to stick to a public weight-training program. To explain any sudden increase in muscle mass."

Jones and Anthony exchanged shrugs. "Guess we might could do that," Anthony said.

"Okay," Loren said. "I'll get you a month's supply. Check with me tomorrow."

Jones didn't look convinced. "What about the grease?"

The question stopped Loren cold. He ticked off the ingredients mentally: lemon juice, sunblock, and cold cream. "No grease," he said aloud.

Jones grunted. "Man, if it's free, how good can it be?"

"Think of this as a trial run," Loren said. "We can talk money later if it works for you. This stuff doesn't come with any guarantees or government warnings. You take it, you take your chances."

"But it made a hitter out of Sound-Off Sammy," Anthony said. "And he passed the piss test."

Loren smiled. "Both those things are true."

"We'll catch up with you tomorrow, then," Jones said. "*Before* the game."

"Before or after, either is fine." Loren started to tell them no steroid cream could work instantaneously, but stopped himself. After all, the cream he was pushing could work any time.

"See you tomorrow, then," Anthony said. He turned and followed Jones's solid stride down the row of lockers, snapping his fingers to his own private orchestra.

Loren watched the two relievers depart. He decided not to increase production. He'd give the pitchers some of the batch he'd planned to give Tancredi. More for them, less for Sammy. Serve the bastard right for blabbing.

Lloyd Keaton popped the tab on a Coke, unwrapped the tuna sandwich he'd bought at the corner deli, propped his feet on a kitchen chair, and used the remote to turn on the TV in the living room of his one-bedroom flat. He flipped quickly through the available movie channels. Ray Milland was cadging drinks from a bartender, zombies were threatening a group of teenagers, and Grace Kelly was kissing Jimmy Stewart. He guessed that *Rear Window* had enough viewing time left until ESPN aired the Mets/Pirates game, so he left the channel tuned to Kelly and Stewart.

Three walls of Keaton's apartment were lined with sagging floor-to-ceiling bookshelves. The lone wall that didn't feature double-shelved books had two windows that looked across an alley to a mirror-image of his apartment building. Between the windows, one framed picture showed Keaton's grandfather in the stands of Comiskey Park with Ring Lardner, while a second showed his father sitting at a banquet table with fellow sportswriters Red Smith and Jim Murray. In the sparsely furnished living room, short stacks of books sprouted like stumps in a forest.

Keaton had long since realized that he'd never read all the books he owned, much less all those he wanted to read. "I can quit any time," he'd told his wife, half jokingly. Now the books and their son Davy were the only legacy from their marriage, which had broken apart over the other habit he couldn't seem to break, gambling.

Keaton looked at his watch. Almost an hour until the first pitch in Pittsburgh. Lots of time to get a bet down. He still knew the numbers of the East Wheeling bookies by heart. They'd be more than willing to take his money.

Oke going against a wild rookie with that tight-ass Bradshaw umpiring behind the plate. As close to a sure thing as he'd ever get. He took out his cell phone. Flipped it open. Stared at it. Snapped it shut. He weaved his way around the stacks of books in the living area and put the phone on top of the first book on the highest shelf he could reach, Woody Allen's *Getting Even.* There was no danger he'd forget where he'd put it. It had been there before.

It helped that he had a "bet" on Oke and the Mets down with David Bowers. After his divorce, he and David had set up a system of barter based on that season's baseball cards. Each of them had bought a full set of Topps cards and assigned values to each card equal to the annual salary of the player shown on the card's face.

It had been five years since Keaton's gambling had cost him his reporting job in Cleveland, and two years since it had cost him his marriage. Two years without putting real money down on the outcome of a game or the turn of a playing card. In that time, though, he was about $220 million in players' salaries ahead in his "bets" with David Bowers. From time to time, he wondered what might have happened if he'd had the wherewithal to back those pretend bets with real money. Tonight, with what his gut told him was a sure thing coming up on ESPN, was one of those times.

Raymond Burr was about to surprise Grace Kelly ransacking his apartment when game time arrived and Keaton switched from the movie channel to ESPN. The game started out following Keaton's script. The umpire gave Oke strike calls on close pitches and withheld them from the Pirates' rookie, who had enough movement on his pitches to hold the Mets scoreless through three innings.

Keaton used his remote to channel surf between innings. He caught the final scene of *Rear Window,* then switched away from a commercial for the Ohio State Lottery to encounter one of the dozens of poker contests that seemed to show up everywhere on TV. The lottery was a sucker game that had never tempted Keaton, but he missed the riffle and splat, bet and bluff, smoke and mirrors of poker. Too bad he couldn't convince anyone to exchange chips for baseball cards.

The Pirates' manager was ejected in the top of the fourth for arguing a ball call in the vicinity of the knees that had been a strike for Oke the previous inning. The call put Mets on first and second, and the clean-up hitter scored them both with a triple.

The two runs were all Oke would need, but the Mets capitalized on the Pirate pitcher's walks to score once in the fifth and twice in the sixth to post a final score of five to one. Keaton watched the game through the final out, then jotted down notes for his next day's column, checked online to see how the players on his fantasy team were doing, and had a Bass Ale while he waited for the West Coast scores to come in. The Indians were shut out at Oakland, their third loss in four games on the road. Keaton doubted that calling up Sammy Tancredi would improve their offense. There had to be a limit to the number of hits you could expect from lemon juice and cold cream.

Before going to bed, Keaton toted up his accumulated winnings from his two years of betting baseball card salaries with David Bowers. The evening's win put him up over $250 million in players' salaries. He'd plunged heavily, risking over $40 million in the back salaries of Alex Rodriguez and Albert Pujols, but he figured the combination of Oke pitching against a wild Pirate rookie with Bradshaw umpiring behind the plate was as close to a sure thing as he'd ever get. If he'd been able to back his bets with even a small fraction of the amount they'd assigned to the cards, he could easily have made enough to upgrade his living quarters and set a little aside for Davy's college fund.

He couldn't let himself think like that. He'd been down that road before. Several times, always hitting a dead end. Still, Bradshaw's umpiring gave him an edge he'd never had before. Given what was left of the season, Bradshaw would have at least twenty more umpiring assignments behind the plate. With any luck, two or three of those should come with pitching matchups like the one earlier that evening. Sure things. All he had to do was wait.

Chapter Three: Cream of the Jest

KEATON'S KORNER

Sammy Tancredi has been up in the majors with the Tribe for more than a month now, and he's oh-for-June. Looks like Sammy is one of those "Four-A" players who burn up the league at the AAA level but fizzle out in the bigs. Maybe Cleveland could send him back down to Menckenburg. Even without Slamming Sammy, the Mammoths are in the hunt for the AAA pennant, and the team could certainly use the bat he was swinging before his call-up.

The steam from the showers mixed with the shouts of happy players as Dale Loren unlaced his spikes and placed them on the top shelf of his locker. The Mammoths had just won a three-to-two squeaker to pull within a game of the first-place Bisons. Bumper Jones, who struck out two of three batters in the ninth to record his third save of the week, left two reporters behind, cinched his towel tightly around his waist, and straddled the bench next to Loren.

Jones rubbed his bare pitching arm with his left hand and said in a low voice, "Man, I need some more of that good goop."

"Already? I just gave you a full jar on Monday."

"Hell, man. I closed out three games since then."

Loren glanced around to make sure no one was listening. "That's still a lot of cream. You're not sharing it with somebody else, are you?"

"You think I'm crazy?"

"It's just that you seem to be going through a lot of it."

Jones scratched his legs on either side of the bench and rubbed his thighs. "I'm spreading it on my legs, too. That's where I get my power, man."

Loren glanced down at the thicket of black hair matted on Jones's legs and briefly considered adding a depilatory to his formula.

Jones patted his crotch through the gray towel. "Tried it on my cock, too, but it stung like a sonuvabitch."

Before the trainer could respond, Jones held up his hand and laughed sharply. "Just kidding, man. I don't need no help in that department."

If the lemon juice didn't sting, the cream probably wouldn't hurt in that department, Loren thought. So long as the user believed, it should work at least as well as an aphrodisiac as an arm aid and homer helper.

"So what about it?" Jones asked. "Can you get me some more?"

"You been keeping up your workouts?"

"Every day. First thing I do when I get to the park. Out where everybody can see."

"All right, then. I'll have your prescription refilled by tomorrow's game."

Jones swung one leg over the bench, adjusted his towel, and stood up. "You're a good man, Train."

Loren finished dressing and was on his way out of the clubhouse when Bait MacFarland poked his head out of his office door. "See you a minute, Dale?"

Loren took a seat while the Mammoths' manager, still in uniform, leaned back in his swivel chair and propped his sweat socks on the corner of his desk. "Saw you talkin' to Bumper."

Oh, shit, Loren thought. He focused on the thin rim of dust that marked the line left on the white socks by the manager's shoe tops. "He looked pretty good out there today."

"He's looked pretty good out there for the last month. Like he got his big-league stuff back."

Loren nodded.

"Says you got him working out."

"Lifting weights. Squats. Stretching his shoulder. He's been at it pretty steady."

"Him and Ants both."

Oh, Christ, Loren thought. One of them talked.

MacFarland picked up a ball from his desk and rotated his wrist as if he were throwing a curve. "Anthony's been pitching pretty good too. Not as good as Jones, but his stuff's moving more."

"He's been pitching in bad luck. An error and a handle hit beat him his last time out."

"Still, he's looking a lot better than when he first came up. Guess your training's got him on track. Him and Jones both."

"They just needed a few good outings to give them a little confidence."

MacFarland examined the stitches on the baseball in his right hand. "You don't think the weight training and all might not be too much?"

"Too much? How?"

"I don't know. Overwork maybe. I don't have to tell you we're in a tight race. I can't afford to lose either of them boys."

"No, you don't have to tell me."

"So you're not worried that what you're doing might sideline them for a spell?"

"I don't see how."

MacFarland made an overhead throwing motion without releasing the baseball. "I mean, arms are fragile. There's a lot more pressure now, what with steroid testing and all. Careers are fragile. But I don't have to tell you that."

Hell no, you don't have to tell me that, Loren thought. If you hadn't overworked my arm twenty years ago, I might have had a real pitching career. "Are you asking me to cut back their training routine?"

MacFarland laid the baseball on his desk carefully, as though it might break. "How can I ask you to cut back when I don't know everything you're doing?"

Oh, you know, Loren thought. You just don't want to say it out loud. "So we'll just keep on the way we're going."

"Seems to be working. I'm letting you know, though, I'll be holding you responsible if anything happens to cost me those arms. Understand?"

"Oh, yeah. I understand."

David Bowers's new house was northeast of Menckenburg, in New Albany, safely beyond the strip malls and one-design-fits-all developments. Keaton knew the area by reputation, but he'd never had many occasions to visit. The home prices had been well beyond his range when he'd had his life uprooted and moved to Menckenburg, and they were even farther beyond his means now. He left a road that ran beside a meandering creek and wound his way up a hill, passing streets whose names emitted an aura of southern elegance: Honeysuckle Lane, Magnolia Way, Pear Blossom Drive. Nothing so prosaic as a Road: only Ways, Lanes, Drives, and Courts.

The Bowers' brand new home commanded the end of a cul-de-sac called Peach Tree Court and looked as if it had been designed by an architect who had seen *Gone With the Wind* a few too many times. The only feature that wouldn't have been found in Tara was the wheelchair ramp connecting the garage to the colonnaded porch.

When Bowers had been a classmate of Keaton's at Notre Dame, he'd fallen in love with one of the few female students in the economics department. Judy Daley was a minority in other ways as well. She was one of the few townies from South Bend registered at the college, and her skin was jet black.

One evening as Bowers was walking back to the campus after seeing Judy home, a blast from a drive-by shooter had shattered his spine. "Wrong place, wrong time, wrong side of the tracks for a white boy," said the local police, who never found the shooter. "Judy's neighborhood was never the wrong place for me," Bowers insisted. He recovered the use of everything but his legs, completed his bachelor's degree one year late, married Judy, and got a Ph.D. in economics that led to the Treasury Department, an early retirement, and his current consulting/bookmaking operation.

Keaton pushed the doorbell and was greeted with the first notes of Tara's Theme. Judy opened the door. Nearly as tall as Keaton, she didn't seem to have aged since their college days. With close-cropped curls fitted tightly to her head, she reminded him of museum engravings of Greek goddesses.

Keaton kissed her cheek and handed her a bottle of Chardonnay, saying, "I think you'll be amused by its presumption." It was the tag line of a New Yorker cartoon Judy had sent him when he'd complained about a wine-tasting course his ex-wife had insisted they take together.

She smiled and cradled the bottle in her arms. "And how is Liz?"

"Give it up. We're not getting back together."

On the right side of the entry hall, an elevator door opened and David wheeled his chair out. "Well, what do you think?"

"All it lacks is Clark Gable. Are you double-billing you consulting clients or skimming your own bookie operation?"

"Neither, actually. I married well."

Keaton smiled at Judy. "You certainly did that."

Judy bowed her head and fluttered her eyelashes. "Aw, shucks. Ah'm just a poor working girl."

"Who happens to be a partner in one of Ohio's biggest corporate law firms," David said.

Keaton mimicked Judy's faux-southern accent. "Mah daddy always said, 'If you don't go out with anything but rich girls, you'll never marry anything but a rich girl.' "

David beat him to the punch line. "Course, your daddy never married."

"You two should take your act on the road . . . and soon." Judy turned and led the way to the dining room.

After dinner, Keaton helped Judy rinse the dishes and load the dishwasher. The kitchen sparkled with chrome appliances set in an inch-thick countertop of flecked white granite. "All the modern conveniences," Keaton said. "Although I really expected Hattie McDaniel to be doing the dishes."

"Shelve the *Gone With the Wind* references, all right?" Judy punched a button and the dishwasher hummed quietly. "I wouldn't have picked this place. But David had a builder client who got in over his head."

Keaton whistled softly. "He must be laying off some pretty big bets."

"Much too big. And he's still doing business with Little Bill Ellison."

"Jabba the Hutt?"

"The man belongs in a sewer, but there's no manhole big enough for him to squeeze through. I wish you'd talk to David about him."

"Talk to me about who?" Bowers rolled his wheelchair through the kitchen doorway.

Judy wiped her hands on a dish towel. "Your dung-pile-shaped friend from East Wheeling."

"Oh, Christ. Do we have to cover that ground again?"

Judy threw the dish towel into the sink. "No. No, we don't have to talk about it." She stormed out of the room, knifing through the small space between the kitchen door and David's wheelchair.

"What was that all about?" Keaton asked.

"The current family argument. Little Bill controls gambling in parts of three states. There's no way I can avoid dealing with him. I'm just a small frog in his pond. I need him to lay off my overages."

Keaton swept his arm in a gesture that took in the whole room. "You may be a small frog, but your own lily pad is getting pretty big."

"It's not so much the company I keep as the whole idea of making book. Judy'd like it if I quit altogether. She doesn't know how much of this place comes from laying off bets."

"Speaking of which, in just three days Jerry Neyer's on the mound with our buddy Bradshaw behind the plate."

"Who's pitching against Neyer?"

"Another one of those Pirate rookies."

David turned his wheelchair and headed back toward the living room. "Neyer's the hottest pitcher in baseball right now. Guess I can expect another run on my baseball cards."

Keaton followed him. "Maybe this time we should bet more than cards."

David shook his head. "Bad idea."

"You've been handling my card bets. You know Bradshaw's close to a sure thing."

"You forget the times you've lost betting that sure thing."

"What? One time."

"At least twice. There was the time the Giants hammered Oke. And the time that Cincinnati rookie settled down and outpitched Neyer."

"All right, twice. But look how far ahead I am overall."

"In little pieces of painted cardboard."

"I'm just saying I'd like to try it with little engraved sheets of legal tender."

"You can't handle it. You know you can't handle it."

"You're my oldest friend. And my bookie. You can help me handle it."

"No, I can't. Don't ask me to. Friend or no friend, if I were a bartender and you were an alcoholic, I wouldn't serve you."

"I'd just find another bar."

"At least I wouldn't have to watch you puking on my doorstep."

"Well, I have to admit it's a handsome doorstep."

The post-game locker room was a raucous mix of shower steam, snapping towels, shouts, and rowdy laughter. The pitching combination of Lee Clifton, Ants Anthony, and Bumper Jones had just shut out the Bisons to lift the Mammoths into undisputed possession of first place.

As the celebration swirled around him, Dale Loren sat quietly at his locker, smiling and contemplating the confidence-building impact of cold cream, suntan lotion, and lemon juice.

He looked up to see a squat man in an ill-fitting blue suit elbowing his way through the clot of backslapping players. The clubhouse attendant, who was even shorter than the squat man, trailed him through the crowd, trying unsuccessfully to catch him as he approached Loren's locker.

The man stopped in front of Loren, allowing the attendant to catch up with him, grab his sleeve, and say, "Excuse me, sir, but you can't come in here."

The squat man ignored the tugging and stared down at the trainer. "You Dale Loren?"

Loren nodded.

The intruder reached into his breast pocket, pulled out a dark envelope, and handed it to Loren. "This is for you."

Loren took the envelope. "What is it?"

"It's a subpoena to appear before Congressman Bloodworth's congressional committee."

"Why?"

The squat man smoothed out his twisted jacket sleeve. "Sam Tancredi has tested positive for steroids. He's named you as his supplier."

CHAPTER FOUR:
STAR CHAMBER

KEATON'S KORNER

It's been nearly a year since any major leaguer tested positive for steroids. That means Congressman Bloodworth's committee has had over a year to store up invective to heap on the heads of steroid users; a year to forge stronger shackles for suppliers; a year to fashion fresh outbursts of outrage.

Pardon me, though, if I'm not impressed. Haven't we heard all this before? Major League Baseball is suspending Sammy Tancredi 100 days for his second steroid offense. Isn't that sufficient punishment? Should he (and we) have to listen to Bloodworth's bombast as well? Doesn't the U.S. Congress have bigger fish to fry than the single miscreant that surfaced after an entire year of testing?

Sitting with the press corps in the gallery overlooking the congressional hearing room in Washington, D.C.'s Rayburn Building, Keaton had to admit the scene was impressive. Senators, congressmen, and their aides sat behind two semi-circles of paneled mahogany desks raised well above the floor of the room. Three long tables strewn with microphones and cables stood in front of the central rows of seats on the hearing room floor. Sammy Tancredi, resplendent in a yellow checked sport coat, sat at the center table with a representative from the baseball commissioner's office and a lawyer from the player's union. The table on Tancredi's left was occupied by a middle-aged blonde woman flanked by two men, none of whom Keaton recognized. Dale Loren sat propped up by his elbows at the right-hand table, listening to a man Keaton assumed to be his lawyer. Loren was too far away for Keaton to read the expression in his eyes, but the trainer's mouth was a grim line as he nodded to the lawyer's words.

The hearing opened with a lengthy prayer that managed to avoid any mention of a deity, followed by a short talk from a Hall of Fame pitcher who had entered politics after retiring from baseball. Then Bloodworth took over the podium to condemn the use of all performance-enhancing drugs and demand that any records tainted by the stain of steroids should be stricken from the record books.

Keaton had heard both the pitcher and Bloodworth speak before, on more than one occasion, and wondered how the former ballplayer felt about records achieved with the aid of cortisone and amphetamines, both of which were clubhouse staples when he was still pitching. The message of the next speaker, however, was much harder to dismiss. The blonde woman related in a shaky voice how her shortstop son Ron had begun juicing in high school when coaches told him he needed to get bigger and touted the use of steroids. When her son graduated from college and failed to be drafted by the majors, he fell into a depression she was convinced was steroid-induced and shot himself. The two fathers who followed her to the podium told similar stories, heartbreaking tales of star athletes whose steroid use was followed by depression and suicide.

The stories of the bereaved parents shook Keaton, who scribbled the details in his notebook and then, in the margin next to the notes, wrote a single word, "Davy," followed by an outsized question mark.

By the time the congressmen called Sammy Tancredi to

testify, the strategy of the hearing was clear. They were going to hang Tancredi and Dale Loren for the deaths of the three scholar athletes. Representative Bloodworth took over the questioning of Tancredi himself. Adjusting his glasses so that they perched on the end of his hawk-like nose, the congressman squinted over the rims until he had the outfielder squarely in his sights. "Mr. Tancredi, you have heard testimony regarding the tragic effects steroids can have on American youth. You were listening, weren't you?"

Tancredi grasped the microphone with his two hands separated, as if he were going to lay down an unaccustomed bunt. "Yes, sir. I was listening."

"And you do understand that as a Major League ballplayer you serve as an example to the youth of America?"

Tancredi clutched the microphone tighter and looked perplexed, as if he'd forgotten the bunt signal. "Yes, sir. I understand."

"Then you must understand that you are setting an abominable example. The record shows that you have used steroids before. And you are still using them. Can you think of any reason why you should not be barred from baseball for life?"

Sammy's head jerked backward as if he were ducking a high inside fastball. He looked around wildly until his lawyer leaned forward, covered Sammy's microphone with his hand, and whispered into his client's ear.

The lawyer leaned back and Sammy grasped the microphone in both hands, near the end of the handle. "Sir, my counsel reminds me that the established penalty for my offense is a hundred-day suspension."

"I'm not interested in the established penalty. I'm thinking of all those high school and college kids who look at you and believe they can't succeed except by cheating. Whatever the established penalty is, it's far too lenient, especially in view of the horror stories we've just heard from bereaved parents. Wouldn't you agree, Mr. Tancredi?"

Tancredi looked to his lawyer for help.

Bloodworth's voice boomed over the hearing room. "I asked you the question, Mr. Tancredi. Not your lawyer."

"Sir. I'm sorry, sir. But a hundred days is the law."

"You seem to have no trouble breaking the law, Mr. Tancredi. I find it more than a little ironic that you choose to hide behind it."

Tancredi was silent.

"Tell me, Mr. Tancredi," the congressman continued, "do you feel that you are the only major leaguer using steroids?"

"I wouldn't know, sir."

"You wouldn't know? Are you saying you don't have personal knowledge of any other players who are using steroids?"

"No, sir. I mean yes, sir. I'm saying that I don't personally know any other steroid users. In the majors."

"I find that hard to believe. Where did you get your drugs?"

"From my trainer on the Mammoths."

"That would be Mr. Dale Loren?"

"That's right, sir."

"And did Mr. Loren supply any other Mammoths with drugs?"

"You'd have to ask him that, sir."

"I intend to do just that."

Keaton watched Dale Loren stand to take the oath. The trainer didn't look comfortable, but he didn't flinch under Bloodworth's glare. He looked, Keaton thought, like a relief pitcher coming in to face the opposition's clean-up hitter with the bases loaded.

After Loren sat, Bloodworth stared down from his roost and said, "You've heard the previous testimony. Did you supply Mr.

Tancredi with steroids?"

Loren met Bloodworth's stare. "No, sir. I did not."

"I remind you, sir, that you are under oath."

"I'm aware of that."

"You've heard Mr. Tancredi's testimony. Are you calling him a liar?'

"No, sir. I'm just saying I never supplied him with any unlawful substance."

"Then how do you account for his testimony?"

"I believe he believed I was giving him steroids."

"You believe he believed. Are we jousting with semantics here, Mr. Loren? Are we back trying to define the meaning of the verb 'is'? Are you making light of the mission of this committee?" Bloodworth swept his arm in a gesture that took in the center table of parents. "Were you listening earlier to the testimony of these poor bereaved fathers and mother?"

"Sir, my heart goes out to those parents. I've lost a teenage son myself. But I will swear on his grave I've never given any player steroids."

"But you did give Mr. Tancredi something."

"I provided Mr. Tancredi with a harmless mixture of cold cream, sunblock, and lemon juice."

"Then how is it he tested positive for steroids?"

"He didn't test positive when he was with the Mammoths. I don't know where he got drugs after that."

"He says he got them from you."

"He's mistaken. I never gave him steroids."

Keaton watched the congressmen and their aides shuffle papers and exchange sly, knowing looks. They obviously didn't believe Loren.

Bloodworth cleared his throat and asked in a slow, cornpone drawl, "Now why in the world would you supply Mr. Tancredi with a harmless cream?"

Loren looked like a hurler whose best pitch had just been called a ball but who didn't dare argue with the umpire. "He was in a slump and kept pestering me for steroids. I knew he had used them before. I was afraid if he didn't get something from me, he'd go back to his old sources."

Bloodworth sat back in his chair and folded his arms across his chest. "So you were saving Mr. Tancredi from himself?"

Loren started to reply, "Well, sir . . ."

Bloodworth held up his hand. "There's no need to reply, Mr. Loren. It was an observation, not a question."

A smirking aide stepped forward and handed Bloodworth a sheaf of papers. With his hand still raised, the congressman adjusted his glasses and read the top sheet. Then he dropped his hand and said, "I see Mr. Tancredi's performance improved immensely under your regimen."

"That's correct, sir."

"And how do you account for that?"

"In addition to the cream, I prescribed weight training. But I believe most of the improvement can be traced to a placebo effect."

"A placebo effect?"

"Yes sir. That occurs when . . ."

Bloodworth cut him off. "I assure you, sir, that I am aware of the definition of placebo." He tapped the sheets of paper he'd been reading. "But if these results are any measure of a placebo effect, you should have lathered up the entire Mammoth team."

The hearing room erupted with laughter. Loren shifted uncomfortably at the microphone.

When the laughter had subsided, Bloodworth said, "Mr. Loren, we're not unreasonable men. All we are after is the truth. Is there any hard evidence that this fable of yours is true?"

Loren looked to his lawyer for guidance. When none came, he said, "Only the fact that Tancredi tested clean when he was with the Mammoths."

"But we all know there are many ways to defeat a random test, don't we? For example, two of Mr. Tancredi's teammates have testified that he boasted he kept a clean urine sample in his locker."

"But he wasn't able to use it."

"Do you know that for a fact, sir? Did you supervise the test?"

"No, but league officials . . ."

"Mr. Loren, you dishonor no one but yourself in your attempt to make a fool of the U. S. Congress. And you greatly underestimate this august body if you expect us to believe this cock and bull story of yours."

Loren squeezed the microphone. "I've told you the truth."

"So you say." Bloodworth took off his glasses and pointed them at the trainer. "Well, Mr. Loren, supplying others with controlled substances is a serious criminal matter. It seems to me you ought to have a chance to plead your case before a grand jury."

Loren winced as if he'd just watched the winning run walk home on a bad call.

"And let me say," Bloodworth continued, "if you are no more successful in convincing a grand jury of your innocence than you have been here today, it's my hope that you will find yourself faced with a long, quiet time in prison to contemplate the evils unleashed on the sport of baseball, its players"—he held out both arms toward the parents at the side table—"and the families of its players, by the poisons purveyed by you and your sorry ilk."

Keaton copied down and underlined the words "your sorry ilk." Jesus Christ, he thought, did the old windbag really say that? He looked up from his notebook in time to see Dale Loren leaving the witness table with his lawyer.

Keaton followed the press corps out to the front steps of the Rayburn Building, where his fellow reporters fired questions at Loren as he left. News cameras snapped and TV cameras bobbed above the crowd like the heads of predators as Loren's lawyer led his client through the swarm of newsmen to a waiting taxicab.

"No comment. My client has no comment," the lawyer shouted over his shoulder as he held the taxi door open, shoved Loren into the back seat, and climbed in beside him.

Keaton moved in front of the cab and laid both his hands on the hood as if he wanted to push it backward. The cabbie honked, yelled, and shook his fist, but Keaton didn't budge. He locked eyes with Loren, who opened the door on his side of the cab so that Keaton could jump in.

"I thought we agreed not to talk to reporters," the lawyer said after Keaton had slammed the cab door.

"It's all right, he's a friend," Loren said.

The lawyer shook his head. "After today, you have no friends."

The cab pulled away, leaving the shoving crowd of reporters in its wake. "That was brutal back there," Keaton said. "Why didn't you give them a sample of your cream mix as evidence?"

"There's no way to prove any mix he gives them now is what he gave Tancredi," the lawyer said.

"I saw the ingredients in your locker," Keaton said. "I can testify to that."

"Are you an expert on drugs?" the lawyer asked. "Did you have the cream tested?"

"No. But I know what I saw and what Dale told me. That should be enough to plant a reasonable doubt in a jury's mind. You're still innocent until proven guilty, after all."

Loren sighed. "Not if Bloodworth has anything to do with it."

"All right," Keaton said, "let's look at it from another angle.

If you didn't give Tancredi steroids, he got them from someone else and lied about the source. Any idea who that source was or why he lied?"

Loren shook his head. "None whatever."

"I'll talk to him," Keaton said. "Bring the power of the press to bear. Maybe I can get him to cave."

"Good luck with that," the lawyer said.

"It's worth a try, at least," Keaton said. "Look, I've heard a few rumors these last weeks. Did you give your cream to any other players?"

"Don't answer that, Dale," the lawyer said.

"Oh, for Christ's sake," Keaton said. "Don't you see how much trouble you're in? If other players have your cream, it can be tested."

"But what he gave other players may not be what he gave Tancredi," the lawyer said.

"Whose side are you on?" Keaton asked the lawyer. "The tests would be a way to pile up evidence on Dale's side of the ledger."

"Ants Anthony and Bumper Jones," Loren said. "I gave them both the mix."

The lawyer shook his head. "Listen to me, Dale. You don't want those names to become public."

"That's right," Loren said. "I don't want to get them into trouble."

"You're the one in trouble here, Dale," Keaton said. "What are Anthony and Jones going to be charged with? Cold cream conspiracy? Loitering with lemon juice? They used your concoction and tested clean for steroids."

"They haven't been tested since I put them on the cream," Loren said.

"Then have them tested," Keaton said. "Go see them. If they have any goop left, get samples. Take somebody with you so you can demonstrate there's been no hanky-panky with the samples." Keaton looked across Loren to the lawyer. "You can do that, can't you?"

"I'm not sure that will stand up in court," the lawyer said.

"Figure out how to make it stand up," Keaton said. "That's your job, isn't it?"

The cab pulled up in front of the Mayflower Hotel. The lawyer opened the door, climbed out, and was immediately surrounded by reporters. Loren pulled the door shut. "Shit, they followed us."

Keaton put his hand on Loren's arm. "We can fight this. You two talk to Jones and Anthony. Threaten them with disclosure if they don't cooperate. While you're doing that, I'll go see Tancredi."

Loren loosened his tie and rubbed his neck. Outside the cab, they could hear the lawyer repeating, "No comment. No comment. I told you guys my client has no comment to make on today's testimony."

Chapter Five: If You Ain't Lyin'

KEATON'S KORNER

The Mammoths have hit the skids since Sammy Tancredi was suspended for steroid use and hauled before the Bloodworth Commission. Their losing streak stands at eight straight games, but it seems reporters would rather cover pharmaceutical matters. Instead of asking, "What kind of pitch did Smith hit to beat you?", sportswriters nowadays focus on signs of steroid use, like bulging biceps, receding hairlines, back acne, and whether those are dimples or puncture marks on our players' butts.

Come on, guys. The Mammoths tested clean all last year and all this year. Even Sammy Tancredi tested clean when he was here in Menckenburg. Besides, if our heroes were really on steroids, shouldn't it be showing up in the win column?

After his hearing, Sammy Tancredi moved back to Menckenburg to the apartment he'd rented as a Mammoth. It was in a complex called the Wild Flower Arms and nicknamed the Wide Open Arms by the single players, since it featured hot- and cold-running Hooters hostesses and late-night pool parties with a minimal dress code.

When Keaton knocked, the door to Tancredi's apartment was opened by a tall brunette barely clad in a fire-engine-red bikini. Her fingernails and toenails matched her swimsuit, and had probably taken enough polish to cover the entire bikini with a little left over.

"Sammy's in the weight room," the brunette told Keaton. "You want, you can come in and wait for him. I mix a mean martini."

"Maybe later," Keaton said. "I'll try to catch him at his workout."

Keaton found Tancredi in the far corner of the workout room, bent over in a poor imitation of Rodin's Thinker, raising and lowering a small weight with his left hand. Sweat poured down his naked torso and pooled above the elastic drawstring on his purple shorts.

He kept working the weight up and down when he saw Keaton. "Got nothing to say to you. You called me a Four-A player in your column."

"Well, now you're a No-A player, and you've got no one to blame but yourself."

"Is that crack supposed to soften me up?"

"I just want to know where you got your steroids."

Sammy stopped working the weight. "I saw you at the D.C. hearing. I told the Commission where I got 'em. Straight from Dale Loren."

"That's bullshit. You and I both know the steroids that showed up in your test didn't come from Loren."

"That's my story and I'm sticking to it."

"You're sinking his career."

"What about my career? Man said he gave me cold cream. How lame is that for a story?"

"Whatever he gave you, it put you on a hitting spree that got you promoted to the majors."

"Ain't nothing he gave me helped me lay my bat on the ball." Tancredi rose and placed the hand weight on the wall rack behind him. As he turned, Keaton saw that his back was pockmarked with acne scars.

Keaton whistled softly. "If your muscles don't say 'steroid user,' your back sure does."

"Yeah, well. I never see my back. I'm always looking forward. Steroids are the future, man."

"Then why are they illegal?"

"You don't want kids taking them. Hell, I can see that. But you get a doctor helping you handle the dosage, eat right, get on a good cycle so your liver can filter out the shit—you do all that, and man, you can live forever."

"So you got them from a doctor?"

Tancredi grabbed a towel from the bench behind him and mopped up the sweat on his shoulders and biceps. "First time, yeah."

"First time. What about the last time?"

Tancredi threw the towel against the wall under the weight rack. "That's it. I been talkin' to you vultures long enough. You can't handle the truth about steroids. You don't want to know the good they can do."

"Okay, tell me this. What did you do to keep from testing positive in Menckenburg?"

"Didn't have to do nothing. Loren said the stuff he gave me was undetectable."

"So how come you got detected using it in Cleveland? You weren't using Loren's cream up there. You ran out. Where'd you get more?"

"You really don't want to know where I got my refills. We're talkin' about guys that'll gobble your guts and then pick their teeth with your pinkies."

"Who, Sammy? Give me a name."

"I give you a name, it's my pinkies they'll be chomping on." Tancredi stood up. "We're through here."

"Sammy, your lies could send Dale Loren to prison."

"Well, he gave me steroids, didn't he?"

"You know he didn't."

"No, I don't."

Keaton fished a business card out of his wallet and handed it to Tancredi. "You change your mind, think of something I might be able to use to help Loren, let me know."

Tancredi took the card and shoved it under the damp elastic of his gym shorts. "Yeah, sure. You think of something that will get me back in baseball, you let me know."

Dale Loren dropped the combination lock on top of the gloves, spikes, sweats, and jock straps he'd jammed down into the large cardboard Gatorade box. Tomorrow would be the first day in nearly thirty years his spikes wouldn't have a home in a professional locker room.

The post-game chatter had a hollow sound that seemed to echo off the clubhouse wall. Maybe it was always that way after a loss. Maybe he'd just never noticed before.

Bumper Jones stopped by Loren's locker on his way back from the shower. "Man, I sure stunk tonight. Didn't have shit or sense enough to keep it off the center of the plate."

"Happens sometimes."

"What's with the box?"

"Packing up. MacFarland just canned me."

"Just because we dropped out of first place? Man, that wasn't your fault."

"More like because Sammy Tancredi tested positive for steroids."

"Oh, yeah, that." Jones cinched his towel tighter around his waist. "Man, I surely appreciate how you kept my name out of that mess."

Loren shrugged and sat down beside his box of possessions. "That's all right."

"Hey, that was some story you told them guys in D.C., though. Cold cream and lemon juice. Some story, all right. Man, if you ain't lyin,' you ain't tryin.' "

"Yeah. Some story. Look, you wouldn't happen to have any of that cream left, would you? You know, from that last batch I gave you?"

"You kidding? I scrapped it all when the news broke about Sammy. Too bad, really. Sure could have used some tonight."

"Well, the sunblock probably wouldn't have helped much under the lights."

"What? Oh, yeah. I get it." Jones faked a punch at Loren's shoulder. "Some story, all right." Then he squeezed past Loren and held out his hand. "Well, good luck, man. Thanks for your help."

Loren shook the offered hand. "You're welcome, I'm sure."

Loren was still sitting in front of his locker when Lloyd Keaton made his post-game tour of the clubhouse. Keaton took one look at the box on the bench and said, "Oh, shit."

Loren nodded slowly. "Two weeks' severance. After twenty-five-plus years. And I can't go on using the team's lawyer."

"That guy was on the Mammoths' payroll? That explains it. Seemed like he was more worried about the Mammoths than about you. And he wasn't too sharp at that. Could be you're better off without him."

"Sharp or not, the price was right."

"Hard to argue that. Did you talk to Jones and Anthony about cream samples?"

Loren's shoulders slumped. "They both dumped everything when Sammy tested positive."

"Too bad."

"Funny thing. I think Jones still believes I was giving him steroids."

"So does Tancredi."

"You saw him?"

"This afternoon."

"Any luck tracking his real source?"

"No, he's running scared about something."

Loren stood and closed the door of his empty locker. "So am I."

Heading for his car, Keaton pondered the limits of credibility. Even in the face of Loren's testimony, Bumper Jones still believed the trainer had really been giving him steroids. And neither Tancredi nor Bloodworth bought Loren's story. People believed what they wanted to believe.

Maybe I'm the one who needs a credibility check, he thought. Maybe the cold cream and lemon juice in Loren's locker were just window dressing, in case someone tumbled to the fact that he was distributing stronger stuff.

Against all his instincts as a skeptical reporter, though, Keaton wanted to believe Loren. After all, what were the chances the trainer had discovered a steroid you could take any time without getting caught? But how could he prove Loren was dispensing harmless cream? Anthony and Jones had both dumped their supplies. His best bet was to find out where Tancredi got the steroids that triggered his positive test.

Keaton reached his car, a dilapidated Ford Escort that had seen better days three years ago when he'd traded his Beemer for it to pay off some gambling losses. Before starting the Escort, he fished his cell phone out of his pocket and switched it on. He always turned it off during games, saying he didn't want to disturb his fellow press box occupants with phantom ringing and disembodied conversations. Actually, he was the one who didn't want to be disturbed.

The cell phone's message display showed that one unanswered call had arrived during the game. He punched voice mail and heard the voice of Sammy Tancredi saying, "I need to talk to you about that stuff . . . you know, that stuff we talked about."

Keaton called the number Tancredi had left, but got no answer. A vague feeling of unease nagged at him. Tancredi should still be up, especially if he'd listened to the game broadcast. Maybe his short stint with the Indians left him uninterested in triple-A ball. Or maybe he was busy with the bikinied martini mixer who'd answered his door.

Keaton switched on the ignition. The Escort's engine turned over with an asthmatic wheeze, and he headed for Tancredi's apartment. When he wheeled his car into the apartment parking lot, his feeling of unease blossomed into outright alarm. An ambulance was pulling away from a crowd of onlookers outside Sammy's front door.

Keaton spotted the martini mixer in the dispersing crowd and caught up with her before she disappeared inside the complex. The bright red colors she had sported earlier were no longer in evidence. She wore a white terrycloth robe, her toes were covered by satin slippers, and her fingernails dug into the palms of her hand. Her mouth was free of lipstick and her eyes dripped mascara.

"What's going on?" Keaton asked.

The girl looked out at the departing ambulance, which had stopped for a traffic light. "It's Sammy," she said. "I stopped in. For a drink. After the game, you know. He was on the bathroom floor. There was a syringe." She wiped at her eyes and a dollop of mascara came away on her knuckle. "I called nine-one-one. But it was too late."

Keaton followed her gaze to the ambulance. Its flasher was dimmed, and even when the traffic light changed it didn't look as if it were in any particular hurry.

Chapter Six: Alea Ludo Ergo Sum

KEATON'S KORNER

The full weight of the federal government, in the form of Representative James Bloodworth and his committee of steroid snoopers, came down on Sammy Tancredi last week when Bloodworth called him a "fine example for the youth of America" and threatened him with lifetime expulsion from baseball.

Sammy was still upset by Bloodworth's threat of expulsion when I interviewed him yesterday. All he wanted was to serve out his hundred-day suspension and get back to baseball. Today we know that will never happen. Representative Bloodworth has another scalp for his belt, another example for the youth of America, and the lifetime expulsion he sought. It's time the voters realize what Bloodworth's sideshow is costing this country in money and, now, in lives.

Keaton watched the flat farmland of central Ohio fly by as he headed his car along the interstate to East Wheeling. Sammy Tancredi's death had been news for two days, until the police decided that there was no evidence of foul play. Just another oxycontin overdose. Hillbilly heroin, the plague of Appalachia, was claiming so many lives that fatal overdoses ceased to be news, even when the victim was an up-and-coming baseball star.

Keaton had to agree that the police verdict of accidental

death seemed reasonable. He'd talked Eddie Oliver, his editor, into letting him track the story and then talked the police into letting him examine Sammy's apartment after they were satisfied the outfielder was responsible for his own death. But Keaton hadn't found anything in the apartment to suggest the police might be wrong. There were no signs of a struggle, and barely enough clothes and personal items in the furnished apartment to fit into the two suitcases the outfielder had brought with him. He'd signed a three-month lease, and evidently left most of his clothes and baseball gear stored in Cleveland, confident that he would return to the majors as soon as his suspension was lifted.

Tancredi's death had left Dale Loren in a bind, since it was now Loren's word against the word of a dead man that he never supplied the young outfielder with steroids. It was tough to impeach a dead man, get him to recant his statement, or identify his real suppliers. With Tancredi dead, Keaton didn't see how the trainer could avoid being crushed by Bloodworth's committee.

As he drove, Keaton forced himself to think about Sammy Tancredi's death and the problems it caused Dale Loren. Otherwise he might find himself thinking about his destination. East Wheeling, West Virginia, was the kind of a city where the bail bondsmen made house calls. Lodged near the center of the upthrust spear of the Mountain State that separated the farms of eastern Ohio from the mines of western Pennsylvania, the tiny city on the Ohio River had been the gambling center of the region ever since World War II, controlled first by Big Bill Ellison and now by Ellison's son Little Bill.

East Wheeling was a two-hour drive from Menckenburg, and on his good days Keaton viewed the distance as a gambling deterrent. He was like an alcoholic who uses a stepladder to hide bottles in the top-most niche of his attic, but keeps the stepladder within easy reach. Interstate Seventy was Keaton's stepladder. If David Bowers wouldn't take his bets, he could always get some action from Little Bill Ellison.

Once Keaton crossed the Ohio River into West Virginia, he told himself there was no turning back. Little Bill's gambling emporium took up two floors of a red brick warehouse on the banks of the Ohio. Noisy slot machines, roulette wheels, and craps tables dominated the downstairs, while the upstairs was given over to quieter pursuits like blackjack, poker, and sports betting. Little Bill himself held forth on two barstools in front of a bank of LED displays listing betting odds and results for the day's sporting events. He was shaped like a melting snowman, and an oxygen canister jutted out under his left arm like a bright red torpedo.

As Keaton cleared the stairwell and left the downstairs slots behind, the harsh rasp of Ellison's breathing could be heard over the soft whisper of cards on green felt and the tinkling of ice cubes in cocktail glasses.

"Haven't seen you in quite a while, scribe. What brings you to East Wheeling?" Ellison's voice was a throaty gargle.

"Got a hot tip."

"Fixin' to break me?"

"Would if I could. Don't quite have the bankroll for it, though."

"That's a load off my mind." Ellison shifted on his two seats and waved his right arm at the odds board behind him, so that the red torpedo under his left arm pointed directly at Keaton. "What's your pleasure?"

"Pittsburgh at San Francisco. Going for the line on the Giants."

Ellison shifted to fix Keaton with a watery stare, causing the oxygen canister to clunk against the bar behind him. "Must have got that tip from your buddy Bowers. He just laid off over a hundred grand on San Francisco."

Keaton avoided Ellison's stare and scanned the odds board behind him. He tried to keep his voice steady, matter-of-fact. "That so?"

"It's a lot of play for a Pirates/Giants game. You boys know something I don't?"

"Not about betting."

"Yeah, well." Ellison nodded toward the cashier's window just behind him. "We're happy to take your money any time."

Keaton fumbled with his wallet, then counted three stacks of hundred-dollar bills onto the cashier's shelf. His hands shook and he had to count the third stack twice. He turned to Little Bill. "Three thousand dollars. Hardly enough to break you." But more than enough to break me, he thought.

Little Bill snorted a half laugh and then rasped, "Every little bit hurts."

Once he got his bet down, Keaton just wanted to leave the casino as quickly as possible. On his way to the stairs, though, he heard a familiar voice behind him. "Back at it, huh, scribe?"

He stopped and turned to see Bull Harding, a squat, totally bald man who was rumored to have been the chief enforcer for Big Bill Ellison. "See you're still around, Bull."

"You know how it is. Every time I try to retire, they keep pulling me back in." Harding nodded toward Little Bill, whose rasping breaths could still be heard across the room. "Somebody needs to keep an eye on the kid there."

"He's not a kid anymore."

"None of us are. He still needs looking after, though. He's not half the man his daddy was."

"Big Bill needed four barstools? That must have been quite a sight."

Harding stretched his thin lips in what might have passed for a smile. "Takes more than barstools to support us. Business ain't what it used to be. Nowadays anybody wants some action just has to find a computer or a teepee. Hard for us to compete."

"Well, I still like doing business with an old, established firm."

" 'Preciate it." He jerked his thumb toward a room separated from the rest of the casino by heavy black curtains. "Stick around. Be some high-stakes poker back there soon."

Most people looked at Harding's broad shoulders and the thick folds of skin that linked those shoulders with his bullet head and saw only a redneck who'd been too brutal and corrupt even for the East Wheeling police force. But Keaton had stared across a poker table at those tiny, feral eyes and knew there was a fierce intelligence behind them. The last thing he needed right now was a high-stakes poker game.

"No thanks," Keaton said. "I just bet all my swag on a ball game."

"Betting Neyer and that tight-ass umpire like your buddy Bowers?"

"Jesus Christ. Does everybody here know my business?"

"Long as you're here, your business is our business." Harding nodded toward the black curtains. "Your Giant game's on the West Coast. They're three hours behind us. Sixth inning here is the third inning there. You've got lots of time before the game starts. Why not pass it playing poker?"

The black curtains undulated like a woman's hips. The game hadn't started, but Keaton thought he could hear the riffle of cards shuffling behind them. He took one step toward the curtains, then pivoted and backed away from Harding, heading for the stairs.

"Sorry," Keaton said. "Can't do it. Got to get back to Menckenburg." He hurried down the stairs, then burst out the revolving door and inhaled great gulps of river air. Lucky he'd left his wad with the sports cashier, or he'd be back gambling for sure.

Keaton ate dinner at a rib joint on the river road and got a late start back to Menckenburg. Lightning flashed in the night sky as he crossed the Ohio River, and rain was cascading down his windshield when the night games started on the West Coast. He tuned in the Giants/Pirates game on his XM satellite radio, and listened as the round, familiar tones of the lead Giant announcer as he lavished praise on the pitching of Jerry Neyer. The announcer didn't say so outright, but it sounded as if Bradshaw was running true to form, giving the Giant pitcher the benefit of close calls on anything near the plate. Through the first six innings, Neyer struck out seven Pittsburgh hitters while walking none and holding the Pirates scoreless.

Bradshaw was much less generous with the Pirate pitcher. By the end of the sixth inning, the rookie had walked five batters. Twice, when the Giants seemed about to score, the Pirate infield had turned a quick double play to keep the game scoreless. The second time that happened, Keaton swore and pounded his steering wheel so hard that his Escort fishtailed on the wet asphalt.

Between innings, as the Giant announcers hawked medical plans and used-car deals, Keaton pondered his talks with Little Bill Ellison and Bull Harding. Both said Dave Bowers had been betting heavily on Neyer, and Harding even mentioned the connection with the umpire Bradshaw. Had Bowers been coining money with real bets all the time the two of them had been diddling with baseball card wagers? Son of a bitch. I'm the one who figured out the edge you could get with Bradshaw behind the plate, and all I've got to show for it is a few lousy baseball cards.

Well, at least he had real money down on this game. But the edge he'd counted on with Neyer pitching and Bradshaw umpiring would be useless as an ashtray on a motorbike if the Giants couldn't score. The Pittsburgh pitcher walked the bases full with one out in the top of the seventh, and it looked as if San

Francisco might break through just as Keaton pulled into the driveway of his apartment building. Since he had no access to the satellite station inside his apartment, he sat in the parked car muttering, "No more double plays. Please, no more double plays," and shouted over the thunder when the Giants' number-five hitter doubled to clear the bases and give the Giants a three-to-nothing lead.

That's more like it, Keaton thought. He unfastened his seat belt and sat back, grinning. A three-run lead with Neyer going strong and Bradshaw giving him the close ones. Money in the bank. Then a Giant error and a seeing-eye single put two Pirate runners on base in the top of the eighth and prompted a visit to the mound from the Giant manager. "This could be it for Neyer," the Giant announcer speculated.

"Leave him in. Dammit, leave him in," Keaton yelled at his dashboard. "He's still got his stuff. They're lucky to have anybody on base." The Giant manager ignored Keaton and replaced Neyer with a hard-throwing rookie prone to control problems. "No. No. No." Keaton clenched the steering wheel. "That's just the kind of pitcher who won't get any breaks from Bradshaw."

The pitcher threw three tight sliders to the next Pirate hitter, and Bradshaw called all of them balls. When the Giant announcer complained about the third call, Keaton asked the announcer, "What the fuck did you expect?"

The Giant rookie grooved his next pitch, and the Pirate hitter connected, driving it into the left-field stands to tie the score. Keaton slumped backward. "Fuck. Fuck. Fuck." A lightning flash lit up his car and he caught sight of his reflection in the windshield. "I could see it coming a continent away. Doesn't anybody in San Francisco understand this game?"

The Giants' pitcher struck out the next three hitters, who obligingly flailed unsuccessfully at marginal pitches instead of taking them. Unfortunately, the Giants' hitters were no more successful in their half of the inning, and the teams went into the ninth with the score still tied.

This is it, thought Keaton. This is what I've been missing. Action. Talking to my dashboard at midnight in the middle of a thunderstorm. He felt alive for the first time in months. Bring 'em on.

Keaton pleaded with the radio for a new pitcher before the Pirates came to bat in the ninth, but the Giant manager stuck with the young fireballer. Hoping that Bradshaw might give the kid a break on the close ones was like hoping for mercy from the IRS. The kid sandwiched a strike-out between two walks before surrendering the go-ahead run on a single and earning a trip to the showers. "*Now* you take him out," Keaton said to the radio. He wondered if Dave Bowers was listening to the game. He stands to lose a lot more than I do. Serves him right for laying money on these match-ups without telling me.

The Pirates went down without scoring any more runs and brought in their closer to protect their one-run lead in the bottom of the ninth. At least we've got the top of the order up, Keaton thought, but the Giants' lead-off hitter grounded out harmlessly.

"Come on. Come on." The next Giant batter walked, bringing up their number-three hitter, Steve Brewer. "Come on, Brewer. Earn your pay."

Brewer took one pitch, then hit the next one into the left-field bleachers. And it was over. Sudden as a thunderclap. Giants win five to four. Keaton pounded the steering wheel with both hands, accidentally sounding the horn.

He rolled out of the car and stood with his face to the heavens, letting the rain drench him. Oh, yeah. Oh, yeah. This was it, baby. Won the bet. He could quit any time, but why would he want to? Lightning flashed and he raised both fists skyward, shouting the Latin he'd learned from a buddy in Gamblers Anonymous, "*Alea ludo ergo sum.*" I gamble, therefore I am.

Chapter Seven: Just Another Damned Thing

KEATON'S KORNER

The fine old American tradition of "innocent until proven guilty" took a hit this week when the Mammoths dismissed trainer Dale Loren after his appearance before Representative James Bloodworth's congressional committee. In his committee appearance, under oath, Loren denied supplying Sammy Tancredi or any Mammoth players with steroids.

Evidently the accusation alone, unsupported by any evidence, was enough to convince the Mammoth brass, since manager Bait MacFarland fired Loren on Tuesday. It wasn't the first time Loren had been treated shamefully by MacFarland and the Indians organization. Nearly twenty years ago, MacFarland was the Indians manager who overworked the pitching arm of one of the most promising young left-handers in the American League. That pitcher was Dale Loren, whose reputation and livelihood have now suffered the same fate as his ruined pitching arm.

Lloyd Keaton threw the front door open with such force it drove David Bower's wheelchair backward through the entry hall into his own living room. "You son of a bitch," Keaton shouted. "You son of a bitch. You've been betting my system with Little Bill Ellison."

Bowers braked his backward-rolling wheelchair. "Whoa there. I thought it was *our* system. And why shouldn't I bet it? It works. You should know. It's won you a big stack of baseball cards."

"Yeah, I've got a stack of baseball cards, and you've got this brand new house. Does that seem fair to you?"

"I risked my own money. You weren't in a position to do that."

"It's my system."

"It's *our* system. We worked it out together."

"And you gave it up to Little Bill Ellison."

"The hell you say. Why would I do that?"

"I don't know. Professional courtesy? One shark to another?"

"Bullshit. What makes you think I tipped him to the system?'

"I had a little talk with him yesterday."

"Did that talk involve betting?"

"Don't change the subject."

"Betting is the subject. Jesus Christ, Lloyd. Are you betting again?"

"It was a sure thing."

"It's *never* a sure thing. That's why they call it gambling. Did you listen to the game, for Christ's sake? The Giants were lucky to pull it out."

"The Pirates were lucky to be in it at all."

"Doesn't that tell you something about sure things? And what makes you think I gave anything away to Little Bill?"

"Bull Harding as good as said so. He remembered your bet. Said you were counting on the combination of Neyer and Bradshaw."

"He mentioned the umpire?"

"By name. That's what I'm telling you."

"I never gave it up. I swear. Why would I give it up to that asshole? They must have figured it out for themselves. They've been taking enough hits to make them pay attention." He jerked his wheelchair around and propelled it across the hall into his office. "What the hell. Bookmaking's my business. I've been doing it ever since college. I've got nothing to apologize for."

Keaton followed him. "In college it was just a sideline."

"In college I got this." Bowers brought both palms down hard on the rims of his chair's tires. "Top of my class, but the only decent job offer I got was from the federal government. None of the big consulting firms wanted to take on my wheelchair."

"You did all right with the feds."

"I put in my time. Eighteen years. Then I just couldn't take it anymore. All those clockwatching cocksuckers counting off the hours till their carpool left, the days till their vacation started, the years till they could retire. The only thing that kept me alive was making a little book on the side."

Bowers wheeled his chair over to face Keaton head on. "Meantime, all those hotshots we were in college with? Half of them have retired already. Remember Harry Cullinan?"

"Sure. Dense as pressed plywood."

"Never could get it through his head that profits could go higher than a hundred percent. 'How can you have more than a hundred percent of anything?' he'd say."

Keaton smiled. "It's like that old joke about the millionaire who's interviewed and says, 'I just buy stuff for a dollar and sell it for three dollars. I figure, what the hell, thirty percent ain't bad."

"Well, hundred-percent Harry just retired as a full partner with McKinsey."

"Harry wasn't the brightest bulb on the marquee, but he could always sell himself."

"Hell, I could sell myself too. Trouble is, the only willing buyers wanted to hide me behind a back-office desk. And anybody who happened to wander back assumed I only got the job to fill some handicapped quota."

Keaton put his hand on Bowers's shoulder. "We like to say 'disabled,' not handicapped."

Bowers shook off the hand. "You're behind the times. The feds wanted to label me 'differently abled.' And God forbid anyone should call me 'wheelchair-bound.' They spent more time worrying what sort of PC sign to hang on me than how to use me effectively.

"Well, by God, that's all behind me. I'm my own boss now. No more GS-whatevers to lord it over me and shout like it was my hearing that was bad and not my legs."

"Yep, you're doing all right, all right. Thanks to my system."

"Will you get off of that." Bowers jabbed his chest with his thumb. "*I* helped out with the system. *I* put up the money. *I* took the risk. *I* get the reward." Each "I" was accompanied by another jab.

"But you wouldn't let me bet *my* money."

"No. And I still won't. You got lucky yesterday. Now call it quits."

"Oh, sure. Look who's talking. You're still raking in the dough."

"Call it quits. You're like an alcoholic watching someone else drink. You can't handle it. You know you can't."

"So I should just sit around and watch while you pay off this house using my system?"

"You lost your own house two systems ago. And your car with the last one." Bowers wheeled himself over to a rolltop desk and returned with an envelope. "Tell you what. Give me what you won last night. I'll act as your investment counselor, parcel it out on future games, using our system. You just steer clear of the betting parlors." He held the envelope out to Keaton.

"So I should just put my money in and you'll let me know when I win? Hell, that's what we tell suckers waiting to be plucked at the poker table."

"Yes, and that's what I'm telling you. You're just another sucker waiting to be plucked by Little Bill and his boys."

Keaton batted away the envelope. "Goddamn it. This time I'm the plucker, not the pluckee."

"The hell you are. I've seen this before. You get one win under your belt, and you think God's on your side. You think you can't lose. Well, here's a flash for you. God doesn't care about your bets, or even about baseball. He may see a sparrow fall, but he doesn't give a shit about Red Birds or Orioles."

"Oh, that's cute. Don't forget about the Blue Jays."

"If God's not watching the Cardinals, He sure as hell isn't paying attention to some expansion team up in Canada. Can't you see we've been here before? You'll take your winnings and plunge again because you think God's on the side of you and your goddamned system. And pretty soon you're going to lose more than you've got."

Keaton stood up. "Oh, fuck you. I don't know why I bothered to come."

"Well, if you don't know, I sure don't."

"Don't bother to see me out." Keaton slammed the door behind him. Shit. All the excitement had been drained from last night's betting. He didn't feel like a winner anymore. He didn't feel like much of anything.

Liz's lower lip moved, almost imperceptibly, and Keaton knew, from years of living with her, that she was biting the inside of it. He also knew, standing there on the porch straddling the bag from the sporting goods store and hefting the box containing a Braun coffee maker, what she was going to say next.

"You've been gambling again."

The box in his arms was just big enough to be awkward. "Can I come in?"

"Of course." She unlatched the screen door and the hydraulic mechanism screeched as she swung it open.

"I'm in the kitchen, ironing." She started toward the rear of the house without waiting for him.

Keaton held the screen open with his foot and set the bag just inside the door. Then he carried the box into the kitchen. "You always wanted a coffee maker," he said.

She stood behind the ironing board, wearing a yellow T-shirt, beige slacks, and sandals. "It was pretty near the bottom of my list. A stable home life, now, that was right close to the top."

A divorce was near the bottom of her list too, Keaton thought. Both their lists. Just another damned thing they couldn't afford. But in the end, she'd insisted. He hefted the awkward box. "Where should I put this?"

She pointed with the iron. "There. On the kitchen counter. Just leave it in the box. It'll make it easier when they come to repossess it."

He put the box down on the counter next to a stack of freshly ironed and folded T-shirts. "Can't you just take it, say thanks, and be happy with me?"

She pressed down hard on the iron, steaming it across the leg of a pair of black slacks. "No. I can't. Because I know the roller coaster will start back down any day now."

"At least I'm headed back to the top."

"Congratulations. So was Icarus."

"You mean Sisyphus."

"Don't tell me who I mean."

"Icarus only had one shot at it."

She attacked the other pant leg with the iron. "And just how many shots did we have?"

"It's not like I'm really gambling. I'm on to a sure thing."

She sat the iron on end and stared at him. "For heaven's sake, Lloyd. When was it ever *not* a sure thing?" She went back to work on the seat of the slacks. "You're right. It was Sisyphus."

A tendril of black hair worked its way free from her bun and fell over her temple. Keaton had always found that vaguely sexy, and enjoyed patting it back into place. But now he was too far away.

"Is Davy here?" he asked.

She set the iron aside, straightened, and nodded toward the ceiling. "Upstairs, in his room."

She puffed out her lower lip and blew the stray tendril out of her eyes. "You better knock first. I keep finding *Playboy* magazines under the mattress when I make his bed."

She patted the tendril back into place, and Keaton noticed a few strands of gray among the black hairs. "He's old enough to make his own bed," he said.

She smiled. "Then I wouldn't find the *Playboy*s." It wasn't a smile you could hang a lot of hope on. But at least it was a smile.

Keaton backed out of the kitchen. He nodded toward the coffee maker. "I got it at Macy's. Take it back if you don't want it. Exchange it for something you do want."

She went back to her ironing. "You know what I want."

Keaton picked up the shopping bag he'd left in the hallway, climbed the stairs, and knocked on the door of his son's room. When he heard "Come in," he shouldered the door open and held the bag in front of him as an offering. "Hey. Brought you a gift."

Davy, who had been lying on his stomach with his feet dangling over the end of the bed, laid aside his English textbook and sat up, swinging his long legs over the edge of the coverlet. "Hey, Dad. Whatcha got?"

Keaton reached into the bag. "A shortstop's glove." He tossed it to the boy.

Davy caught the glove and fitted it onto his left hand. "Wow. A Wilson A3000."

"Well, you'll be moving from the outfield to the infield next year."

Davy pounded his fist into the pocket of the glove. "This is great. Thanks, Dad."

"In my day, infielders and outfielders used the same kind of glove."

Davy smiled over the leather webbing. "Did they have gloves in your day?"

"A few players wore them. We called them 'sissy-boys.' "

Davy stood up. "Let's go try it out. You can use my old glove."

"Actually, I can't use it." Keaton raised his left hand and flexed his fingers. "Wrong hand."

"Oh, yeah. That's okay. There's an old lefty glove of yours in the garage."

"Surprised your mom keeps it around."

"She thinks it's mine."

"I guess if you don't watch a lot of baseball, a left-handed claw looks pretty much like a right-handed claw."

"Yeah, those first-baseman's mitts all look alike. But, hey. There's still some other stuff of yours in the garage. A couple of boxes, at least."

A couple of cardboard boxes. Not much to show for sixteen years of marriage. Still, there was Davy. "Let's go get my old glove," Keaton said. "If we can find a bat too, I'll hit you some grounders."

Davy pounded down the stairs with Keaton just behind him. Even with the advantage of being one or two steps higher, Keaton couldn't help notice how tall his son had become. But that wasn't all he noticed.

When they reached the foot of the stairs, Keaton said, "We better tell your mom where we're headed."

Davy led the way into the kitchen, while Keaton lagged behind and stood blocking the doorway. The boy held up his glove. "Hey, Mom. Dad and I are going over to the field to test out this new glove he got me."

Liz looked up from her ironing. "That's nice, dear. Don't forget your homework."

"That's a good looking shirt you're wearing," Keaton said from the doorway. "Maybe you ought to change into one of those T-shirts your mom's ironing."

"Oh, I'm okay," Davy said.

"I intend to run you pretty hard. That shirt's going to get all sweaty," Keaton said. He didn't want to be right. And he didn't want to cause a fuss if he was wrong.

"Maybe *you* ought to change," Davy said. "You're the one wearing a dress shirt."

"Got a T-shirt there that'll fit?" Keaton asked Liz.

"Davy's an extra-large now," she said.

"Pretty broad through the shoulders there, young man," Keaton said.

Liz pulled a blue T-shirt from the pile and threw it to Keaton. "You're broad in other places. Extra-large should fit just fine."

Still standing in the doorway, Keaton unbuttoned his shirt, turned his back on the kitchen, and pulled on the T-shirt. He turned again to face the two in the kitchen. "Your turn," he said to Davy.

"I'm fine with this shirt," Davy said.

"Let's go then." Keaton stepped out of the doorway, motioning Davy through.

As Davy went through the door, Keaton grabbed the tail of his son's shirt and yanked it above his head. The boy's back was pitted with ugly scabs.

Keaton swore and jerked on the shirttail, pulling Davy back into the kitchen.

Liz stopped ironing. "Lloyd, what on earth are you doing?"

"It's what *he's* doing." Keaton dug his fingers into Davy's arm and spun him around. "How long have you been doping?"

"I'm not doping!"

"Don't lie to me. I used to see acne like that in the Mammoths' locker room. How long have you been using steroids?"

"I told you, I'm not doping."

Keaton dug his fingers deeper into his son's arm. "Come on, Davy. I know better."

"Lloyd, you're hurting him. Didn't you hear him say he's not using steroids?"

"That acne says he is."

"He's had acne all over his face for over a year," Liz said. "He's a teenager. We've been using cream on it. I never thought to use it on his back."

Keaton relaxed his hold on Davy's arm without turning it loose. "Do I have to get you tested? I will, you know."

Davy looked down at the linoleum. "No. I tried some pills. But I only used them once."

"How about the rest of the team?"

"Some guys have a regular thing going."

"Does your coach know?"

"No."

"Doesn't know or doesn't want to know?"

"Doesn't want to, I guess."

"Where did you get the pills?"

"Dad, come on."

"Tell me."

Davy raised his eyes from the linoleum. "Hulk Anderson. He was bragging on his biceps and handing out samples."

"Where did he get his samples?"

"I don't know."

"Take a guess."

"I told you, I don't know."

"Leave him alone, Lloyd," Liz said. "Can't you see he's not lying?"

Keaton released his son's arm. "God help you, you'd better not be."

Davy rubbed his arm. "What are you going to do?"

Keaton sighed. "I don't know what I'm going to do. But I know what you're going to do. You're going to steer clear of that junk. For the rest of your life."

Chapter Eight: Don't Ask, Don't Tell

KEATON'S KORNER

Maybe we've got the wrong end of the stick with all these stories about steroids. No matter what we say about side effects, the message that gets across to kids is, "They help you hit home runs."

It's a little like those TV ads for pills that promise "natural male enhancement" and, in the obligatory listing of side effects, warn that you should see your doctor "if erections last more than four hours." (Gee whiz, Doc, please don't throw me in THAT briar patch.)

The current congressional hearings and news stories are telling kids that steroids will give you big muscles, but BE CAREFUL, excessive use may lead to home-run records and batting championships. No wonder we're finding high school kids hooked on steroids.

Lloyd Keaton heard the familiar sound of infield chatter and the unfamiliar ping of an aluminum bat meeting a baseball before he rounded the corner of the high school and saw the wire mesh backstop and green bleachers that enclosed the school's baseball diamond. Davy's high school coach, Stu Lammers, had kept many of his key players together over the summer by forming a team in the local American Legion league.

Today was a practice day, and Keaton had timed his arrival so that he could watch the end of the practice session before confronting the coach about steroids. Lammers, a stocky man whose beefy arms and pot belly bulged out of a tattered blue sweatshirt, stood at home plate hitting grounders to a group of gray-shirted boys on the edge of the infield grass. Out in center field, Davy took turns with other outfielders catching looping fungoes off the bat of a tall boy in gray sweats standing just beyond first base. As Keaton approached the field, his son ran down a long fly, returned the ball on one hop to the hitter, and ran back to the line of outfielders without acknowledging his father.

Keaton was about to settle into a bleacher seat behind the fungo hitter when he saw Dale Loren sitting alone behind home plate. Loren waved, and Keaton walked along the edge of the bleachers to join him.

"My son's out in center," Keaton said. "You got a boy on the team?" He remembered that Loren's teenage son had been killed and was immediately sorry he'd asked.

"Bobby Lewis is my nephew." Loren nodded down the left field line, where a group of pitchers took turns throwing to two squatting catchers. "He'll be a sophomore next year. Coach Lammers invited him to come out for the Legion team."

"What do you think of Lammers?"

Loren pursed his lips. "Seems to have inherited the worst traits of Casey Stengel and Captain Bligh. He doesn't communicate well and overworks the boys."

"Not exactly a positive recommendation."

"I'm not in a very positive mood right now. Got a lot of free time on my hands. Looks like nobody wants any part of a steroid-peddling ex-trainer."

"It's a bum rap."

"You and I seem to be the only two people in Ohio who believe that. Thanks for mentioning it in your column, anyhow."

On the field, a lanky infielder gloved a grounder and sailed his throw over the first baseman's head. While the first baseman ran after the ball, the coach turned toward the bleachers, saw Keaton, nodded, and called Davy in from the outfield to join the infielders.

Davy ran to the bench, picked up his new glove, and ran out to the shortstop position, trying not to look at his father in the stands.

"Any follow-up on the hearing?" Keaton asked Loren.

"Besides my being fired?"

"Bloodworth was talking grand jury."

"That's all I'd need right now."

The coach hit a skipping grounder to Davy that ticked off the webbing of his glove and bounced between his legs. The boy looked at the ground, kicked the dirt, and then inspected his glove closely for possible signs of malfunction as an outfielder retrieved the ball.

"Get that butt down, Keaton," the coach shouted. "Try for two this time."

The coach lashed a hard grounder far to Davy's right. The boy took three quick steps, backhanded the ball cleanly, pivoted, and unleashed a perfect throw to the second baseman.

"Attaboy, Davy," Keaton yelled.

Davy didn't look up, but Keaton could see a slight grin poking at the corners of his mouth.

"Nice play," Loren said.

"Any idea where Sammy Tancredi got those steroids he was using?" Keaton asked.

Loren shook his head and sighed. "None."

"Or the hard stuff?"

"Hell, no. That bothers me, though. Sammy didn't seem like a hard-core doper when he was with the Mammoths."

"How so?"

"Because he'd been caught once, I was watching him for needle marks or any other sign of illegal drug use. Never saw a thing. And he was really happy when I gave him my cream mixture. He'd been afraid I'd give him something he'd have to inject. Sammy was finicky about needles."

"Maybe we can help each other. I'm trying to track down local steroid sources. If we can locate Sammy's real suppliers, it'll clear you."

"I'm guessing Sammy's suppliers were closer to Cleveland, but I'll do whatever I can."

"You must have seen some steroid traffic here in Menckenburg back when they were legal."

"Not much. We had a couple of players on andro, but they didn't get it through me."

"Maybe you could find out who supplied them. What about amphetamines?"

"Oh, we ordered them by the carload. Handed them out like jelly beans."

"Where'd you get them?"

"A local distributor. OgrowSport. I'd order vitamins, amphetamines. Aspirin, ibuprofen, holistic stuff, anything non-prescription."

"They still supply you?"

"Everything but amphetamines. Lots of holistic stuff now. Glucosamine. Condroitin. Every year there's something new. A couple of players are trying something called Vitamin O."

Keaton smiled and shook his head. "Any sign it works?"

Loren shrugged. "Austin Reed is burning up the league. He's likely to be the next Cleveland call-up."

The coach yelled, "Bring it in," and hit a high bouncer to Davy, who fielded it, threw it to the catcher, and charged the plate as the catcher rolled the ball back onto the field to simulate a bunt. Davy scooped up the rolling ball in his bare hand, rifled it back to the catcher with a single fluid arm movement, and trotted over to the first row of bleacher seats. He glanced quickly over his shoulder at his father as the coach went through the same drill with the rest of the infielders.

"Would these local guys have handled steroids back when they were legal?" Keaton asked.

"Possibly. I know they batched amphetamines for us."

"Think they might be dealing steroids now?"

"Where's the percentage? There can't be many users. It's illegal. And anyone who juices is likely to be caught by the league's testing program. Company like that would be risking too much for not much gain."

"What if a league has no testing program?"

"Organized ball tests at all levels now."

"Not all levels." Keaton nodded toward the only two players left in the infield, the catcher and first baseman. "Those two boys built like anybody you went to high school with?"

Loren's face clouded over. "You think . . . ?"

"I've heard rumors."

They watched Hulk Anderson return the ball to the catcher and lumber off the field, his biceps bulging through the slit sleeves of his gray T-shirt.

Loren looked from the first baseman to Keaton. "You think the coach knows?"

Keaton stood and dusted off the seat of his pants. "That's what I came to find out."

Trophies of various sizes featuring bronze baseballs, bats, and posed players topped the metal file cabinets lining the walls of Coach Lammers's office. The coach had taken off his spikes and greeted Keaton in his stocking feet, settling into a swivel chair and waving his hand toward the folding chairs on the other side of the green metal table that divided the room.

Keaton took the chair closest to Lammers. "Team looks pretty good."

"Good bunch of kids. Your boy Davy's going to make a fine shortstop."

Keaton moved forward to the edge of his chair. "I couldn't help noticing that several of your boys are pretty big for high school."

"They grow 'em big in this part of the state. Same as the corn and wheat."

"Fertilizer helps the corn and wheat grow big. Think your boys might be getting a little help growing as well?"

Lammers took a toothpick from a mug on his desk that read WORLD'S GREATEST COACH. "What are you saying?"

"Some of them looked like they might be on steroids."

"Which ones? They by God know I'll kick their asses off the team if I catch them juicing."

"I'm guessing that policy might cost you half your starting lineup."

"That's bullshit. There's no way half my boys are juicing up."

"Then you wouldn't be averse to having their urine tested?"

The toothpick in Lammers's mouth dipped below his chin stubble. "By who?"

"My newspaper. Of course, we'd want to sample all the teams in the league. Kind of level the playing field."

"You got no call to do that. You could ruin some boy's ball-playing career. I've got a lot of these kids on my high school team."

"Then you better wean them off steroids before your high school season starts."

Lammers took the toothpick out of his mouth and smiled over its frayed end. "We got kind of a 'don't ask, don't tell' policy around here."

"Well, you'd better start asking, or I'll start telling."

"Who you gonna tell?"

"The hundred thousand readers of the *Menckenburg Herald*,

for starters."

Lammers pointed the frayed end of the toothpick at Keaton. "Maybe you ought to think twice about that. Your boy, you sure he'd pass a steroid test?"

"You want to start testing, he'll be ready when your high school season starts."

"Could be he'd pass then. But could be he won't be good enough to play shortstop then. Assuming some newspaper decides to collect piss samples and spotlight my program."

Keaton stood and pressed his fists so hard into the metal table that his knuckles whitened. "Let's be clear here. Are you saying Davy might not get to play if I sound the steroid alarm?"

"Not at all." Lammers fixed his face in the smile of a beauty pageant loser. "I'm just saying he might find the competition to make the team a little tougher if he's not in top-notch physical shape."

"Now that would make a great lead for my story: LOCAL HIGH SCHOOL COACH SAYS BOYS MUST USE STEROIDS TO MAKE THE TEAM."

Lammers's smile vanished. "I never said no such thing. You're twisting my words."

"I think I heard you pretty clearly. I bet I could even quote you verbatim."

"It's my word against yours, and I'll deny saying anything like that."

"Well, in that case, it's a good thing I have this little device to prod my memory." Keaton pulled a small recorder from his shirt pocket, pushed two buttons, and held it out toward Lammers. The recorder whirred and repeated, "I'll deny saying anything like that."

Lammers's face reddened. "You can't do that. You didn't tell me you were recording. You can't do that without my permission."

"I am dreadfully sorry you feel I've transgressed the ethics of my profession." Keaton pulled the recorder back and cocked it beside his ear, his finger on the *record* button. "Why don't I ask you now? Is it all right if I record our conversation?"

"It sure as shit isn't all right. And if you turn that thing on again, I'll cram it up your ass."

"I'll take that as a 'no' answer."

Lammers pointed at the recorder. "That'll never stand up in a court of law."

"Well, then, it's a good thing we're not in a court of law."

Lammers stood up. "This here interview is over."

Keaton didn't move. "You must have me confused with someone you can kick off your team. This interview is over when I say it's over." He turned on the recorder. "Now let's talk about steroid use among high school athletes."

Lammers folded his arms across his chest and clamped his mouth shut. After a few seconds, he opened it to say, "I ain't saying shit," and clamped it shut again.

Keaton shrugged. "You're wrong, Coach Lammers. You've been saying shit all morning. But you're right about one thing." He switched off the recorder. "This interview is over."

Chapter Nine: Covering the Key

KEATON'S KORNER

Well, Congressman Bloodworth and his Committee on Governmental Reform continue their drive to make the world safe from millionaire steroid users. Having wasted the time of the legislative branch of our government, they have now arranged for a grand jury to waste the time of the judicial branch.

Major League Baseball has put steps in place to deal with the steroid offenders in its ranks. Do we really need to watch preening public officials hounding players who have already suffered loss of reputation, pay, and playing time?

I don't deny that the Committee on Governmental Reform has the right to investigate steroids in baseball, hamburgers and fries in the teenage diet, or gum chewing in kindergarten. But shouldn't the aim of the committee be, as its name implies, the reform of the government itself? Once it's managed to accomplish that, I will happily applaud their expansion into baseball pill popping, school lunch calories, and kindergarten nap times.

Dale Loren squatted on his garage roof, trying to patch the leaks from a three-day rainstorm before they spread to his house. Following the advice of the *Menckenburg Herald*'s Fix-It column, he laid long planks on the flat asphalt surface so that he wouldn't do more damage to the roof by walking on it. Now he hunkered along the planks, looking for cracks beneath the scattered gravel and the blackened remains of last year's leaves. The dark puddles left by the rain didn't seem to be anywhere near the leaks he'd seen earlier dripping onto the garage floor.

He found a few suspicious-looking cracks and spread thick gobs of black sealer over them with a putty knife. When he couldn't find any more cracks within reach of the planks, he smeared half the can of black glop around the base of two beams that had been nailed into the roof by a previous owner. The beams supported a basketball backboard that stuck out over the edge of the roof. A frayed net clung to the hoop and dangled over the driveway.

While he was still caulking around the support beams, his wife came into the driveway and called up to him, suggesting that they get a professional roofer.

"Look, Robin, I'm out of work," he answered. "I've got the time, and there's no money coming in. It's only the garage. Let's just wait and see whether my patch job works."

"I don't want to wake up some morning and find the living room drenched."

"We'll never find a roofer now that the summer rains have started. Besides, I don't want to take down the backboard with the basketball season so close."

"Tess says she's not going to play this year."

"She'll play. She said that last year."

Robin shook her head. "Last year she did it just to please you. Because of Tommy."

"She's got to play. If she doesn't, she can't expect to make the high school varsity."

"Well, you'll have to talk to her. God knows she doesn't listen to me."

Loren's daughter, Tess, started playing basketball in the fifth grade. Nearly all the girls in her class at St. Mary's went out for the team that year. Positions and playing time were divided equally among fifteen pigtailed novices more intent on controlling their dribbling than on passing or scoring. That first year, Tess was so excited to get the ball that she would hop with glee, which ensured that she didn't keep it very long. The sequence of catch-hop-whistle-traveling call-turnover happened so often that Harry Simmons, father of another of the pigtailed players, saddled Tess with the nickname "Turnover Tessie."

By the seventh grade, Tess hit a growth spurt and became St. Mary's starting center. Slender and intense, she played with a gangly grace that set her apart on the court. Covering the key instinctively, she blocked opponents' shots with a frequency that put a backspin on her nickname and gave "Turnover Tessie" an entirely new meaning. Her premature hop vanished, replaced by a shy post-play one-step. After forcing a turnover, or after scoring herself, she would cock her head, flash a palms-down "safe" sign, and kick out sideways. To Loren, she looked like a bashful crane determined to learn the Charleston.

In the eighth grade the pigtails were replaced by a ponytail and frizzy blonde bangs. Most of her friends, studious girls who were more interested in James McEvoy than in LeBron James, stopped playing basketball. Tess wanted to stop too, but the grief counselor thought it would be better for her to play. And for Loren to watch.

Loren moved the planks and looked for more cracks, without much luck. Across the street, his neighbor was loading his whole family into their SUV. Loren waved, but they didn't see him. It looked as if they were going away for the weekend. Loren remembered doing that, back when he had a whole family. He looked down at his empty driveway and thought about Tess's brother Tommy. He'd gotten so he could go five or six hours without thinking about Tommy, but when he did, he repeated the same internal dialog he'd had going for nearly two years.

It's just so hard to know about kids. You tell them not to do so many things. "Don't do drugs." "Don't drink and drive." "Don't draw to an inside straight." "Don't swing at a three-and-oh pitch." He never thought to tell Tommy not to leave his taillights on when he had to stop beside a freeway. Drunks can lock on them and try to follow you. You assume kids know so much. Tommy hadn't even been driving long enough to know a car needed water. Or how to read a temperature gauge. He never thought to tell his son, who was conscious long enough to tell Loren he was sorry. Jesus, *he* was sorry.

Loren and his wife tried grief counseling. A starched woman who'd probably never lost so much as an earring tried to get them to ". . . let their loss find expression." Loren went for a month, then gave it up. It wasn't that he couldn't scream. He just couldn't scream on demand. Robin was still going, though. There, and to MADD meetings and SADD seminars where she trotted out their story as an object lesson to other high school kids. He didn't know why. It was the other guy who had been drinking.

But the counselor had been right about Tess's basketball games. They turned out to be good therapy. Robin was busy with her own projects, and on those afternoons when the Mammoths were at home with a night game, Loren was generally the only male parent at his daughter's games. Except for Harry Simmons, of course. He had his own brokerage firm, and left work before the markets closed to get to the games. Tess said he came to practices as well. At games, Simmons stalked St. Mary's side of the court, yelling at the girls and waving folded sheets of white note paper. He had shown Loren his notes once. Play diagrams and scouting reports on other teams in the league.

"Looks like you're all set for the NBA draft," Loren said. "Too bad eighth-grade girls aren't eligible."

"Our girls shouldn't lose a game," Simmons said. "Back up

there, Cassie! With good coaching, there could be college scholarships out there someday."

Loren sat happily with the mothers, cheering St. Mary's baskets and Tess's shot blocking. Watching her on the court had been the best part of the year for him. And Harry Simmons had turned out to be right. Their team went undefeated.

"Have you talked to her yet?" Robin asked as Loren was getting ready for bed. His wife was already under the covers, reading.

"Not yet."

"Well, don't expect me to do it. I think she hates me. I found out today she's been menstruating since March. She didn't even tell me. She must hate me."

"She doesn't hate you. She's just feisty and independent. You prepared her . . ."

"Why do you always argue with me?"

"I'm not arguing."

"You are. I'm just trying to tell you how I feel."

Loren crawled in on his side of the bed and turned off his light. But Robin wasn't through talking.

"I don't know why you insist she play basketball, anyway," she said. "Tess is healthy, gets mostly As, and has a nice group of friends. We should be happy for that. You can't turn her into another Tommy."

"Tommy didn't play basketball."

"Well, then, you can't relive your own youth through her."

"Jesus Christ, I'm fed up with this psychobabble. I didn't play basketball either. I just think it's a shame for her to chuck something she's so good at."

"Stop yelling."

"I'm not yelling. I'm explaining."

"Well, explain in a lower voice. The children are sleeping."

No, he thought. The child. The child is sleeping. But he didn't correct her. He did it all the time himself. The children are sleeping.

Loren was still awake two hours later. Even with his back to Robin, he sensed she must be awake too. From her side of the bed he heard a rustling, a rubbing. A short, soft moan. He lay still, embarrassed by something he didn't understand.

After another half hour, he got out of bed and prowled the dark house, wearing only his shorts. He found a blanket in the hall closet and sat on the living room couch. Furniture formed ominous shapes. Windows made gray holes in black walls.

He just wanted to limit the damage. To stop it from spreading. Before he lost Robin and Tess too. He couldn't say exactly why he wanted Tess to play. But he was dead certain none of Robin's reasons were right. Somehow, it had to do with learning. Tess was good at it, but she'd never be as good as she could be if she didn't go on playing. She was entering one of the power schools in the area, and if she wanted to play any varsity sport, she had to play it year-round. If Tess didn't play, she'd miss something. Something important. But he didn't know what. If he knew, he could just tell her. It was so hard to know what to tell kids. He couldn't puzzle it out. He felt as if *he'd* missed something. He just wanted to make sure she knew everything she needed to survive. And he'd already blown it once.

He stretched out on the couch, pulled the blanket around him, and tried to sleep. He knew the night sounds by now. The sound lone cars made turning down their street to come home. The sound when they don't turn down their street. When they don't come home.

The counselor said to concentrate on a clock's ticking when he had trouble sleeping. Shows how up-to-date she was. There wasn't a ticking clock in the whole damned house. She'd have him sitting in the kitchen watching the microwave flash off the seconds. Instead, he focused on the refrigerator motor.

Ka click click ah. Ka click click ah. Ka click click ah.

For the first time, he was conscious of a steady drumming on the roof. The refrigerator's mantra changed.

Ka click click ah, drip. Ka click click ah, drip. Ka click click ah, drip, drip.

He grabbed the blanket and stumbled through the kitchen to the garage. Rainwater beaded on the ceiling and puddled on the cement floor.

The man at the hardware store had a different sealer for him.

"It's asphalt cement. It pours, see. You don't have to spread it on with a putty knife. You just wait until the roof is dry and pour it on. It finds the leaks just like water does. Seals 'em right up. It'll solve all your problems."

It's going to take more than asphalt cement to solve all my problems, Loren thought. But he bought two big cans. He also bought a new red, white, and blue basketball net.

He put the net up first and tried to interest Tess in a game of elephant. It was their family's extended version of cow. Follow-the-leader with a basketball. When a player made a shot, you had to match it exactly or get one letter toward elimination. Ever since Tess grew into her center position, the three letters of cow had made for too short a game. Loren shot left-handed, and Tess had a deadly two-handed flip that started just above her frizzy bangs. Tommy shot right-handed. When the three of them played, none of them could match the others' shots. Tess wasn't comfortable shooting one-handed, and neither Tommy nor Loren could outshoot Tess with two hands. In a three-letter game, the first person to make a shot almost always won. Cow became as predictable as tic-tac-toe. So they extended the number of letters to horse, and finally to elephant.

★ ★ ★ ★ ★

Tess sat cross-legged on her bedroom floor, her narrow feet shoved into laceless tennis shoes.

"Net's up. What about a game?" Loren said.

"Don't feel like it."

"We can go for ice cream afterwards."

"Okay, but I get first shot. And it doesn't mean I'll play this summer."

"We'll talk about that later. Over ice cream."

Tess quickly ran off a string of two-handed baskets from the center of the key Loren had painted on the driveway. He caught up with a run of left-handed jump shots from the corner. When they were both one letter from elimination, he switched hands and tried a right-handed hook from the key. It caromed off the backboard and dropped through the hoop.

"That's Tommy's shot," Tess said. "Why'd you switch hands?"

Loren handed her the ball. "It's time you learned to shoot with your right hand."

"Geez, dad, you're getting to be as bad as Mr. Simmons."

"Just try the shot. For the ice cream."

She balanced the ball awkwardly in her right hand, pivoted, and flung it toward the basket. It missed the backboard and landed on the garage roof.

Tess shouted, "I'll get it" and started toward the ladder that stayed propped behind the garage for the duration of the basketball season.

"Tess, stop. Come back here." She stopped at the corner of the garage. "Come back here. I'll get it."

"But I always get it down."

"It's you kids clomping around up there that caused those damned leaks." Loren edged past his daughter, rounded the corner, and headed for the ladder. "I'll get it."

"It's not my fault," she shouted as he started up the ladder.

Then she disappeared in the direction of the house. "It's not my fault." Her voice was fainter. A door slammed, and Loren was alone on the roof.

As long as he was on the roof, Loren started the new patch job. He hacked away blisters and covered the worst cracks with layers of asphalt cement and roofing felt. The smaller cracks he just filled with the asphalt cement. The pitch black cement poured on easily, spreading in all directions. It seemed so much easier than hunting down every little leak and caulking it with lumpy glop. He poured on one whole can and part of the second. Then he went to find Tess.

The ice cream store had been remodeled to look like a nineteenth-century soda fountain. A teenage girl in a frilly apron standing behind an imitation marble counter asked, "Are you two together?"

"I'm together." Loren pointed down a row of ice cream vats toward his daughter. "But she's kind of flaky."

"Oh, Dad."

Neither Loren nor Tess quite fit into the wrought-iron chairs. A glass-topped table perched on three iron legs wobbled between them. Tess licked circles around the bottom of her scoop of rocky road, leaving a narrow waistline between the cone and ice cream. Loren lapped his butterscotch upwardly, bringing the ice cream to a point. He wondered if the way people ate ice cream revealed some deep-seated psychological difference between men and women.

Two tables away, a middle-aged man was staring at Loren and whispering to the woman with him. He tried to ignore them, to focus on Tess. He'd been aware of the same sort of attention just after Tommy died, but it had only lasted about a month. He wondered how long his current notoriety would last.

He turned his attention to Tess and tried to explain why it

was so important that she play basketball. His daughter listened impassively, licking in circles.

"See, you'll miss something," he said for the umpteenth time. "Something important. I just don't know what."

"If I do play, how do you know I won't miss something by being away from my friends? I don't even like basketball anymore."

"You played for ice cream this afternoon. What if I bribe you?"

"There's not enough ice cream in Baskin Robbins." She poked at his stomach over the glass tabletop. "Besides, you can't afford the calories."

"No, seriously. Is there something else you want?"

"A cell phone of my own. But Mom'd never go for it."

"I'll handle Mom. Would you play then?"

"I don't know."

"Come on. Would you play then?"

"Cassie Simmons whines all the time. And her dad yells at us."

"That hasn't stopped you before."

"Okay, I'll play. For the phone."

In the car on the way home, Tess asked, "How'll you get Mom to go for the phone?"

"I don't think it will be too hard. She wants what's best for you."

"She spends more time in her car than with me."

"You're too hard on her, Tess. She loves you very much. She just hasn't had a lot of time lately. She's been pouring herself into all these causes."

"She might as well have died with Tommy."

Pinpoints of rain dotted the windshield. They grew and multiplied before Loren turned on the wipers.

As they pulled into the driveway, Robin was running into the garage with handfuls of plastic garbage bags. Loren parked and ran after her. As promised, the asphalt cement had found the leaks. But it hadn't sealed them. Black stalactites hung from the garage ceiling. Water and tar both dripped onto the cement floor. And onto the overhead garage door. And onto Robin's white Volvo.

It took a week before they could get a roofer to come and give an estimate. Loren watched from the window as the man parked his pickup, checked the hitch on the trailer of tar he was towing, and headed up the driveway. When he saw the black streaks of runny asphalt cement on the garage door, he stopped, retreated, and motioned toward the passenger in the pickup. The passenger, a husky man with a tar-stained T-shirt advertising something Loren couldn't make out, joined the roofer at the garage door. They ran their fingers over the black streaks, shaking their heads and grinning. Finally, the passenger returned to the pickup and the roofer rang the doorbell. He was still smiling when Loren answered the door.

Loren followed the roofer up the ladder at the rear of the garage. The man stalked across the roof, ignoring the planks laid out as walkways. He stopped, toed one of the patch jobs with a worn work boot, and took a stubby pencil from behind his ear. Then he began moving again, asking questions without looking at Loren. "How old's the house?" "This the original roof?" "Ever get rid of these dead leaves?" "Mind holding this tape?" "Know you've got asbestos here?"

Every now and then he wrote something on his clipboard, but the pencil movement seldom followed Loren's answers. The man's terse, preoccupied questions remind Loren of someone, but he couldn't think who.

The questions continued when the two men were back on solid ground. Looking at the black streaks on the garage door, the roofer asked, "You try to get this out?" Loren showed him the corner where he'd tried scouring the streaks. The tar was gone, but the redwood surface was stained and discolored. The roofer sucked his pencil thoughtfully. "Guess you'll have to live with it, huh?" Then he stuck the pencil back behind his ear and said his estimate would be ready in a couple of days. When asked how soon he'd be able to get to the roof itself, the roofer answered, "Dunno, we're pretty busy."

As the roofer drove away, his passenger had his head laid back on the seat, laughing. Loren was back in the house before he figured out what the roofer's questions reminded him of. Their grief counselor. He also remembered something he'd meant to ask the man: "What did I do wrong?"

Loren was late picking Tess up after her first afternoon of basketball practice. He spotted her sitting on one of the low kindergarten swings beyond the outdoor courts. With her long legs almost parallel to the ground, she swayed from side to side, holding a basketball in her lap. Head down, she didn't see him arrive.

He started across the courts toward Tess when her coach intercepted him. She fingered the whistle around her neck nervously. "May I speak to you a minute, please?" she asked. Before he could answer, she took his arm and led him back toward his car.

"We had a little scene this afternoon," she explained. "Mr. Simmons was helping me. He took Tess off to one of the side baskets. He was trying to make her—to teach her—to shoot one-handed. I was with the other girls, so I'm not sure exactly what happened. But she threw the ball at him. By the time I got there, she was crying and shouting 'I hate you.' "

"She threw a basketball at Harry Simmons?"

The coach gave a short laugh and pulled the whistle from

side to side. "Well, she didn't hit him." The whistle's chain chafed her neck. "But, you know, he gives so much to the school. And the summer program." She looked back over her shoulder. By now Tess had seen the two of them talking. She leaned forward on the swing, trying to hear what they were saying.

"I understand," Loren said, watching Tess. "I'll talk to her."

"I really want her to play this year. And she's still welcome to. I just don't feel we can force her."

"I didn't think I was forcing her. Has anything like this ever happened before?"

"Not with Tess."

"I'll talk to her as soon as we get home." Loren waved Tess over. She stood and started toward him, dropping the basketball. It bounced once and rolled into the rut under the swing.

Tess fastened her seat belt defiantly, as if daring her father to have a collision. "I told you I didn't want to play."

"You can still play. But you'll have to apologize to Mr. Simmons first."

"He's an asshole."

"That may be. But he spends a lot of his own time helping out with school sports."

"He'll still be an asshole after I apologize."

"You're right, Tess. Apologizing to assholes won't change them. But sometimes you have to do it." And sometimes they ought to apologize to you, he thought. "Look, Tess, I'm sorry. It'll be okay. You don't have to play if you don't want to."

"What about Mr. Simmons?"

"You'll still have to apologize."

"What about the phone?"

"Maybe for Christmas. We'll see."

"I know what 'we'll see' means."

" 'We'll see' is the best I can do right now. Apologize to Mr.

Simmons first."

"And then what?"

"We'll see."

When they arrived home, Loren opened the trunk to help Tess unload her things. As she shouldered her backpack, he handed over her basketball kneepads. She handed them back. "It's okay, daddy. I'll still play soccer. You can come to those games next spring."

Loren reached out and hugged her. Her bangs brushed against his forehead. She hugged back for a few seconds and then wriggled away. "I'll let you go," he said.

Tess turned at the door, cocked her head, and flashed her palms downward. Safe. I'll let you go, my darling child.

Loren climbed the ladder to the roof. Before he could do anything, a black Pontiac pulled into the driveway. It must be one of the other roofers I called, he thought, come to give a second opinion on this asphalt money drain. Loren climbed back down the ladder. By the time he'd reached the driveway, the Pontiac driver was out of the car. The driver looked familiar, but Loren couldn't quite remember where he'd seen the beefy man. Then the man reached inside his jacket pocket and pulled out a thin white envelope, and Loren remembered immediately.

"Dale Loren," the man said as he pushed the envelope into Loren's hands. "I'm serving this subpoena directing you to appear before the grand jury convened to investigate the use of drugs in professional baseball."

Inside the house, Loren stuck the subpoena to the refrigerator door with a strong magnet. Robin had already left a note on the refrigerator. The first roofer had called with his estimate. The repair would cost more than two months of Loren's salary, if he still had a salary. The contractor was busy for at least two months, but would get to them eventually. Eventually. That must be a contractor's way of saying "We'll see." He went into the garage and mixed the rest of the runny asphalt cement with the thick black glop he'd used at first. Then he climbed the ladder to the roof. Ignoring the garage leaks, he spread the new mixture over any suspicious-looking seams and cracks above the living room. The leaks never seemed to come where the cracks were, but it was the best he could do for now. He climbed down, retracted the ladder, and put it away in the garage. He wouldn't need to leave it out this summer.

Chapter Ten: Flattened Pennies

KEATON'S KORNER

Well, the Mammoths have won six of their last seven and are back in the race. Second-baseman Austin Reed is on a tear, sporting a twenty-game hitting streak and carrying the team on his spindly shoulders.

Reed tells me he attributes some of his success to an over-the-counter organic vitamin supplement. If that's the case, the rest of the team should find that counter and belly up to the bar.

From the press box, Keaton saw David Bowers wheel his chair into his accustomed slot just as a local firefighter started to sing, "Oh say, can you see . . ." over the public address system. The second the umpire shouted "Play ball!" Keaton made his way under the stands, coming up behind Bowers in time for the first pitch. It was a strike, and Grace Hanson's cowbell echoed throughout the park.

Bowers glanced over his shoulder. "Should be a good game."

"How's the betting running?"

"Betting here always favors the Mammoths. But there's enough down on the Mud Hens so I don't have to lay anything off."

"You see the Mets started a series in Denver last night? Bradshaw was umpiring third base. That means he'll be behind the plate Sunday for Oke's next start."

"Who's Oke going against?"

Keaton was pretty sure Bowers already knew the answer, but he told him anyhow. "Half the Rockies' starting pitchers are on the DL, so they're bringing a kid up from AAA. Name's Don Kyle. He pitched against us late last year."

"Oh, yeah. Big right-hander. Terrific fastball. No control."

"Averages six walks a game in the minors. If the Major League hitters don't eat him alive, Bradshaw will. Looks like a sure thing for the Mets. Ought to bet it big time."

Bowers turned his chair to look at Keaton. "I take it you're not talking baseball cards?"

Keaton edged himself into the attendant's space beside Bowers's wheelchair. "No. I want you to take my money."

"We've been through this. I won't take your money."

"Then what about this? Since you've been doing so well betting *my* system, how about staking me to a little loan?"

"It's *our* system, remember? What happened to the money you won last time?"

"Still got most of it. I plan to put it all down on the Mets. But I'd like to beef up my bet a little. Get at least ten grand down."

Bowers turned his chair back toward the field. "If I won't take your money across my counter, I'm sure as hell not going to give you any of mine to pass to some other bookie."

On the field, the Mammoths' pitcher set the visitors down one-two-three, and the Mammoths' lead-off hitter, Austin Reed, tripled to start the home half of the first. The crowd stood as Reed rounded second, and Grace Hanson's cowbell sounded a duet with ex-mayor Tony DiCenzo's ooga horn.

"Talk about a sure thing," Keaton said as the crowd sat down again. "That kid's hit in twenty-one straight games now."

"He's been on fire ever since they started wearing those black arm bands for Sammy Tancredi."

The mention of Tancredi nagged at Keaton like a sore tooth. "Team's sixteen and four since they started wearing them. Maybe they ought to sacrifice a player every year, just so they can wear those lucky bands."

"Didn't the Indians win the Series the year they lost a player?"

"Yeah, nineteen twenty, when Carl Mays beaned Ray Chapman. Team wore black arm bands from mid-August through the series. See, there's precedent. Sacrifice a player a year."

"Doesn't seem like too much if those arm bands guarantee a championship," Bowers said. "Still, it might make it hard to attract players."

"Good point." Keaton shook his head. "Seems like you managed to steer the conversation away from betting."

"I'm here to watch baseball. Not to bet on it. Look at that."

On the field, the Mammoths' clean-up hitter singled Reed home with the first run of the game. Bowers joined in the crowd's applause. "You ought to be watching yourself. Not thinking about betting dough you don't have."

Keaton stood up. "You'll be betting the Mets game Sunday. You know it."

"Leave it alone. It's my business, damn it."

"Well, mine's reporting. Maybe I better get back to my computer."

By the seventh inning, the Mammoths had built a commanding eight-to-two lead. Keaton left the press box and walked outside to the parking lot, fingering his cell phone. He knew what he was going to do. There was no point in putting it off any longer.

He found some shade beside a tour bus, flipped his cell phone open, and called the number for Little Bill Ellison. He wasn't surprised to find he knew the number by heart.

"Lloyd Keaton, Bill. I want to put ten grand down on the Mets this Sunday. Can you start a tab for me?"

Ellison had a voice like gears grinding. "Sure thing. Just like old times." Keaton could hear the ruffling of papers at the other end of the line. Then Ellison's voice came back on. "That's Oke's game, isn't it? Your buddy Bowers beat you to the betting line. You guys know something I don't?"

Dale Loren sat at the conference table in the Federal Office Building in Cleveland. The table was long enough to accommodate sixteen chairs with plush purple upholstery, seven on either side and two on the ends. At twenty after two on Friday afternoon, all the chairs but two were empty. Loren was accompanied by his lawyer, Mario Biancalana, a short, handsome Italian with a moustache and a goatee.

Biancalana was a criminal lawyer, and he looked to Loren as if he were about eight parts criminal and two parts lawyer. At first, Loren had balked at hiring a criminal lawyer, and still couldn't come to grips with the fact that he needed one. Even here in the Federal Building, contemplating a grand jury subpoena and a lot of empty purple chairs.

Loren checked his watch for the tenth time since they'd come into the room. "The man's twenty minutes late."

"Believe me, when Hamilton Jeffords gets here, you'll wonder why you were so anxious to see him."

"Tell me again what I should watch out for."

Biancalana stroked his goatee. "Jeffords says he wants to meet to let you know the charges he'll be bringing against you. But it's really a fishing expedition. Before he goes to the grand jury, he wants to be sure he's got every possible charge he might make stick. So he'll tell you the charges he's sure of and make up a few he's not so sure of, just to see if you flinch."

"Can he do that? Legally, I mean."

"Oh, yeah. Try not to flinch. Just be honest and straightforward. But don't try to be too helpful. If you give him lots of info, and some of it is contradictory, you could find yourself facing perjury charges on top of everything else."

"Can I just refuse to answer? Plead the fifth amendment?"

"You can try, but that just means he'll bring a broader list of charges before the grand jury and let them know you didn't deny any of them. Probably best to help him narrow the list of charges. You'll have less to defend yourself against when the grand jury indicts you."

"You mean *if* the grand jury indicts me."

"No. I mean *when* they indict you. Our grand juries pretty much rubber-stamp whatever our prosecutors want."

"If it's all preordained, and you won't be allowed at the grand jury hearing, why do I even need a lawyer?"

"You'll need me to represent you at the trial after you're indicted."

Loren waved at the empty chairs. "So all this is just to make sure the noose fits?"

"In my experience, nooses are pretty much 'one-size-fits-all.' "

Loren felt a nervous, queasy stirring rising from the pit of his stomach. It wasn't the nervousness he'd once felt approaching the pitcher's mound, which he somehow converted to adrenaline. No, it was the nervousness he felt as he was being anesthetized before his first shoulder operation, a nervousness born of the knowledge that so much depended on the outcome of a procedure he had little control over. He remembered his left leg kicking out uncontrollably as he lay on the gurney, counting backward from one hundred. He reached under the conference table and ground his left hand into his thigh to steady its trembling.

A young black man carrying sheaves of paper came through the conference room door and held it open for a tall man with a knife-thin nose and a receding hairline and a petite young woman carrying two stuffed briefcases.

Biancalana nodded toward the knife-nosed man and whispered, "Jeffords."

The young black man continued to hold the door open as Jeffords and the young woman were followed by two short bespectacled men wearing nearly identical blue suits, a tall sandy-haired man in a seersucker jacket, a pudgy bald man, and a pants-suited woman carrying a laptop.

Jeffords introduced his retinue as they spread out and took seats at the table across from Loren and his lawyer. The two blue-suited men were with the FBI, while the sandy-haired man was with the IRS and his balding companion represented the Ohio Tax Board. The petite woman and young black man were both attorneys on Jeffords's staff, and the woman carrying the laptop was a stenographer.

Loren was grateful to see Biancalana writing the names of Jeffords's people on a seating chart he'd sketched on his legal pad. The ex-pitcher was so stunned by the range of government agencies represented by his adversaries that he hadn't absorbed any of their names except that of Jeffords. Justice Department, FBI, IRS, Ohio Tax Board. And the man from the IRS represented its Criminal Investigation Division. Jesus Christ, Loren thought. He dug his fingers into his left leg again to keep it still.

When everyone had been seated, Jeffords said, "Thank you for coming. I want to go over the charges I'll be bringing against you to the grand jury and make sure that you understand their full range."

"I appreciate that," Loren said.

Jeffords looked at Loren as if his response had been an unwelcome intrusion. "Yes, well," the prosecutor continued, "the primary charge will of course be the illegal distribution of steroids and other controlled substances."

"What other controlled substances?" Biancalana asked.

"In due time," Jeffords said. "These charges are substantiated by the statements of the late Samuel Tancredi and several others."

"What others? My client has a right to know the names of all his accusers."

Jeffords turned to his young female assistant, who had taken a seat against the wall directly behind him. She handed him a typewritten sheet of paper. The prosecutor glanced at the paper. "Numerous others. I see the names of at least two major leaguers." He went on to read the names of two veteran players currently on the Indians' roster.

"When those men were with the Mammoths, steroids were legal," Loren said. "And I wasn't the one who supplied them."

"But you did supply them with amphetamines," Jeffords said.

"Amphetamines were legal then. I made them available to anyone who asked for them."

"You'll have a chance to make that point at your trial." Jeffords smiled and tapped one of the briefcases on the table. "We have more than enough evidence here to guarantee an indictment. The only question is the number of charges. In addition to dealing steroids, for example, there is the matter of their manufacture."

Loren couldn't believe his ears. "Manufacture?"

"Don't act so surprised. The supply chain for steroids is typically vertically integrated. Most suppliers are tied to their manufacture in one way or another."

"Then it's lucky I'm not a supplier."

"So you say." Jeffords tapped his briefcase again. "The evidence suggests otherwise." The prosecutor took several sheets of paper from the sandy-haired man and frowned as he riffled through them. "You also appear to be something less than a faithful taxpayer."

"I pay my taxes," Loren said, trying not to stare at the sheets in the attorney's hands. "Faithfully."

Jeffords adjusted his glasses and read from the top sheet. "For the past five years, at least, you have neglected your tax obligations in the states of New York, North Carolina, South Carolina, Indiana, Kentucky, Virginia, Rhode Island, and Pennsylvania."

Loren closed his eyes, trying to control himself. "Oh, for Christ's sake."

"Kindly do not blaspheme," Jeffords said. "These are all states visited by the Menckenburg Mammoths in completing their league schedule. I'm sure that you're aware you owe income taxes in these states."

"I've never broken it down. I claim all my income in Ohio and pay all my taxes here."

"I'm afraid that's not an option." Jeffords looked to the IRS and Ohio Tax Board representatives for confirmation. They both shook their heads disapprovingly.

"It would be a lot simpler if everyone did it that way," Loren said. "In any case, I actually pay more taxes by filing everything here in Ohio. Rates in those other states tend to be lower than ours."

"The fact that you overpay in Ohio doesn't reduce your obligation to these other states." Jeffords set the sheets of paper aside. 'So it seems we can add tax evasion to the charges of manufacturing and distributing an illegal substance."

Loren bridled. "I've never manufactured an illegal substance."

"Or distributed one," his lawyer added.

"Or distributed one," Loren repeated.

"But you admit you distributed amphetamines to players," the prosecutor said.

"When they were legal, yes."

"When did you stop distributing them?"

"The date, you mean?"

"The date."

"I don't remember."

"Then how can you be sure you didn't distribute illegal amphetamines?"

"I stopped when baseball made them illegal. I just can't recall the exact date."

Jeffords squared up the stacks of paper on the desk in front of him. "I can make it a lot easier for you if you just give me the names of everyone you supplied with steroids."

"I didn't supply anyone with steroids."

"And tell me where you got your supplies."

"Because I never supplied anyone with steroids, I didn't need any supplies."

"You'll have to do a lot better than that." Jeffords lifted one of the stacks of paper in front of him. "We've got sworn statements from your customers."

"That's impossible. I have no customers. No customers and no suppliers."

"And I suppose your flagrant tax evasion is a fabrication as well."

Loren was silent.

Jeffords began loading the stacks of paper into his briefcase. "If you have nothing else to say, I believe we're finished here. I'll see you at the grand jury hearing."

Jeffords's young female assistant stepped forward to take his briefcases and lead the procession out of the conference room. Before Jeffords left, he turned in the doorway and said, "If you change your mind and decide to cooperate, your lawyer knows how to reach me."

Loren stared at the closed door. His jumping leg was keeping time with his nervous stomach. "Jesus Christ. He wasn't listening at all."

Biancalana flipped through the pages of his yellow legal pad. "Let me spell it out for you. He doesn't have to listen. He doesn't even want to listen. This is a high-profile case. All he wants to do is pound you flatter than a penny on a railroad track for all the world to see."

"But I haven't done anything."

"Doesn't matter. I'm afraid he'll charge you with tax evasion, steroid distribution, maybe pushing amphetamines, and anything else he thinks might stick."

"But amphetamines were legal when I handed them out."

"You weren't clear on the exact dates. We'll have to figure them out, build a defense." The lawyer scanned his notes. "It wasn't all bad. I don't think you said enough for him to trump up a perjury charge."

"I didn't say enough? What about you? You said what, maybe nine words. At your rate that works out to about a hundred dollars a word. Not bad for an afternoon's work."

"I understand you're upset. But the only thing we could do this afternoon was find out what he's up to, try to limit the damage. Force him to narrow his charges."

"Narrow his charges? Listen to me. I didn't do anything."

"You listen to me. It doesn't matter. He'll indict you on whatever charges he chooses."

"You're saying the grand jury is his home field."

"Home field, hell. I'm saying it's his casino, his dice, his tables, his croupiers, his rules, and his audience."

"And he's playing with house money while I'm paying a hundred dollars a word for a lawyer."

"Welcome to the U.S. justice system."

Loren slumped in his chair.

"You'll get your day in court," Biancalana said. "Our job is to win over a jury of your peers. But we have to wait for your trial to have any shot at all."

The late-afternoon heat was sweltering inside Keaton's Ford Escort. He'd gone straight to his car after the Mammoths' win and had tuned in the Rockies/Mets game on his satellite radio. They were in the fourth inning in Denver, and the Mets were behind two to nothing. The Rockies had gotten to Oke in the bottom of the first, when the number-two hitter followed a leadoff walk with a home run.

Two runs didn't seem like a lot to overcome in the rarefied Denver air, but the AAA call-up Kyle, whose wildness Keaton had counted on when he bet $10,000 he didn't have, was getting a lot of strike calls from plate umpire Bradshaw and hadn't walked a batter.

Keaton pulled up in front of his apartment house, opened all his car windows, laid his hat on the passenger seat, and mopped his brow. The local TV channels weren't carrying the game, so the only way he could catch the play-by-play was to swelter in his air-conditionless car or find someone with a cable subscription. When the fourth inning ended, he plugged his cell phone into his lighter outlet and called David Bowers.

"What the fuck's going on?" he asked as soon as Bowers answered. "Oke's walking every other batter and the kid's throwing nothing but strikes."

"Goddamned if I know," Bowers said. "It's like Bradshaw hasn't read the script."

"You watching on cable?"

"What I can see through my fingers."

"Mind if I come over? I can only get it on my car radio."

"Come ahead. I'll leave the door unlocked."

Keaton found Bowers in his den, hunched over in front of his high-definition TV. His shirtsleeves were rolled up, and large patches of perspiration showed under his armpits.

"Want a beer?" Bowers asked without looking up from the TV.

"Sure."

"You know where it is."

"Get you one?"

Bowers pounded his chair's front wheels with both hands as a Denver batter took ball four, tossed away his bat, and trotted toward first. "Get me two or three."

Keaton draped one arm over the refrigerator door and let the cold air wash over his sweaty face. He stood that way, not actually seeing the refrigerator's contents, when Judy came into the kitchen wearing shorts, sandals, and a tank top.

"Lloyd," Judy said, "I didn't know you were here."

When Keaton didn't respond to her greeting, she said, "Is everything all right?"

"Could be better." Keaton grabbed two bottles of Budweiser. "Thanks for asking, though."

"Anything I can do?"

"Not unless you've got some magic that can cause a pitcher in Denver to crash and burn."

"I thought you'd sworn off betting."

"Not quite. I've been limiting my bets to sure things."

"Then you shouldn't need magic."

Keaton closed the refrigerator door. "You couldn't be more right." He returned to the den and handed one of the beers to Bowers, who opened it and took a long pull without taking his eyes off the TV set.

"Bottom of the sixth," Bowers said. "Only one out and Oke's already walked two batters. At this rate he won't make it out of the inning."

The Mets turned a double play to keep the score at two to

nothing, but Oke was lifted for a pinch hitter in the top of the seventh.

"There goes half our edge," Keaton said. "He wasn't so sharp this time out."

"He did all right," Bowers said. "Two runs in six innings. It's the other half of our edge I'm worried about. The kid pitcher is still going strong."

Oke's pinch hitter doubled, and the next batter drew the first walk issued by Kyle. "Maybe the kid's human after all," Bowers said.

Kyle ran the count full on the next batter, then threw a pitch wide of the plate that looked like the fourth ball. But the umpire raised his right fist, thumb extended, and called it strike three.

The Mets' batter threw down his batting helmet in disgust and was immediately ejected from the game. That brought the Mets' manager from the dugout, jutting his jaw at the umpire and gesticulating wildly.

While the argument grew, the TV instant replay showed that the pitch in question was at least four inches wide of the plate. "The Rockies really caught a break there," the home-team announcer crowed, as Bradshaw ejected the Mets' manager as well.

Keaton slumped back on the couch. "Evidently Bradshaw didn't get the memo."

"I don't know what the hell is going on," Bowers said.

"Well, the Mets still have two more innings to catch up. The fat lady hasn't sung yet."

"I hate to say it, but I think I hear her warming up."

The Mets' relievers shut the Rockies down in the seventh, but the young Rockies' pitcher did the same for the Mets in the top of the eighth. Keaton's right arm twitched and jerked with each pitch. When the inning ended, he pulled two more beers from the refrigerator and stood fanning himself in front of the open door until the commercials were over and he could hear the play-by-play announcer come back on the TV.

Two Mets' pitchers held the Rockies scoreless in the eighth inning, and the visitors came to bat in the ninth inning needing two runs to tie the score.

"Come on, come on," Keaton pleaded with the TV set. "Give us a comeback that will leave the fans gasping."

Bowers hunched forward in his wheelchair, elbows on his knees.

The first Mets' batter singled, and when the next one walked the Rockies manager trudged to the mound and replaced Don Kyle with the team's closer. Kyle got a standing ovation as he headed for the dugout.

"All right, now we're going," Bowers said, more to the TV than to Keaton. But when the next Mets' hitter popped out trying to bunt, he slumped back in his chair. "Can't anybody there play this game?"

Another walk and a sacrifice fly left the Mets with one run in, two men out, the tying run on third, and the clean-up hitter coming to the plate.

"Couldn't ask for a better scenario," Bowers said, leaning forward to coach the hitter. "Come on, earn your exorbitant pay."

The hitter took the first pitch for a ball and then smoked a screaming line drive into the gap between left and center field.

Keaton leapt to his feet.

The Rockies' center fielder was off with the crack of the bat, raced into the gap, threw himself forward parallel to the ground, and thudded to earth with the ball in his glove. Game over.

Keaton slumped back onto the couch. "Holy shit."

"I take it because you didn't bet any baseball cards with me, you must have actual legal tender down on the game."

"More than I could afford. I bet on the cuff."

"Welcome to the club."

Keaton patted his inner thigh. "You don't suppose there's any truth to those rumors that Bull Harding got his nickname using bull snippers on the balls of deadbeats who couldn't pay up?"

"How much did you lose?"

"Ten grand."

"A piddling amount in their eyes. My guess is they won't bother with your balls. Maybe just take a couple of fingers."

Keaton spread his fingers and stared at the backs of his hands. "Shit. I need my fingers for typing."

Chapter Eleven: Half Empty or Half Full?

KEATON'S KORNER

I see they've revived the old argument about tacking asterisks onto the home-run records set by Mark McGwire, Sammy Sosa, Barry Bonds, and other alleged steroid users in order to "level the playing field."

I've got news for them: The playing field has always been tilted one way or another. Babe Ruth never had to suit up against black ballplayers. (And the Babe was known to relax with a controlled substance—whose use was forbidden at the time—composed of malt, barley, and hops.) Roger Maris has already been saddled (short term) with an asterisk by Ford Frick because his season was longer than the Babe's and expansion had weakened the available pitching corps. And let's not forget that Hank Aaron finished his career as a designated hitter, an option unavailable to the Babe.

Best to take our records as they come and not try to wedge matchbooks under one corner or another of the playing field to level it. Some guys will do better, some will do worse. Asterisk you take.

Keaton felt like hiding, so he wheeled his office chair into the corner of his cubicle where he couldn't be seen by passersby. Since the Mammoths had the day off, he could stay in his office all day and into the night. But the flimsy cubicle walls didn't afford much protection. And that was the first place they'd look for him. There was no point in hiding, anyhow. Little Bill and his boys were likely to find him no matter where he went.

Still, he told himself, it wasn't likely they'd be chasing him. David Bowers was right. Ten grand wasn't a big bet to them. Just to him. Jesus Christ, what had possessed him? He could get half of the ten grand easily, but he had no idea where he'd find the rest.

The phone on his desk rang, startling him. He stared at it for two rings, then three. He'd have to talk to them eventually. Better to talk on the phone than to face them in person. He picked up the receiver.

An unfamiliar female voice said, "Mr. Keaton?" When he grunted yes, the voice said, "This is Essie Utonen." The name didn't make the voice any more familiar. At least it wasn't Little Bill Ellison. When he didn't respond, the voice explained, "I live in Sammy Tancredi's apartment building. We talked the night he died. You gave me your card and asked me to call if I thought of anything having to do with Sammy's death."

Keaton smiled, thinking of the red bikini. "Of course, I remember you. Have you thought of something?"

"Well, not me, exactly. But Sammy's sister is here at the apartment. She doesn't think he'd kill himself with a drug overdose."

"What makes her so sure?"

"She's certain Sammy would never have taken hard drugs. She went to the police, but they wouldn't listen to her. I convinced her to talk to you."

"Where are you now?"

"At Sammy's apartment."

"I can be there in about an hour. Will that be soon enough?"

He heard muffled voices on the other end of the line, then "She says that will be fine. She's sorting through Sammy's things. We'll be here a while."

Keaton had just hung up the phone when it rang again. Thinking it was the Red Bikini calling back, he picked up the phone right away and said, "Did you think of something else?"

A deep male voice said, "Keaton?"

He recognized the voice immediately and felt his testicles shrink. "Hello, Bull."

"I'll be in your neck of the woods this afternoon. You should have a little something for me. Thought I'd stop by. Save you a trip to East Wheeling."

Keaton winced. "Mighty thoughtful of you." Considerate as a snake rattling before it strikes.

"What time's good for you?"

"The later the better. I still have to pull everything together."

"Is there some problem?"

"No problem. Come by my office. Around five." While there are still people around, so we won't be alone.

"See you then."

Keaton hung up and stared at the phone. Why had he told Bull he'd have the money? He knew why. He hoped Bull would leave his ball snippers at home. Buy a little time.

Maybe he could even pull the money together. He ran through his options. They were so limited he could count them on both thumbs. There was Liz. She might have put a little aside, but he'd rather face Bull's snippers than ask his ex-wife to raid Davy's college fund again.

The only other person who might float him a loan was David Bowers. Bowers picked up his phone on the first ring, as if he'd been expecting a call.

"Just got a call from Bull Harding," Keaton said.

"No surprise there. Man wants his money."

"Says he'll be in town this afternoon."

"Passing the collection plate at the Church of the Wayfaring Gambler."

"Like I told you yesterday, I can't cover my losses."

"You only bet ten grand. How short are you.?"

"I can raise about half."

"Maybe he'll only take one testicle. Then you'd have a barometer for your daily outlook on life the minute you wake up. Just ask yourself whether the sac is half empty or half full."

Keaton groaned. "Do you hear me laughing?"

"You always were a half-empty kind of guy."

"I was hoping maybe you could help me keep it full."

"You want me to loan you five grand?"

"I know it's a shitty time."

"It's about to get shittier. Harding's coming to see me too."

"Oh, Christ. Don't tell me I wasn't the only one betting on the cuff."

"Like you said, it looked to be as sure as sunrise."

"Jesus, Dave. I'm sorry. If I'd known I never would have called. I mean, if I have to guard my crotch, you must be far enough in so you have to watch your crotch, head, torso, and any spare appendages."

"Oh, I don't really think they'll try any rough stuff with me. I'm too good a customer. We'll work something out."

"Well, good luck with Bull anyhow. I'll find my five grand somewhere else." Like the lottery, Keaton thought. That's all that's left.

"I don't recall turning you down," Bowers said.

"But you owe them too."

"I owe them so much, an extra five grand isn't going to make any difference. It'd be like adding pennies to the national debt."

"Are you sure? You'd actually lend me the five grand?"

"With a few strings attached."

"What strings?"

"You go back to GA. And you don't bet anything bigger than baseball cards again. Ever."

Keaton closed his eyes. "You know my track record. I don't see how I can promise . . ."

"That's the deal. Take it or leave it."

"I'll take it."

"Good. What time do you meet with Harding?"

"Five o'clock."

"Fine. Stop by any time before then. I'm not going anywhere."

Sammy Tancredi's apartment was even emptier than it had been when Keaton went through it with a police escort. Essie Utonen, Tancredi's bikini girl, sat on a couch next to a dark-complexioned young woman with jet black hair.

Two packing boxes and a suitcase sat in front of the couch. One box had been taped shut. The other was half full. The checkered sport coat Tancredi had worn to Bloodworth's hearing was folded on top of the open box.

Essie introduced Tancredi's sister, whose name was Sara. "There wasn't as much in the apartment as we had thought," Essie said.

"My brother did not have much, despite his boasting," Sara said. "But I do not think he kill himself."

"I don't think so either," Keaton said.

"Sammy was raised Catholic. He still went to mass, at least when he visit mother. For a Catholic, suicide leads to eternal damnation." Sara fingered the gold cross hanging from her neck. "I explain this to the police."

"They probably weren't too impressed," Keaton said.

"It's not only his religion," Essie said. "I never saw him do any drugs. And there were plenty of parties here where drugs were offered."

"My brother, he did not like needles," Sara said.

"He did take steroids," Keaton said. "And lied about their source. It might help if we knew who was really supplying him.

Did he have an address book? Or any sort of diary?"

"There was that little black book, remember, Sara?" Essie said. "With those notes penciled next to a few of the names."

"Oh, yes," Sara said. "It was embarrassing to read."

"May I see it, please?" Keaton asked.

Sara reached into the black purse at her side, retrieved a well-thumbed, pocket-sized address book, and handed it to Keaton.

Keaton flipped through the pages. Names and numbers had been entered in a childish scrawl that bore no relationship to the lines printed on the pages. A few names had stars and exclamation points in the margin, and underneath one name, taking up a full half page, was the notation GREAT HEAD!

Keaton closed the book. "I'd like to have my office make a copy of this, if it's all right with you."

"Of course," Sara said.

"If Sammy had a cell phone, that would be helpful too. There are probably some telephone numbers programmed into it."

Sara's face clouded. She reached back into the purse and handed Keaton a cell phone.

"I'll get both these things back to you," Keaton said. "How long will you be around?"

"Not long. I must get back to my mother."

"Where do you live?"

"Paterson, New Jersey."

Keaton smiled. "Home of Larry Doby."

"Who?"

"A baseball player."

"Was he one of Sammy's teammates?"

"Not quite. He was the first black player in the American League."

Sara bowed her head. "You will have to excuse my ignorance. I do not follow baseball."

"Where are you from originally?"

"San Pedro de Macoris. In the Dominican Republic."

Keaton nodded and looked at the two storage boxes. "Was there anything else that might lead us to Sammy's steroid supplier?"

Sara shrugged.

Essie said, "There may be more stuff in Cleveland. We found a key to a storage locker there."

"That's right. I did not think of that," Sara said.

"Will you be going there?" Keaton asked.

"I guess so. I have not thought very far ahead."

"How are you traveling?"

"I came by bus. From New York City."

"Do you have a place to stay?"

"The apartment manager said I could stay here. Sammy prepaid the rent through the end of his suspension."

"Tell you what," Keaton said. "I have something to do this afternoon. But I could drive you to Cleveland tomorrow morning. We could look through the storage locker together."

"I would not want to put you to any trouble."

"It's no trouble. And it might help to clear your brother's reputation. I could bring you back here afterward. Or you could return to Paterson from Cleveland."

"That would be nice."

Keaton stood. "Good. Maybe I could take a quick look through those boxes. See if anything occurs to me."

"There is not much besides clothes," Sara said.

Keaton bent over the open box. "All the same, I'd like to look." He went through the two boxes methodically, finding only clothes, baseball gloves, a portable CD player, CDs from groups he didn't recognize, two pairs of spikes, an assortment of hotel towels, and various award plaques. Nothing that looked as if it would lead anywhere but the local Goodwill outlet.

He closed the second box and stood up. "Thank you for letting me look through these," he said to Sara. "I'll pick you up tomorrow morning at eight o'clock. All right?"

"I will be waiting."

Keaton pulled up in front of David Bowers's home at three o'clock. Plenty of time to get a check from Bowers, take it to the bank, and meet Bull Harding at five o'clock.

He'd tried calling Bowers from his car on the way over, but had gotten no answer. So he was relieved to see the black van that accommodated Bowers's wheelchair in the driveway. He parked beside the van and walked up the wheelchair ramp.

When no one answered the doorbell or his loud knock, Keaton assumed Bowers was working in his upstairs study, out of earshot. He tried the front door, found it open, stepped inside, and called out Bowers's name.

No one answered. He could hear the drone of a baseball broadcast coming from upstairs. The Mammoths were off, but the Indians had an afternoon getaway game. That was probably why Bowers hadn't heard the doorbell.

Keaton pushed the elevator button and the doors slid open. But there was no elevator. Just cables dangling in an empty shaft. In the half light at the bottom of the shaft, he could see the underside of a wheelchair. And poking out from under the upended chair were the pale, unused legs of David Bowers.

Keaton called nine-one-one as he raced downstairs and opened the elevator doors. Then he lowered himself into the shaft and lifted the wheelchair off the body of his friend. Bowers lay face down, his head canted at an unnatural angle.

Keaton pushed his cheek down next to Bowers's slack mouth. He thought he could feel weak puffs of breath. He grabbed Bowers's wrist, found a faint pulse, and slid his own hand down to squeeze his friend's palm. "It's all right, Dave. I'm here.

Help's coming."

Keaton sat and stared at the lime-green walls of the hospital corridor while Judy paced in front of him, stopping from time to time to spew expletives. "I didn't want that goddamned house. Or that goddamned elevator."

More pacing, then, "He told me once the door sometimes opened with no elevator. How could that happen, anyhow?"

Keaton shook his head. He didn't know *how,* but he was pretty sure he knew *who.*

"And even if they do open by accident, you don't just wheel your chair into an empty shaft without looking."

Keaton shrugged as if he had no idea. Actually, he didn't want to think about it.

Still more pacing. "I guess it's lucky you were there to find him. I wouldn't have gotten home until seven." She stopped in front of Keaton's chair. "What were you doing there in the middle of the afternoon, anyhow?"

Keaton shrugged again. "Betting stuff."

"Betting stuff. God help us." She checked her watch. "Shouldn't we know something by now?" She stared at the swinging doors at the end of the corridor. "He's been in there, what? Two hours?"

"Just about."

A young man in green scrubs came through the swinging doors and said, "Mrs. Bowers?"

Judy hurried to the doctor. Keaton rose from his chair and followed her, fearing the worst.

"I'm Dr. MacDougall," the man said with a faint Scottish burr. "Your husband has suffered a broken collarbone, a fractured wrist, and a severe concussion, but we've managed to stabilize his physical condition."

"Then he's going to be all right?"

The doctor frowned and looked down at the green booties covering his shoes. "We really can't say. Physically, he's fine. But I'm afraid he's not responding mentally."

"Mentally?"

"He's in a comatose state. Blows to the head have caused traumatic brain injury."

Judy stiffened. "Oh, my God."

Keaton took Judy's shoulders in his hands, "You said blows. There was more than one blow?"

Before the doctor could answer, Judy pulled free of Keaton's hands and whirled to face him. "Blows? You son of a bitch. This was no accident. It's those bastards from East Wheeling. And you know about it."

Keaton shook his head. "He owed some money. I don't know how much."

Judy pounded on Keaton's chest with her fists. "You son of a bitch. You guys and your macho games."

Keaton threw up his arms and backed away, but Judy pursued him, raining blows on his forearms. "Get the fuck away from me," she shouted. "I never want to see you again."

The doctor grabbed Judy's arms from behind and stopped the shower of blows. Two nurses materialized out of nowhere and pulled Keaton backward, out of striking range.

"Get him the fuck away from me," Judy shouted. "He's got no business here."

The taller of the two nurses stepped between Judy and Keaton, holding up both arms like a fight referee. "I'm sorry, sir," she said to Keaton. "But I really think you better leave."

Keaton backed away. "But he's my friend."

"Friend? Fuck that." Judy sneered over the nurse's shoulder. "Fine friend. You and your sure things have put him in intensive care."

The taller nurse kept a restraining hand on Judy's chest while the shorter nurse tugged at Keaton's arm, pulling him backward.

"Get him the fuck out of here," Judy shouted.

Keaton allowed the shorter nurse to lead him to the exit. "I'm sorry, sir," she said as he pushed his way out of the door. "As you can see, though, this whole thing is very upsetting."

Keaton sat on a stone bench outside the emergency room entrance and rubbed his forearms, trying to erase the sting of Judy's flailing blows. Two nurses on a smoke break regarded him with casual disinterest, as if violent evictions from the hospital were an hourly occurrence.

He checked his watch. Seven o'clock. He was two hours late for his meeting with Bull Harding. He wondered if Bull would still be at the *Herald* office. Didn't matter, really. He was still $5,000 short of the money he needed to cover his lost bet, and the crowd of newspaper workers he'd counted on for protection would have gone home some time ago. He didn't relish the thought of facing Bull alone with only half of what he owed him. Especially after seeing what had happened to David. He decided to bypass the press room and go straight home. An easy choice.

Twilight was casting shadows throughout his apartment when he arrived home. As he reached for the light switch, one of the corner shadows spoke. "Missed you at your office."

Keaton switched on the light. "Hello, Bull."

Harding sat with one thick leg draped over the arm of Keaton's favorite easy chair. "Waited for you over an hour."

"I was at the hospital." Keaton didn't bother to ask how Harding had gotten into his apartment.

"Nothing serious, I trust."

"You know damned well it was serious."

"Now, how would I know that?"

"Somebody shoved Dave Bowers down an elevator shaft."

"Guess that's why he didn't make his appointment either."

Harding lifted his leg over the arm of the chair and edged forward in the seat. "He hurt bad?"

"Pretty bad. You don't seem too surprised."

"Why shouldn't I be surprised?"

"He owed you money he didn't have."

"So you think we shafted him?"

"Seems like a pretty big coincidence. First he drops a big bet he can't cover. Then he drops a big distance."

"You've been watching too much TV. We don't go around trying to kill private citizens. Makes it hard to collect what they owe."

"You're saying you didn't have anything to do with his fall?"

"Where's the percentage? If he can't pay right away, we just add the vig and set up a payment schedule."

Keaton watched Harding's slate gray eyes as he talked. He'd sat across the poker table from that hooded stare. There was absolutely no way of knowing whether or not he was telling the truth. Every sentence came out in the same measured monotone.

The monotone continued. " 'Course, if a guy starts missing payments, that's another matter. It's not like we can take the debt to a court of law."

"But Bowers hadn't missed any payments?"

"We hadn't even cut him a coupon book. Hell, I had no idea he was coming up short. How big a fall did he take?"

"Two stories."

Harding muttered "ouch" without much feeling. "Well, two stories would be a good start. If we did it. But you see where that'd leave us. Man's in a hospital bed, he's not likely to be keeping up with his vig. It's not like Aflac offers insurance to cover our kind of debt."

Keaton stayed near the door. It seemed like Harding was alone, but he couldn't see into the bedroom.

Harding stood up. "I take it from the tenor of the conversation that I'm going to have to work out a separate payment schedule for you."

Keaton backed so close to the door he could feel the knob against his butt. "I'm on the first floor here. Not much of a drop."

"Oh, for Christ's sweet sake. How long have you been betting with us? Vig's ten percent per month. Don't miss, or we'll find a way to bounce you off the first floor."

"I've got five grand I can give you right now."

"In that stand beside your bed. Glad you didn't forget about it. That'll cut your debt in half."

Keaton paused at the bedroom door, not knowing what to expect. But the room was empty, and the five grand was still stashed in his bedside stand. He brought the money out to Harding.

Harding riffled the bills, then dropped them in his briefcase. "This'll make it easier all round. First vig's five hundred bucks. Due in a month."

"I understand."

Harding took two steps toward the front door, then stopped. " 'Course, there's a way you might make it easier on yourself."

"How's that?"

"You're in the Mammoths' locker room. You hear something we can use, you pass it along, maybe we forgive that month's vig. Maybe you know something already. Like about umpires?"

"If I knew anything, you wouldn't be here."

"Still, maybe you hear something. Like in the locker room. And maybe you pass it along."

"Right now, I hear a lot of maybes. What if I do pass something along?"

"Depends on how good the intel is." Harding stopped at the door. His gimlet eyes never left Keaton.

Keaton had seen that look before, many times. It was a look that said he absolutely knew he had you beat. That you'd fold your hand. A look that dared you to do anything different.

"Don't do me any favors," he said. "I'll get your money without ratting on the team."

"Suit yourself." Harding stopped just outside the door and pressed two pudgy fingers against his bald head in a half salute. "See you next month."

Chapter Twelve: In-Laws and Out-Laws

KEATON'S KORNER

I'm getting a little tired of the controversy over the status of records set by alleged steroid users at a time when baseball hadn't outlawed steroids.

Suppose we applied the same logic to other fields where performance-enhancing drugs are in common use. During World War II, the U.S. government regularly provided amphetamines to pilots and bomber crew members to help them stay awake during grueling long-distance flights. Should we give the Sudetenland back to Germany? (Before you answer, remember Hitler took amphetamines as well.)

Opium was Edgar Allan Poe's drug of choice. Should we affix an asterisk to every stanza of "The Raven"? Or perhaps just to the title, with a cautionary footnote explaining the circumstances surrounding the poem's creation.

And what about all those boozing southern authors? Should we reclaim Faulkner's Pulitzer Prize and give it to a writer who was a comparative teetotaler? (My vote goes to Flannery O'Connor.)

Seriously, folks. There certainly are valid reasons for concern over steroid use. But the validation or invalidation of records set on a playing field that has never been dead level isn't one of them.

The ringing eventually woke Keaton, who rolled over and pushed the button on his snooze alarm. When the ringing didn't stop, he pushed it harder, sending the clock radio off the side of the bedside stand. When the ringing still didn't stop, he answered the phone.

"Mr. Keaton?"

Keaton stared at the numbers glowing up at him from the fallen clock. It was four fifteen in the morning. He grunted into the receiver.

"This is Essie Utonen. I'm sorry. Did I wake you?"

"No. That's all right. I had to get up to answer the phone anyhow."

"I'm really sorry. I thought you ought to know I just saw Sara Tancredi drive away with one of those boxes we loaded this afternoon."

Keaton sat bolt upright. "She said she didn't have a car. I was supposed to pick her up at eight o'clock to drive her to Cleveland."

"I know. That's why I called you."

Keaton flung his feet over the side of the bed. "Shit."

"I was coming home from a party and saw her lights were on. I thought she might like some company, so I dropped my purse off at my apartment, changed my shoes, and started back down the outside stairs to her place—well, Sammy's place—when she backed out of the door, carrying one of those boxes."

Keaton swore again, pushed the *speaker* button on his phone, and struggled with a pair of jeans.

"I called out, asked if she wanted some help. You know how narrow those apartment walkways are, and it was a pretty big box. Well, she looked up, startled like, and shook her head no."

Keaton shoved an arm into the sleeve of a light blue polo shirt. "Then what?"

"I leaned on the railing and watched while she put the box into the trunk of her car. Then she looked up at me, waved, and drove away."

"Don't suppose you got her license number?"

"No. At first I didn't think anything was wrong. Then I remembered what she'd said about not having a car."

Keaton retrieved a pair of crumpled black socks from under his bed and pulled them on. "Did you get the make of the car she didn't have?"

"All those new cars look alike to me. I think it was red. But those parking-lot lights make everything look different. She looked different too. She wore a bandana tight around her head. Made me think she might have been wearing a wig yesterday afternoon."

Keaton shoved his feet into a pair of black loafers. "Wake up your apartment manager. Tell him what happened. I'll try to roust some law enforcement and get over there as soon as I can."

"I'm sorry. I didn't realize what was going on until it was too late."

"You did just fine. You were right to call. I'll see you in a bit."

"She showed me a valid driver's license. It said Tancredi on it. What was I supposed to do?" The apartment manager wore a New York Yankee uniform top pulled over a pair of striped pajama bottoms and flip-flops. He was addressing Keaton, who had just arrived, but he'd evidently rehearsed by saying the same thing to Essie Utonen and two uniformed policemen, who nodded in sympathy.

Keaton looked around the room. "Detective O'Donohoe not here yet?"

"Somebody call Detective O'Donohoe?" the taller of the two officers asked.

"I did," Keaton said.

"May I ask why?" The officer, whose name tag read MAYHEW, said in a tone of voice that suggested Keaton might have been guilty of a crime.

"He was the detective assigned to investigate Sammy Tancredi's death," Keaton said. "Tancredi's apartment was a crime scene for a while, before they decided there was no crime involved."

"I see," said Mayhew, as if Keaton's explanation was somehow unpersuasive.

"O'Donohoe didn't call you?" Keaton asked the officers.

"I called nine-one-one," the manager said. "These men are our local beat police."

"And that means we've got at least two extra people on what sure sounds like a wild goose chase." Detective O'Donohoe pushed his way through the door of the manager's office, blinking bloodshot eyes and scratching at a half-night's worth of gray stubble. "Go ahead, Keaton, convince me there's some good reason for getting us all up in the middle of the night."

Keaton outlined the events of the previous day, from the appearance of the woman claiming to be Sammy Tancredi's sister to her disappearance with a box of his personal effects.

"The woman showed me a valid driver's license," the apartment manager said.

"Of course she did. She always does." O'Donohoe grimaced at Keaton, giving him his best "why-the-hell-are-you-wasting-my-time-with-this-shit?" look. "We call her 'Sister Susie.' She's just under six feet with frizzy red hair. We get this all the time. She scans the death notices looking for one with no mention of relatives. Then she shows up a couple of days after the funeral claiming to be the sister-in-law of the deceased and takes whatever isn't nailed down."

"Except that the woman wasn't tall," Keaton said. "She was short, wore a dark wig, called herself Tancredi's sister, and showed up two weeks after the funeral."

"So we've got ourselves a 'Sister Sara,' " O'Donohoe said. "It's the same goddamn MO. And from what you tell me, all she got away with was a box of baseball stuff."

"And some papers," Essie said.

Keaton looked at her. She was wearing a black strapless gown and tennis shoes. It was an effort to turn his attention back to O'Donohoe. "Calling her 'Sister Sara' instead of 'Sister Susie' doesn't make it the same MO. And doesn't it strike you as a little strange that the looting occurred in the apartment of a young man who died under mysterious circumstances?"

"We've been over this before," O'Donohoe said. "There was nothing mysterious about the circumstances. Young hotshot turns doper and ODs. We get five or six every month."

"Still," Keaton said. "You've got to admit a crime has been committed here. And it's not too much to expect the Menckenburg police to try to apprehend the culprit."

O'Donohoe shook his head. "Oh, yeah. A crime. Somebody stole a few baseball shoes and gloves. We'll get our very best people right on it."

Keaton stifled the impulse to say, "At least get your very worst person right off it." Instead he said, "Well, if you did put someone on it, you might prevent a recurrence of this scene in Cleveland."

"How's that?" O'Donohoe asked.

"That's right, I forgot," Essie said. "The woman found a key to a Cleveland storage locker in Sammy's effects. She seemed really excited about it."

"And she didn't want to give it up," Keaton said. "The only way I could get close to it was to offer to drive her to Cleveland."

"I'll bet she's headed there right now," Essie said.

"So, just where exactly is this storage company?" O'Donohoe asked. "Do we have a name? Or an address?"

Keaton looked at Essie, who looked at the ground, blushed, then shook her head and said, "It was one of those store-it-yourself places. I don't remember the name."

"Still, that shouldn't be too hard to run down," Keaton said.

"No. Can't be more than a hundred of them in the greater Cleveland area," O'Donohoe said. "I'll just call up there, get the commissioner to pull a hundred of the Forest City's finest off their beats to prevent any more baseball equipment from going missing."

"She's not much more than an hour ahead of us," Keaton said. "Can't we get a little cooperation out of you?"

"Not without more information than you've given me," O'Donohoe said. "Or more reason to follow up on a trivial theft."

"Even if that trivial theft involves evidence in a murder case?"

"You haven't convinced me that there was a murder, let alone that some baseball equipment might be evidence."

"What the hell," Keaton said. "I'll go up to Cleveland myself."

"I'll go with you," Essie said.

"Good idea. Then the rest of us here in Menckenburg can get back to real police work." O'Donohoe nodded to the two officers. "Let's go, boys."

"I still need a little information for my report, if you don't mind, Mr. Keaton," Officer Mayhew said.

"Christ Almighty," Keaton said. "If you won't help us, at least don't hinder us. We need to get on the road."

"You're the one who soaked up the time of these officers," O'Donohoe said from the doorway. "Give them what they need."

Officer Mayhew watched O'Donohoe leave, then gave Keaton a slip of paper with a name and phone number on it. "I played college ball with Gerry Waldron," he said, nodding toward the paper. "He just made detective in Cleveland. I'll call him, tell him what you're up to. He's only one guy, but he'll do whatever he can."

"Thanks," Keaton said. "I was beginning to think nothing I said was making sense."

"Expecting help from O'Donohoe is like expecting mercy from the IRS," Mayhew said. "The man has delusions of mediocrity."

"Leaves his fly open in case he has to count to ten and a half," Mayhew's partner said.

Keaton laughed and held up the slip of paper. "Well, thanks again." Then he hurried out the door with Essie following close behind.

"You don't have to come," Keaton said to Essie as they crossed the apartment parking lot.

"I want to. I can help make phone calls while you drive. I feel as if this is my fault. I never asked the woman for any ID. I just assumed she was who she said she was."

"It wasn't your job to check her ID. The apartment manager should have been more careful. Hell, I should have known she wasn't from Paterson when she'd never heard of Larry Doby."

"Maybe she's not a baseball fan."

"His name's on one of the main roadways." Keaton stopped in front of his Ford Escort. "Here's my car."

Essie looked at the gray primer covering the dented door and the twisted wire keeping the exhaust pipe from dragging. "Maybe we ought to take my car and put this one out of its misery."

"Show a little respect for your elders." Keaton opened the passenger door for Essie. "This'll get us where we're going. It hasn't failed me yet."

The car started with an asthmatic wheeze and Keaton pulled out of the parking lot. "It's about two and a half hours to Cleveland. Our girl's got almost an hour-and-a-half head start on us. If she's headed to Cleveland, she ought to be pulling in about an hour from now."

He handed Essie his cell phone. "See what you can find out from Information about self-storage companies. Maybe a name will ring a bell. If not, we can start calling a few."

Essie took off two pearl earrings, dropped them into her purse, and took out a pencil and a small notebook. "I don't remember Sara ever mentioning the name of the storage company." She punched 4-1-1 into the cell phone and asked the operator for the numbers of a few self-storage companies in the Cleveland area.

"No, I don't have a name," she told the operator. Her face darkened. "How many?" Then she said, "I see. Well, can you give me the numbers of a few that advertise twenty-four-hour service?"

Essie wrote down a handful of numbers in her notebook, then thanked the operator and snapped the cell phone shut. "Seventy-five numbers in the Cleveland metropolitan area. Lots of names like U-Haul, U-Store, U-Lock, U-Keep-It." She punched a number into the phone. "Guess I better start calling."

"U-Go, girl." Keaton listened to Essie's first call.

"U-Store-It? This is Officer Mayhew of the Menckenburg police. We've had a rash of burglaries here by people pretending to be relatives of recently deceased individuals. We have reason to believe that a woman representing herself as the sister of Sammy Tancredi, the deceased Indians' outfielder, is heading to Cleveland to claim the contents of his storage locker. We're contacting all the major self-storage companies in the hope of catching her."

Keaton marveled at her smoothness as she followed up her introduction with the question, "Do you have any storage space registered in the name of Sammy Tancredi?"

Essie glanced over at Keaton as she waited for an answer, then shook her head and mouthed the word *no.* Then she spoke into the phone. "I see. Well, thank you for your time. We are calling from Menckenburg and don't have a complete listing of all the firms offering storage space in Cleveland. Can you give us the names and numbers of a few of your competitors where Mr. Tancredi might have rented space?"

She scribbled a few lines in her notebook. "I see. Well, thank you very much for your time. You've been most helpful."

After making ten calls, Essie had gotten no answer from two firms, reached four recordings asking her to call back during regular business hours, and talked to four firms that said they had no record of Tancredi.

The eleventh place she called was reluctant to give out any information on their renters over the phone. Finally, Essie said, "If you would like local verification, please call Detective Gerald Waldron of the Cleveland PD." She held her left hand out to Keaton and mouthed the word *number.* When Keaton provided it, she passed Waldron's number along to the wary storage operator.

Essie snapped the cell phone shut. "Guess we better call Detective Waldron and let him know what we're up to." She reopened the phone, punched in Waldron's number, and passed the phone to Keaton.

Waldron didn't sound old enough to have a badge, let alone a detective shield, but after Keaton outlined their current situation—stressing his belief that the woman might somehow be connected with Sammy Tancredi's death—the detective wasted no time in laying out a plan of attack.

"He thinks we're doing the right thing, contacting storage companies," Keaton reported to Essie when he'd finished talking to Waldron. "He's going to start in the middle of the alphabet and work his way to the end while we start at A and work our way down. Whoever finds Tancredi's storage unit first will call the other."

"So he believes us," Essie said.

"Seems he's an Indians fan."

Essie took the phone, called a number, then made a sour face. "Only about half the numbers I call are answering. Mostly, I'm getting recordings telling me to call during regular business hours. That woman could have emptied Sammy's storage unit and be gone by then."

"It may not be all that easy for her. Waldron says about half these companies have caretakers or combination locks you have to get past just to gain entry to your locker."

The sun had come up, framing Essie's head in a bright glow. "Well, she won't have any trouble getting past a caretaker. Look how easily she handled my apartment manager. And me."

"Not much point in worrying about that," Keaton said. "Then too, she may not be in a hurry. She doesn't know we're on her trail. If she stops for breakfast, we might even pass her." He looked at his dashboard and said, "Oh, shit. I'm almost out of gas."

He pounded the steering wheel. "Fuck. Nobody ever runs out of gas in a movie chase."

"If they did, it wouldn't be much of a chase."

"This isn't much of a chase either. We're not even sure whether our target is ahead of us, behind us, or headed in a completely different direction."

Essie held up Keaton's cell phone. "That's okay. We're really chasing her with this. As long as it doesn't run out of gas, we'll be all right." She looked at the phone display. "Do you have a charger here in the car?"

Keaton shook his head.

Essie smiled. "I knew we should have taken my car." She pointed to a gas station on the edge of a shopping center. "Pull in there."

Keaton turned into the gas station. As soon as he stopped at the pump island, Essie jumped out and shouted, "I'll be right back."

"Where are you going?" Keaton called.

Essie just waved at him and started running across the shopping center parking lot toward a 24-hour Wal-Mart.

Keaton finished pumping gas and checked his watch. Six thirty. The woman calling herself Sammy's sister could be in Cleveland by now. If that was where she was headed. He squeezed behind the wheel of the car and had barely pulled away from the pump when he saw Essie come through the Wal-Mart door carrying two plastic shopping bags. She began to sprint toward his car, and he wheeled it across the nearly empty parking lot to meet her.

Essie slid into the passenger seat, fished a cardboard and plastic container out of the first shopping bag, broke it open, and plugged a phone charger into the Escort's cigarette lighter. She attached the cell phone to the charger and said, "There. Now we don't have to worry about the phone running out of gas."

Keaton wheeled the Escort back onto the highway. While he accelerated to sixty-five, Essie took a pair of jeans from the second shopping bag and wriggled her hips into them under her strapless dress. Then she unzipped the dress and pulled it over her head, revealing a push-up bra.

Keaton tried to keep his eyes on the road, but he liked her for not telling him to do so. Instead, she said, "You saw more of me when I was wearing my bikini," as she took a red T-shirt from the bag and pulled it on.

She tugged the T-shirt down over her hips and fastened her seat belt. "I thought we might have to sweet-talk our way past a security guard and I'd be more believable if I was dressed to move some boxes."

Then Essie propped one foot on the dash and rotated her ankle as if she were admiring her tennis shoe. "The alternative was to find a pair of shoes that went better with my dress, and that could have taken all morning."

Keaton took his eyes off the rotating ankle and scanned the road ahead. "Good decision."

Essie reached back into the second plastic bag and pulled out three yellow pages torn from a phone book. "Thought it might be simpler if I called the companies with big ads first rather than take things alphabetically. That's probably what Sammy did."

"Another good decision."

Keaton concentrated on his driving and listened as Essie called more Cleveland storage companies. Over half the numbers she called hooked her up with recordings. When she'd failed to reach a live operator on five consecutive calls, she let the phone drop to her lap, closed her eyes, and massaged her eyelids with her thumb and forefinger.

Just then the phone in her lap announced an incoming call with the "Gambler" refrain "You've Got to Know When to Hold 'Em." Essie picked up the phone and mouthed "Waldron" to Keaton. Then she said, "You found her? Where?" She repeated Waldron's end of the conversation so that Keaton could hear. "A place called SpaceSavers. Seventy-second and Forest. The owner says she's there right now."

After a pause, Essie said, "We're on I-Seventy-Seven just past Broadview Heights." Another pause. "All right. I understand."

She snapped the phone shut and pulled a street map of Cleveland out of the second Wal-Mart bag. As she unfolded the map, she explained, "It's on the outskirts, so we're closer than Waldron is. He's on his way, and he'll send in another patrol car. If we get there first, he wants us to hang back and watch. Whatever we do, he says not to let her see us."

SpaceSavers Storage was surrounded by a chain-link fence with a gate wide enough to accommodate two lanes of traffic. Beyond the open gate a narrow guardhouse straddled the two lanes. A sign announced that all visitors needed to stop and show proper identification.

Instead of driving through the gate, Keaton turned onto a pock-marked street that paralleled the fence. He drove slowly, so that he and Essie could scan the rows of concrete block storage units inside the fence.

"There she is. That's her car," Essie said, pointing to a red Pontiac Grand Prix parked in front of a storage unit about halfway down the fourth row of structures.

"Just about the only customer this early in the morning," Keaton said. "She'll spot us in a second if we sit here watching, though." He backed into the lot of an auto-body repair shop across the road from the chain-link fence and parked under a sign reading "MAY WE HAVE THE NEXT DENTS?"

"That's good protective coloring," Essie said. "This car looks as if it belongs in a body shop."

They watched as the woman calling herself Sara Tancredi loaded a box into her trunk.

Keaton rummaged around in the back seat of his car and retrieved his own Panama hat and a Mammoths baseball cap. "She's never seen my car," Keaton said, "but she's seen us."

Essie put the cap on and tucked her brunette hair up under it. "Well, this works for me, but half the times I've seen you, you've been wearing that thing."

"I don't think our friend with the Grand Prix has seen it, though."

"Oh, God, look," Essie said. "She's leaving."

"The woman slammed her trunk shut, locked the door of the storage unit, and started her car toward the guardhouse and the exit gate.

"Where the hell are the cops?" Keaton asked.

"I'm calling them," Essie said. Then, into the phone, "She's leaving. Where are you?"

There was a pause while she listened to the detective. "Okay, I guess we can do that." Essie closed the cell phone. "He's still a couple of miles away. Says we should follow her if he doesn't get here before she leaves."

As the Grand Prix approached the guard house, the custodian emerged and signaled for the car to stop. "That must be the guy Waldron talked to," Essie said. "He knows she's a phony."

"Looks like he's trying to stall her."

The custodian, a tall, stooped man who looked to be in his late fifties, propped his right elbow on the driver's window and gestured with a clipboard in his left hand.

The Pontiac lurched forward suddenly, spinning the custodian around. He dropped his clipboard and took two steps backward to steady himself as the car roared out of the compound.

"She knows something's up," Essie said. "Follow her."

Keaton pulled out of the auto repair parking lot, skirted the chain-link fence, and turned onto the exit road in the wake of the Grand Prix.

"Don't get too close," Essie said.

"There's nobody else on this road," Keaton said. "She must know we're following her. At any rate, the guard sure spooked her."

The Grand Prix turned north, headed for Lake Erie. She was doing fifty-five in a thirty-five-mile zone.

"Don't let her get away," Essie said. "What street is this, anyhow?" She put her mouth to the cell phone and shouted, "We just turned left on Main."

Ahead of them, the Grand Prix ran a red light, causing a black SUV to honk and swerve to a stop.

"Did you see that?" Keaton braked and waited for the SUV to clear out of the intersection. "She ran that red light."

"You run it too," Essie said. "Otherwise she'll get away."

"Jim Rockford never ran a red light."

"Steve McQueen never stopped for one. Will you please get after that red car?"

Keaton left tread marks on the road accelerating through the red light. He hadn't gone more than a block when he heard the wail of a police siren. He looked in his rearview mirror to see a patrol car with its light bar flashing on his tail. The driver motioned for him to pull over.

Keaton swore and slowed down.

"You can't stop," Essie said. "Speed up. Keep after her. Lead the cops to her."

Keaton sighed and pulled over to the curb. "It's no use. I'm just not Steve McQueen."

As he stopped, the patrol car whipped around him and went after the Grand Prix with its lights flashing and siren blaring.

"He's after our girl," Essie said. "It must be Waldron."

Keaton pulled away from the curb and started after the patrol car. As he did so, another siren sounded behind him.

"What the hell?" He pulled back to the curb and checked his rearview mirror again. A plainclothes officer left his patrol car and approached Keaton's Ford Escort. As the officer drew closer, Keaton could see that the man had the smooth, rounded face of a high school sophomore. He'd tried to age his face by growing a thin moustache, but all that did was make him look like a high school sophomore just learning to shave.

The officer/sophomore bent down and stuck his hand through Keaton's rolled-down window. "I'm Gerry Waldron. You guys did real good."

Keaton shook the extended hand. "Shouldn't we keep after her?"

Waldron shook his head. "Nah. Let my guys finish the job. They get paid for handling pursuits and bringing in baddies. Besides, I wouldn't want to write you up for any more infractions than I've already seen."

"You're kidding, I hope," Keaton said.

Waldron smiled. "Well, I suppose I can let you off with a warning this one time." The short-wave radio on his belt beeped and he answered it.

"That's good," he said into the speaker as he gave a "thumbs-up" sign to Keaton and Essie. "Is she hurt?" After uttering a couple of noncommittal "uh-huhs," he clicked off the unit and returned it to his belt. "She sideswiped a car and broadsided a tree about a mile from here."

"Is she hurt?" Essie asked.

"Shaken up but alive. Not in any danger my guys can see. Guess we can get on down the road and see for ourselves." Waldron looked at Keaton. "Suppose you'll be wanting to look at all the stuff she took from the storage unit?"

"That and her cell phone," Keaton said. "I'd like to know who she's been talking to."

Chapter Thirteen: The Bashful Crane

KEATON'S KORNER

The whole question of performance enhancement and cheating can't be answered without entire teams of philosophers, clergymen, and lawyers. Rafael Palmeiro was presumably seeking to enhance his performance if he took the Viagra he was advertising, but was he cheating? We presume not. Yet when he used steroids to enhance his performance on the diamond, we presume he was cheating, even if he slathered them on, scarfed them down, or shot them up before baseball outlawed their use. Is it just the timing that made him a cheater? And what about all those players who gobbled amphetamines like jelly beans before baseball outlawed them? Were they cheating? We presume not, perhaps because there were too many to prosecute.

And what about Austin Reed of the Mammoths, who is tearing up the league and attributes his enhanced performance to a legal (at least for now) dietary supplement called Vitamin O. Will we brand him a cheater and block his path to the majors if some future commission decides that the use of Vitamin O is unfair? The entire debate reminds us of the quandary over what happened to those Catholics who were lodged in hell for consuming meat on Friday when the Church lifted the ban on meat-eating. Come on, folks. Let's get back to baseball. The Mammoths are one game out and playing their best ball of the season. Who cares how many steroid users can dance on the point of a syringe?

Detective Waldron stood over two cardboard boxes, one suitcase, and a steamer trunk on the loading dock behind his precinct station. "This is everything we got from her car."

Keaton lifted the lid of the steamer trunk enough to see four baseball bats lying on two Cleveland Indians uniform tops, one gray and one white. He let the lid drop back into place. "Doesn't look much different from the stuff he moved to Menckenburg."

"Bats," Essie said. "There weren't any bats in Menckenburg."

"Must have thought he'd be coming back here after he served his suspension," Keaton said to Waldron. "Can we look through this stuff?"

"It's evidence," Waldron said. "I need to get it checked in properly. After that, you're welcome to take a look."

What about her cell phone?"

"She surrendered it to the booking officer. That would be me." Waldron took a slim phone from his pocket. "Mayhew says you're okay, so I'll let you take a look before I check it in. But legally, you've never seen it. If you want to use it in a court case, you'll have to come back and request it formally."

"I understand," Keaton said.

Essie held out her hand. "Give it to me. I'll copy all the phone numbers I can find." She flipped open the cell phone, sat down on the edge of the loading dock, and took her notebook from her purse. "Where's our girl now?"

"Waiting in our interrogation room," Waldron said. "She's called a lawyer."

"Be nice if we could quit calling her 'our girl,' Keaton said. "Do we know her name?"

"She had two drivers' licenses. One says she's Sara Tancredi. The other says she's Nora Smith. My careful detective logic tells me that at least one is a phony."

The phone on Waldron's belt buzzed. He snapped it open,

listened, frowned, said, "I'll be there," snapped it shut, and said, "Shit."

"Trouble?" Keaton asked.

"She's got Highpockets Hufford for a lawyer. He's with her now. He's a partner in one of the biggest criminal law firms in the state."

"That's a sign that this is more than simple larceny, isn't it?"

"Could be. Can't imagine Highpockets doing pro bono work." Waldron clipped his phone back onto his belt. "Want to take a look before I start the interrogation?"

"Absolutely." Keaton raised his eyebrows at Essie.

She looked up from her copying task. "You go ahead. I'll come when I've finished with these phone numbers."

Waldron led Keaton to a room with a one-way mirror adjoining the interrogation room. Through the mirror, they could see Nora Smith sitting at a green metal table. Tufts of red curls peeked through her yellow bandanna. Highpockets Hufford towered above her, an imposing figure with wavy gray hair.

"I can see why they call him Highpockets," Keaton whispered.

"Yep. He's six-foot-eight. Played center for Ohio State. All-American his senior year."

"Oh, yeah. I remember him. Fred Hufford. Drafted by the Cavs."

"Never made it in the NBA. Story was he wasn't tough enough. Plenty tough enough for the league he's in now, though."

"I wouldn't want to go up against him."

"On the court or in court." Waldron shook his head. "Funny thing, he married an Asian woman who can't be more than four-feet-nine. Word is, she has to go up on him."

Keaton laughed.

"That's the only funny thing I can think of about him," Waldron said. "Well, it's time for me to take him on. Afraid I can't let you watch that. Anything you want me to ask?"

"Find out why she picked Sammy Tancredi. And who's behind her."

Keaton watched as Waldron entered the interrogation room and then joined Essie on the loading dock. She was bent over Nora Smith's cell phone, shielding her eyes against the sun and copying numbers into her notebook.

"Woman had lots of friends," she said. "At least there are a lot of numbers here. Some with no names attached."

"Customers, probably." Keaton leaned over her so she wouldn't be bothered by the glare. "Can I help?"

"I've got it under control."

After about five minutes, Waldron joined them on the loading dock.

"Good timing," Essie said, handing him the cell phone.

"A little quick, wasn't it?" Keaton said.

The detective shrugged. "Fucking Hufford. He argued that the 'allegedly' stolen goods barely constituted a respectable Goodwill donation, and that our officers endangered the life of his client by initiating a high-speed chase against force policy. He insisted that his client undergo a thorough medical examination before being interrogated. Strictly a delaying tactic, but we have no choice but to go along with it."

"What happens next?" Keaton asked.

Waldron shrugged. "She'll be arraigned. Hufford will argue that she should be released on her own recognizance with no bail pending a trial date. We'll argue against the 'no-bail' part, but it's hard to paint the woman as a threat to society. Hufford's right about the size of her haul. It's pretty skimpy."

"What if you argue she's part of a larger crime ring?" Keaton asked.

"I wasn't aware there's been an epidemic of missing baseball bats," Waldron said. "And I read the sports section pretty carefully."

"No. But there's been a rash of burglaries in Menckenburg with the same MO, women passing themselves off as relatives of recently deceased locals."

"Smith's ID says she's from Menckenburg. Think she's a part of all that?"

"I'd say it's about as likely as winning the lottery with last year's ticket. But claiming Smith's a part of it might up the stakes, get the bail set higher."

Waldron smiled. "I'll make sure the judge is aware of the similarity of MOs. Got nothing to lose, and it will be nice to surprise Highpockets."

"How they hangin', Keaton? Doin' any good? Keepin' out of trouble?"

The questions were posed by Alex Keith, a program developer at EEYAH.com, one of the most successful dot.com ventures that had sprung up along the outer freeway belt, Menckenburg's answer to Silicon Valley. A self-proclaimed geek, Alex's scheme for fitting in socially was to pepper people with a series of stock phrases.

Keaton ignored the first two questions, preferring to keep the disposition of his testicles to himself and not wanting to think too hard about whether he was doing any good. He did address the third question, saying, "If I were keeping out of trouble, I wouldn't be here."

Alex smiled. "What can I do you for?"

"Like I said on the phone, I want you to compare a couple of lists of phone numbers for me and find any duplicates."

"Easy enough. Can I see the lists?"

Keaton handed over the list of numbers Essie had transcribed from the cell phone of the woman calling herself Nora Smith and a separate list compiled from Sammy Tancredi's address book and cell phone.

Alex scanned the two lists. "Mind telling me what it's all about?"

Keaton filled Alex in on the death of Sammy Tancredi, the appearance of his pseudo-sister, her capture, and her subsequent release on $25,000 bail.

"So," Alex said, "you think there's some direct connection between Tancredi and the woman who claimed to be his sister?"

"Either they knew one another or they both knew someone in common."

Keaton knew from past experience that when Alex immersed himself in a problem, the trite expressions vanished from his speech and a keen intellect and offbeat sense of humor showed themselves. He'd first come to know Alex when interviewing him about a mathematical technique, called changepoint detection, the analyst was using to pinpoint the times at which the home-run outputs of Mark McGwire, Sammy Sosa, and Barry Bonds had undergone enough statistical change so that they might be suspected of using steroids. Since that initial interview, Keaton had returned regularly to get statistical insights into hitting streaks and pitching performance, sometimes for his columns, sometimes to bolster betting theories.

Keaton nodded toward the lists in Alex's hands. "So you can handle the comparisons?"

"Piece of cake. With a little hacking, I can also print out the names behind most of the numbers."

"That'd be great."

Alex riffled the pages. "You've got about a hundred and fifty numbers in one list and over two hundred in the other. With that many samples, I'm guessing you're bound to get a couple of matches."

"Statistically, I guess the math is the same as for that old problem of figuring out how many people you need in a room before it's likely that at least two have the same birthday?"

"Something like it. With random birthdays, the odds start to favor a match when you've got at least twenty-three people."

"But there you've only got three hundred sixty-six different possibilities. The Menckenburg phone book has that many numbers on what? Two pages? There must be a quarter of a million numbers in that region alone. And Sammy's phone book has listings stretching from Cleveland to Menckenburg. Doesn't that lower the odds of a match considerably?"

"I'm still betting I'll get a couple of hits. Hell, I'd be willing to bet that your cell phone has numbers that match the ones on these lists."

"For how much?"

"What?"

Keaton took his cell phone from his pocket. "I'll bet you my cell phone doesn't have any numbers that match these lists. You name the stakes."

Alex's eyes traveled from the cell phone to Keaton's face. "Why do I feel like I'm being hustled?"

"Easiest way to find out is to take the bet."

"All right. Fifty bucks says one of the numbers on your cell phone will have a cousin on these lists." Alex held out his hand. "Give me your phone."

Keaton handed over his phone.

"Why are you smiling?" Alex flipped the phone open and called up the address book. "What the hell? There are only ten numbers here."

Keaton's smile widened. "My carrier called me in to have a new chip installed. When they put it in, they erased every number in my address book. I've been re-creating it one number at a time whenever I need to make a call."

"So that's why you were smiling like a contented crocodile.

You *were* hustling me. You come here to ask a favor and wind up hustling me."

Alex was nearly thirty, but he had a round, kewpie doll face that made him look no older than a teenager. Now he looked like a teenager whose fake ID had just been torn up by an unsympathetic bartender.

"Forget the bet," Keaton said. "You're right. I had an unfair advantage."

Alex studied the face of Keaton's cell phone. "No. Let it ride. I made the bet. I'll stand behind it."

"You sure?"

Alex copied the ten numbers into his computer. "I'm sure."

Alex's face was so smooth and doll-like it was hard for Keaton to tell whether the analyst was hurt, angry, determined, or confident. He decided to change the subject. "So, is there anything new I should know about on the analytic front? Still tracking performance measures? Anything off the charts?"

"You called a real chartbuster yourself in one of last week's columns. Something's going on with Austin Reed in Menckenburg. Batting average is up fifty points. Home-run output has doubled."

"He's not using steroids, though. At least, not anything they can detect."

"He's one of a group of players trying a dietary supplement called Vitamin O. Its manufacturers are paying us for a matched-pair analysis to test whether it helps their performance."

"Must be working. Reed is burning up the league."

"Kids that age, though, you can't tell whether the improvement comes from a new batting stance, a different bat, a growth spurt, vitamin supplements, steroids, or just getting laid regularly."

"I assume as an objective scientist, you're monitoring all those factors."

"Just the vitamin intake and the batting output. You'll have to ask Homeland Security how often he's getting laid." Alex looked up at a vent in the ceiling and said, his voice raised, "If you're listening out there, that's just a joke."

"But you say you've got a matched-pair test going. That must mean other players are using this Vitamin O stuff and some players are getting placebos."

Alex made a lip-zipping motion, then said, "That's about all I can tell you for now. I only brought up Reed because you'd already mentioned him in your column."

"When can you talk more about it?"

"We should have reportable results by the end of the season. I'll fill you in then."

Keaton pointed at the lists he'd brought in. "When do you think you'll have reportable results on those phone numbers?"

Alex pursed his lips. "Shouldn't take more than a day or so. Come back Wednesday." The pursed lips opened into a smile. "Bring fifty dollars."

Keaton stood to leave. "See you then."

"Take it easy. Or take it any way you can get it. But don't do anything I wouldn't do."

Dale Loren's wife Robin looked up from the breakfast table. "Is that what you're going to wear to the grand jury hearing?"

Loren stopped in the doorway of the breakfast room and looked down at his navy blue suit. "What's wrong with it?"

"There's a spot on the lapel. And another on the right sleeve. I can see them from here."

"Nuts. I haven't worn this in at least a year." He went to the kitchen sink and dabbed at the offending spots with a damp dishrag. Then he filled a mug with water, dropped in a teabag, and put the mug in the microwave.

When his tea was ready, he joined his wife at the breakfast

table and held out his right sleeve for her inspection. "That better?"

"Well, at least that blob will be dry by the time you reach the court."

"I'll throw myself on the mercy of the court. Tell them I couldn't afford a dry cleaner."

Robin dabbed at an egg yolk with a piece of toast. "That might be funny if it weren't true."

"I'll be sworn in. Have to tell the truth."

"I still don't see why you can't take that lawyer in with you."

"It's the rules. They don't want anyone but me in front of the prosecution's steamroller. Lawyers might gum up the works by insisting on proper rules of evidence."

"But we've been paying the guy."

"If the case goes to trial, the money won't be wasted."

"If the case goes to trial, he'll want much more than we've already paid."

The hot tea burned the roof of Loren's mouth. He didn't want to tell her that the grand jury would almost certainly vote to send his case to trial.

"And they'll bring up that business about the unpaid taxes?"

"Seems likely."

"I don't see why they have to do that."

"They want to make me look like a really bad guy, dodging taxes in all those cities where the Mammoths played."

"But my signature's on those tax forms along with yours. They'll get me as well."

"The amount we owe is piddling. And we paid more in Ohio than we would have if we'd filed in all those other states."

"So you get the worst of both worlds. You overpay and you're still a tax evader. I told you we should have paid those other states. Maude Gibbons says her husband always does."

"Jerry Gibbons was in the majors. He has teams of accountants helping with his taxes. I don't. And filing in all those other states is a goddamned nuisance for the amount we'd have to pay. That's not what the hearing's about, anyway."

"No. It's about your giving steroids to that dead player."

"But I didn't give him steroids. That's the whole point."

"No. You say you gave him cold cream instead."

"It's the truth."

"Good luck with that defense. My God, what were you thinking?"

"I was thinking that if he thought the cold cream worked, he'd lay off steroids."

"It just sounds so unbelievable." Robin rose, took her half-eaten egg to the sink, and washed it down the drain.

The room was silent after the disposal unit stopped grinding. Then Tess's footsteps pounded down the stairs and their daughter appeared in the doorway saying, "Hey, you look nice, Dad."

Loren smiled and rubbed at the spot on his sleeve. "Thanks, hon."

Tess shrugged off her backpack. "Can somebody take me to Mary Gil's?"

Robin looked up from the sink. "I've got my MADD meeting. But it's on Dad's way."

Loren checked his watch. "If I'm taking you, we'll have to leave right now."

Tess grabbed her backpack by the straps and lifted it off the floor. "Let's go then."

Loren nodded to Robin from the doorway. "See you this evening."

Robin didn't look up from the sink, but just raised her right hand off the drain board in a "whatever" gesture.

Tess threw her backpack onto the rear seat of the Accord and fastened her seat belt. "Big day, huh, Dad?"

Loren nodded. "Big day."

"Gonna notch a win?"

"We'll see." Loren realized "we'll see" was parent-speak for "not very damned likely." He knew Tess was fluent in parent-speak and quickly changed the subject. "When does school start?"

"About three weeks."

"Ready for it?"

"Oh, yeah. They'll have parents' day the first week. Kind of a get-acquainted thing. Think you can come?"

"I don't have much else on my calendar."

"You're always a big hit. Half the boys in my class want to be big-league pitchers."

"Think they'll want me this year, with all the steroid stuff in the news?"

"You kidding? They'll all ask if you know Albert Pujols or Mark McGwire."

"Know McGwire? I struck him out."

"That's all you need to say." Tess retrieved her backpack. "Here's Mare's house."

Loren stopped and his daughter hopped out of the car, saying, "Good luck today."

Instead of running up the walk to her friend's house, Tess stood and watched her father pull away from the curb.

Loren caught sight of her in the rearview mirror and waved.

Tess smiled, cocked her head, kicked one leg sideways, and spread both palms downward in her bashful-crane "safe" sign.

Chapter Fourteen: All Roads Lead to East Wheeling

KEATON'S KORNER

Well, those of you who think pro wrestling is on the up-and-up would have enjoyed yesterday's grand jury hearing. In a ritual as rigged as a WWF title match, former Mammoth trainer Dale Loren was indicted on the strength of circumstantial evidence, innuendo, and the hearsay testimony of a deceased baseball player.

Prosecuting Attorney Hamilton Jeffords paraded the testimony of parents who had lost children to steroid abuse—none of whom had any connection with Loren; cited the unsupported accusation of Sammy Tancredi—who is well beyond the reach of cross-examination—that Loren had provided him with steroids; and badgered Loren with the startling revelation that the former trainer had failed to pay a miniscule amount of back taxes in a few of the many states visited by the Mammoths.

My sources tell me it was a performance worthy of the late Senator Joseph McCarthy or Thomas Newton, who prosecuted the Salem Witch Trials. In a nation where the threat of costly litigation can lead to extorted settlements that have no bearing on the merits of a case, isn't it reassuring to see the full force of the legal system hammering an ex-jock accused of handing out performance-enhancing drugs to a single player? The arrayed might of the judiciary would be misplaced and misused even if Loren were guilty; but it's ridiculous to ruin the career and reputation of a man whose only offense was to distribute cold cream to one of his charges to keep him from using steroids.

"Shouldn't there be a guard at this door?" Keaton asked. "After all, somebody tried to kill David."

Judy stood in the doorway of her husband's hospital room. "Police think it was an accident. There were no signs of a struggle, and no indication that anyone else had been in the house. The elevator door had a history of malfunctioning."

"Did you tell the police David owed a lot of money to some nasty people?"

"I think they caught on to his gambling debts from that little scene you and I played out right here at the hospital." She backed into the room, inviting Keaton in. "I'm sorry about that, by the way."

Keaton raised his left hand, palm outward. "No need to apologize. You were upset."

Keaton hesitated at Bowers's bedside. The IV drip, oxygen tube, and the starched sheet drawn tight across his friend's chest reminded him of something. He glanced back at Judy, and it came to him.

"What is it?" Judy asked.

"This whole scene. It reminds me of college. After the drive-by." Keaton reached down and clasped Bowers's hand, taking care not to disturb the finger clamp. "He's a tough guy. He survived that. He'll survive this."

"I don't know. He's still comatose."

"What do the doctors say?"

"They don't know either. But his vital signs are good."

"How are your vital signs?"

"Oh, you know. I'm coping." Judy shrugged. "Keeping busy at work. Your friends from East Wheeling contacted me."

"They're not exactly my friends."

"They claimed David owed them money. Quite a lot of it, in fact. We could have lost our house."

"What did you say to them?"

"I told them to fuck off."

Keaton released Bowers's hand. "You did what? Judy, these aren't people you mess around with. You don't tell them to fuck off."

"I translated 'fuck off' into legalese. They have no legal standing. Any debt they claim my husband owed them was incurred through illegal activity. No court of law would hold me liable."

"And what did they say to that?"

"A few threats. Nothing serious."

"Judy, those guys don't make casual threats. Forget about hiring a guard for David. You need one for yourself."

"I'm a lawyer, Lloyd. I'm used to threats. They haven't a legal leg to stand on. And they gain nothing by hurting me."

"They don't lose anything either. But they do lose face if word gets out somebody threw up a legal screen and dodged their payments."

"You're not listening, Lloyd. I'm not about to pay any debt my husband incurred through illegal activities. David's been getting calls from Vegas, too. I assume those are more debts."

"Who's calling him from Vegas?"

"They call themselves SportsBook, SportsBet, something like that. I haven't been taking their calls."

"Your legal argument won't work in Vegas. Betting's not against the law there."

"So I've heard. That's one reason I haven't been taking their calls."

"I doubt if David would have been laying off bets in Vegas. That's a couple of rungs above him in the pecking order. We have a mutual friend at SportsBook. I'll call and see what I can find out."

"I'm still not taking any calls from them."

"Even if David was into them, they're not likely to dispatch any collectors across the country right away. But East Wheeling's only a hundred and twenty miles away. I wouldn't take them so lightly."

Judy tapped her glasses with a red fingernail. "You could be right. Bru's been around for the past week. I've been thinking about asking him to stay full time."

"How long's he been out?"

"For over six months."

"What's he doing?"

"Trying to stay out."

Keaton formed a mental image of Judy's brother, a hulking linebacker who lost his college scholarship when he was caught looting an armory with some Black Muslim buddies. "Bru would be a formidable presence, all right."

"More than a match for any of those East Wheeling rednecks."

"For any one of them, maybe. But they'll keep sending more."

"I don't care. I'm not about to pay what they're asking. It would bankrupt me."

"Might not be a bad idea to call in Bru. He could watch out for David as well."

Judy pursed her lips and seemed to look well beyond her husband's bed. "Bru never got along very well with David."

"Let him think he's just guarding you. He can't help but look after David too."

"I suppose it's likely that the rednecks who threatened me are the same ones who put David in that bed."

"They claim that's not the case."

"You saw them?"

"They came to collect from me."

"Oh, that's right. You would owe them too."

"They said it wasn't in their interest to hurt David. It would only make it more difficult to collect what he owed them."

Judy nodded. "Well, that's certainly true. What about you,

though? Did you pay them what you owe them?"

"I paid them half. It was all I could afford."

"And did they threaten you?"

"Not with physical violence. They wanted me to run some pretty demeaning errands. When that didn't work, they set up what they felt was a reasonable payment schedule. With interest."

"How much interest?"

"Ten percent."

"Well, that's not bad. My credit cards charge more than that."

"It's ten percent per *month.*"

"That's outrageous. How much do you owe them?"

"Five thousand dollars."

"Is that all? Let me lend it to you. I can offer half their interest rate." Judy reached out and touched Keaton's shoulder. "No. Seriously. Let me bail you out. Pay me back whenever you can. It's what David would have done."

"I don't know. You owe them so much yourself."

"But I don't intend to pay it. Even if I did, your five grand is a drop in the bucket compared to what they claim I owe. It'd be like adding pennies to the national debt."

"That's funny. That's exactly what David said."

"Then it's settled. You'll take the money."

Keaton didn't understand why he was hesitating. He certainly hadn't hesitated when David made the offer. Finally, he said, "That's very generous. Thank you."

"Come back tomorrow. I'll have the money. And you can help us move David. The doctors think he'd be better off at home."

"All right." Keaton patted David's shoulder and scanned his face and hands for any sign of a reaction. When he saw none, he gave Judy a quick hug and left the hospital.

★ ★ ★ ★ ★

Alex Keith looked up from his computer. "Hey there, Keaton. Still hangin' in? Still causing trouble?"

"Trying to stay out of it. Did you run those computer matches?"

"Did you bring your fifty dollars?"

"You found a match for one of my numbers, huh? I thought you were pretty quick to take the bet." He made tight "gimme" motions with his fingertips. "Show me what you found."

Alex took six sheets of printout from a stack of papers on his desk and fanned them out for Keaton to see. "What I've got on these first three sheets is all the numbers from each of the three phones and Sammy Tancredi's address book." He nodded toward the remaining sheets. "And then these three sheets have those numbers that showed up on more than one phone. One sheet for each combination of two pairs."

Alex smiled broadly and offered one of the fanned-out sheets to Keaton like a magician starting a card trick. "Here's all the numbers you and Sammy Tancredi had in common."

Keaton glanced at the sheet. "Only one number. Who's it go to?"

"Only one number, but it'll cost you. You and Sammy both had United Airlines' number programmed in your phones."

"I knew I should have switched to Southwest." Keaton fished in his wallet for two twenties and a ten and laid them on the corner of Alex's desk. Losing the bet didn't faze him, since he was happy to pay Alex for his trouble, but he was disappointed that the match of airline numbers told him nothing useful about Sammy Tancredi. "What about matches between Sammy and his so-called 'sister'?"

Alex nodded toward another of the fanned sheets. "Got a few more hits there. In fact, they had each other's numbers."

Keaton took the offered sheet from Alex's hands and studied

it. "So they knew each other. How did Sammy have her listed?"

"Under the name Sara in his cell phone."

"Just 'Sara'?"

"That's all. No last name. But her phone was issued to a Sara Galardi on West Thirty-Second Street in Menckenburg."

"That's not the name she gave the Cleveland police."

"She and Sammy both had three unlisted numbers in common. I couldn't find out who they belonged to."

Keaton took out his pen and circled the three numbers. "I'll call them. See what I can find out. Anything else of interest?"

"It's not a number that matches any of yours or Sara's, but Sammy had written the number for OgrowSport in his address book."

"OgrowSport?"

"They manufacture vitamin supplements. They're the folks who produce Vitamin O, the pill that Austin Reed's been popping. I told you, they asked us to help test it."

"Wonder if Sammy was trying to go straight? Substitute a legal drug for steroids?"

Alex shook his head. "No idea."

"Sounds as if I ought to interview those folks for the paper. Get the inside slant on vitamin supplements in pro sports." Keaton nodded toward the two printout sheets left in Alex's hands. "What about the lady's phone numbers?"

"Hairdresser, manicurist, couple of spas. Lady liked to take care of herself. Several men listed only by their first names, including Sammy Tancredi."

"Could be the lady liked someone else to take care of her too."

"Lots of unlisted numbers. One she has in common with you. So you would have lost our bet even if you'd switched to Southwest Air."

"With me? Whose number is it?"

Alex shrugged. "Can't tell. It's unlisted. You should recognize it, though. It's a three-oh-four area code."

Keaton grabbed the sheet from Alex. "Three-oh-four is West Virginia. That's the number of my bookie in East Wheeling."

Chapter Fifteen: Six to Five Against

KEATON'S KORNER

In news related to Menckenburg sports, a woman falsely identifying herself as the late Sammy Tancredi's sister recently tried to misappropriate Tancredi's belongings in both Menckenburg and Cleveland. With the help of this newspaper, she was apprehended by the police in Cleveland and only yesterday skipped out on $25,000 bail.

The miscreant has subsequently been identified as Ms. Sara Galardi, whose most recent address was on Thirty-Second Street here in Menckenburg. Anyone having information regarding Ms. Galardi's current whereabouts should contact Lieutenant Gerald Waldron of the Cleveland Police Department.

Our own Menckenburg police had closed the book on Tancredi's untimely demise, attributing the cause to an accidental drug overdose. We can only hope that Ms. Galardi's suspicious activities will convince them to reopen the case and look more deeply into the real causes of the young slugger's death.

Keaton waited until he got to his office to try contacting the list of phone numbers he'd gotten from Alex, because he didn't want his home number registering on the recipient's caller ID. Seated at his desk, he scanned the list, but decided to start with the Las Vegas number given him by Judy Bowers. He recognized it as the number of a friend, Mike Brown, who ran one of the largest sports books in Vegas. Might as well start with an easy call to a friendly voice, and leave the heavy lifting of Alex's list for later.

Mike Brown had evidently been trying to call Dave Bowers for several days. Judy had ignored his calls, assuming that he only wanted to collect more losing bets, but Keaton doubted that was the reason behind the phone messages. He picked up his phone and dialed Vegas.

Mike Brown answered right away. "Hey, Lloyd. What's up?"

"That's what I'm calling to find out. You've been leaving messages at Dave Bowers's home."

"Yeah. That was before I heard about his accident. That's really tough. Man's not safe in his own home."

"Eighty percent of all accidents happen there."

"And that probably doesn't count the wrong lipstick on your collar, Internet betting, or unplanned pregnancies."

Keaton smiled. "Probably not. How'd you hear about Dave's accident?"

"I was talking to Bull Harding. Guess Dave owed the East Wheeling boys *beaucoup* bucks."

"Did he owe you too? Is that why you were calling him?"

"God, no. He called me to ask if I'd seen or heard anything funny about last week's Mets/Rockies game."

"The one Oke pitched."

"Yeah. That one. Dave said he'd lost a bundle on it."

"He wasn't the only one. What did you tell him?"

"Told him I hadn't heard a thing. We didn't get much play on it here. Big game that day was the Yankees/Red Sox."

"That's funny."

"Surprised Dave too. He thought Little Bill Ellison would have laid off some of his bets with us.

"He didn't?"

"Not with me. 'Course, there are lots of other sports books

here in Vegas."

"But Little Bill usually comes to you when he has more than he can handle on one side or the other of the betting line?"

"Far as I know. He laid off over a hundred grand on Sunday's Yankee/Red Sox game."

"The one on ESPN."

"Yeah. Guess there are a lot of Red Sox fans in his neck of the woods."

"More likely a lot of Yankee haters. But little Bill didn't lay off anything on last week's Mets/Rockies game?"

"Not with me."

Thunder boomed outside and the phone line crackled.

"What's going on there?" Brown asked.

"Thunderstorm." Keaton's office windows were opaque with rain.

"Think it'll rain out the Mammoths game?"

"Hope so. I could use a day off. Look, why were you trying to reach Dave? Is there something I can help you with?"

"Dave was so surprised Little Bill hadn't laid off anything on the Mets/Rockies contest, he asked me to check some other games."

"Can you do that?"

"Oh, yeah. Computers have revolutionized our business. We keep all the data. Look for betting patterns. It's all there. I couldn't get at it right away, though, so I told Dave I'd call him back."

"What'd you find out?"

"He gave me five games from the last two years. Four of the five, Little Bill had more than he could handle and laid off some bets with me." Brown read off a list of four names. The most recent was the Giants/Pirates game that had marked Keaton's successful return to gambling.

Keaton copied down the dates and games. "What was the

fifth game?"

"Let's see. It was a Dodgers/Giants game two years ago. July first."

"Shit."

"You remember it?"

"God, yes. Cost me my car and sent me to Gamblers Anonymous. Sure didn't feel like celebrating on the Fourth."

"Maybe David took a big hit on it too. Maybe that's why he asked me to check it out."

"Could be. But you say Little Bill didn't lay off any of his bets on that game."

"Not with us. Think he knew something?"

"Knew enough to keep our losses for himself," Keaton said.

"What about the other four games?"

"I'm guessing Dave bet them big and won."

"So Little Bill used us to help cover his losses," Brown said.

"But he didn't cut you in on his wins."

"Life's tough that way."

"Damon Runyon said, 'All of life is six to five against.' "

"Think maybe Little Bill has found a way to turn those odds around?"

"On baseball, maybe. Not on life."

"Well, it's only two games out of six. But the pattern is clear. He laid off the bets and shared the risk on the four games he lost, and kept everything for himself on the two games he won. Think Dave was onto him?"

Thunder crashed and lightning flashed outside Keaton's window. "Dave didn't say anything to me. But then, he didn't have a chance to."

"Think maybe his drop down that elevator shaft wasn't an accident?"

"I've always thought that. But the local cops don't see it that way."

"What are Dave's chances?"

"Damon Runyon said it. Six to five against. They're bringing him home today. But he's still comatose."

"I'll hold some good thoughts for him. And for you."

"For me?"

"You know at least as much as he knew. Better steer clear of elevator shafts."

Keaton hung up and stared at the phone. It sure sounded as if Little Bill had some advance notice about the outcome of the two big bets he and Dave had lost since tracking Bradshaw's calls and working out their system. Still, as Mike Brown pointed out, it wasn't a big sample. But it was the only two times they'd lost out of what? Ten to twelve bets? Little Bill was on the list of people he wanted to call today, since his phone number was in Sara Galardi's address book. He reached for the phone, then pulled his hand back. He'd better work out a good cover story for the call before he dialed it, or he could have to spend the rest of his life avoiding elevators.

The rain was still sheeting on his office window, so he called the Mammoths' business office and learned that the afternoon's game had been rained out. Then he called Judy Bowers to say that the game was no longer an obstacle and that he could help bring David home any time that day. Judy told him she'd already scheduled an ambulance pick-up for six o'clock to accommodate the game, and that Bru was supposed to meet them at the hospital at that time. Since she was having trouble contacting Bru, they decided not to reschedule the ambulance.

Keaton got a Coke from the vending machine and retrieved the three unlisted numbers that Sara Galardi and Sammy Tancredi had in common. Before he called the numbers, though, he needed some pretext that wouldn't arouse suspicion and would provide him with some basic information. The people on the other end of the line would probably hang up if he pretended to be a telemarketer, and they would certainly be leery of providing personal information to a stranger over the phone. He could tell them they'd won some sort of a prize and solicit their addresses, but that was just a small step up from telemarketing. If the prize was too small, they'd hang up on him, and if it was too attractive, it would arouse some suspicion.

Finally, he hit upon an approach that he thought might work. He jotted down six questions on his writing pad and called the first number. When a soft female voice answered, he said, "Good morning. I'm calling from the Central Ohio Transportation Authority with six quick questions about your daily commute. The questions shouldn't take more than three minutes of your time, and our answers will help us plan the future of Menckenburg's transportation network. Can I ask the questions now, or would you prefer that I call back later?"

The woman hesitated, then said, "Ask them now, I suppose."

"First," Keaton said, "I'd like you to rate the congestion during your morning commute on a scale of one to five, where one is uncongested, and five is heavily congested."

"Oh, five. Easily."

Keaton could tell he had her hooked. As a reporter, he knew that people loved to talk about their traffic problems. He followed the first question with, "And how long does it take you to get from your home to your place of employment?"

"About a half hour. If the merge onto I-Seventy-One is backed up, it could take forty-five minutes."

"Do you drive alone, carpool, or take public transit?"

"I drive alone. I'd like to carpool, but I don't work regular hours."

"Finally, so that we can model your commute in our computer, I'd like your home and business addresses. First, your home address:

"Two zero five West Thirty-Second Street in Menckenburg."

"And your business address?"

"Thirty-five sixty-two Nosler Drive."

"Well, that's all the questions I have. Thank you very much for your time." Keaton hung up, feeling pleased with himself. West Thirty-Second Street was the address Alex had found for Sara Galardi. Sara and the soft-voiced woman were probably neighbors.

He tried his survey routine on the remaining two numbers and got one recorded message and a surly male who refused to cooperate. He could call them both later. For the present, he popped open a second Coke and started writing the next day's column, finishing just in time to meet Judy Bowers at the hospital.

Two orderlies were transferring David to a gurney when Keaton entered the hospital room. "Bru's on his way," Judy said, "and the ambulance is waiting outside."

When Keaton tried to help the orderlies, they shook their heads and waved him off. "They're responsible for anything that happens here in the hospital," Judy said. "Until we get to the ambulance, you're just in the way."

The orderlies wheeled the gurney to the emergency room entrance, where an ambulance was parked under a concrete canopy. The rain hadn't let up, and the wind pelted the side of the ambulance with sheets of water and soaked both orderlies as they loaded David into the back. When the orderlies had finished, Keaton helped Judy into the rear of the ambulance and climbed in beside her as she wiped droplets of rain from her husband's forehead and immobile eyelids.

The sheeting rain and gathering dusk made it impossible to see the street at the end of the hospital's driveway. Judy peered out into the murk and said, "I don't understand what's holding Bru up."

The ambulance driver, a slim black man, slid open the window that linked the driver's cab to the rear compartment. "I can't sit here much longer," he said. "They need this entrance for real emergencies."

Judy punched a number into her cell phone, then stared at it and shook her head. "No answer. Where are you, Bru?"

A siren sounded behind them. The driver looked back through his window, hoping for guidance. "Pull ahead, but don't leave this driveway," Judy said.

The driver nodded and inched the ambulance out from under the protection of the canopy. Rain pelted the vehicle's roof and obscured the road ahead.

An ambulance pulled into the space vacated by the driver and silenced its siren. Keaton and Judy watched out of their rear window as orderlies transferred a woman wearing a neck brace from the parked ambulance onto a gurney and took her into the hospital. As the emergency room doors closed behind them, a pair of headlights pierced the gloom and stopped under the canopy beside the newly arrived ambulance, boxing it in.

"Thank God, it's Bru," Judy said.

Judy's brother Brutus left his car motor running and sauntered over to the rear of his sister's ambulance as if the wind and rain didn't exist. "Fucking accident on every corner," he said. "Lucky I wasn't in one myself."

"Well, you're here now at least," Judy said. "I tried to reach you on your cell phone."

"Out of juice," Bru said. "Forgot to plug it in last night." He nodded to Keaton without offering his hand. "Hey there, White Bread."

Keaton nodded.

"You'll follow us home," Judy said. "Stay close."

"I got your backside covered." Bru opened his black raincoat to show the handle of an automatic pistol jutting from his belt.

The tails of his raincoat flapped in the wind as he turned to Keaton and shouted, "What about you, White Bread? You packing?"

Keaton shook his head.

"What the hell, man. How you expect to protect my sis?" He shook his head. "Motherfucking writer. Pen might be mightier than the sword, but it's no match for an Uzi."

"Can you give him something?" Judy shouted over the storm.

Before Keaton could protest, Bru said, "Fuck, woman. I'm on probation. I get caught carrying, I'm in deep shit." He tapped the handle of his automatic. "So I just pack enough for me. You're lucky I could find that popgun for you."

The driver of the ambulance behind them loosed a short burst on his siren and shouted to Bru, "Hey there, fella. Will you move that heap so we can get back on the road? We're two calls behind."

"Chill, motherfucker," Bru said. "Unless you want to be an accident statistic yourself."

"Tough guy, huh?" the driver answered.

Bru set his jaw in a tight smile that allowed just one gold tooth to peek through. He turned and walked slowly toward the ambulance behind theirs. The driver started to open his door, but Bru kicked it shut. Then he reached through the open window, grabbed the back of the driver's head, and pulled it forward so that the window glass was an inverted guillotine under the driver's neck.

Neither Keaton nor Judy could hear what Bru said to the ambulance driver. But it was clear that the driver was listening intently. When Keaton started to go to the driver's aid, Judy grabbed him by the elbow and said, "Wait. We need Bru."

Bru finished talking, grabbed a handful of the driver's hair, jerked his head up so it cleared the window, and shoved him back inside his cab. Then he walked back to Keaton and Judy with his black raincoat flapping in the wind.

"He'll be all right," Bru said. "Learnt that white trash not to disrespect my Caddy. He apologized for calling it a heap." He buttoned his raincoat and nodded to Judy. "You can take off now. I'll be right behind you."

Judy knocked on their driver's window and gave him a thumbs-up sign.

As the driver inched forward, Keaton said, "Did I hear right? Are you carrying a gun?"

Judy opened her purse and showed him a small .45-caliber automatic. "You're the one who thought Dave might need protection."

The ambulance reached the street and rolled slowly forward, its headlights barely penetrating the wall of rain and darkness. Through the rear window, Bru's headlights swam in and out of their occluded vision.

Keaton leaned back against the ambulance wall and stretched his legs under David's cot. "I see Bru hasn't changed."

"He better," Judy said. "Another conviction will make his third strike."

"Couldn't tell that by the gun he's carrying on his hip or the chip he's carrying on his shoulder."

"He's had a hard time of it."

"Comes from a bad family, does he?"

"Don't make fun, Lloyd. He got in with a bad crowd and never really had a chance."

"He had the same chance you had."

"No. Not nearly." She shook her head. "But I don't want to talk about it."

They rode for a while with only the sound of the pelting rain for company. Then Judy leaned forward and peered intently out of the back window with a puzzled look on her face.

"What's the matter?" Keaton asked.

"I haven't seen Bru's headlights for the last four blocks."

"He's back there. He knows the route. We couldn't lose him if we tried."

"Something's wrong. I can feel it. Maybe that ambulance driver called the cops on him."

Their ambulance stopped so suddenly that David shot forward on his cot until his feet slammed into the driver's partition.

Keaton looked through the front window. The driver was nowhere to be seen, and a late-model Chevrolet sat catty-corner across their path. He looked through the back window and saw nothing but rain.

An amplified voice cut through the storm. "You in the back. Come out with your hands in the air and no harm will come to you. Just open the rear door and come on out."

"No harm. Bullshit," Keaton said. He looked at David. "They sure mean to harm somebody."

"I don't understand what's happened to Bru," Judy said.

"To hell with Bru. Call nine-one-one." Keaton upended the spare cot next to David and propped it against the front window so that no one could see in from the driver's seat. Then he covered the rear windows with the cot's bedding.

"If you don't come out, we'll start shooting," the voice said.

"Oh, God," Judy said.

"Get flat on the floor and dial nine-one-one," Keaton said.

Judy stretched out on the ambulance floor and fumbled in her purse. She dumped the contents on the floor and picked up the cell phone in one hand and her brother's .45 automatic in the other. "Do you think they'll really shoot?"

Keaton pulled David's legs off the cot and struggled to wrestle his upper body over the edge so that he could get him onto the floor. "How the hell would I know? Call nine-one-one."

Keaton jerked David's body free of the cot in a tangle of sheets and lowered him to the floor beside Judy. Then he covered his friend's body with his own.

Judy fumbled with the cell phone. "Dammit. I misdialed."

Keaton held out his hand. "Let me do it."

Judy put the .45 in his hand. "No, you take this."

A thunderclap exploded, and the back window of the ambulance shattered.

"Oh fuck, it's a recorded message." Judy stabbed at the phone with her finger.

Keaton stared at the automatic in his hand. He didn't know where to look for the safety, or how to tell if it was on.

"Operator. Operator." Judy shouted into the phone. "We're at the corner of Fifth and Jefferson. Someone is shooting at us."

The disembodied voice behind them cut through the storm. "Will you come out now?"

Two shots rang out, followed by a third. A car engine started. Then all they heard was the pelting rain.

Keaton rose to one knee, pulled the sheet over the back window to one side, and peeked out. A shadowy figure trailing a wind-whipped raincoat approached the ambulance.

Keaton's hand tightened on the automatic and he pointed it at the rear door.

"Sis. Sis." The figure shouted through the rain. "You all right in there?"

Judy grabbed Keaton's gun hand and pulled it down. "It's Bru. Open the door."

They swung the rear doors open and Bru hefted himself over the threshold, dripping water. He looked at David's body, tangled in sheets on the floor of the ambulance. "He get shot?"

"No. Lloyd pulled him down on the floor," Judy said. "What happened? Where were you? I had to call the police."

"The police?" Bru took the automatic pistol from his belt.

"I've got to get out of here."

He looked at the gun and returned it to his raincoat pocket. "You guys better leave too. Can you drive this thing, White Bread?"

"Probably easier than I could use this." He handed the .45 back to Judy. "But why don't we just wait for the cops?"

"Night like this, they could take forever." Bru nodded toward the shattered ambulance window. "Besides, this is just too hard to explain without involving me. I'll follow you home."

"I don't know," Keaton said. "Those gangsters are still out there with their guns."

"You're sitting ducks if you stay put," Bru said. "I scared them off for a while, and they're not likely to try again long as I'm with you. But I sure as shit can't stay, so let's get out of here."

"Do what he says, Lloyd. We can sort it out later." Judy knelt beside David. "Let's get him back onto his cot."

"No time," Bru said. "Let him ride on the floor. Man don't know the difference. I'll help lift him when we get home."

Keaton hesitated.

Bru hopped out of the ambulance and held his hand out. "Come on. Be a driver."

"Please, Lloyd," Judy said. "Bru can't be any part of this."

Keaton took Bru's hand, let himself down into the rain, and hurried to the driver's door of the ambulance. The door was open and the key was still in the ignition.

"Okay," he shouted to Bru's departing back. "Guess I'll see you at home." He turned on the ignition and pulled out into the rain-splattered street. There wasn't any opposing traffic, and he couldn't see much more than five feet in front of the ambulance.

That's all right, he thought. If I can't see anything, no one can see me either.

Chapter Sixteen: Arnolds and Cream

KEATON'S KORNER

Congressman Bloodworth announced yesterday that his Committee on Governmental Reform will be producing a detailed report on its findings regarding the current use of steroids in professional baseball. Pardon me if I don't seem excited by this piece of manufactured news. This committee has long since evolved into a political entity with a single aim: to further the career of Representative James Bloodworth.

While baseball's management and the players' union were jointly delinquent in taking much too long to address the problem of steroids, there seems little doubt that the testing program they finally put into place is working just fine without the peripheral meddling of Congress. Since the testing program has been operating, however, barely two major leaguers per year have tested positive for drug use, and so far this year the program has unearthed only one user, the tragic Sammy Tancredi.

Still, the Bloodworth committee is busy generating headlines, producing reports, and railroading honorable ex-players on the flimsiest of hearsay evidence. Representative Bloodworth may wish to be remembered as a revered statesman, but the congressional models he most resembles are Senator Joseph McCarthy of the infamous Army/McCarthy hearings, and the indicted and jailed Representative J. Parnell Thomas of the House Un-American Activities Committee, which instigated the notorious blacklist that ruined the careers of many innocent bystanders.

The rain was still pelting down when Keaton pulled the ambulance into the Bowers's driveway and they installed David in the bed prepared by his in-house caregivers.

"We've got to call the police," Keaton said as Judy fixed them drinks from the wet bar.

Water dripped from the hem of Bru's jeans as he stood in the hallway at the foot of the stairs. "You do, and my ass is in a sling for packing while I'm on parole."

"But somebody just tried to kill David," Keaton said. "For the second time. The police can give him protection."

Bru shook his head. "Shit, man. They won't give no more protection than a busted rubber. Me and my guys can do lots better than that."

Judy handed Keaton a scotch and carried a bottle of Budweiser over to her brother. "Bru's right, Lloyd. The police aren't going to extend themselves to protect a bookie."

"Especially one with a black wife," Bru said.

"Ex-bookie," Keaton said. "With a wife who's a respected member of the bar. And even if they won't protect him, they can try to find the people who shot at us."

"Not much chance of that," Bru said. "It was raining so hard I didn't see enough to ID anyone."

"I can't believe this," Keaton said. "You're an officer of the court, Judy. You're also in charge of your husband's welfare. And you propose to let this ride without reporting it. What makes you think these people won't try again?"

Bru slugged down a long pull of Budweiser. "They do, I'll be ready for them. Me and my boys can watch David twenty-four-fucking-seven. Cops won't come close to that."

Keaton's scotch tasted bitter. "Come on, Judy, you need to report this."

"You do, you leave me out of it," Bru said.

Judy poured herself a glass of red wine. "Can we concoct a

story that doesn't involve Bru?"

"Well, let's see," Keaton said. "Thugs stop the ambulance, scare off the driver, order us out, and then start shooting. How exactly did we escape without Bru's help? Moral suasion?"

Bru sat down on the hallway stairs. "What the hell's that?"

"Lloyd's being sarcastic," Judy said. "He's suggesting we tell the police we used logical arguments to convince the shooters they were wrong and get them to leave."

"Oh, yeah," Bru said. "That'll work for sure."

"Maybe help came from your nine-one-one call and scared them off," Keaton said.

Judy shook her head. "But it didn't. The police will be able to check that."

"There was more than one shot fired," Keaton said. "Why don't we claim you returned their fire and that scared them off?"

"Returned their fire with what?" Judy asked.

"That forty-five Bru gave you. I assume it can't be traced to anybody here."

"Not to me," Bru said. "But it's still not such a hot idea."

"Why not?" Keaton asked.

Bru shrugged. " 'Cause there's no telling where it's been."

"Oh, Christ," Keaton said. "Does David have a gun?"

Judy nodded. "I never wanted a gun in the house. But in his business, he thought he needed one. He couldn't be sure some sore loser wouldn't come gunning for him."

"That's it, then," Keaton said. "Take it out back and fire it a couple of times. We'll tell the police your shots scared them off."

Bru pointed the neck of his beer bottle at Keaton. "I still think it's a mistake to bring the police into this. You hearin' me, White Bread?"

"You really don't have a choice," Keaton said. "Your

ambulance driver has been wandering around without his vehicle. Once he checks in and tells his story, it's likely his boss will call the cops."

"Oh, Lord. That's right. We've got to be ready for them. I'll get David's gun." Judy started upstairs, then stopped. "Wait. What if the ambulance driver saw what really happened?"

"He was probably long gone by the time Bru arrived," Keaton said. "Even if he hid and tried to watch, he couldn't see anything in all that rain. If he was close enough to hear the extra shots, that'll fit our story."

"That's right. That's right. Lloyd, you call the police right now. We'll beat the driver to the punch." Judy left the stairs and shoved her brother's shoulder lightly from behind. "Bru, you better make yourself scarce."

Detective O'Donohoe sported the same gray stubble at seven in the evening as he had the last time Keaton had seen him, at five in the morning on the day the woman calling herself Sammy Tancredi's sister had run off from Menckenburg to Cleveland. The man was either too lazy to shave or had been watching too many cop shows without realizing that the rugged and stubbled TV stars were twenty-five years younger and had better writers.

The rain had slowed to an occasional drizzle as O'Donohoe ran his finger lightly along the shattered rear window of the ambulance. "So this is where the bullet entered."

"That's right," Keaton said.

Peering through the shattered window, O'Donohoe said, "And it went out through the roof, just before it got to the driver's cab."

Keaton nodded.

O'Donohoe rested his elbow on the edge of the window, lined up his forearm with the bullet's trajectory, and sighted along it. "So the shooter must have been standing about there," he said, pointing at a streetlamp about 200 feet away.

"Actually, the shooter was standing at the corner of Fifth and Jefferson," Keaton said.

"But about as far away from you as that street lamp," O'Donohoe said, ignoring Keaton and addressing Judy.

"I guess so," Judy said. "It was raining so hard it was difficult to see anything."

"But you returned their fire anyhow."

"That's right."

"Even though you couldn't see anything."

"I was pretty scared."

O'Donohoe lifted a Walther PPK automatic from the floor of the ambulance by inserting a pen through the trigger guard. "And this was the gun you used."

"Yes. It's my husband's."

"I assume he has a permit to carry this weapon?"

"He must. But I don't know where it is."

O'Donohoe laid the PPK back on the ambulance floor. "But you were carrying it."

"That's right."

"And lying on the floor of the ambulance."

"That's right."

"So you just got up, opened the rear door of the ambulance, and fired blindly."

"Yes. I told you, I couldn't see anything in the rain."

"And you don't have a permit to carry that gun."

"I don't, but my husband does. And the state recognizes the right to use firearms in self-defense."

"Look," Keaton said. "You're acting as if we're the criminals here. I'd like to know what you're going to do to find the people who fired on us."

"Well, you haven't given us much to go on. The bullet is somewhere west of Fifth and Jefferson, and you can't describe your assailants."

"We just couldn't see much in the rain," Judy said.

"What about the ambulance driver?" O'Donohoe asked.

"He lit out before the shooting started," Keaton said.

"So there's a good chance he saw something," O'Donohoe said. "How can I contact him?"

"Through the ParaPrivate Ambulance Service," Judy said.

O'Donohoe took a pen and a small notebook from his pocket. "Could you spell that, please?"

"It's right there on the side of the vehicle," Keaton said. "Along with their phone number."

O'Donohoe copied down the information and pocketed his notebook. "The trail is pretty cold by now. Why'd you wait so long before calling the police?"

"We dialed nine-one-one right away," Judy said. "Then we brought David home and called your office."

"Nine-one-one never responded. Unless the driver saw something, there's not much we can do. The shooters have had more than enough time to get away."

"What about providing protection for Mrs. Bowers's husband?" Keaton asked.

"You certainly can't expect my department to do that," O'Donohoe said. "Mrs. Bowers's husband is a law breaker, a known bookmaker. For all we know, this attack is some sort of turf war. That's not something my department wants to be a part of."

"Mrs. Bowers's husband is a tax-paying citizen. And in his current comatose state, he's hardly in a position to conduct a turf war. There've been two attempts on his life in less than a month. How many does it take to get your attention?"

"We concluded that the fall in the elevator shaft was accidental."

"Well, don't you think you might reconsider that conclusion

in light of the current shooting?"

"We'll certainly keep the books open on the case. Even if we thought the elevator shaft accident was attempted murder, though, we wouldn't provide police protection for a known bookie."

Judy stepped between O'Donohoe and Keaton and put her hand on the reporter's arm. "That's all right, Lloyd. We can take care of David ourselves, now that he's home."

O'Donohoe looked up into the gray skies. "Looks like it's fixing to come down in buckets again. I'm going to get back on the road. Let me know if your ambulance driver shows up here. He'll probably be looking for that vehicle."

"We'll do that," Judy said.

O'Donohoe checked his cell phone. "It's been a bad night for ambulance drivers. We got a report that one was assaulted in St. Vincent's parking lot."

"That's terrible," Judy said. "Did they catch the assailant?"

"Not yet. Another case of too little information. Although we do have a partial license plate number. Too bad you couldn't have gotten one of those."

Keaton and Judy watched as O'Donohoe drove away. "Man's got a mind like a steel trap," Keaton said. "Unfortunately, it rusted shut several rains back."

"The way you kept baiting him, I'm surprised he didn't arrest you."

"Well, he might still arrest Bru. Better call your brother and tell him they're on the lookout for his license plate."

"Oh, I imagine he's ditched that car by now. It wasn't his to begin with."

Keaton's cell phone rang just after he'd slid behind the wheel of his Ford Escort. He knew the voice. He'd always know the voice.

"Lloyd. Can you come home?"

"What's happened?"

"It's Davy. I caught him using steroids. He swore at me and locked himself in his room."

Keaton closed his eyes and exhaled something like a sigh. "Shit. I'm on my way."

Liz had the front door open before he was out of the car. As soon as he reached the porch, she held out a handful of green and yellow capsules. "I caught him taking these."

Keaton took two capsules from her hand, glanced at them, and said, "Arnolds."

"Arnold's what?"

Keaton nodded toward the capsules. "Arnolds. It's what they call them in the locker room."

"Charming." She brought up her other hand and held out an unmarked jar of what looked like cold cream. "What do they call this?"

"Just 'the cream.' He's using that too?"

"I found it in his room. You were right not to believe him."

"I wish I'd been wrong."

Liz closed her fist over the remaining capsules. "He's never sworn at me."

"Those pills can change your personality. He still in his room?"

Liz nodded.

Keaton took the stairs two at a time and knocked on his son's bedroom door. "Davy, open up. It's Dad."

Keaton heard a chair scraping the floor on the other side of the door, followed by Davy's voice saying, "Go away."

"You know I won't do that."

"Get the fuck out of here. I don't want to see you."

"Well, you're going to have to see me sooner or later, because I'm not leaving this hallway until you come out."

"Stay as long as you want. I'm not coming out."

Keaton sat down facing the door, his back braced against the hall banister. After ten minutes of silence, he said, "Davy, open up. Don't make me take the hinges off the door."

When there was no answer, he said, "All right. If that's the way you want it. I'll go get my tools." He made a maximum amount of noise descending the stairs, removed his shoes, put his finger to his lips to shush Liz, went back up the stairs, and quietly resumed his position in front of the door.

After fifteen minutes of silence, Davy said, "Dad?"

When Keaton didn't answer, the bedroom door slowly cracked open. Keaton threw his shoulder into the door, blasting it open and driving his son backward onto his bed.

"Get out of my room!" Davy shouted from the bed. "You've got no right to come in here."

Keaton swept his arm toward the window on the wall opposite the bed. "I'm paying for that half of the room. Your mother's paying for the other half. Exactly which half are you paying for?"

"I've got a right to my privacy."

Keaton held out the two capsules he'd taken from Liz. "You'll have the privacy of an early grave if you go on taking these."

"That's bullshit. They just help me bulk up."

"That's not all they do. Look in the mirror. Your acne wasn't that bad a month ago, and that's just one of those pills' side effects."

"My acne's not that bad."

"No. But it's getting worse. How long have you been taking this junk?"

Davy shrugged. "Since the summer season started."

"That's what? Four weeks? What kind of a schedule are you on?"

Davy's face clouded over. "Schedule?"

"Yes. Schedule. The pros take these for a couple of weeks, then lay off for a while. How are you timing your dosage?"

"I just take them whenever I get them."

"Jesus Christ. You're not on a schedule. And you're stacking them with the cream. You're lucky your dick hasn't fallen off."

"Come on, Dad. Give me a little credit. That's not a side effect."

"No. But sterility is. And muscle deterioration. And impotence. That stuff can stunt your growth in two directions, up and out. So no, your dick won't fall off. But you might not be able to use it when you want to. And some of those effects aren't reversible. You want to be a eunuch all your life?"

"What's a eunuch?"

Keaton closed his eyes. He was letting his mouth run ahead of his mind. He needed to focus, not froth over. "Never mind," he said. "But you've had other side effects already. Your mom says you've had mood swings. And you've been swearing at her."

"Just once. When she came into my room."

"Once is twice too often. You still think your coach doesn't know you're using?"

"I don't know what he knows."

"But other kids are taking them."

"About half the team. And we're in first place. And I'm hitting four hundred. You didn't mention that in your list of side effects."

"All that could be happening without steroids. You've had a growth spurt. And another year of experience. You're bound to be getting better."

"I've never hit over three-thirty before. And coach is letting me play short."

"Well, here's the deal. You stop using or I'll tell your coach you're on steroids. He'll have no choice but to throw you off the team."

"But if I don't play in the summer league, coach might not let me on the school team next spring."

"You heard the deal. Stop using or stop playing."

Davy's eyes roamed from the ceiling to the bedroom walls as if he were seeking an escape route. Finally, he said, "I'll stop using."

"All right. I'll be around every evening to make sure you're keeping your word. And I'll know if you're not. I see this stuff at the professional level every day." He knew he wasn't likely to detect steroid use without a urine test, but he was fairly confident Davy wouldn't know he was bluffing. After all, his son didn't know the first thing about scheduling steroids. Hell, he didn't even know the meaning of the word *eunuch.*

"And that's not all," Keaton said. "I want to know where you're getting this stuff."

"I can't tell you that."

"Then you can write off summer league baseball."

"I don't want to get anybody in trouble."

"You're already a poster boy for trouble. And whoever's supplying you is no better than a cocaine peddler."

"It's not like that."

"That's the way the law sees it. He's pushing illegal drugs."

Davy shifted his gaze to the bedroom floor.

Keaton said, "I'm going to find out where this stuff's coming from. With you or without you. The difference is, if I do it with you, you'll still be playing ball."

"The team manager gets it for us. I don't know where from."

"The team manager? And the coach doesn't know?"

"He's never said anything."

"I'll just bet he hasn't. What's the manager's name?"

"Crain. Johnny Crain."

"Wouldn't happen to know where he lives?"

"No. He brings the stuff to our practices. We get together with him afterwards."

"You mean you used to get together with him afterwards."

"What are you going to do?"

"Dam up your supply line. Cut it off if I can." Keaton backed out of the bedroom. "See you tomorrow night."

Liz stopped Keaton at the foot of the stairs. "How did it go?"

"I'm hoping I scared him off the stuff. To make sure, I'm going after his supplier. But I told Davy I'll be stopping by nightly to check on him."

Liz sighed. "Come around dinner time. Maybe we can pretend to be a family again."

Before interviewing Johnny Crain, Keaton enlisted the aid of Robert Mayhew, the Menckenburg police officer who had helped him connect with the Cleveland police when he was tracking Sara Galardi. As they drove to Crain's address in Mayhew's squad car, Keaton briefed the police officer, saying, "I don't necessarily want to arrest the kid, just scare him a little, find out what we can about his source of supply, and dry it up."

"Just parking this patrol car in front of his house is likely to discourage his suppliers," Mayhew said.

Johnny Crain lived in a dilapidated frame house backed up against the wrong side of the railroad tracks. Through the screen surrounding the front porch, Keaton could see a set of mismatched lawn chairs, a large plaster duck wearing a gray Mammoths cap, and a bicycle that looked as if someone had taken a club to its front wheel.

Keaton pushed the doorbell and listened for the sound of buzzing or movement without hearing either. He knocked hard on the screen door and called out, "Johnny. Johnny Crain."

Dark curtains parted slightly in the window next to the front door, but the door still didn't open.

"Johnny, we know you're in there. Open the door, please."

When the front door stayed closed, Keaton took one step down from the screen door and called out, "All right. We'll come back when your parents are home."

The door opened. A short, pudgy boy stood in the doorway. He had four angry-looking stitches on his lower lip, and his right arm was in a cast that he held in front of his face as if he wanted to ward off a threatened blow.

"My God," Keaton said. "What happened to you?"

The boy nodded toward the dented bicycle on the screened-in porch. "Fell off my bike."

"I'm Lloyd Keaton, Davy Keaton's dad. I work for the *Herald.* This is Officer Mayhew of the Menckenburg Police."

"I know who you are," the boy said to Keaton. "Seen you at our games last season."

"Can we come in?"

"Got nothing to say to you."

"I think you do."

The boy poked his head out the front door and looked up and down the empty street. "Well, you're wrong."

"If you're worried about someone seeing us, it's probably better if we talk inside."

The boy stepped through the front door, crossed the porch, and opened the screen door. "Let's just talk here on the porch."

Keaton and Mayhew stepped inside the screen door. "You manage the Lancers and Coach Lammers's American Legion team?"

"Yeah."

"So you haul equipment, carry water, and give out aspirin."

"Somebody needs aspirin, yeah, I give it out."

"They tell me you give out steroids too. For money."

The boy looked away and directed his answer to the plaster

duck. "You can't prove it."

"It's against the law, you know," Mayhew said. "Selling controlled substances without a license."

"You can't prove it. They said you can't prove it."

"Johnny, you're in big trouble," Keaton said. "There are people who will testify under oath that they bought drugs from you."

"I never sold no drugs."

"Steroids are drugs."

"Anybody who says I gave them steroids is in trouble themselves." He spoke haltingly, as if he'd memorized a difficult passage of Shakespeare without quite understanding it. "Because that makes them steroid users, and they won't be able to play anymore themselves."

"Who told you that?" Keaton said. "Your coach? Does your coach know about the steroids?"

"Nobody told me. I just know it. Like I know I don't have to talk to you lessen you got a warrant."

Lyrics from a rap song sounded from Crain's side pocket. The boy took his phone out, looked at the screen, flipped it open, and said, "Can't talk now."

Keaton caught the boy's left wrist before he could return the phone to his pocket. "Nice-looking phone."

Mayhew snatched the phone from Crain's hand. "Looks like evidence to me."

The boy swiped at Mayhew with his free hand. "Hey. Give that back. You can't do that."

"We'll return it after we've had a chance to examine it," Keaton said. "Maybe you'll feel more like talking to us then."

"Like hell I will."

"Save us a lot of trouble if you just give us your supplier's name and address right now," Mayhew said. "If we have to hunt for it in your phone records, it'll go harder with you."

"Kiss my ass."

"I wouldn't go bandying invitations like that around," Mayhew said. "You keep up the way you're going, you'll find yourself behind bars where lots of folks will take you up on that offer."

"Shit, man. You don't scare me."

"We'll leave then," Keaton said. "But you can be sure we'll be back. Meantime, you should think seriously about telling us where you get your stash of steroids."

As the squad car pulled away, Keaton punched a number into Johnny Crain's cell phone and smiled to see that it had already been programmed into the phone.

Officer Mayhew nodded toward the phone. "A sharp lawyer's likely to disallow that evidence as the fruit of an illegal search and seizure."

"That's okay," Keaton said. "I'm just using his numbers to triangulate a target I've already got in my sights."

Chapter Seventeen: Employee of the Month

KEATON'S KORNER

Well, here we are in the dog days of August and with two weeks left in the AAA season our Mammoths are two games up with twelve games left to play. That makes their magic number ten—any combination of Mammoth wins or Bison losses that adds to ten will clinch at least a tie for the pennant. But the real magic number is Austin Reed's .380 batting average. If he keeps it up, it will be the highest ever in Mammoth history.

We're lucky the Indians already have an established second baseman on their roster, or Reed would have been called up long ago. As it is, the Huntington Flash has certainly earned a call-up to the big show when the AAA season ends.

Keaton remembered that the male voice on the phone had been surly and uncooperative the first time he'd called, but he persisted. "I know you've turned us down once, sir, but your phone number was selected at random and we have to get a suitable percentage of responses in order for our survey to be valid."

"That's not exactly my problem, now, is it?"

"No sir, it's not. But we just have five quick questions about your daily commute, and we really need your responses here at MTA."

The other end of the line went silent. For Christ's sake, don't hang up, Keaton thought. The number he'd called had come from Johnny Crain's phone and matched one that had appeared in both Sammy Tancredi's address book and Sara Galardi's cell phone.

Finally, the voice said, "I suppose you'll keep calling back if I hang up."

"At least one more time, sir. It's the specified procedure."

"Well, then, go ahead. But make it quick."

"Thank you, sir. First, I'd like you to rate the congestion during your morning commute on a scale of one to five, where one is uncongested, and five is heavily congested."

"Five. Isn't everybody's?"

Keaton copied down the answer as if he were really compiling a survey. "And how long does it take you to get from your home to your place of employment?"

An audible, impatient sigh, followed by "Twenty-five minutes."

"Do you drive alone, carpool, or take public transit?"

"Drive alone. Tried carpooling once, but couldn't find anyone compatible."

Why am I not surprised? Keaton thought. "Finally, so that we can model your commute on our computer, I'd like your home and business addresses. First, your home address."

"Twelve oh one Morningside Heights."

The address meant nothing to Keaton. "And your business address?"

"Two nineteen East Third Street." Keaton wrote down the address, followed by the notation WAREHOUSE DISTRICT. "Well, that's all the questions I have. Thank you very much for your time."

"Don't you want to know my age, gender, occupation, religious persuasion, salary, length of residence, and party affiliation?"

Keaton was so deep into his role playing as a survey taker that he began writing down all the categories the respondent suggested. When he realized what he was doing, he stopped after he'd written "religious persuasion" and said, "No sir, that won't be necessary. We don't seem to need any of those categories."

"Well, that's good, because they're none of your damned business."

"I quite agree, sir." After the last category he'd copied—religious persuasion—Keaton wrote the word ASSHOLE in block capitals.

"Are we done, then?"

What the hell, Keaton thought; might as well go for it. "There is one other thing, sir, although it's entirely optional. I seem to have reached you at your place of business. I wonder if I might have your name in case my supervisor needs to verify the authenticity of this call."

"My name?"

"Yes sir. As I said, it's entirely optional."

"My name's Gordon Arthur. But I'll tell you right now, if you or your supervisor interrupts me at work again, the mayor is going to hear about it."

"That shouldn't be necessary, Mr. Arthur. Thank you for your time."

The line went dead as Arthur hung up.

Keaton unfolded his map of Menckenburg and smoothed out the section just east of the downtown area. The work address Arthur had given was within a block of OgrowSport, the firm that was supplying the vaunted Vitamin O to Austin Reed and other AAA players. Maybe it was time to offer some free newspaper space in the form of a behind-the-scenes interview with the supplement manufacturer.

★ ★ ★ ★ ★

The two-hundred block of East Third Street linked Menckenburg's expanding downtown with the warehouse district that had once housed the products of the city's now defunct manufacturing plants. The end of the block nearest the downtown was well lit and had been refurbished with glass fronts. OgrowSport stood in the middle of the upgraded section, flanked by a gymnasium on the corner and, near the center of the block, a day spa that had begun life as a beauty parlor.

The glass facade of the corner gymnasium revealed a row of spandex-clad women of assorted shapes and sizes on treadmills, all marching to different drummers. The gym occupied two stories, with brightly lit rows of exercise equipment extending over the OgrowSport offices and the adjoining spa. On the other side of the spa, at the end of the block farthest from the downtown, the owners either hadn't gotten the word about urban renewal or had chosen to take a stand against gentrification. Where the glass walls of the spa ended, a windowless brick facing took over and stretched to the end of the block, broken only by a corrugated garage door and a black metal door accented with the faded yellow numerals 219, the workplace address given by Gordon Arthur.

Keaton punched the buzzer next to the black metal door, took out his pocket notebook, and waited. When nothing happened, he punched the buzzer again.

A sliding panel in the door squealed open and two eyes shaded by bushy eyebrows peered out. Then the door opened just enough for a mouth framed by a bushy beard that matched the eyebrows to push its way through and say "Yeah?"

"I'm Lloyd Keaton of the *Menckenburg Herald,* here for the interview."

"What interview?"

"The three o'clock interview we'd scheduled on the phone."

"What the hell are you talking about?"

Keaton checked his notebook and tried to peer inside the darkened building, but the man's bulky form blocked his view. "The three o'clock interview with Mr. Cleary of OgrowSport."

A greasy thumbnail appeared under the bushy beard. "Two doors down."

"Then you're not affiliated with OgrowSport?"

The man stretched his neck far enough through the door to scan the chipped bricks surrounding it. "We look like we're affiliated with them?"

Keaton checked his notebook again. "Guess I must have written down the wrong address. Sorry to have bothered you."

The bearded man grunted and disappeared behind the metal door as it rasped shut.

The OgrowSport reception area was flanked by two ceiling-high windows and glass doors leading to the workout gym on the right and the day spa named Seana on the left. The row of treadmills behind the fully occupied row in the front window was unoccupied except for a pony-tailed blonde wearing mauve shorts who seemed grimly intent on covering the distance between Menckenburg and Cleveland with long, powerful strides. Through the spa windows on the left, Keaton could see two manicures and a pedicure in progress. Directly ahead of him, a brunette wearing a red polo shirt with OgrowSport printed in blue and white script over her left breast sat behind a long, curved Plexiglas desk.

"Can I help you, sir?" The brunette asked.

"I have an appointment with Preston Cleary."

The brunette smiled. "Oh, then you'd be Mr. Keaton of the *Herald*. Preston is expecting you. Take a seat and I'll let him know you're here."

Keaton perched on a stool at the end of the Plexiglas desk and scanned the wall behind the receptionist. It was the only wall in the room you couldn't see through, and it was covered with autographed pictures of sports figures, a framed full-page ad from *USA Today,* product endorsements, and employee award plaques. He recognized pictures of Austin Reed and Sammy Tancredi in their Mammoth uniforms, but he had trouble identifying all the sprinters, swimmers, and cyclists who shared the wall with the baseball players, and his eyes weren't good enough to make out the autographed inscriptions from a distance.

A tall blonde man in a crisp blue OgrowSport blazer came through the door behind the reception desk and held out his right hand. "Mr. Keaton? I'm Preston Cleary."

Cleary led Keaton through the door behind the reception desk into an office lined with still more photos of sports celebrities, politicians, civic recognition plaques, and employee awards. There were no windows, however, so they wouldn't be distracted by pedicures or peddling blondes.

Keaton sat in an armchair of leather stretched over curved metal tubing and said, "I was surprised by all the activity. How long have the gym and spa been a part of your OgrowSport operation?"

"The exercise equipment, trainers, and beauticians are fairly recent additions, actually. We acquired a lot of private investment and became a full-service operation when Vitamin O began receiving so much positive press. I was glad to see you mention it in your column, by the way."

"How long have you been producing Vitamin O?"

"Over four years now. But the big rush of publicity has come this baseball season with our series of blind tests."

"How are those going?"

Cleary smiled and gave a slight shrug. "We won't really know until the AAA season ends and we have a full year of statistics from all the players involved in our sample. That's why I told you I felt this interview was a trifle premature."

Keaton flipped open his notebook. "Well, there's already been a lot leaked to the press about your tests. What can you tell me about the process?"

"Before the season started, we selected twenty-eight players—a pitcher and position player from each team. Half have been taking Vitamin O, while the other half are being given a placebo."

"I didn't realize placebos were involved. What's the incentive for players getting the placebo?

"Well, the players don't know whether they're getting Vitamin O or a placebo. We've promised all the participants a free supply of Vitamin O so long as they remain in professional baseball. In return, we ask that they be willing to give us paid endorsements."

"The players don't know what they're getting?"

"That's correct. Our statistical consultants told us the test wouldn't be valid otherwise."

"But the names of some of the players have leaked out."

Cleary managed another shrug. "I'm afraid that's unavoidable."

"I saw Austin Reed's picture in the outer office. He's been telling interviewers that he's taking Vitamin O."

"Austin is a part of the program. But I'm afraid he doesn't actually know whether he's getting the placebo or the real thing."

"Do you?"

Cleary stiffened, frowned, and said, "Of course not."

"Well, let me tell you, the way that kid's hitting, if he's not getting Vitamin O, you better be prepared to market the placebo when the season ends."

Cleary's face stayed set in its frown. "Of course, we hope that won't be necessary."

"Of course."

Cleary seemed to relax. "I guess that was a little of your *Keaton's Korner* humor. Would you like to see the production process?"

"If I could, sure."

Cleary led Keaton out a side door into a long, narrow hallway. Three doors marked EMPLOYEES ONLY lined the right side of the hallway. Cleary opened the nearest door and stepped aside to allow Keaton to enter.

A narrow conveyor belt ran half the length of the room, carrying small plastic cylinders about two inches high. The cylinders entered the room in batches through a wall opening draped with thin strips of black rubber. Metal guides funneled the batches into a single file and guided the containers under two tubular arms that sealed and capped them.

The capped containers passed over a small digital scale and were gathered in groups of four and shuttled into a waiting box partitioned to receive three groups of four cylinders. A stout woman wearing a white apron and rubber gloves stood at the end of the line, gathering the filled boxes and replacing them with empty cartons.

Cleary nodded to the woman and said, "Afternoon, Maria." Turning to Keaton, he said, "Maria there controls the speed of the belt. She usually averages three boxes a minute, but can do five or six in a pinch. "That right, Maria?"

Maria smiled. "That's right, sir. We've gone as high as eight, but it's hard to keep that up."

"So each box has a dozen vials," Keaton said. "How long will that last a player?"

"There's two ounces per vial. The box should last the whole six-month season."

As Keaton watched, a buzzer sounded and a cylinder was shunted out of the main line into a cloth bag at the edge of the conveyor belt.

"Didn't meet the weight specs," Cleary said. "Maria will recycle the bag's contents when it fills up."

Keaton reached into the bag and retrieved the rejected vial. "Mind if I take this with me?"

Cleary hesitated for an instant, then smiled and said, "Be my guest. You should realize, though, that you won't get much of a performance boost from a single vial. It usually takes a month or two of continuous use before your body begins to respond."

"That's the dosage you need if you're playing second base for the Mammoths. My job's not nearly so strenuous." Keaton put the plastic vial in his shirt pocket and patted it twice. "Maybe I can get a little inspiration for my column from just two ounces."

"Could be," Cleary said. "Let's hope so."

Keaton nodded toward the strips of black rubber that the conveyor belt passed through on its way into the room. "What goes on beyond that wall?"

"That's our mixing room, where all the ingredients come together. I'm afraid I can't show you that. It's a closely guarded secret until we can get it patented."

Keaton turned a page in his notebook. "What *can* you tell me about it?"

"Vitamin O was originally developed for use by our astronauts to ensure that they received enough oxygen to maintain their health. The ingredients are all natural, and are designed to maximize your nutrients, prevent disease, promote health, and improve physical performance."

Keaton wrote down "astronauts" and "oxygen," then realized Cleary was just parroting the text of the *USA Today* ad in the reception area. He wrote down USA TODAY and said, "So, Vitamin O stands for oxygen?"

"That's right. It consists of stabilized oxygen molecules in a solution of distilled water, sodium chloride, and trace elements of a few other ingredients I'm not at liberty to divulge."

Keaton wrote down "O + distilled H2O + NaCl + ? = Snake Oil?" and closed his notebook, saying, "I guess I've seen enough here."

Cleary thanked Maria and led the way back to his office.

Keaton sat down in the tubular chair and fished the vial of Vitamin O from his breast pocket. "So tell me about dosage. Suppose I did want to play second base for the Mammoths. How much of this should I take?"

"What you've got there is about a two-week supply."

"And what's its retail value?"

"We sell it for twenty-five dollars, plus taxes and handling charges, with discounts for large lots."

"How are sales?"

"Not bad. But we expect them to take off when the AAA season ends, the results of our tests are known, and we have some solid science to back our claims."

"Do you manufacture any other products?"

"Some shampoos, conditioners, and moisteners for the spa."

"No other performance pills though?"

"No. Not anymore. We did quite a business in amphetamines before baseball banned them."

"So you've been around a while."

"Over twenty years."

"And you've manufactured amphetamines. What about steroids?"

"We produced andro when it was still legal. But we stopped when baseball banned it." Cleary frowned. "Look here. I hope you don't have to mention our past production of steroids in your article."

Keaton didn't respond. Instead, he said, "One of the arguments against steroids was that they created an uneven playing field by giving some players an unfair advantage. If Vitamin O gives its users an edge, aren't you afraid it might be banned as well?"

Cleary smiled. "No way. Vitamin O isn't a controlled substance. We use strictly natural ingredients."

"Steroids have some pretty nasty side effects. Any side effects with Vitamin O?"

"No record of any. As I said, we only use natural ingredients, so we wouldn't really expect any harmful side effects."

"Socrates might argue that point with you," Keaton said.

"I'm sorry. I don't see it as a philosophical issue."

"I was thinking of history, not philosophy. I believe hemlock is a natural ingredient with some mildly fatal side effects. Belladonna's another one."

Cleary managed a tight smile. "Oh, I see. Well, I can assure you that you won't find either of those ingredients in Vitamin O."

"That's a load off my mind." Keaton reopened his notebook. "Tell me a little about yourself."

"Not much to tell. Educated at Ohio State. Got a BA in phys ed."

"How long have you worked for OgrowSport?"

"Over ten years now."

"So you were around when they were distributing steroids and amphetamines?"

"Yes. Not many of our current employees can say that. We had to let a lot of people go when baseball banned those products. They cut off most of our customer base."

"Were the Mammoths a good customer back then?"

"For amphetamines, yes. Not so much for steroids."

"Did you work with Dale Loren?"

"Yes. But not for steroids. Even before baseball banned juicing, any Mammoth who wanted andro had to come directly to us. They couldn't go through the team and Loren."

"Then you must find it surprising that he's been indicted for distributing steroids."

Cleary shrugged. "Somebody must have made it worth his while. That's what happens when you ban something. The price skyrockets. Look at Prohibition."

Keaton flipped his notebook shut. "Well, that's all I need. I'll have a staff photographer contact you. We'll want some pictures of your operation to accompany the article."

"I look forward to reading it."

Keaton stopped in the reception area to copy a few details from the framed *USA Today* ad. Through the glass door leading to the gym, he could see that the blonde in the mauve shorts still hadn't made it to Cleveland.

He was about to leave when a series of plaques next to the *USA Today* ad caught his eye. The plaques displayed the names of OgrowSport's EMPLOYEE OF THE MONTH for the last ten years. Preston Cleary's name appeared twice on the plaque covering the past year. Ten years ago, though, a single employee had won the award for three consecutive months. That employee's name was Gordon Arthur.

Chapter Eighteen: Research by the Yard

KEATON'S KORNER

It's about time that Congressman Bloodworth and his committee recognized that the real problem with steroids is their unsupervised use by the youth of this country. For the past week, the Congressman and his cohorts have been playing Perry Mason, grilling retired players, trainers, and clubhouse boys about their involvement with steroids at a time when professional baseball hadn't bothered to outlaw their use. The ostensible purpose, outside of political preening, seems to be to ask enough questions so that some poor schnook will eventually be caught in a lie and sent to the slammer on charges of perjury.

These proceedings aren't related to any conceivable issue of public policy, or to the stated purpose of the oversight committee, which is government reform. Let me propose that if the committee really wanted to do some public good, they could put their time and money to better use by initiating random testing of high school athletes. It's not as glamorous as gong on TV to ask retired stars where they were on the night of October 13, or what they said to one another in spring training ten years ago, or what they thought was in those needles stuck in their butts, but it might actually do some good.

"So how long will it take to get this analyzed?" Keaton asked.

Alex Keith held the plastic vial of Vitamin O up to the light. "Shouldn't take more than a day. What is it?"

"It's Vitamin O, the magic mixture that's supposedly pushing Austin Reed's batting average through the roof."

"So that's what it looks like."

"You mean you've never seen it? I thought OgrowSport hired you guys to run tests on it."

Alex set the vial down carefully, as if it might break. "They hired our statistical guys to oversee the matched pair tests they were running with players, not to test the magic waters. But they pulled the plug on us."

"Pulled the plug? Why?"

"Your Congressman Bloodworth. He snuck some money into the Feds' Environmental Appropriations Bill to analyze and detect performance-enhancing substances. He earmarked the funding for Dixon State University."

"Never heard of them. Do they have any experience with steroid testing?"

"None at all. But they're in Bloodworth's home district."

"Can he do that?"

"Happens all the time. A couple of months ago we were all set to bid on a two-million-dollar motorcycle safety study we'd been tracking for two years. We'd done some pioneering work in the field and thought we had the inside track in an open competition. But the head of the Transportation Committee was from North Nowhere, and he earmarked the money for his state university."

"So the job was never bid."

Alex's baby face clouded over as if someone had puked in his sandbox. "Nobody asks whether the grant recipient can actually do the job. Congress pretends you can buy research by the yard from anybody with a shingle and a Ph.D. They turn these appropriation bills into a fiscal Christmas tree and dangle ornaments for all their buddies."

"I remember reading about Bloodworth's bill," Keaton said.

"I thought he just wanted to develop tests that could detect human growth hormones and other steroids that were slipping through the current screenings."

"That was the initial idea. But the language of his rider was pretty broad. Dixon State can do almost anything they want with the money. Spend it trying to figure out the impact of drugs on performance, for example. Maybe just develop ads designed to keep kids off steroids."

"What kind of money are we talking about?"

"A million and change."

Keaton whistled silently. "Lucky Dixon State."

Alex shrugged. "When Dixon State got the federal money, OgrowSport figured they could get more exposure from a nationally recognized program with Bloodworth's imprimatur."

"So they pulled the plug on your work."

"What the hell. There was no way we could compete with the low overhead of a university program riding on earmarked funds."

"So when the AAA season ends next week, whatever the statistics show about the effectiveness of Vitamin O will come blessed by a national testing program with Bloodworth's seal of approval."

Alex tossed the vial of Vitamin O into the air with his right hand and caught it with his left. "It's your tax dollars at work."

The Mammoths had the day off, so Keaton planned to catch Davy's summer league game in the late afternoon. He spent the rest of the morning working on his OgrowSport story and making follow-up phone calls.

"I don't care what you think," Officer Robert Mayhew said in his faintly southern accent. "No judge is going to issue a search warrant on the strength of a phone number you got using fairly dubious tactics, and I'd personally rather not have those tactics subjected to judicial scrutiny."

"They're still producing steroids," Keaton said. "Sure as sunrise. The guy who's in everybody's phone book, this Gordon Arthur, used to work for OgrowSport back when they were turning out andro. I'm betting he still does. I'm betting that whole block is one big juice factory."

"The betting odds might be in your favor. But all you've really got is a hunch, and that's not enough to convince either my boss or a judge."

"What would I need to convince them?"

"Hard evidence that steroids are coming out of that block. Testimony from a juicer or dealer that OgrowSport's been supplying them. Anything that links OgrowSport to the current stream of steroids."

Keaton drummed his fingers on his laptop. "Johnny Crain had Gordon Arthur's number in his phone. I'm betting Arthur is his steroid supplier. My son will testify that this Crain kid's been dealing dope to his summer league team. Won't that give us an entrée?"

"We might be able to scare the kid into revealing his source, I guess. But only if we catch him dealing or stashing big batches of the stuff. If your son is willing to testify, we could probably get a warrant to search the Crain kid's home. If the kid's smart, though, he would have dumped anything incriminating after our first visit."

"He didn't register too high on my smart meter. He probably doesn't get much of a cut from his sales, so dumping product would seem like burning big money to him. I think he could be our link to OgrowSport."

"Get a formal statement from your boy and I'll try for a warrant to search the kid's house."

"In the meantime, what about keeping OgrowSport's plant under surveillance?"

"I can keep an eye on them while I work my beat. But my boss isn't likely to assign manpower to full-time surveillance on the basis of your hunch."

"What about using a camera to keep track of comings and goings?"

"You've got at least three entrances on the street and three more in the alley. You'd need quite a few cameras, and that eventually boils down to manpower I can't get. You're with the media. Maybe you could pull it off."

Keaton managed a half smile. "I'm at the wrong end of the media chain. Maybe you haven't heard, but TV and the Internet are gobbling up newspapers."

"If we get enough evidence for a search warrant, we'll have enough to argue for surveillance cameras too. But we need to start with a statement from your son."

Keaton knew that might not be as easy as he'd made it sound. But he said, "I'll see what I can do."

After hanging up, Keaton phoned Preston Cleary to make an appointment for a *Herald* photographer and finagle a thirty-day gym membership for himself while he was working on the OgrowSport story. He'd always viewed exercise machines with all the enthusiasm of an Inquisition victim contemplating the rack—at least Torquemada's torturers hid their machines in dank cellars and didn't display them behind brightly lit windows in full view of the passing population. But a gym membership would give him an excuse to do a little of the surveillance he couldn't get from the local police. Maybe he could bypass the exercise machines and go straight to the steam room.

Keaton was so busy with his phone calls and writing that he didn't make it to Davy's game until the bottom of the second inning. The players on the field outnumbered the fans in the stands, and the infield chatter was louder than the sporadic crowd noise.

He stood at the edge of the wooden grandstand, watching the sunlit puffs of dust kicked up by the fidgeting infielders, listening to their choruses of "C'mon babe," "C'mon boy," "Little life, little pep, little hustle," and realizing once again that there was no place he'd rather be than a baseball diamond with a game underway. Any diamond. Any game. It was a feeling that never left him, even in the middle of his losing streaks, and he knew he was lucky to be able to make a living on the fringes of the game he loved.

Davy's team was at bat, and Keaton spotted him at the far end of the dugout, leaning forward and shouting at the opposing pitcher. When he finally caught his son's eye, the boy stopped shouting and stared down at the dugout floor.

Keaton saw Dale Loren in the stands behind first base and joined him on the hardwood planks.

"Mammoths' day off," Loren said, more as a statement than a question.

"Last home stand starts tomorrow. Good chance they'll wrap up the pennant before they go on the road." Keaton nodded toward the field. "What'd I miss here?"

"One to nothing, favor of the good guys. Your boy laid down a nifty bunt single in the bottom of the first. He's been doing fine."

"What about your nephew? How's he doing?"

"Lammers cut him from the team. He was a little young for the competition."

"You're still coming to the games, though?"

"Need to get out of the house."

"How's it going for you?"

Loren shrugged and sighed. "Losing sleep. Losing weight. Losing friends. Losing money."

Keaton took a long look at Loren. The ex-trainer's eyes stared out through two burnt holes, and his faded red polo shirt looked as if it had been handed down by an older, bigger, roughhousing brother. "The lost weight shows."

"It's the indictment diet. I'd recommend it, except bulimia is probably a more pleasant way to lose weight." Loren ran the back of his wrist across his mouth. "Hell, starvation is probably more pleasant."

"Got a court date yet?"

"No. My lawyer is trying to maneuver for a sympathetic judge."

"Seems like you ought to do okay. The only thing they've got against you is the word of a dead man."

"That didn't stop the grand jury from indicting me."

"In my experience, grand juries figure it's their job to indict regardless of the evidence. You should do better when you get your day in court with your own lawyer."

"I don't know. Some days it seems like I'm the one-legged man in the ass-kicking contest. And my lawyer's lost my crutches." Loren propped one leg on the bleacher seat below them and extended both arms like a man fighting to maintain his balance. "I want to thank you for the support you've been giving me in your column, though."

"Least I can do. You know, I'm still trying to figure out where Sammy Tancredi actually got his steroids. Any ideas you might have would be a big help."

"All I know is where he didn't get them."

The home team's catcher popped up for the third out, and Davy ran out to his shortstop position, where he fielded warm-up grounders without looking up into the stands.

Keaton watched his son warm up, but turned to Loren when it became obvious the boy wasn't likely to acknowledge his presence. "Had an interesting conversation about you the other day with the head marketer for OgrowSport."

"Preston Cleary."

"That's the man. He said you refused to handle steroids for the Mammoth players even before they were banned."

"That's right. Didn't seem to me that the risks were worth the potential pay-offs."

"Think it might be worthwhile to get that into the court record?"

"Depose Cleary, you mean?"

"Don't see how it could hurt."

"Shows I knew some players were using steroids."

"But it shows you steered clear of them even when they were legal. I have to think that would impress a jury."

Loren shrugged. "Could be. I'll talk to my lawyer. See what he says."

The first batter up for the visiting team hit a sharp grounder between short and third. Davy glided to his right, backhanded the ball smoothly, and threw the batter out at first by half a step.

Keaton stood, whistled shrilly, and clapped. "Attaboy, Davy."

A few spectators turned their heads in the direction of the cheer. Coach Lammers emerged from the dugout, looked up into the stands, saw Keaton, and returned to the dugout without acknowledging him.

Keaton sat down. "What about OgrowSport? Think they might still be turning out steroids?"

Loren shrugged. "Hard to tell. The only player on the Mammoths with a history of juicing was Sammy Tancredi, and they weren't supplying him."

"When he was red hot with your cold cream, you mean."

Loren nodded.

"What about before and after the cold cream? He'd tested positive once before. And he had to get steroids from somebody after Cleveland called him up."

"I don't know that the supplier was OgrowSport, though. I heard they had a really tough time right after baseball banned juicing. Once they got back on their feet, it wouldn't have made much sense to go on producing an illegal substance if they were getting enough business from a legal one. And it looks like they were."

"You mean Vitamin O. What do you know about it?"

"Not much. Austin Reed asked me about it when he started on their program. All I could find out was that they guaranteed it was all natural and wouldn't trigger a steroid alarm."

"I'm having it analyzed."

"Then you'll know lots more than I do."

The visiting team went down one-two-three, and Davy's team came to bat in the bottom of the third inning. The visitors' pitcher walked the first two batters and got a force out at third on a bungled bunt attempt with Davy kneeling in the on-deck circle.

As his son sifted dirt through his hands and stood up to head for the plate, Keaton shouted, "Wait him out, Davy. Wait him out. He's wilder than the March Hare."

Davy gave no sign he heard Keaton. Standing at the plate, he took two balls and a strike, and then lined a fastball into the gap between the center and right fielders.

Keaton and Loren both leapt up at the solid ping of the aluminum bat and stood cheering as Davy rounded first and second and slid into third with a triple. The boy bounced up, dusted himself off, clapped his hands twice, and stole a hurried glance in his father's direction.

"Way to go, Davy!" Keaton shouted.

Davy quickly looked away, said something to his third-base coach, and then scored standing up as the next hitter grounded out to deep short.

When the home team took the field for the top of the fourth

inning, a stocky blonde boy ran out to the shortstop position.

Keaton looked into the home team dugout and saw Davy slumping on the end of the bench farthest from Coach Lammers, dangling his glove from his left hand. "What the hell? He's benched Davy."

"Doesn't make sense," Loren said. "Your boy's been the best player on the field for the last three or four games."

"The coach is sending a message to me," Keaton said. "I had an argument with him about kids juicing and then caught Davy using steroids he'd gotten from the team manager. I'm trying to cut off that source of supply."

"The team manager? That little pudgy kid?"

Keaton nodded. "That's the one."

"I didn't see him around today."

"I sicced the local law on him."

"Think the coach knew about the kid's dealing?"

"He must have. Look at that infield. Every kid out there is bulked up to big-league proportions."

"Yeah. Now that you mention it, your boy looks a little top-heavy as well."

"I think we've finally got him to stop using. But he looks different today. Grim. Like he's not enjoying himself. That's not like him. Ever since we first started playing catch, he's been happy and smiling whenever he comes into contact with a bat and ball."

"Yeah. I've noticed that about him. And you're right. He's sure not enjoying himself right now."

In the top of the fifth, Davy's replacement botched a double-play grounder that let in two runs.

"Has that kid at short been playing much?" Keaton asked.

"First time I've seen him," Loren said. "Your boy Davy didn't miss an inning while you were on the road with the Mammoths."

So the coach is sending me a message, Keaton thought. A veiled threat, reminding me that he had some power over my son. Just in case I wanted to make a fuss over his players' steroid use. What the hell, best to ignore it. I don't want to turn into one of those nagging parents who hounded me about their kids' playing time when I was coaching Little League.

Davy's team hung on to win four to two. As they were standing to leave, Keaton said to Loren, "Haven't seen you around the Mammoths' games lately."

"Can't find any place to sit where people don't stare at me."

"Come up to the press box with me. I'll leave a pass at the gate."

"Thanks. I'll do that."

Keaton held out his hand. "Good luck with your trial."

Loren's mouth tensed into something that could have been the start of a smile. "Good luck with your boy."

Davy was still on the end of the dugout bench, changing his spikes for tennis shoes, when Keaton caught up with him. "Nice game," he said. "Need a ride home?"

His son nodded without looking up from his shoelaces. "Sure."

"Car's in the lot behind first base. Wait for me there. I want to talk to your coach."

"Aw, Dad. Leave it alone."

"Don't worry. I won't be long."

Coach Lammers was loading aluminum bats into a dusty duffel bag at the other end of the dugout. When he saw Keaton coming, he straightened and said, "Well, looky who's here. Bring your tape recorder again?"

Keaton shook his head. "Got everything I needed on tape the last time we talked."

"What brings you out then?"

"Wanted to watch my boy play shortstop. Was wondering why

you took him out in the fourth inning." He hadn't meant to sound like a whiney, pushy parent, but the words just seemed to tumble out.

"Got to give everybody a chance. Assess my talent before the high school season starts."

"I thought it might be because I've been looking into steroid use by high school teams."

Lammers zipped up the duffel bag. "We've plowed that ground before. I'm not aware any of my boys are using steroids."

"Then you wouldn't object to them taking a urine test."

"I think you're bluffing. But I wouldn't object if you could get permission to test every team in the league."

"Might be easier if I just wrote an article about a certain local high school coach who has a laissez faire attitude toward steroid use."

"What the hell's that supposed to mean?"

"It's French. It means your 'don't ask, don't tell' policy won't play too well with the public when we shine a light on the pipeline that's been shipping steroids to your players."

Lammers slung the duffel bag over his shoulder. "Better check your sources, Mr. Reporter. I'm not a part of any pipeline. I don't got anybody using steroids."

"Then you won't object if my paper tests your players' urine?"

"Just so long as your boy lines up at the piss pot with everybody else." Aluminum bats clanked in the duffel bag as Lammers turned and walked away.

"How'd it go with the coach?" Davy asked as Keaton slid behind the wheel of his Ford Escort.

"Not too bad, really." But not too well, either, Keaton thought. "I think we understand one another."

"Meaning what?"

"Meaning he's not going to bench you for fingering your

steroid supplier."

"Oh, great. You told him I fingered Johnny Crain. Thanks a lot, Dad."

"The subject of you and Johnny Crain never came up. Not in the same sentence, anyhow."

"You weren't with Coach for more than a couple of minutes. If our names weren't in the same sentence, they had to be in the same paragraph."

Keaton reached out from behind the wheel to pat his son on the shoulder, but Davy was slouched well out of reach against the passenger door. "Actually, I never mentioned Johnny Crain at all. But take my word for it, Lammers isn't going to bench you. For one thing, you're head and shoulders better than that kid he put in your place."

"What's the other thing?"

"What other thing?"

"You said 'for one thing,' I'm his best shortstop. What's the other thing?"

"It's just a figure of speech. But I'm pretty sure he doesn't want my newspaper on his back for running a program where half his players are juicing."

"That's it? You're going to bring down my buddies if Coach doesn't cooperate? That'll make me real popular."

"Davy. Your coach is sanctioning steroid use by underage kids."

"So's every other coach in the league."

"Do you know that for sure?"

"Not about every coach."

"Well, it's got to stop with your coach."

Davy squirmed and shifted his position against the passenger door. "Why are you looking at me like that?"

"If I do have to bring his program down, I need to be sure you're clean."

"Of course I'm clean. Mom took away all my pills. And even if I wanted more, Johnny Crain hasn't been around to supply them."

"That's another thing. I need you to sign a statement saying you got your steroids from Johnny Crain."

"Oh, yeah. Sure. That's gonna win me lots of points with the guys."

"There's no reason they have to know about it."

"Somebody's gonna know, though. Otherwise you wouldn't need my signature."

Keaton held up four fingers. "Four people. That's all who need to know. You, me, a local policeman, and a judge. We need an affidavit from you to support a search warrant."

"Who are you gonna search?"

"Johnny Crain's house. What did you think?"

"And if I don't sign?"

"Then Coach Lammers won't have a chance to bench you. I'll do it myself."

Davy was quiet the rest of the way home. As soon as the car stopped in his driveway, he jumped out, slammed through the front door, and headed upstairs to his room.

Liz was waiting by the stairway as Keaton followed Davy through the front door. "Our son just breezed right by me without so much as a 'Hi, Mom.' Was it something you said?"

"Yeah. I said I needed a written statement identifying his steroid supplier."

"That's a pretty tall order for a kid."

"I wouldn't ask for it if it weren't important."

"Important to you. But not to Davy."

"Important to Davy. It will cut off any connection he has with steroids."

While Liz fixed dinner, Keaton told her about the need for a search warrant to dam up Johnny Crain's supply of steroids, and about his suspicion that those steroids might be coming from the OgrowSport complex.

Liz took a break from tearing lettuce and held the back of her left hand up to the light. "Looks like I could use a manicure. What did you say the name of that spa was?"

"Seana. But you don't need to . . ."

Liz cut him off with a wave of her unmanicured hand. "If you can join a gym I can sacrifice my fingernails. Should I wear a disguise and make up a phony name?"

"No. Tell them I sent you. That I recommended the place. It might get you special treatment while they're still waiting for my article to appear."

"What should I be looking for?"

"Anything that strikes you as a little off. See if you really believe they could make it as a day spa."

Liz went back to tearing lettuce. "Sounds exciting."

"Don't get carried away. If these people are dealing drugs, they're likely to be pretty touchy about their privacy." Keaton stood up. "Is there paper in your printer?"

"Of course."

"I think I'll go type up a statement for Davy to sign while you're finishing the salad."

"Good idea. It's a safe bet he'll be down for dinner."

"How's he been the last week?"

"Full of testosterone. Excited about playing shortstop."

"Not still moody?"

"Not so's I noticed. Why?"

"I'm worried he might still be on steroids."

Liz paused with a paring knife poised over the skin of an avocado. "What makes you think that?"

"I don't know. The way he looked on the diamond today. The way he behaves toward me."

Liz pointed the knife blade at Keaton. "Well, you're asking

him to snitch on a friend. That's a pretty big deal for a teenager. For anybody."

"I guess so. I hope that's it. I'll go type up a statement to make it easier for him."

When Davy came down to dinner, two neatly typed copies of a statement identifying his team manager as a steroid distributor had been placed under his napkin and a ballpoint pen sat next to his fork. "What's this?" he asked.

"A statement that Johnny Crain sold you steroids," Keaton said. "I need to have you sign it."

"Why two copies?"

"One for the police and one for the judge."

Davy put his napkin on his lap, then scribbled a signature on both copies and handed them to Keaton.

"Don't you want to read what it says?" Keaton asked.

"You wrote up what you wanted it to say. Bad enough I have to sign it without having to read it too."

Davy endured the meal in sullen silence, effectively cutting off any attempts at conversation. When he finished eating, he left the table without excusing himself.

"Well, that was just great," Keaton said as he listened to his son stomp up the stairs to his room.

Liz stood and cleared the plates from the table. "You got what you wanted."

"I got what I needed." Keaton carried two empty wineglasses to the sink.

"You treated him like a criminal."

"He's been involved in a criminal activity. I'm trying to get him through it and punish the people responsible."

"He's stopped using steroids. Isn't that enough?"

"Liz, I'm not at all certain he's stopped juicing. But one way to make sure he stops is to turn his supplier over to the cops."

"I just don't like to see you bullying our son."

"I gave him two pieces of paper to sign. How is that bullying him?"

"You really don't see it, do you?" Liz turned on the tap with such force that water splattered off the dirty dishes onto her slacks. "You're threatening to ban his baseball playing. You're forcing him to snitch on his friends."

"For Christ's sake. The team manager is no friend of Davy's. He's a dope peddler."

"Davy sees it as snitching on his teammates too."

"Well, maybe he should." Keaton knew from past experience he'd better leave before one of them said something they'd regret. He snatched up Davy's signed affidavits and said, "Thanks for dinner."

Before Liz could say, "You're welcome," Keaton's cell phone rang, sounding the chorus of "The Gambler," "You've got to know when to hold 'em."

"God, I hate that song," Liz said as Keaton fumbled to retrieve the phone from his jacket pocket.

"I'm sorry," Keaton said. "I'll take the call in the car."

He was down the porch steps by the time he got the phone to his ear and the voice on the other end of the line said, "Keaton? It's Alex. I thought you might like to know what our lab analysis showed for that sample you dropped off."

"That was quick."

"Turns out there wasn't much to analyze. There's some vitamin B-twelve there, but it's mostly just salt water with a little lemon flavoring."

"Salt water? I wonder if Cleary gave me the placebo by mistake." Keaton thought back to Cleary's conversation beside the conveyor belt. "No. I'm sure he said it was the real thing. We joked about how much I'd have to take to play second base for the Mammoths."

"My guess is a reservoir full wouldn't help you."

"Jesus. They've got this big *USA Today* ad that's filled with testimonials and says Vitamin O consists of 'stabilized oxygen molecules in a solution of distilled water and sodium chloride.' "

"Well, that's salt water."

"I guess we can't nail them for false advertising."

"Not unless they made up some of the testimonials."

"Will you be at your office for a little while? I'll stop by and pick up the sample."

"I'll be here. Like I said, though, I doubt if it will make a second baseman out of you."

"Well, I never really expected it to. I'm left-handed."

Keaton had put his cell phone back in his pocket and started his car when the phone rang again. A deep, rasping voice said, "This Keaton? Lloyd Keaton?"

"Yeah."

"You want to stay healthy enough to keep turning out those cutesy columns and watching your boy Davy play baseball, you better stop your steroid snooping."

Chapter Nineteen: Shampoo or Real Poo?

KEATON'S KORNER

Although they failed to do it before their hometown fans, the Mammoths managed to wrap up the AAA pennant with one game yet to play. So the only suspense left before the playoffs is whether Austin Reed can keep his batting average above .387 and set a new Menckenburg record.

Since Reed's average currently sits at .388, Bait MacFarland tells me that he's thinking of benching his star second sacker for the final game to make sure that his stats stay above the record level. There is, of course, a precedent for this sort of thing. In 1941, Ted Williams entered the last day of the season with an average of .39955, which would have rounded up to .400, an average nobody had reached since Bill Terry in 1930. When Red Sox manager Joe Cronin offered to let Williams sit out the final day of the season to protect his record, Teddy Ballgame said, "Hell, no," played both games of a double header, got six hits in eight times up, and raised his average to .406. Nobody has hit over .400 since.

Thirty-one years before Williams's decision to play out the string, Detroit's Ty Cobb was in a race with Cleveland's Napoleon Lajoie for the batting championship and a car promised to the winner by the Chalmers Automobile Company. Cobb took the last two days of the season off, confident that his lead could not be overcome so long as his average did not drop below its then-current level of .385. Lajoie nearly caught him (with the aid of a sympathetic St. Louis defense that allowed five bunt singles) but fell one hit short with an average of .384. The Chalmers Company gave cars to both Cobb and Lajoie, but Cobb's decision to opt out of the contest early added to his already low popularity outside of Detroit.

If Austin Reed is thinking about a last-minute sitdown, I'd ask him to consider whether he'd rather be remembered as Ted Williams, who put his title on the line, or Ty Cobb, who put his butt on the bench.

Officer Robert Mayhew slid Davy Keaton's signed statement inside a large blue folder and laid the folder on the passenger seat of his squad car. Then he asked Lloyd Keaton, "What can you tell me about this guy's voice?"

Keaton ducked below the forearm he'd rested on the roof of Mayhew's vehicle and spoke into the open window. "He didn't say much. Just my name. Then he called my column 'cutesy' and threatened me."

"So you've been doing something that's registered on the radar of some nasty folks. Any idea what that might be?"

"Well, you and I rousted Johnny Crain. And I had a little heart-to-heart with Davy's coach."

"And you've been poking around OgrowSport."

"And chasing after Sara Galardi."

Mayhew sucked on the earpiece of his Ray-Bans. "At least one of those activities must have brought you pretty close to something."

"Yeah. Pretty close to the end of my tether. They're all connected to steroids somehow. But I haven't been able to pull all the pieces together."

"Somebody must think you have been able to."

Keaton shook his head. "Worst of all possible worlds. Somebody I don't know wants to keep me from telling something I don't know."

"If you're right about Sammy Tancredi being murdered, what you don't know can certainly hurt you."

"That's your professional opinion, huh? What's your professional advice?"

"Watch out. Be careful."

"Let me take my notebook out so I can write that down."

"My boss isn't going to detail anyone to watch you on the strength of one anonymous call." Mayhew put his Ray-Bans back on, took a business card out of the blue folder, and scribbled something on its back. "Here's my cell number. Call me if you think of anything else or feel like you're being shadowed. In the meantime, try not to make an easy target. Vary your routine. Stay around crowds of people." As an afterthought, he wrote something else on the back of the card before he handed it to Keaton, saying, "Now you don't need your notebook."

Keaton flipped the card over and read the back. Under his cell phone number, Mayhew had written BE CAREFUL in block capitals.

Keaton nodded to the OgrowSport receptionist, located an empty locker for his gym bag, and headed back to the gym itself, where he viewed the array of torture instruments with some trepidation.

In the far corner of the room, sweat gleamed on the forehead of a woman in a bright red running suit who was spread-eagled on what looked like an upright medieval rack. She suddenly gathered her strength and bent forward, raising rope-bound weights through a contraption of pulleys that had seemed to imprison her. Then gravity took over and the weights dropped, returning the woman to her initial spread-eagle position

Near the center of the room, three young hunks in tank tops and shorts hunched over stationary bicycles, pedaling furiously and checking each other's progress as if they were in the Tour de France.

The row of treadmills nearest the front window seemed to be occupied by the same gaggle of middle-aged women who had been using them on the occasion of his first visit. The second row of treadmills, however, was unoccupied. Evidently the determined blonde wearing mauve shorts had finally reached Cleveland.

Keaton stepped onto the treadmill that the blonde had been using and was confronted by an instrument panel that might have come from a 747. What the hell, he thought, I just want to turn the damned thing on. He finally found a *start* button alongside several sliding levers that regulated speed. He pushed the button, felt gears mesh under his feet, and began trudging reluctantly in the direction of the women striding and chatting in the row ahead of him.

Keaton hadn't been on the treadmill for more than a minute when his distaste for solitary exercise came flooding back to him. If he were playing tennis, which he loved, there was an opponent to beat. It had been the same when he'd played in a pick-up softball league. But here, there were just two digital displays, whose functions he didn't understand, blinking on the instrument panel.

He tried to focus his thoughts on upcoming columns, but there was no way to take notes. Next time, he'd bring a tape recorder. He supposed he could stand to lose a little weight, but who would know or care? He'd never owned a bathroom scale, so his exact weight was an ongoing mystery that was solved once yearly at his annual checkup.

He knew his jacket size had ballooned from a forty-two-long to a forty-eight-long in the ten years before he'd turned forty. But when his gambling habit took over he'd dropped back to a forty-four-long. Maybe they should spice up those TV ads for state lotteries with before-and-after photos of the weight losses recorded by addicted gamblers.

He scanned the instrument panel for some indication of how long he'd been on the treadmill, but there was nothing so obvious as a clock to be seen. He checked his watch and found that only five minutes had elapsed. Time wasn't moving any faster or farther than he was walking.

Who was it who said he really enjoyed long walks, especially when they were taken by people who annoyed him? Sounded like Fred Allen. Maybe all this could be worked into a column. Have to check the quote, though.

When his watch told him he'd passed the ten-minute mark, he stepped down from the treadmill. No sense in overdoing it. Besides, he was really here to check out OgrowSport operations, not to maximize his calorie burn.

He went to the men's locker room, draped a towel around his shoulders, and let himself out into the corridor. Turning away from the arrows leading to the steam room, he headed toward the corridor that paralleled the Vitamin O assembly line. He passed the first of the doors marked EMPLOYEES ONLY, which led to the end of the assembly line that Cleary had shown him, and tried the second door, which presumably led to the start of the line.

The second door was locked, so he continued down the corridor and opened the third EMPLOYEES ONLY door. A woman seated behind a computer in the nearest of several cubicles looked up and said, "May I help you, sir?" in a tone that barely veiled her annoyance.

Keaton grabbed both ends of the towel draped around his neck and swung the ends outward. "Looking for the steam room."

The woman nodded in the direction he'd come from. "Other end of the corridor."

"Oh. Guess I must have taken a wrong turn. Sorry to have bothered you."

Keaton returned to the locker room, where he stripped down, wrapped a towel around his midsection, and stuffed his warm-up suit into his gym bag. As an afterthought, he slipped his bare feet into unlaced tennis shoes before heading into the steam room.

A wall of heat met Keaton as he opened the door to the steam room. Wooden walkways laid out over the tile floors led to slatted wood benches set against the three walls opposite the door. There was no one else in the room. Keaton tightened the towel around his waist and followed the central wooden walkway to the bench directly opposite the door.

Keaton's only prior experience with steam rooms had come from movies, where they either served as trysting places for lovers or meeting places for gangsters bent on rubbing one another out. He leaned back against the wall and stretched his legs out in front of him. Not too bad, really. Roughly the same soothing sensation as a hot bath without the need to accordion his six-foot frame into a space designed for shorter mortals.

Puffs of steam came from metal generators on either side of the room and formed a visible mist just above Keaton's eye level. Beads of sweat formed on his forehead and upper lip as he closed his eyes and breathed in the aroma of eucalyptus trees.

He heard the steam-room door squeak and opened his eyes to see a pair of stocky male legs standing on the wooden walkway. Raising his eyes past the towel around the visitor's midsection, he found himself staring into the cold, impassive face of Bull Harding.

Harding gave no sign that he was surprised to see Keaton. Instead, he followed the wooden walkway to the bench against the wall on Keaton's right, sat down, and deposited a folded towel he'd been carrying under his left arm on the bench next to him. The folded towel hit the bench with an audible clunk that caused Keaton to sit bold upright.

When Keaton finally found his voice, he said, "Aren't you a little out of your territory, Bull?"

Harding gave a barely noticeable shrug. "Friend of mine has an interest in this place. And we've got a lot of customers in this area. You should know that."

Keaton tried to keep his eyes off the bulky towel on the bench next to Harding. "Customers. Yeah. Right. I'm one of them."

"In good standing. Little Bill tells me you paid us off."

"Yeah. I had a friend who offered better terms than you and Little Bill."

"You're lucky. Ask my friends for money and all you'd get would be a kick in the balls."

The mention of balls reminded Keaton that Harding had allegedly gotten his nickname by threatening to castrate a recalcitrant loser with a farm implement called a bull snipper. Even in the overheated steam room, he could feel his own testicles shrink.

"Something wrong?" Harding asked.

The towel at Harding's side didn't look big enough to conceal a farm implement. Still, Keaton wasn't sure how big the implement in question might be. "No. Nothing's wrong. Why do you ask?"

"Seems like you're staring at me."

Keaton could feel sweat forming on his sweat. "Was I? Guess it must be your face. I remember you had that look when you bluffed me off a straight in a game of seven card."

"How'd you know I was bluffing?"

"You showed me your cards after I'd folded."

"Oh, yeah. I remember now. Just a little advertising to set you up for a time when I wasn't bluffing."

"Don't think that time ever came."

"We miss you at the poker table."

Keaton shifted on the bench, moving a little closer to the wooden walkway. "Well, you know how it is. Gamblers Anonymous tells us to avoid old haunts."

"You've been betting the sports book though."

Keaton managed a short laugh. "That didn't turn out too well. For me or Dave Bowers."

"How is Bowers?"

"Still comatose."

"Tough break."

Maybe I'm overreacting, Keaton thought. Why would the East Wheeling mob send an enforcer after me? Hell, I'm not even sure Harding's an enforcer. All I've ever heard are rumors. And nobody could have known I was coming here. Still, what'll I do if he goes for whatever's in that towel?

The door to the steam room opened and the three Tour de France bicyclists entered, flicking towels at one another. One of the bicyclists stepped off the main walkway to dodge a flicked towel, winced as if he'd stepped on hot coals, and stepped up onto the walkway spur leading to Bull Harding.

Keaton rose quickly, skirted past the two bicyclists on the central walkway by stepping onto the heated floor with his tennis shoes, and left the steam room without looking back.

He rescued his gym bag from the locker room and headed out through the men's toilet area, pausing just long enough to grab a plumber's helper at the restroom door. It wasn't much of a weapon, but at least he wasn't empty handed.

The men's room door opened into a corridor that offered Keaton three choices: out through the reception area, deeper into the complex toward the production line, or straight ahead into the ladies' restroom.

Still clad only in a towel and tennis shoes, Keaton headed

straight into the ladies' room and locked himself in a toilet stall before anyone saw him. Climbing up onto the toilet seat so his hairy legs couldn't be spotted under the stall door, he balanced precariously and slipped into the jacket of his warm-up suit. He risked sitting on the seat just long enough to pull on his sweatpants, then climbed back up and stood hunched over on the toilet seat while he used his cell phone to call Officer Mayhew.

When Mayhew answered, Keaton whispered into his phone, "It's Lloyd Keaton. Can you come get me? I think I'm being shadowed by a mob hit man."

"Where are you?"

"The ladies' room at OgrowSport."

"The ladies' room?"

"I'm hiding in a stall and nobody knows I'm here. This guy Bull Harding from the East Wheeling mob followed me into the steam room. I got out before he managed to do anything, but the ladies' room is as far as I could get."

"Bull Harding?"

"Yes. You know him?"

"Only by reputation. Why's he after you?"

"I don't know. I'm not even sure he is. He had something heavy wrapped in a towel, and I didn't feel like playing twenty questions to identify it."

"I can be there in five minutes. Try to stay put."

Keaton closed his cell phone and checked the time. He heard female voices approaching and tried to shrink back into the toilet stall.

A hand rattled the latch on his stall. Then, when the door failed to open, he heard the door rattler settle into the stall next to his. Keaton held his breath to make as little noise as possible as the woman in the adjoining stall carried on a rapid-fire conversation about wrinkles and Botox with someone in the adjoining locker room.

The paper roll in the next stall squealed, and just when he thought he'd succeeded in escaping the notice of his neighbor, Keaton's cell phone sounded the opening bars of "The Gambler" theme.

He swore under his breath and answered in a high-pitched whisper. "Yes?"

"Lloyd? Is that you?"

It was Liz. He was aware of a sudden silence in the adjoining stall. Still trying to maintain a high-pitched whisper, he said, "Yes. But I can't talk right now."

"It certainly sounds like you can't talk right. I've got to see you. I think I've found another stash of Davy's steroids."

Keaton whispered, "I'll be there as soon as I can" and flipped his cell phone shut.

The room outside was still quiet. Imagining at least two sets of eyes on his stall, he climbed down from the toilet seat, lifted the lid, and plunged the plumbers' helper furiously in and out of the ceramic bowl.

He flushed the toilet once, unlatched the stall door so it swung open, and went back to work with the plunger. After one more flush, he shouldered the plunger and turned to find two middle-aged women covering themselves with towels and staring at him.

"Now, you ladies should know Tampax just don't flush," Keaton said as he edged past them and left the ladies' room without looking back.

Once in the outer corridor he cracked open the door to the reception area just enough to make sure that Bull Harding wasn't waiting there. When he didn't see Harding, he dropped his plumbers' helper, scooted past the reception desk, and ran into the street just as Officer Mayhew's patrol car pulled up.

Keaton scrambled into the patrol car and said, "Boy, am I glad to see you," as Mayhew accelerated away from the curb.

"Where are we going?" Mayhew asked.

"My car's around the corner. But why don't you circle the block and see whether anybody followed me out of the gym."

Mayhew turned right at the corner. "Okay. Want to tell me what's going on?"

Keaton started by telling Mayhew about Bull Harding's appearance in Menckenburg the day David Bowers was found at the bottom of his elevator shaft and concluded with the steam-room adventure that had just ended.

While Keaton was talking, Mayhew circled the block and double-parked in front of the OgrowSport complex. There was no sign of any activity anywhere on the block. "Doesn't make sense," Mayhew said when Keaton finished. "What are those East Wheeling folks doing with OgrowSport?"

"Harding said a friend of his owned a piece of it. Maybe they're using it to launder gambling money. Seems like way too much of a coincidence, Harding's appearing just after somebody threatened me."

"Hell, maybe East Wheeling owns the whole OgrowSport complex. If they are manufacturing steroids it would give Little Bill's gambling operation an edge just to know which players are juicing."

A call came in on Mayhew's car radio. Keaton heard static, a string of numbers, and the address 215 West Third Street.

Mayhew laughed. "Somebody's reported a Peeping Tom at OgrowSport. I better take the call to keep it from getting out of hand. Why don't I drop you at your car first? Might not do to have a witness see the peeper himself sitting in my car."

"They'd sure be impressed with Menckenburg police efficiency. But I'm just as happy not to be an object lesson. I've got to go see my ex-wife and son."

"Be careful. Call me when you get there. If I don't hear anything from you in the next half hour, I'll come straight to your house."

"You think that's necessary?"

"You said the caller threatened your boy too. If they're serious, you both make pretty easy targets."

Liz met Keaton at the door. "Come on in. I've got something to show you." She led the way to the kitchen table and motioned for him to sit. Then she gripped the sides of her leather purse and said, "I went to that Seana spa today. Just to see what was going on."

"I just came from the gym next door."

Liz paused as if she expected him to say more. When he didn't, she flipped her short black hair with the back of her right hand. "I had my hair done."

"Oh. Yeah. It looks nice."

Liz nodded without smiling. "Thanks for noticing."

"I'm just guessing here, but I'm thinking that's not what you got me here to see."

"No, you're right. You wanted a report on their operation. Well, for a Saturday morning, they were doing surprisingly little business. There was only one other customer in a chair when I arrived, and none when I left. No matter how low the rent may be in that area of town, I don't see how they can make it at the rate they were going today."

Liz reached into her purse and pulled out a small vial with a cylindrical cap. "In addition to the beauty treatments, they manufacture their own brand of shampoo." The label on the vial read SEANA SHAMPOO. "Or at least repackage it. I found out they buy it in bulk and put it up in different-sized containers with their name on it. This is the smallest size."

"Looks like the samples you get in hotels."

"Yes. That's exactly what I thought. I knew I'd seen a container like this somewhere, but I couldn't remember where.

Then it came to me. It was in Davy's bathroom. In the medicine cabinet."

She pulled another small container from her purse and held it up. The label read ELENA SHAMPOO. "I thought this must have been something you brought home from one of your trips."

Keaton shook his head. "Never seen it before."

Liz held up both vials. "See how the caps are exactly the same but the plastic containers are different." She opened the cap of the Elena Shampoo container and squeezed a creamy glob onto her fingertips. "The contents are different too."

She went to the sink and held her hand under hot tap water, massaging her fingertips with her thumb. "This stuff, the stuff from Davy's room, isn't shampoo."

When lather failed to form on Liz's fingertips, Keaton swore. "Shit. It's some sort of cream. He could still be on steroids."

"I asked Davy. He says it's acne medicine. But he couldn't explain why it came in a shampoo bottle."

"Steroid creams are acne medicine, all right. They'll create acne where he didn't have any."

"That's what I was afraid of."

"Where is Davy?"

"Upstairs in his room. He expects to be grounded pretty good."

Keaton took the container of sham shampoo from Liz. "I can have this analyzed, but I'm sure it must be steroid cream." He turned the container in his hand, examining it. Then he laid it on the kitchen table, saying, "I'll be right back."

"Where are you going?"

"To get something from my glove compartment."

Keaton disappeared through the front door and returned with the vial of Vitamin O that Alex's lab had analyzed. He set the vial on the table between the two containers bearing shampoo labels.

"The containers are all different," Liz said.

"But except for their color, the caps are all the same." Keaton picked up the vial of Vitamin O and pointed to a small horizontal indentation just below the flip-top on the cylindrical cap. "And look at this. Each cap has this same little nick on it."

"In exactly the same place," Liz said.

"I'm betting there's a small burr on the capping machine I saw operating when this container was filled."

"So all three of these came from the same place."

"Exactly. The place I just came from. OgrowSport." Keaton took out his cell phone and called Officer Mayhew.

"Keaton," the voice on the other end of the line said. "You make it home okay?"

"Yeah. Can you stop by? I've got something here that may get us into OgrowSport with a search warrant."

"That's where I am right now. Seems they had a Peeping-Tom scare earlier this evening. Some pervert hid in the ladies' bathroom."

"Did you get a good description?"

"Descriptions vary. Nobody could put a name to him. Sounds like a real desperado though. Seems he threatened two nearly naked ladies with a plumbers' helper. He left the weapon behind, so we may have some prints."

"God. I hope not."

"Probably take us a while to process any prints. Then, of course, we need to find a match. I'm thinking that's likely to be a real long shot."

"You're a good man, Mayhew."

"I interviewed a lot of people here to see if they saw the peeper. Your friend Harding was one of them. He didn't mention your name. Could be he didn't make the connection. Said he hadn't seen anything unusual. Turns out he's been a member of the gym ever since it opened."

"How much longer will you be there?"

"I'm about to finish up. What've you got for me?"

"I think I can assemble enough evidence that OgrowSport's still producing steroids to support a search warrant." Keaton described the three miniature containers on the kitchen table, one filled with Vitamin O, one with shampoo, and one, he was almost certain, with a steroid cream. "And the caps are identical, with similar nicks that suggest they all came from the same assembly line."

"Like a fingerprint ID," Mayhew said.

"Exactly," Keaton said. As he held up the vial of Vitamin O, he suddenly recalled something that had been nagging at his consciousness ever since he'd seen the vial come off the OgrowSport assembly line.

"Listen, Mayhew," he said. "Before you come, call up your friend Waldron in Cleveland and have him look in Sammy Tancredi's Dopp kit. The one that Sara Tancredi tried to take. I'm betting the little shampoo containers in that kit are filled with something besides shampoo."

Chapter Twenty: Uncorked

KEATON'S KORNER

Former major leaguer Jose Canseco offers a sad illustration of the dangers of steroid abuse. Canseco admitted to using anabolic steroids in his 2005 tell-all book, *Juiced,* which specifically identified a number of former teammates, including Mark McGwire and Jason Giambi, as steroid users. A recent cable TV documentary shows the one-time all-star on the brink of bankruptcy, ostracized by his former baseball friends, and suffering bouts of depression linked to low testosterone levels. After 25 years of steroid abuse, his body can't manufacture enough testosterone on its own, and he has gone to great lengths to reverse these effects, including trying to import fertility drugs illegally from Mexico.

In spite of the fact that Canseco has told interviewers that his biggest regret in life is writing *Juiced,* he has followed it with a second book, *Vindicated,* that, according to publicity releases, reveals "details even more shocking than his controversial first book." Actually the pickings in the second book are pretty slim, identifying several players who had done little more than discuss steroid use with Canseco. To be fair to Jose, most of the insider details in his first book, which were initially received with a lot of skepticism, subsequently proved to be accurate. The trouble with tell-all books, though, is once you have told all, there's nothing much left for a sequel.

Officer Mayhew examined each of the three containers on Keaton's kitchen "Three of a kind," he said.

"At least as far as the caps are concerned," Keaton said. "Is that enough to support a search warrant for OgrowSport?"

"If that middle container is really a steroid cream, a warrant shouldn't be a problem."

"Let's get it analyzed then. Did you hear back from Waldron?"

The cell phone in Mayhew's belt holster buzzed and he checked the screen. "That's him now."

As soon as Mayhew put the phone to his ear, Keaton heard two quick "Yeahs," followed by a slower, drawn-out "Yeah." Then the officer smiled, held up four fingers, and said, "Looks like Tancredi's Dopp kit gives us four of a kind."

"Tough hand to beat," Keaton said. "Tell him I'll be there first thing tomorrow to pick up a sample."

Mayhew relayed Keaton's message, listened, then covered the mouthpiece and said, "Waldron wants to keep the container. Says it looks like evidence in a murder case, which trumps your steroid search."

"That's okay. I'd just like a sample of the contents. What do you need for your search warrant?"

"A sample and a photo of the container should do the job. Waldron says he can courier them down."

Keaton took the phone. "Detective Waldron, this is Lloyd Keaton. I'd like to come pick up the evidence myself. I have a feeling there must be something we missed in Tancredi's belongings."

"Didn't we just find it?" the detective said.

"Maybe. Maybe not. I'd still like to look through the rest of his stuff one more time."

"Come ahead then. I'll be here at eight tomorrow morning."

After Keaton hung up, Mayhew said, "You think there's more

to find in Tancredi's stuff than just steroids?"

"I think there has to be. Sara Galardi was looking for something, but I don't think it was just the steroids. Everybody knew Sammy was a juicer, so nobody would be surprised at finding steroids in his effects."

"But the steroids in his Dopp kit could be traced to Ogrow-Sport."

"At the time, nobody knew the container caps were marked. They still don't. Sara had links to OgrowSport, so it's a good bet she knew where to find Sammy's steroids, and she took his Dopp kit."

"She couldn't have had time to dispose of anything big. Weren't you and Waldron on her as soon as she left the storage locker?"

"When we picked her up, she didn't have anything incriminating on her person." Keaton shook his head. "I don't think she found what she was looking for."

"But what do you think that was?"

"OgrowSport had to be concerned that Sammy would crack under the pressure of the congressional committee and reveal the real source of his steroids. Maybe he threatened to do just that. Maybe he had squirreled away evidence identifying Ogrow-Sport as his supplier."

Mayhew pointed to the three containers on the kitchen table. "But we've got that evidence in hand."

"Sammy wouldn't have known the containers could be traced back to OgrowSport."

"And we're still not sure that the shampoo from his Dopp kit or your son's bathroom will check out as a steroid."

"Assuming they test out, what else do you need for your search warrant?"

"I just need to be specific about the precise addresses and what I expect to find."

Keaton nodded. "Okay. You're looking for steroids, so grab samples of every cream or ointment they've got under their roof. Make sure some of the samples have the marked shampoo caps. See if you can't confiscate the capping machine itself, before they get wise and shave off the burr that's marking their product."

"That could be construed as interfering with their livelihood. Which shouldn't be a problem if their livelihood involves illegal drugs. I'll list the machine in the warrant. At the very least, I'll take enough photos of the capper so we can nail them in court."

"And you probably ought to list every address on the block in your warrant. They're all connected by an internal corridor."

"All right. Do we still want to get a warrant for Johnny Crain's house?"

"Oh, yeah. He's supplying high school kids. And I'm guessing his coach knows it. But let's hold off on him until you've had a chance to hit OgrowSport. If you hit Crain first, it might scare OgrowSport into cleaning up their act and dumping any steroid inventory they've got in-house."

Mayhew started toward the door. "Good point. I'll pull both warrant requests together as soon as we know for sure what's in those shampoo bottles."

As soon as Mayhew left the house, Liz reappeared in the kitchen. "Stay for dinner?" she asked. "I'm about to nuke some day-old lasagna."

"Sounds delightful," Keaton said. "Almost as delightful a prospect as confronting Davy about his acne medicine."

"Both jobs will go down a little easier with some red wine." Liz opened a bottle of merlot while Keaton set three place settings around the three plastic containers at the center of the kitchen table.

Keaton was halfway through his glass of wine and the timer on the microwave was buzzing when Davy appeared in the kitchen door. The boy stared at the three plastic containers and asked, "What were the cops doing here?"

Keaton held up the shampoo container that had come from Davy's bathroom. "They heard somebody in the house was using illegal drugs."

"Well, it wasn't me. Like I told mom, that's acne medicine."

"Come on, Davy. If it's acne medicine, why does the label say shampoo?"

"I don't know. That's just the way it came."

"Where'd you get it?"

"Johnny Crain. He said it would cover up the acne that came from the steroid pills."

"Oh, for Christ's sake, Davy. It's a steroid cream."

Liz put a trivet on the table and set a casserole dish containing warmed-over lasagna on it. "You don't know that for sure, Lloyd."

Keaton slipped the container into his shirt pocket. "Not for sure, but I can find out fairly quickly. It'll be tested tomorrow."

"Well, until it is tested and you know for sure whether it's a steroid cream, maybe you shouldn't be so quick to accuse our son."

"Whose side are you on here?" Keaton said. "We know Davy's been taking steroids."

Liz poured herself a fresh glass of wine. "But you confiscated the pills—the Arnolds—and Davy says the cream in that container isn't a steroid."

"Well, it sure as hell isn't shampoo."

"Johnny Crain told me it was acne medicine," Davy said.

Liz put her hand on Keaton's arm. "Lloyd. Maybe Davy didn't know. Can't you give him the benefit of the doubt? Shouldn't he be innocent until proven guilty?"

Keaton drew his arm out of Liz's reach. "I see where this is going. Roger Clemens claimed he thought his trainer was injecting him with Vitamin B-twelve. Barry Bonds insisted his trainer was giving him flaxseed oil and a pain killer for his arthritis. And you say you thought you were getting acne medicine."

Keaton paused, then continued. "All right. You're aping big leaguers by using steroids. And you're even aping their excuses. Why don't we just invoke the big leaguers' penalty system as well?"

"What's that supposed to mean?" Davy said.

"If they catch a big leaguer using steroids, they suspend him for about a third of the season." Keaton retrieved the shampoo vial from his pocket and held it up. "This will be tested tomorrow. If it's acne medicine, I'll apologize. But if it's steroids, we'll see to it that you're suspended for the rest of the summer season."

Davy's voice rose nearly an octave. "You can't do that."

"Why not?" Keaton said. "You're actually getting a good deal. There's only a couple of weeks left in the season."

"Coach is depending on me. If I don't play, he'll find somebody else. And he probably won't let me play short when the high school season starts."

"We'll tell the coach you're sick," Liz said. "Or that we're going on a family vacation. You won't have to tell him the real reason you're not playing."

Keaton set his wineglass down on the table. "Maybe we should tell Coach Lammers. Maybe it would make him pay more attention to what his players are doing off the field."

Davy shook his head back and forth. "No. Don't do that."

"He already knows, doesn't he?" Keaton said. "Davy, if you're sure of that, you'd be better off with a different coach."

"Your dad's right, honey," Liz said. "Don't you see that?"

"No, I don't see that. First you get me to snitch on Johnny Crain. Now you want me to snitch on Coach Lammers?"

"We can save that discussion for another day. Let's make sure you understand what we're saying today." Keaton tapped the lid of the shampoo vial. "If these are steroids, you're through playing ball this summer."

"What if I play anyhow?"

"Look at me, Davy," Keaton said. "If you play anyhow, we'll see to it that you don't play high school ball this coming year."

"How can you stop me?"

Keaton wiped his mouth with his napkin and refolded it. "Davy, you're fifteen years old. Your mom and I have to sign a consent form agreeing to let you play high school sports."

"And you're saying you might not sign?"

Keaton set his napkin beside his plate. "I'm only repeating what we've told you several times. You've got to stop using steroids. If you don't, we'll see to it that you stop playing ball."

"It's not fair," Davy said. "That is acne medicine."

Keaton put a dab of the contents of the vial on his forefinger and pointed it at his son. "Davy, I'm sure you want to believe this is acne medicine. Hell, Roger Clemens wanted to believe those shots in his butt were vitamin injections. Maybe this gob on my finger really is acne medicine. But we have a foolproof way of finding out. And if it is steroids, you've got to be prepared to face the consequences."

"It's just not fair." Davy bolted from the table and stomped upstairs to his room.

Liz picked up Davy's napkin, which had fallen onto the floor. "Well, that was a sterling performance. If I'd known you were going to bully him, I never would have asked you to stay for dinner."

"Liz, I told him. When we first knew he was juicing. If he didn't quit steroids, he'd have to quit baseball. There are serious side effects. The stuff's illegal, and we've got to get him off it."

"You could have faith in him. Take him at his word. Give him a second chance. God knows I gave you plenty."

"That's different."

"Oh, it's different all right. So far the only downside I've seen from Davy is a little acne. Your gambling wrecked our marriage. And probably did our son more harm than a few specks on his face and back."

"It's more than a little acne. There's depression. Mood swings. Read my columns. The effects are starting to show up in big leaguers. Davy's a lot more vulnerable than they are. Cut me some slack here."

"I cut you so much slack when we were married, there's none left."

Keaton wanted to say, "That's not fair." But that was the argument Davy had made before he stomped out. Keaton knew it was a losing argument. He'd lost it a long time ago.

Detective Waldron lifted the lid of Sammy Tancredi's steamer trunk to reveal four baseball bats lying on two Cleveland Indians' uniform tops, one gray and one white. The edge of a Dopp kit peeked out from a tangle of clothing stuffed into one corner of the nearly full trunk.

"We've been through all this pretty carefully," Waldron said. "Once before the Galardi woman disappeared and once after. Don't see how you expect to find anything we missed."

Keaton held up the plastic bag Waldron had just given him containing a sample from the "shampoo" vial found in Sammy's Dopp kit. "Missed this the first two times through."

"Well, we didn't exactly know what we were looking for back then."

"I'm hoping we can turn up more surprises." Keaton picked up one of Tancredi's bats, turned it in his hands until the trademark was up, then pretended he was standing at home plate and executed a half swing, stopping at the point where the bat would meet the oncoming ball.

The reporter smiled as Waldron went through the same ritual with another of Tancredi's bats. "Funny," he said. "Hand a grown man a baseball bat, and nine times out of ten he'll take a stance as if he's facing an imaginary pitcher. You suppose it's some sort of genetic imprint?"

"Probably goes all the way back to our caveman ancestors fending off attackers with clubs."

Keaton picked up a second bat and pretended to use it as a microphone. "Now facing the dinosaurs for the Cro-Magnon Tar Pitters, the clean-up hitter . . ." He stopped and stared at the barrel of the bat he'd been speaking into, then hefted it by the handle with his left hand. He picked up the bat he'd originally swung in his right hand and held the two bats in front of him, comparing them.

"Something wrong?" Waldron asked.

Keaton nodded toward the bat in his left hand. "This one's lighter." He handed the two bats to Waldron. "See what you think."

Waldron hefted one bat in his right hand and the other in his left. "You're right. One seems lighter."

"Same make. Same model number. But one's lighter. What's that suggest to you, detective?"

"Well, Sammy was willing to cheat with steroids. Corking a bat probably wouldn't have given him too many ethical problems."

Keaton picked at the indented top of the lighter bat with his fingernail, looking for signs of tampering. "Easy way to find out. Got a saw somewhere in your office?"

"Wait here," Waldron said.

After Waldron left the evidence room, Keaton took his car key and scraped at the wood in the indented bat head. It didn't take long to uncover the outline of a wooden plug about an inch and a half in diameter.

Waldron returned carrying a small scale and a hacksaw. He was followed by a short, redheaded female officer whose nametag read SCOBBA. He introduced the officer, saying, "So long as we're tampering with evidence, I thought we ought to have a witness."

Keaton showed both Waldron and Scobba the outline of the circular plug he'd uncovered in the barrel head of the suspect bat. "Somebody has already tampered with this evidence."

"Why would anyone do that?" Scobba asked.

"Lighter bat means a quicker swing," Keaton said.

Waldron closed the lid of the steamer trunk and set the scale on top of it. "Let's do this right." He weighed the bat Keaton had originally picked out, jotted down the results in his pocket notebook, and then weighed the bat Keaton had been picking at with his car key.

"The suspect bat is an ounce and a half lighter," Waldron said, making another notation in his notebook. He took the hacksaw and made an incision about an inch from the heavy end of the plugged bat. "Let's see what we've got inside."

While Waldron was sawing, Scobba asked, "What do you expect to find?"

"About six inches of cork," Keaton said. "Or maybe sawdust. The last couple of major leaguers caught doctoring their bats used cork."

Scobba ran her hand through her short red hair. "If the object is to make the bat lighter, why use anything?"

"If you don't fill the cavity with something, you'll get a hollow sound when the bat meets the ball," Keaton said. "A dead giveaway."

Waldron paused with his saw about halfway through the barrel of the bat. "Almost as bad as having the bat splinter and expose the cork when you make contact."

"Has that ever happened?" Scobba asked.

Waldron resumed sawing. "Happened to Sammy Sosa a couple of years after he was ringing up big homer numbers with Mark McGwire."

"What became of him?"

"Umpires called him out and ejected him from the game. Then the league suspended him for seven games." Keaton raised his voice so he could be heard over the grating noise of the saw. "Funny thing is, physicists say corking a bat doesn't get you any more distance on your hits. You may pick up a little bat speed, but the cork absorbs energy like a sponge, so the ball doesn't go as far."

"Wonder if Sammy Tancredi knew that," Waldron said.

"Probably not," Keaton said. "But the corking might have given him a mental edge, thinking he was getting away with something."

"Like Yogi Berra said, 'Ninety percent of baseball is half mental.' " Waldron's hacksaw bit through the bat head and the tip of the bat dropped to the floor, followed by six brightly colored rubber balls. The balls bounced around the evidence room with Scobba and Keaton in pursuit.

"Superballs," Waldron said. "That's a new one on me."

Keaton headed off a bright yellow ball before it disappeared behind ceiling-high shelves of file boxes. "Been tried before, he said. Graig Nettles got caught loading his bat with superballs over thirty years ago."

"Before Tancredi was born. Surprised our boy had that much knowledge of history." Waldron poked his finger into the hole in the barrel of the bat. "There's something else in here."

Keaton watched a bouncing red ball vanish under a rolltop desk. "What is it?"

Waldron extracted a lined sheet of paper from the cylindrical hole and unrolled it. "Looks like a note from Sammy Tancredi.' "

Keaton left the ball under the desk and joined Waldron. "What's it say?"

Waldron read the note.

I got some steroids from Dale Loren, but I got more from OgrowSport in Menckenburg. OgrowSport is really a front for East Wheeling gamblers who threatened to kill me if I said they sold me steroids. Whoever finds this note should take it to the police.

Keaton whistled silently. "That should be more than enough to get the investigation of Sammy's death reopened."

"No doubt about it." Waldron held the letter up to the light. The writing was scrawled without much regard for the ruled lines. "But why hide this so well that nobody was likely to find it?"

Keaton pointed to the number four beside Tancredi's signature. "Could be he made four copies. The others may have been so easy to find that Sara Galardi got them and destroyed them."

"We'd better get back to tracking her down," Waldron said.

Keaton put the yellow ball he'd retrieved back into the hole in the sawed-off bat. "In the meantime, can you get me a copy of that note?"

"I don't know about that." Waldron slid the note into a plastic envelope. "This is serious evidence in what looks like a murder case. You're not exactly law enforcement, and 'finders keepers' isn't a principle the Ohio courts are likely to recognize."

"That's okay," Keaton said. "I'd like you to do two things, though. First, get a copy of the note to your friend Bob Mayhew in Menckenburg. It should help him get a warrant to search OgrowSport's office."

"I can do that."

"Next, keep this as quiet as you can until Mayhew and the

Menckenburg police have had a chance to search OgrowSport. If and when you do decide to go public with it, though, I'd like you to give my paper a head start."

"I can do that too." Waldron looked at Officer Scobba, who was on her hands and knees trying to retrieve the red ball that had bounced under the rolltop desk. "Just help me get the rest of these damned balls back into this bat."

"How they hangin', Keaton?" Alex Keith asked when Keaton brought shampoo samples from Tancredi's Dopp kit and Davy's medicine cabinet in for analysis.

"Varies with temperature and handling," Keaton said. "What's new with you?"

"You see where OgrowSport announced the results of their Vitamin O test? They claim the performance of those players taking it was significantly better than the performance of those taking the placebo. I claim they're full of shit."

"Is 'full of shit' a valid statistical measure nowadays? Or can you translate that comment into something I can print in the *Herald*?"

"Their published results claim that Austin Reed was taking Vitamin O."

"Are you surprised?" Keaton said. "With the year he had, if he'd been popping placebos, OgrowSport would have had to junk Vitamin O and figure out how to market whatever they were giving Reed."

"I think they rigged the sample."

"How could they do that?"

"At the start of the season, when they hired us to consult on their testing process, they sent us a sealed envelope with a list of the players who were getting Vitamin O and those who were getting placebos. Then, when Dixon State was awarded their analysis contract, OgrowSport fired us and ordered us to return all their materials, including the unopened envelope."

"Let me guess. You opened it."

"Steamed it open and resealed it." Alex pulled a sheet of paper from his top desk drawer. "Here's a copy. It's a list of the twenty-eight players they signed up for their test."

Keaton examined the list. It was typed on OgrowSport letterhead and divided into two columns. The players in the left-hand column were to be given Vitamin O, while those in the right-hand column were to get a placebo. And Austin Reed's name was in the right-hand column.

Keaton handed the list back to Alex. "But this doesn't square with what you say Dixon State reported."

"No. Dixon State has Reed in the Vitamin O column."

"So you think OgrowSport switched what they were giving Reed in mid-season when he started burning up the league?"

"Hell, all they had to switch was the column his name was in. Vitamin O is nothing but salt water. How much different can it be from the placebo?"

"So when Bloodworth earmarked funds for Dixon State, it gave OgrowSport a chance to regroup."

"Exactly. They switched Reed's name with a player whose season wasn't going very well." Alex pointed at the left-hand column of his list. "Tommy Goheen of the Bulls."

"But they couldn't have known about Bloodworth's plans for Dixon State at the start of the season. If they had, they never would have hired you in the first place."

"No. But I think they planned to rig the results from the get-go. They weren't taking any chances. A friend of mine at Menckenburg State says they hired them at the same time they hired us. Sent them a sealed list too."

"But you think they gave Menckenburg State a different list."

"I think they probably signed up three or four evaluators at the start of the season and sent them all different sealed lists, intending to publish the results from the list that looked best after the season ended. All they wanted was a responsible testing lab to give them a positive result they could quote in their marketing materials."

Keaton let loose a short, sharp laugh. "Like hiring actors in white coats to show up on TV and tout the virtues of the latest wonder drug."

"You got it. The coats smile at the camera and intone solemnly, "Laboratory tests have conclusively proven that four out of five . . ."

"Is eighty percent." Keaton shook his head. "But you can't prove they were planning to cook the results going in."

"No. My buddy at Menckenburg State sent their list back unopened when OgrowSport asked for it. But I can show that the list OgrowSport gave us is different from the list Dixon State was using." Alex shrugged his shoulders. "If anybody cares, now that they've already made a big splash advertising the wonders of Vitamin O."

"Oh, I think I can find somebody who cares." Keaton nodded toward the samples he'd brought in. "How long will it take to get those analyzed?"

"Day or so. Why?"

"Quicker the better. And I'd like you to keep quiet about this until I've had a chance to get the local law involved and lay out a few options for one of the people who's likely to care the most about your findings."

"And who might that be?"

"The congressman that earmarked public funds for Dixon State."

Chapter Twenty-One: Graymail

KEATON'S KORNER

Today's column comes from an unusual source, the London-based journal *The Economist*. For several years, *The Economist* has been following stories of doping in sports, taking a scholarly approach that traces the practice all the way back to the ancient Greeks, who used potions to fortify themselves before athletic contests.

The Economist recently reported the results of a placebo experiment published in the *Journal of Neuroscience*. Experimenters at the University of Turin found that a team of competitors who had received regular injections of morphine (legal as a painkiller but illegal in competitive sports) followed by a placebo described as an illegal injection of morphine just before they entered competition significantly outperformed competitive control groups in endurance tests. This led the investigators to speculate that an unscrupulous but legalistic coach might prepare his team for a crucial contest by providing them with placebos advertised as illegal performance-enhancing drugs.

There's a local angle to all this foreign research. Sworn testimony suggests that Sammy Tancredi's early season spurt with the Mammoths was the result of a placebo effect. He thought he was cheating when he was actually applying a mixture of cold cream and lemon juice to his workout-strengthened biceps. And Austin Reed attributes his record-breaking late-season surge to the use of Vitamin O, a homeopathic medicine produced right here in Menckenburg.

Keaton called Officer Mayhew from Alex Keith's office as soon as Alex showed him the test results. The minute Mayhew answered, he said, "The lab reports are in. Those shampoo containers are filled with anabolic steroids."

"I know," Mayhew said.

"How do you know?"

"Detective Waldron had Tancredi's sample tested in Cleveland. We didn't want to screw up the evidence chain in a murder investigation by relying on outside tests."

Keaton smiled. "Well then, you must have enough evidence to support an OgrowSport search warrant."

"I do. And I've got the warrant. And one for Johnny Crain's house as well."

"When will you serve the OgrowSport warrant?"

"As soon as I can. I'd say around noon tomorrow."

"How firm is that time?"

"Give or take a half hour. I need to muster the troops and prepare them. Why? Do you want to be there?"

"No. I want to be somewhere else when the search goes down. Somewhere that will take me a while to get to. But I want to know what you find as soon as you find it, so my paper can cover it. You've got my cell number."

"I guess you're entitled to a courtesy call. You're the one that smoked these guys out."

Mayhew's call reached Keaton the next day as the reporter emerged from the Capitol South Metro Station in Washington, D.C. The Metro Station was located behind the Library of Congress and three House office buildings, and by the time Keaton had reached his destination, the Cannon Office Building, Mayhew had informed him that the OgrowSport search had yielded everything they'd hoped for, including a stash of steroids and the telltale capping machine.

The Cannon Office Building is the oldest of the office buildings occupied by members of the House of Representatives. Across Independence Avenue from the U.S. Capitol, it is faced with a marble and features evenly spaced rows of Doric columns. All pretty impressive, Keaton thought, until one reflected that the building had cost eighty-six million dollars more than its initial two-million-dollar appropriation, and that the people who worked there had given the nation the House Un-American Activities Committee.

Congressman James Bloodworth sat behind an uncluttered oak desk that looked long enough to support a full-court basketball game. After Keaton had been escorted to a chair at mid-court by an attractive blonde receptionist, he said, "I want to thank you for seeing me on such short notice."

The congressman tilted his eyeglasses down to the end of his hawk-like nose and peered over them. "Always glad to accommodate a member of the press. Even one from a town outside my jurisdiction. Would it be too optimistic to hope that you've come to apologize for all those unflattering remarks about me that you've put in your column?"

Keaton smiled. "Way too optimistic, I'm afraid."

"Well, we live in hope. What brings you to Washington?"

"I've come to give you a heads-up."

"I wasn't aware that anything dangerous was headed my way. Why do you think I need a heads-up?"

"A little after noon today, the Menckenburg police served a warrant on the owners of a local firm called OgrowSport, found a large stash of illegal steroids on the premises, and arrested their marketing manager."

Bloodworth gave no indication that the news affected him in any way. He removed his glasses and made a show of cleaning them with his handkerchief. "As you well know, I've always taken a strong position against steroid abuse. So I congratulate the Menckenburg police force. But I fail to see how their actions affect me or warrant a trip to Washington on your part."

"Well, I'll tell you. Even though OgrowSport is, as you say, outside your jurisdiction, they've been heavy contributors to your campaigns. Public records show they've given you over a hundred thousand dollars in the past."

"Even assuming that's true, you can hardly hold me responsible for the actions of all my campaign contributors. And since you of all people should be aware of my public opposition to steroids, you can't possibly be suggesting that their contributions swayed me in any way?"

"No. I'm not suggesting you flip-flopped on steroids. But OgrowSport's steroid business has been under the counter until now. Their primary product is a dietary supplement called Vitamin O."

Bloodworth nodded. "Oh, yes. I've heard of Vitamin O."

"That's something of an understatement. You've mentioned the supplement in several of your press releases."

The congressman gave a slight shrug. "As one of a number of legal alternatives to steroid use."

"In fact, you not only gave Vitamin O a glowing recommendation, you earmarked federal funds for Dixon State University so that they could test its effectiveness."

"That's true. In view of the manufacturer's claims, I thought it important to have an independent third party validate the product's effectiveness."

"Well, then, you'll be pleased to learn that Dixon State has reported that Vitamin O significantly improved the performance of a group of Triple-A players participating in a matched pair test."

"I had heard that." Bloodworth tilted his chair backward and crossed his arms. "You'll excuse me, but I don't see where you're headed with this recitation of recent history."

"I'm sorry if I'm boring you. But here's a piece of recent history you're probably not aware of. Those test results were rigged. Vitamin O is nothing but salt water."

The congressman's chair snapped back into an upright position. "Let me get this straight. You're telling me Dixon State fabricated those findings?"

"It's not clear whether Dixon State was culpable or just duped. It is clear that OgrowSport fudged their claims about who took what after the fact. They waited until the season ended and batting and pitching records were in, and then linked the best results to Vitamin O."

"I assume you can prove this?"

"I can."

"Excuse me a moment." Bloodworth swiveled his chair and punched a single digit into a phone on the cluttered desk behind him. "Harry, there's a Menckenburg firm called OgrowSport on our donor list. I'd like you to contact them as soon as possible and confirm whether they've recently been subjected to a police search. Find out whatever you can and get right back to me."

Bloodworth hung up the phone, stared out his window at the Capitol building, and then swiveled his chair to face Keaton. "Even if what you say is true, I don't see how it affects me."

"Well, you have to admit it certainly looks suspicious." Keaton moved one hand in front of his face as if he were tracking a running headline. *"Noted congressman repays large donor by directing tax monies to fraudulent tests."*

"All you've got is circumstantial evidence. Hardly admissible in a court of law."

"It's the court of public opinion I'm interested in."

"And how do you propose to affect the court of public opinion?"

"The story will break tomorrow. The newspapers will play up the raid, the steroids, and the composition of Vitamin O. They won't necessarily have the information on campaign donors, earmarked tax money, and rigged tests. Not unless I give it to them."

"And I suppose you'd expect some reward for concealing my connection to OgrowSport and the Dixon State tests."

"I would indeed."

The phone rang and Bloodworth turned his back on Keaton to answer it. The congressman said, "Speak," then repeated "I see" three times and finally said, "No. We mustn't get involved." He hung up and turned back to Keaton, saying, "Well, at least your story about a police raid checks out."

"Are you surprised?"

"I learned early in my career not to trust reporters. But you're asking me to trust you to keep quiet about potentially damaging information. Let me ask you this. How do I know some other reporter won't piece together the same chain of circumstantial evidence and publish it?"

"You don't. But it's not very likely. I just happened to be interested in both you and OgrowSport. And no one else is likely to know about the rigged tests. Obviously, though, all I can guarantee is my own silence."

Bloodworth sighed audibly. "And what do you want in return for that silence?"

"I want you to drop all your charges against Dale Loren."

"Well now, I certainly didn't see that coming. You must know, though, that Mr. Loren has been indicted by a federal grand jury. If he's innocent, he'll get his day in court to set the record straight."

"At considerable psychic and monetary expense. And there's always the risk that a jury will find him guilty just because they feel the need to send a message about steroid use. The government's case is based entirely on circumstantial evidence. And you've just made it clear that you are leery of such evidence."

Bloodworth managed a tight smile that wasn't reflected in his eyes. "What reason can I give for dropping the charges against Mr. Loren?"

"Tell the public that new evidence has come to light."

"And has it?"

"Definitely. Police in both Cleveland and Menckenburg are investigating Sammy Tancredi's death. They've found out he was getting steroids from OgrowSport. Not from Dale Loren. That takes away the testimony of your key witness."

"And if I drop the charges against Loren, how do I know you'll keep your end of the bargain?"

Keaton smiled. "You'll just have to trust this reporter."

"There's that word 'trust' again. Isn't it customary in cases like this for the blackmailer to surrender all the incriminating evidence to the blackmailee?"

"Don't think of this as blackmail, Congressman. It's more like graymail. Think of it as a prod from the voters to see that justice is done."

"Well, then. How do I know that I won't have to endure more such prods?"

"You don't. In fact, I can assure you that more prods will be forthcoming."

A sound halfway between a laugh and a bark came from Bloodworth's throat. "If I understand you, sir, what you are proposing would leave you with a lifelong hold on me. I can assure you that is quite unacceptable."

"I don't intend to abuse the privilege, Congressman. Just think of me as any other constituent asking you for a favor. You can decide whether the favor is worth the contribution I will make to your well-being."

"That contribution being your continued silence."

Keaton grinned and nodded. "Exactly."

"And how often are you likely to ask for these favors?"

"I can't tell you that. I can tell you, though, when I'm going to ask for the next one."

"And when might that be?"

Keaton made a show of looking at his watch. "Right about now."

"Why am I not surprised? What other favor do you have in mind?"

"I want you to change the focus of your committee's investigation for a while. I want you to take a look at the use of steroids in high school sports."

Bloodworth removed his glasses and stared at the ceiling. "This is absurd."

"I'll grant you the media isn't likely to be as interested in high school sports as in the rumor that some major leaguer is juicing. But since they finally started paying attention to the problem, the majors' testing program is putting your committee out of business. You haven't had a big-league player to pillory since Sammy Tancredi died. But there are real problems with steroids at the high school level."

Bloodworth went back to polishing his glasses. "And how do you see my committee making a dent in those problems?"

"Shine your light on one or two programs. The Menckenburg police have evidence that the student manager of the Central High School baseball team has been supplying steroids to certain players. It's a good bet that their coach is aware of this.

I'd suggest you subpoena the coach. His name is Lammers. Treat him the same way you treat the ballplayers you interview. Ask him so many questions he'll either convict himself or perjure himself."

Bloodworth stopped polishing his spectacles and examined the lenses. "That's a rather cynical view of my committee's methods."

"All right then, look at it this way. Coach Lammers has either been sanctioning his players' steroid use or turning a blind eye toward it. By shining a light on his actions, you will be illuminating the problem, putting a stop to steroid abuse in one high school, and broadcasting a warning to other high schools."

"A high school program is pretty small potatoes. How do I justify turning a full congressional committee on to one?"

"Oh, for Christ's sake. We're talking about the youth of America here. You weren't above calling the parents of dead high school athletes to testify before your committee. Why not try to intervene and spare a few parents the grief of losing their children to steroids."

"You misunderstand me. I'm merely concerned that the local focus might not produce news of national interest."

"I'll see to it that your probe is big news in Menckenburg, and a number of out-of-state newspapers pick up my syndicated column. You've had no trouble making national headlines in the past. And the news that you're looking into one high school program might be enough to scare several others off of steroids."

Bloodworth pointed the earpieces of his spectacles at Keaton. "Can I ask how you happen to know about this coach and his manager?"

"My son plays shortstop for their team."

"Is your son one of the steroid users?"

"He was. He isn't anymore."

"So you are, in effect, asking my committee to participate in a personal vendetta."

"I'm asking you to point your committee's cannon where it will do the most good. If you can find a suspect high school program somewhere outside of Menckenburg, feel free to aim at it."

"That won't be necessary. It seems you and the local police have put in a lot of spadework loosening the ground in Menckenburg. I'll see what we can harvest at our end. In the meantime, I trust you'll keep me up to date with the local investigation."

"I'll be happy to do that."

Bloodworth returned his glasses to the bridge of his nose. "I take it we're through then."

"For now."

"Implying that you are likely to have more requests in the future. By then, it's my fervent hope that OgrowSport will be old news." Bloodworth swiveled his chair and stared out at the Capitol building.

"I expected to find Bru on guard duty," Keaton said to Judy as she led him into her husband's bedroom.

"Bru can't be here twenty-four/seven. We do have round-the-clock nursing care, an internal alarm system, and a baby monitor with speakers in both Bru's room and mine."

Keaton looked at his friend lying peacefully on his back, tethered by fingertip clamps and suction cups to two monitoring screens. "I don't think you're likely to hear David greeting intruders on the baby monitor."

"No, but the caretakers have been alerted to the possibility of intruders."

"From the trouble we had getting David here, I hope you're

giving the caretakers combat pay."

Judy nibbled at the edge of a red thumbnail. "We're doing the best we can, Lloyd. The police haven't been any help. I work full time, but Bru has a friend who helps with security. And no one has tried to get at David since we brought him home. I'm inclined to think the attack on the ambulance was a one-time thing. Bru's convinced he scared the attackers off for good."

"I hope you're right. Certainly if all the attackers wanted was to silence David, there's no need for them to return right away." Keaton nodded toward his friend's bed. "He looks quiet as death."

"He's been that way ever since we brought him home. It's good of you to come. I don't know whether anything we do or say registers on David, but if it does he must be awfully tired of my act by now."

As Judy retreated to a corner of the room, Keaton sat beside the bed and took Bowers's right hand, the hand that was free of fingertip clamps, in his own. His friend's hand was warm and pliable, but there was no response when Keaton squeezed it.

"Hi, guy," Keaton said. He waited for some sort of reaction. A fluttering eyelid, a wiggling finger, even a change in the repeating pattern of the electrocardiogram. When none came, he said, "So, how's your day been?"

After pausing a beat for a non-answer, he said, "Same old, same old, huh? Well, let me tell you I've had a day for the record books. You'd have been proud of me. I pressured a congressional bigwig into dropping the charges against Dale Loren and going after some local steroid peddlers instead."

Keaton tried to remember everything that had happened in the Tancredi case since he'd found Bowers at the bottom of his own elevator shaft. He told his friend about following Tancredi's phony sister to Cleveland, locating the phone numbers that led to OgrowSport, uncovering steroids in OgrowSport's shampoo vials, finding superballs and a note in Sammy's corked bat, and, finally, raiding OgrowSport and confronting Congressman Bloodworth.

"So long as Bloodworth's eating up tax dollars, I figure he might as well put them to good use locally." Keaton found it hard building to the climax of the Bloodworth story and getting no reaction from his audience. He started to release Bowers's hand, but continued to hold it, deciding to go on talking if there was any chance at all he was being heard.

He squeezed Bowers's hand. "Hey, here's a news flash. I haven't placed a bet on anything for any amount since we lost our shirts, shorts, and everything else on that last game Oke pitched with Bradshaw umpiring."

Keaton paused to take a breath, then started again. "Oh, yeah. That reminds me of the most important thing I need to tell you. I talked to Mike Brown in Vegas. He said you'd been phoning him to ask about patterns in the bets the East Wheeling boys had been laying off. I think I figured out what you were after. It looks like East Wheeling had laid off our bets on all those games we won, but didn't bother on those two games we lost.

"You must have thought it was a pretty big coincidence that they only took a chance they'd have to pay us off on those two games we lost. It's a little farfetched, I know, but it's almost like they had Bradshaw in their hip pocket. Is that what you were thinking?"

Keaton looked from Bowers to the monitors above the bed. There was no apparent reaction either from his friend or from the machines linked to him. "Anyhow, I'm thinking I'll do some columns on umpires after the Mammoths' season ends and before the World Series starts. Give me a chance to interview Bradshaw and size him up. What do you think of that?"

Keaton used his free left hand to give Bowers a playful tap on the shoulder. "Great idea, huh?"

Bowers remained impassive, but the impact of the tap made the electrocardiogram blips jump. "I'll take that as a yes," Keaton said.

Chapter Twenty-Two: A Cluster of Blow Flies

KEATON'S KORNER

Well, the Mammoths are down two games to one in the first round of the AAA playoffs against Richmond. One more loss and they're through for the season. A best-of-five series between two top teams is a crapshoot at best, but Menckenburg has been about one die short of a full roll ever since their elixir of choice, Vitamin O, was exposed as salt water. The chief consumer of that elixir, second-baseman Austin Reed, has gone oh-for-the-playoffs.

On reflection, the Mammoths' magical season seems to have been framed by placebo-inspired performances, with Sammy Tancredi's early season heroics attributed to a cold-cream mixture he believed to be steroids, and Austin Reed's late-season run fueled by Vitamin O. Too bad the elixirs seem to have passed their sell-by dates now that the Mammoths have their backs against the wall.

The fourth game of the Mammoths' playoff series was scoreless in the bottom of the seventh inning when Dale Loren appeared in the press box. Lloyd Keaton closed his laptop, stood up, and extended his hand. "Well, look who's come calling."

Loren shook the offered hand. "Last time we talked, you invited me to watch a game from the press box. Kind of a sanctuary from hecklers."

Keaton slid a folding chair in Loren's direction. "You're welcome to our hospitality, but I'm surprised you still need sanctuary. I see the feds have dropped the charges against you."

"There's always somebody who doesn't get the word. Guy sitting behind me in the stands kept poking me and suggesting I slip some steroids to the Mammoth hitters whenever one of them struck out."

On the field, the Mammoths' clean-up hitter popped up for the third out of the seventh inning, leaving the game in a scoreless tie. Keaton shook his head. "Well, if you can't slip them steroids, maybe you ought to mix up some cold cream and lemon juice. They sure need some kind of help."

"Not my job anymore, I'm afraid." Loren rested his hand on Keaton's shoulder. "I want to thank you again for all the support you gave me in your column."

Keaton shrugged. "Least I could do."

"I never did get to depose that guy Cleary from OgrowSport like you suggested. He was in jail before my lawyer could set anything up."

"Turns out you didn't need his deposition. Or anybody's, for that matter."

"I'm curious, though. Did you know OgrowSport was crooked when you suggested I get Cleary to swear I'd always refused to handle steroids?"

"I had my suspicions. I'd been tracking them for a while. Turns out that's where Sammy Tancredi actually got his steroids when he tested positive."

"Then why'd he tell the feds he got them from me?"

"He thought you had been giving him steroids. And he knew OgrowSport was mobbed up. Pretty easy choice when you think about it."

Loren extended both arms, palms up, as if he were weighing options on a scale. "Hmm. Inform on me? Or inform on the mob? Guess he didn't have to think too hard about it."

"Even a dim bulb like Sammy could figure that out. Going

against the mob is like playing Russian Roulette with six bullets."

Loren shook his head. "None of this is public knowledge."

"Those who need to know, know."

"Including Congressman Bloodworth?"

"Especially Congressman Bloodworth."

"How can you be sure of that?"

"I told him myself. In person."

Loren drummed his fingers on the press table. "It seems I have more to thank you for than this press-box seat."

Keaton waved his hand. "Forget it. You never should have been in Bloodworth's sights."

The crowd noise shifted from rhythmic clapping to a concerned murmur. Richmond had just loaded the bases with two men out in the top of the eighth inning. Bait MacFarland trudged to the mound and signaled to the bullpen for Ants Anthony.

"If anybody can stop them, it's Ants," Loren said. "He's been nearly unhittable lately."

"Been that way ever since he thought you were giving him steroids. Turned his season around. Probably his career as well."

"And he never ratted me out. So some good came of all this."

They watched as Ants Anthony finished his warm-up pitches, toed the mound, went into his herky-jerky motion, and threw a fastball that was so high the catcher had to leave his feet to keep it from going all the way to the backstop.

"Nerves," Keaton said. "He was lucky Kerrane caught it."

Anthony's next pitch bore inside on the Richmond hitter, who swung awkwardly and shattered his bat, but still managed to loop the ball in a shallow arc just over the first baseman's head. Two runs crossed the plate, giving Richmond a two-nothing lead. The home-town crowd groaned and fell silent.

"Lucky hit," Loren said.

"The way Richmond's going, though, it could mean the ball game. And the season."

Ants Anthony mopped his brow with his shirtsleeve and looked in to get the signal from his catcher. He laid a curve on the outside corner for a strike, then followed up with two sinkers that the Richmond hitter swung at and missed by a wide margin, ending the half inning.

Loren stood and clapped. "Attaboy, Ants. Now let's get those runs back."

The Mammoths' leadoff hitter in the bottom of the eighth walked, but the next batter hit into a double play and the Richmond pitcher finished off the inning with a strikeout.

"One more inning to go," Keaton said. "I feel like I jinxed the Mammoths by exposing OgrowSport. The team was riding high, thinking Vitamin O was giving them an edge."

"Not your fault," Loren said. "And not your problem. Some of those Richmond players were using Vitamin O as well."

"But none of them was having the season Austin Reed had. And he's been useless in the playoffs."

"Reed's a professional. He's a young hitter on his way up. He might have had just as good a season if he'd never heard of Vitamin O. And you sure can't beat yourself up for shutting down OgrowSport. News reports say they were shipping steroids all over the state."

"That's true. They had a lot of local high-schoolers hooked too."

"So you did a world of good even if you happened to put a small crimp in Austin Reed's career. And I'm not convinced you can take full credit for that." He nodded toward the diamond. "Since I've been sitting out the season, I've been asking myself how much impact we really have on those overpaid phenoms down there."

"Who's we?"

"You. Me. Trainers. Coaches. Reporters. Managers. Look at Bait MacFarland in the Mammoths' dugout. What he knows about pitching you could write on the head of a pin and still have enough room left over for the Baseball Encyclopedia. But he's managed to get the Mammoths into the playoffs."

"Not entirely his doing. There's a lot of talent on the team."

"That's my point. We give ourselves more credit than we deserve when things go right. And the press sure gives Bait more credit than he deserves. The average reporter knows even less than Bait does, and regurgitates his cockamamie explanations just to fill space."

"Well, you can't deny that Sammy Tancredi went on a tear when he thought you were giving him steroids. And you turned Ants Anthony's season around with your cold cream." Keaton waved his hand toward the pitcher's mound. "Look at him down there. All the confidence in the world. He looks like Satchel Paige in his prime."

On the mound, Ants Anthony's unorthodox delivery and baffling assortment of pitches were tying Richmond hitters in knots. The leadoff hitter struck out chasing a change-up that broke well off the plate, while the next batter grounded out to short and the third fouled out feebly to the catcher.

As the Mammoths came in to bat in the bottom of the ninth, Keaton drummed his fist on the press table and announced, "Last chance for the good guys." Even after all his years in the press box, a close game still dried his mouth, tightened his stomach muscles, and left his hands trembling.

The Richmond closer, a rail-thin fireballer whose fastball topped out around 100 miles per hour, appeared to have the game well in hand. He struck out the first Mammoth batter, walked the second on a close three-and-two pitch, and coaxed a weak pop-up to short out the third hitter.

"What's really jinxing the Mammoths is the Richmond pitching, not anything you did," Loren said.

"It's not over yet." Keaton braced his hands against the press table. "The old horse ain't dead till the blowflies come."

Loren laughed. "Does that happen before or after the fat lady sings?"

"It's a saying of my grandfather's. He grew up on a farm and was never much for operatic imagery."

The Mammoth hitter steered a grounder just out of the shortstop's reach, putting runners on first and second. "Tying runs on base," Keaton said.

The hometown crowd rose to its feet, stomping and clapping. As Austin Reed dug his spikes into the batter's box, the crowd's cheers turned into a rhythmic chant of "Reed! Reed! Reed!"

"Lot of pressure," Loren said. "Kid still hasn't had a hit in the playoffs."

At the plate, Reed corkscrewed awkwardly as he missed the first pitch, which registered 101 miles per hour on the stadium radar gun.

The crowd quieted down just long enough for a throaty voice behind the Mammoth dugout to yell, "Get the kid some salt water!"

A smattering of laughter from the crowd was drowned out by more stomping and clapping as the rhythmic chant of "Reed!" resumed.

The sound of bat meeting ball echoed above the chant as Reed sent the next pitch rocketing toward the center field bleachers.

Keaton leapt to his feet. "That's it. That's it."

The Richmond center-fielder turned his back on home plate, sped straight to the fence, and seemed to run halfway up it, extending his glove over the wall just as the ball was about to clear it. With the crowd still roaring, the outfielder tumbled to the ground, rolled over once, and held his glove up to show the ball exposed like a snow cone in the webbing.

The crowd noise stopped as if someone had jerked a plug out of its socket.

Keaton sat down. “Shit. He caught it. Four hundred and ten feet and he caught it.”

“Well, there goes your season,” Loren said. “They win on a broken bat blooper and we lose on a four-hundred-and-ten-foot drive. Hardly seems fair.”

“Fair is what you worry about on buses.” Keaton opened his laptop. “I’m not looking forward to writing this one up.”

Loren stood up. “I’m going to beat it before the blowflies get here. Thanks for your hospitality.” He extended his hand. “And for getting me my life back.”

Keaton shook Loren’s hand. “Any idea what you’ll do with your life now that you’ve got it back?

Loren shrugged. “So far I haven’t exactly been showered with offers.”

Keaton turned back to his laptop. “Now that really doesn’t seem fair.”

Chapter Twenty-Three: Strike Zone or Twilight Zone?

KEATON'S KORNER

The first sentence of the *Official Rules of Baseball* stipulates that: *Baseball is a game between two teams of nine players each, under direction of a manager, played on an enclosed field in accordance with these rules, under jurisdiction of one or more umpires.*

Maligned though they may be, umpires are essential to the game. On a good day, nobody notices the umpires. On a bad day, though, thousands of fans boo them, players confront and curse them, and managers kick dirt on their shoes. A Major League umpiring team makes upwards of 300 decisions a day, many of them close enough to go either way, ensuring a disagreement from one side or the other.

Disputed calls by umpires have changed the outcome of games, pennant races, and the World Series. Since professional baseball began in 1871, roughly forty managers, players, coaches, and trainers have been banned from the game for a variety of gambling offenses, bribery attempts, and contract disputes. In view of the importance of the umpires to each game, however, it's remarkable that only one umpire, Richard Higham in 1882, has ever been banished for conspiring to throw a game. Leo Durocher once said, "I never questioned the integrity of an umpire. Their eyesight, yes."

With the Mammoths' season ended and the Major League playoffs nearly a month away, I'll be using a few of these columns to explore the world of the professional umpire in an attempt to gain some insights into the minds and hearts that are essential to the integrity of the game of baseball.

Keaton caught up with Larry Bradshaw in the lobby of the Netherlands Plaza Hotel in downtown Cincinnati. The umpire was much smaller than he appeared on TV, with precise features and tiny, delicate hands.

"Thanks for taking the time to be interviewed," Keaton said. He made a mental note not to comment on Bradshaw's short stature. He wanted to put the umpire at ease, gain his confidence, get him talking comfortably so that he wouldn't bolt if the subject of gambling was broached.

"Happy to do it," Bradshaw said. "We umpires generally only get press attention after a bad call."

"Then this should be a day in the park for you." Keaton took out his pocket tape recorder. "Mind if I record what we say?"

Bradshaw shrugged. "Fine with me. Who else have you interviewed?"

"You're the first active umpire. I've talked with a couple of retirees. Interviewed Chalk Reston last weekend after the AAA playoff games ended."

"Reston's quite a character. Probably gave a good interview."

"He had a lot to say about the managers of his day. Not much of it good. He did admit to making a bad call. Said he'd called an outside pitch a strike once in nineteen eighty-two."

Bradshaw smiled, crossed his legs, and ran his thumb and forefinger along the crease of his pants. "Well, the home-plate umpire makes about three hundred calls a game. Anybody who claims he never missed one is either a fool or a liar."

Keaton was about to ask Bradshaw whether he'd ever made a bad call but decided not to. Not yet, anyhow. Instead, he said, "Reston says the toughest calls he ever had to make were on high, tight pitches when the catcher jumped up and obscured his view."

"They're tough, all right." Bradshaw raised the palm of his hand over his head as if he were measuring his height. "You may have noticed I'm vertically challenged, so a catcher doesn't have to be too tall to block me out. But I think the toughest call for me is the half swing. Especially because you know the TV cameras have a better angle than you, and the announcers can replay the tape to see whether the bat went far enough to warrant a strike call." Bradshaw paused, then nodded. "Yeah, that's the toughest everyday call for me. You know the worst call I have to make, though?"

"No. What is it?"

"Throwing a guy out who's arguing a call I suspect I got wrong. Doesn't happen very often, but you've got to show everyone you're in control of the game."

"So you've made some bad calls."

"At least twice as many as Reston. Mine were July ninety-nine and August oh-four."

Keaton smiled. "Ever try to make amends for a bad call?"

"With an even-out call, you mean? Favoring the other team? You can't do that. It only makes things worse. Why follow one bad call with another one? The game and the fans deserve better than that."

"Do you hear the fans when they get on you? Or do you manage to tune them out?"

"Oh, you hear them. You can't help but hear them. Usually they question your eyesight." Bradshaw cupped his hands around his mouth and dropped his voice an octave. " 'Hey, Blue, use your good eye.' Or 'Try cutting eye holes in that mask, Blue.' "

"Nothing too original."

"They can be. One guy in the stands right here in Cincinnati almost made me laugh out loud when he shouted, 'Hey, Blue, is that your strike zone or the Twilight Zone?' and then gave me that Twilight Zone 'Do-do-do-do' after every call that went against the Reds."

Keaton laughed. He was beginning to like Bradshaw. "Now that's funny."

"If you want to be liked by everyone, umpiring is the wrong job for you. Close calls always make you twenty-five enemies on one team or the other."

"What kind of advice would you give an umpire starting out?"

"What they teach us in umpire school. 'Call 'em fast and walk away tough.' "

Keaton copied the quote into his notebook. "So be decisive."

"You've got to stay in control. There's no room to dither. You've only got two choices. Ball or strike. Safe or out. Fair or foul. Fans and players will kill you if you seem indecisive."

"I've seen a few surveys where players rate umpires. They seem to value strike-zone consistency above everything else. Umpires that rate lowest are either inconsistent or hard to get along with."

Bradshaw nodded. "You can have a double-wide strike zone and get away with it if you're consistent."

"The ratings I've seen rank you just below the top. Well above the middle."

"That's fine with me. I don't mind being anonymous. As far as I'm concerned, a perfect game is one where nobody notices the umpire."

"What about favoritism toward certain players?" Keaton asked, steering the conversation back toward his target. "My dad told me a story about a rookie pitcher facing Ted Williams for the first time. The kid's first three pitches are close to the plate, but the umpire calls them all balls. The catcher goes to the mound to settle the kid down, and the umpire follows to break up the conference. When the umpire gets to the mound, the kid says, 'Give me a break here. Those pitches were pretty good,' and the umpire responds, 'Don't worry, son. Mr. Williams will let you know when you put one in the strike zone.' "

Bradshaw smiled. "I know your dad was a famous sportswriter, but I'm guessing that story is apocryphal. The fellow who told it to me had Rogers Hornsby batting."

"I have heard, though, that there are some umpires who won't ring up marquee hitters."

"I haven't seen that. Some great hitters have reputations for their exceptional strike-zone judgment. Williams did. Barry Bonds too. Those hitters walk a lot, partly because they know the strike zone, and partly because pitchers are afraid to throw them strikes. But I've never seen an umpire fail to ring up someone like Bonds on an obvious third strike."

All right, Keaton thought, let's get to the heart of the matter. "What about the other side of the coin? There are some control pitchers, like Jerry Neyer or David Oke and, in the past, Greg Maddux, who seem to get more than their share of strike calls."

"That's a little different. They're always around the plate, so they tend to get the close calls."

"Calls that a less consistent pitcher wouldn't get?"

"Put it this way. A pitcher who is all over the place won't get as many close calls as a pitcher who's always around the plate."

"I hear sportscasters saying that all the time. And it certainly affects pitcher's records. Strikeouts, walks, wins, losses, and ERA will all reflect close calls."

Bradshaw nodded. "It's fairly basic."

"Speaking of ERAs, I see that there's at least one group that keeps track of the earned runs allowed with different umpires behind the plate."

"I've heard that."

"There's a pretty wide range. Dick Freedman, with his wide strike zone, has an ERA just under three runs per game, while some umpires, like Paul Cote, nearly double that."

Bradshaw shrugged. "Those two umpires have widely different strike zones. But they're consistent. Pitchers love Freedman and hitters love Cote, but both pitchers and hitters know what to expect."

"Your own numbers put you right near the middle again."

"That so? Can't say I'm too surprised."

All right, Keaton thought, let's get to the point and watch how he reacts. "When I break down your ERA numbers, though, they're pretty interesting. For control pitchers like Oke and Neyer, your ERAs are half that of the next most pitcher-friendly umpire."

Bradshaw rubbed his temple. "Like I said, they get the close pitches."

"But for young pitchers with a lot of stuff but less control, their earned run averages with you behind the plate are higher than those of the most hitter-friendly umpires."

"So it all averages out, leaving me right in the middle. What's your point?"

Careful now, Keaton told himself. "Well, if I were a betting man, I'd wait until you were behind the plate with somebody like Neyer or Oke going against a young fireballer with control problems and bet the farm on the control pitchers."

Bradshaw's lips pinched into a tight half smile. "And are you a betting man, Mr. Keaton?"

"I was. Too much of a betting man, actually. Now I'm in Gamblers Anonymous."

"But you still think like a betting man."

"Like an alcoholic reading wine labels. But I checked out my theory. If I'd followed it the past three years, I'd have won every bet I put down."

Bradshaw's eyes widened with surprise and his pursed lips parted. "That's impossible."

"No, I checked it out." Well, it was pretty close to the truth, Keaton thought.

"I mean, I can't believe it. Let me think about it." Bradshaw's eyes drifted to the ceiling, then focused on Keaton. "There was a game in Colorado. A little over a month ago. A young pitcher named Don Kyle beat Oke."

"You sure?" Keaton asked, knowing the answer. It was the game that cost him his stake and nearly cost David Bowers his new home.

"I ought to be sure. I was there."

"I must have missed that one." But you remembered it, didn't you? Keaton thought. No trouble at all remembering that game.

"But there must be other games," Bradshaw said. "I can't believe I'm that predictable."

"Like I said, I went back three years in the record books."

"But you missed a game that came off not two months ago. I'm guessing you missed a couple more. Maybe it's a good thing you're no longer a betting man."

"That's for sure." Keaton smiled. "If I was, though, I'd be willing to bet I didn't miss any others."

"I'd take that bet. But you'll have to give me a little time to think about it."

"Let's talk about gambling. There've been a few recent scandals over officials on the take in other sports. The NBA, for example. But in the whole history of professional baseball, there's only been one umpire banished for rigging games. And that was way back in the eighteen eighties. That speaks pretty well for the men in blue."

"Well, we are pretty well paid at the Major League level. Umpires start at eighty-four thousand per year and can make as much as three hundred thousand. I think the average salary is well over two hundred fifty thou. So long as the majors pay us well, there's not much financial incentive to cheat."

"But umpires weren't always well paid. Bill Klem was offered two thousand dollars to rig the Cubs/Giants playoff game in nineteen oh eight. That would be worth over two million in today's dollars. That's nearly ten years of salary."

"But Klem turned it down. And reported it to the league." Bradshaw smiled. "We umpires are a feisty bunch. We've got a lot of pride and have been pretty well screened before we make it to the bigs. And our situation has improved dramatically since the umpires went on strike in seventy-nine. We've got pensions, benefits, and get promoted on merit rather than just length of service. I'm not surprised we've steered clear of any gambling scandals.

"Suppose somebody did try to bribe an umpire, though. It's not like bribing a fighter to lie down or a jockey to hold his horse back. The umpire's not in total control of the game. Not even the home-plate umpire. There are eighteen players on the field. And any one of them could make an error or get a bloop hit that would turn the game around."

"I guess you're right," Keaton said, thinking that it was pretty clear Bradshaw had thought about it.

Bradshaw rubbed his middle finger and thumb together as if he wanted to make a snapping noise. "Neyer. The Dodgers lit up Neyer in a game last year. Young Oquindo was on the mound for Los Angeles. That's another game you would have lost betting your system."

"You mean I missed more than one?"

"At least two. And I'm still working on it."

"You're right. Probably a good thing I stopped betting."

"I'd say so."

"Still, I found eight games where the system would have worked. Add the two where you say it would have failed. That's still eight out of ten wins."

Bradshaw shifted in his chair. "You know what? I'm not comfortable sitting here and talking about gambling. Do you have any other questions?"

"Oh, sorry. Guess I got off on a tangent there." Keaton

checked his note pad. "Let me finish by asking you to name the best thing and the worst thing about being a big league umpire."

"Best thing, huh?" Bradshaw stroked his chin and smiled. "There was a famous umpire who said, 'You can't beat the hours,' but he said that before night games and coast-to-coast travel. I'd say the best thing is just being a part of baseball."

"And the worst thing?"

"The worst thing is the loneliness. It's not a profession where you make a lot of friends."

"No. I suppose not." Keaton turned off his recorder. "Look, thanks again for your time."

Bradshaw stood up. "I look forward to reading your columns on umpiring."

"Don't worry. I'll stay in touch. And I'll see that you get copies of the columns."

"I tell you, Dave, without even trying, he came up with the two games we lost." Keaton was sitting at David Bowers's bedside, angling his chair so that he could see both his friend's still face and the life-sign monitors beside the bed.

"I pretended our system had just occurred to me and ran it by him. He shot it down by pulling the examples of the two games right out of his memory bank. The Oke game we just blew and last year's Neyer debacle. The only two games where East Wheeling didn't lay off our bets."

The monitor screens droned on, giving no hint of a change in the patient's status.

"Okay, I can see you're not impressed. I mean, I know it's not a smoking gun. Hell, it's barely a leaky water pistol. It sure doesn't prove without a doubt that Bradshaw is in the pocket of the East Wheeling mob. He could just be one of those guys with an encyclopedic memory."

Keaton reached out to grasp Bowers's hand. Disturbed by its

cool stillness, he ran his own hand up his friend's forearm and let it rest on the sleeve of his pajamas. "And I have to admit the guy didn't act like he had anything to hide. Although he made it clear he didn't want to talk about gambling. So I guess we still don't have anything but our suspicions."

Keaton smoothed Bowers's pajama sleeve. "Hell, I feel like I set the trap and came back to find it sprung with the cheese missing. I even liked the guy. But I tell you, I would have liked him a lot better if he hadn't come up with those two games so easily."

Judy gave Keaton a warm hug on his way out the door. "Thanks for coming by," she said. "I like to think he hears us, and he must be awfully tired of me by now."

"I'll be back soon," Keaton said. He hurried down the wheelchair ramp to find Bru leaning against the door of his Ford Escort. His arms were folded across his chest, and his bald head glistened in the morning sunlight.

"Been seein' a lot of this here heap recently," Bru said.

"I've been coming to talk to David."

"Sure you have. Like he can hear you." Bru made no move to step away from the Escort's door. "You ain't foolin' me."

"Wasn't aware I've been trying to fool you."

"You're here to hit on my sis. I saw you hugging her just now. She's pretty well fixed, and that white bread husband of hers ain't getting no better."

"Don't be silly. That baby monitor by David's bed runs to your room as well as hers. Come chaperone my visits if you're so concerned."

"I'm just sayin,' I don't want to hear you've been seein' Jude outside of visiting hours. Am I clear?"

"Judy's an old friend. I'll see her whenever I want."

"She's already had half a lifetime of trouble with you white boys." Bru still lounged against the Escort's door. "Am I clear?"

"Oh, for Christ's sake. You're clear. Now will you step aside? I've got to get to work."

"Just so's I'm clear." Bru stepped away from the car door. "I don't want no misunderstandings between us."

Chapter Twenty-Four: Players to Be Blamed Later

KEATON'S KORNER

For some time now, this column has been critical of the Bloodworth committee's investigation of steroid use by Major League Baseball players. Ever since the major leagues took the matter in hand and instituted a regular testing program, the committee has been behaving like the drunk who lost his wallet on a dark street two blocks away but is looking for it on a street closer to home where the light is better.

The light of publicity may be brighter where the major leaguers are playing, but the real problem with steroids is several streets down, where high school athletes are taking the field. A recent Kaiser Family Foundation study found that over fifty percent of the youths surveyed believed that it was ". . . common for famous athletes to use steroids or other banned substances to get an edge on the competition." The youth of America model their behavior after famous athletes. They emulate their heroes' batting stances, eat the cereals they recommend, and buy the equipment they endorse. If they think their heroes are bulking up on steroids, you can bet that high school athletes will follow their example.

I commend Representative Bloodworth's committee for turning its focus on the dark alleyways of teenage steroid use, starting with an investigation of high school programs right here in Menckenburg.

The gallery overlooking the congressional hearing room in Washington, D.C.'s Rayburn Office Building was only about half as full as it had been when Congressman Bloodworth was using his committee to pillory Sammy Tancredi and Dale Loren. The section reserved for members of the press had so many empty seats that Keaton was able to have Liz and Davy join him at his press table. Besides his wife and son, other seats in the press section were occupied by three reporters from other Ohio newspapers, stringers from the *New York Times* and *Washington Post,* and a few others Keaton didn't recognize.

On the floor of the hearing room, Bloodworth, his fellow committee members, and their aides sat behind two semi-circles of raised mahogany desks that looked down on several long straight tables strewn with cables and microphones. The last time Keaton had been in the hearing room, Sammy Tancredi and Dale Loren had been seated at the front tables with their lawyers and other witnesses. Today, the only two faces Keaton recognized at the front tables belonged to Davy's coach, Stu Lammers, and his team manager, Johnny Crain. Neither looked happy to be there.

Bloodworth opened the hearings in the same way he'd opened the previous hearings on steroid use among major leaguers. After a prayer that studiously avoided any mention of a deity, three parents took the podium to tell heartbreaking tales of the loss of their children, star athletes whose steroid use led to tragedy. Keaton recalled two of the parents from the previous hearing. The third parent, whose story Keaton knew but hadn't heard firsthand, was a tall, gaunt woman whose son had attended Central High School in Menckenburg. The boy, Buzz Fitzhugh, went on to be a star shortstop and wide receiver at Ohio State University. When he graduated from Ohio State, he was already experiencing violent mood swings that his mother attributed to steroid use. Drafted by both the Toronto Blue Jays and the New England Patriots, he elected to play baseball and was cut by the Blue Jays after two undistinguished seasons in the low minors. He celebrated his release by driving the Corvette he'd received as a signing bonus head-on into an onrushing train.

Davy sat impassive through the harrowing tales of the bereaved parents, but Liz clutched Keaton's arm and whispered, "Oh, God, Lloyd. Oh, God," as the Menckenburg housewife left the podium.

Representative James Bloodworth followed the housewife to the podium and began by reviewing his committee's accomplishments. "In the past, this committee has focused on steroid abuse by Major League Baseball players. I think we can be justly proud of the fact that the drug testing program instituted by Major League Baseball under our prodding has been undeniably effective in reducing steroid use at the professional level."

Bloodworth paused to acknowledge a smattering of applause, then continued. "Having achieved this major victory, the committee now turns its attention to the impact that steroid use by Major League ballplayers has had on the youth of America. We will do this by subjecting a few representative high school and college programs to the same intense scrutiny we extended to professional baseball."

The congressman held up a sheaf of papers and tapped them with his eyeglasses. "I have here sworn testimonies of steroid use from over twenty-five amateur players at the high school and college level."

As Bloodworth fanned out the statements, Keaton glanced over at Davy, who was staring down at his feet.

"Because most of these players are underage," Bloodworth continued, "It is the intent of this committee to hold their identities private and sacrosanct, and to use their statements to shine a light on the underground chain that has supplied them with illegal drugs."

After going over a few more ground rules, outlining committee procedures, and taking credit one more time for all but eradicating steroid use among major leaguers, Bloodworth announced that the first local operation to come under committee scrutiny was the baseball program of Central High School in Menckenburg, Ohio.

He stipulated that the committee's investigators had found evidence of significant steroid use among the program's teenage ballplayers, and called on the team manager, Johnny Crain, to be the first witness of the day.

As Johnny Crain took his position behind one of the standing microphones and was sworn in, his lawyer, a short, balding man in a crisp blue suit, addressed the room through one of the table microphones. "If it please the committee, I would like to emphasize that my client has cooperated fully with the investigation currently undertaken by the Menckenburg Police Force, and likewise intends to cooperate fully with this committee."

Bloodworth responded to the lawyer by saying, "Duly noted," and then turned his attention to Johnny Crain, adding, "Welcome to Washington, son."

The lowest setting of the standing microphone left it slightly higher than the head of Johnny Crain, who had to tilt his head upward to respond, "Thank you sir."

"Let's get right to it then," Bloodworth said. "Son, you've been accused of distributing steroids to several members of the Central High School baseball team in Menckenburg."

Crain's lawyer interrupted. "I'd like to advise my client that his Fifth Amendment rights mean that he does not have to answer that question."

Bloodworth tilted his glasses forward on his nose and peered over them at the lawyer. "It wasn't a question yet, Counselor.

You just advertised your client's wish to cooperate with this committee. Well, sir, why don't you just stand aside and let the boy cooperate."

The lawyer pulled his microphone closer and said, "I merely wanted to inform my client . . ."

Bloodworth silenced the lawyer with a wave of his hand. "I'm aware of what you wanted to do, Counselor. But if you keep interrupting, we'll be here all week just trying to establish the facts of this case. We're not trying to indict your client, who I understand in any case has been granted immunity from prosecution."

The lawyer reddened. "Yes, sir, that's true."

"Now then, son," Bloodworth continued, "How many players on the baseball team did you supply with steroids?"

Johnny Crain hitched the right sleeve of his sport coat back so it cleared his thumb and reached up to tilt the microphone head downward. "It varied from year to year, sir. Last year there were six. This year I've had as many as eight customers."

"So business is growing."

"That's right, sir."

"And just how did you get those steroids you were distributing?"

"I called a number and ordered them."

"And who did you order them from?"

"I never knew, sir." Crain paused. "Well, until recently, that is. After the police raided OgrowSport, the number I had was disconnected and no one took my orders."

"So you concluded that OgrowSport was your ultimate supplier?"

"Yes, sir. I did."

"And once you placed the order, how were the steroids delivered to you?"

"Usually they were left on my back porch. But sometimes

they come by mail."

The committee member to Bloodworth's left, a representative from South Carolina, asked in a soft drawl, "Did you evah see the person leaving them on your back porch?"

"No, sir. They come when I was in school."

Bloodworth resumed questioning. "And how did you pay for these shipments?"

"I left money in a lunch box on my back porch. Hollis Theiro helped me set up the system."

"And who was Hollis?"

"He was the team manager before me. He was a senior when I was a sophomore."

"So this Hollis showed you where to buy steroids. And then you marked up the price and sold them to team members at a nice little profit."

Crain smiled. "Yes, sir."

The South Carolina representative asked, "How much of a profit?"

"Two or three hundred dollars a week during the season. Less after the season ended."

Most of the reporters in the press section wrote down the profit number or entered it in their laptops.

Bloodworth took over the questioning. "That's quite a handsome sum for a high school junior. Tell me, son, did you sell anything besides steroids?"

Crain nodded. "Arnolds."

Bloodworth removed his glasses and asked, "Arnolds?"

"Yes, sir. Arnolds. You know, poppers. Pep pills. Greenies."

An aide seated behind Bloodworth whispered in his ear. The representative nodded and said, "I see. Amphetamines."

"Yes, sir. And aspirin."

"Aspirin?"

"Yes, sir. The Arnolds—I mean, the amphetamines—come in

little aspirin containers. So usually they topped them off with real aspirin. Especially when they sent them by mail."

"So you offered all the services of a regular pharmacy."

"Well, some. Not all. Didn't have no sodas or magazines."

Crain's answer provoked laughter from the audience behind him, and he turned and smiled at the spectators. Liz sighed and shook her head.

Bloodworth allowed Crain to enjoy his moment, then said, "Your pseudo-pharmacy didn't require prescriptions, either. Tell me, son, how did you find your customers?"

"They mostly found me. I started with the fellows Hollis supplied. Then when new players made the team, word got around."

"I see. Word of mouth. Tell me, did the word get as far as your coach?"

"He never ordered no steroids, if that's what you mean."

Another burst of laughter came from the observers. Out of the corner of his eye, Keaton saw Davy smile.

"That's not what I meant," Bloodworth said. "And I suspect you know it. Now this is important, son. Did you ever discuss the players' steroid use with your coach?"

Crain shook his head emphatically. "No, sir!"

"In your opinion, was your coach aware that some of his players were using steroids?"

Crain looked over at his lawyer before answering. His lawyer lowered his head in a half nod, and the boy replied, "I have no knowledge of what the coach knew about steroids."

"I see." Bloodworth looked up and down the panel of congressmen. "Do any of my fellow committee members have further questions for this young man?"

The committee members all shook their heads. Keaton reflected that they hadn't been so reticent when Sammy Tancredi was on the witness stand and there were more cameras present.

"Well, then," Bloodworth said. "Since there are no further questions, the witness is excused."

Liz nudged Keaton and whispered, "They let the little shit off way too easy."

Keaton shrugged. "That's what the word 'immunity' means. Little shits get off so they can catch bigger shits."

Bloodworth next called Coach Stuart Lammers to the witness table. Lammers's lawyer, a man as tall and broad as his client but with a full head of wavy silver hair, took a seat next to the microphone.

When the coach had been sworn in, Bloodworth asked, "Mr. Lammers, how long have you been the coach of the Central High School baseball team in Menckenburg?"

"Sixteen years."

"Have you been fairly successful over that period?"

"Quite successful, sir. We've been to the state championships six years and won it outright twice."

"Pretty big boys on those championship teams?"

"Yes, sir. A few of them."

"You've heard the previous witness testify under oath that at least eight players on your current team are steroid users. Were you aware of this?"

"Most certainly not."

"So it comes as a complete surprise to you?"

"A complete surprise, yes, sir."

"Mr. Lammers, I'd like you to look at a few photographs." Twin screens appeared on either side of the raised platform where Bloodworth and his colleagues sat and the house lights dimmed.

The left-hand screen showed what appeared to be a yearbook photo of a skinny teenage boy. The right-hand screen showed a hefty person in a baseball uniform with muscular arms and a neck as thick as a redwood trunk. In both photos, black bars masked the mouth and eyes of the subjects to conceal their identities.

"Mr. Lammers," Bloodworth said, "Do you recognize the subjects of either of these photos?"

"Those bars over their faces make it difficult to say, sir. I do recognize the uniform of the player on the right. It's one of ours."

"But you don't recognize the players?"

"No, sir. Not with those bars across their faces."

"Would it surprise you to learn that the same person posed for both photos? The photo on your left appeared in the Tower yearbook when the boy was a freshman, while the photo on the right was taken last year when the subject played for your baseball team."

Keaton was too far away to see Lammers's expression, but the coach said something that sounded like "Hmppf" into the microphone.

"The subject," Bloodworth continued, "is one of the players who has confessed to using steroids when he was in your charge."

"As I said, sir, I was unaware of any such use. Had I been notified, I certainly would have put a stop to it."

"But you saw nothing suspicious in the player's appearance?"

"No, sir."

At a signal from Bloodworth, both screens flashed and another pair of photos replaced the first two. Once again, the photo on the left showed a skinny teenage boy with thick black bars shielding his face. This time the photo on the right showed a broad, muscular back covered with acne scars.

Davy slumped deep in his chair. The picture on the left was his freshman yearbook photo, while Keaton had taken the photo on the right just last week.

"Do you recognize this subject?" Bloodworth asked.

Once again, Lammers answered no.

"Would it surprise you to learn that the photos depict the same teenager before and after he joined your team?"

Lammers was silent.

"And you still maintain you detected no signs of steroid use among your players?"

"No, sir. I mean, yes, sir. I detected no signs of steroid use."

"Yet these pictures show life-altering changes in the subjects' physiques."

"With all due respect, sir, you're showing photos taken during heavy growth years for male teenagers. You'd naturally expect to see major change between a boy's freshman and senior years."

"The photos we're looking at now document changes between an admitted steroid user's freshman and sophomore years, but I take your point. Let's try another set of pictures."

The two screens flashed white for an instant, and then the left-hand screen showed a photo of a rail thin African American boy with his face half hidden by masking bars. A picture of what was presumably the same boy, his face still half hidden, flashed on the right-hand screen. In this picture he was wearing a baseball uniform that looked much too big for his slight frame.

"What about these photos, Mr. Lammers?" Representative Bloodworth asked. "Recognize anyone here?"

"No, I don't," Lammers said. Then he half smiled. "But I doubt that I'm looking at photos of a steroid user."

"I commend you on your powers of observation," Bloodworth said. "You show a remarkable grasp of the obvious. As it happens those are pictures of the young Henry Aaron in that heavy growth period between his freshman and senior years in high school. Decidedly and demonstrably *not* a steroid user."

Bloodworth paused. "I do find it curious, though, Mr. Lammers, that you are so quick to recognize a case in which no steroid use exists, but so slow to recognize cases in which that possibility seems self-evident."

Lammers opened his mouth to reply, but shut it without saying a word. His lawyer spoke up instead. "If it pleases the committee, my client is naturally reluctant to accuse teenagers of steroid use on the basis of a pair of photographs."

"It's hardly a matter of accusation, counselor," Bloodworth said. "The teenagers in those first two pairs of photographs were self-confessed steroid users. Furthermore, they both began using steroids supplied by Mr. Lammers's team manager after joining his baseball team."

"I had no knowledge of any of that," Lammers said.

"And no suspicions that the players in question were using steroids, even in the face of remarkable physical changes?"

"I saw nothing remarkable. It's a time when boys that age can experience huge growth spurts."

"And you never discussed steroid use with your team manager, young Mr. Crain?"

"No, sir, I did not."

"Or with other team managers or players in the course of your tenure?"

"No, sir, I did not."

"Mr. Lammers, I must say I find it quite remarkable that at a time when steroid use has arguably been the biggest story in baseball, you, as a baseball coach, never found the time or inclination to discuss it with your teams."

Lammers stood silent.

"Is it fair to say, then, Mr. Lammers," Bloodworth continued, "that you exercised a 'don't ask, don't tell' policy toward steroid use among your players?"

"I guess you might say that."

"Mr. Lammers, while that policy may or may not be the best we can do regarding gays in the military, it is hardly ideal for someone charged with the well-being of teenage boys."

"No, sir. I'll see to it that the boys are disciplined."

"What boys?"

"The boys in the pictures you just showed. The steroid users on my team."

Davy slumped still lower in his chair, both fists pressed hard against his reddening face.

"Excuse me," Bloodworth said. "But didn't you just testify under oath that you didn't recognize the subjects of those photographs?"

"When you first showed me the pictures, I didn't realize they were boys on my team."

Lammers's lawyer stood and maneuvered the coach away from the microphone. "My client naturally assumes that you will share the identity of those boys with him."

"Mr. Boggs, if that's what you assume, neither you nor your client has been paying very close attention to these proceedings. The boys in those photographs are well under eighteen years of age, and we intend to protect their identities. They came forward voluntarily and have announced their intention to quit using steroids. If your client wants to discipline someone, I suggest he try to seek out the remaining steroid users on his team. According to young Mr. Crain's testimony, there are still three or four left."

Liz patted Davy's arm. He straightened somewhat, rising from full slouch to half slouch.

Bloodworth shuffled through the papers in front of him and asked whether other committee members had any questions for Mr. Lammers. When none did, he excused the witness, asking that he and his lawyer remain in the hearing room in case further questions arose.

After agreeing to remain, Lammers and his lawyer beat a hasty retreat from the witness table.

Bloodworth next called Robert Ramella to testify. Ramella was a slight, fidgety man who drummed his fingers on the Bible while being sworn in. He was joined at the witness table by a burly, balding man whose tweed sport coat bulged over his hips and a shorter, bespectacled man carrying a battered leather briefcase.

Keaton didn't recognize any of the newcomers and leaned forward in his chair.

At Bloodworth's request, the two men flanking the witness identified themselves. The burly man was a deputy warden at the Ohio State Penitentiary, while the briefcase carrier was a lawyer from the public defender's office.

"Mr. Ramella," Bloodworth said. "I understand you have been accompanied by a representative of the state penitentiary because that is your current residence. Is that correct?"

"Yes, sir."

"May I ask what activities led to your incarceration?"

"Narcotics possession, sir. And distribution."

Ramella scratched at his right arm as his lawyer interposed, "Alleged distribution."

"And how long have you been a resident of the state penitentiary?"

"Four years."

"When did you first begin using drugs?"

Ramella shifted from one foot to the other. "About ten years ago. I was a junior in high school."

"And where did you attend high school?"

"Central High School in Menckenburg."

"Your drug use aside, did you participate in any school activities?"

"I was manager of the baseball team for three years. We made the state finals my senior year."

"Was Mr. Lammers the coach then?"

"Yes, he was."

"And was he aware of your narcotics habit?"

"I don't believe so. But he was responsible for it. In a way."

"How is that?"

"When I was a sophomore, just starting out as team manager, he got me together with a drug distributor, OgrowSport."

"Why did he do that?"

"They distributed poppers . . . amphetamines, I mean, and he thought they might help some of our players focus."

"So you procured amphetamines for the high school team."

"That's right."

"With the full knowledge of your coach."

"Yes. He said it was all right because they weren't illegal at the time and all the Major League teams passed them out like candy."

"Did you get anything else for the team?"

"Vitamins, aspirin, stuff like that. Then about the end of my sophomore year, Coach Lammers asked me if I could get some andro."

"Androstenedione."

"Yeah. Coach said a lot of big leaguers were using it, so he thought it might help some of our players."

"And were you able to obtain androstenedione?"

"Yes. From OgrowSport. At first I just made it a part of my regular order. Then when my junior year started, they asked me to get andro and poppers from a go-between."

"A go-between?"

"Yes. A woman. I never knew her name. We met a few times, but I usually contacted her by phone. She had other stuff too. Designer steroids. Stuff like that."

Keaton flipped open his notebook and wrote, *Ramella Sup-*

plier = Sara?

"And you supplied these pills and steroids to your team?" Bloodworth asked.

"To whoever wanted them. They weren't a hard sell. If a big-league first baseman was using andro, our own first basemen would want lots of it. Business grew when the guys saw their buddies grow."

"And your coach knew about this?"

"Well, my junior year he said it would be best if I just dealt directly with the players and left him out of it." Ramella finished scratching his right forearm and went to work on his shoulder. "That way I could build a little more profit into the action, so I was happy to do it."

"You're currently serving time for possessing and distributing narcotics," Bloodworth said. "Did you start by offering drugs to the guys on your high school team?"

Ramella's lawyer shoved his briefcase between his client and the microphone and said, "I'll have to advise my client not to answer that question."

Ramella deflected the briefcase and said into the microphone, "I can tell you I started using hard drugs in my junior year, and my source was the woman Coach Lammers set me up with to get steroids."

"And did you continue with that contact after you graduated from high school?"

"For hard drugs, yes. After I graduated, though, I turned the steroid business over to the manager that followed me."

"And that was?"

"Hollis Theiro. He was a sophomore when I was a senior. I trained him and hooked him up with my contact."

"And Mr. Lammers was aware of this business transfer?"

"He suggested it. Asked me to take care of it."

"To your knowledge, did Mr. Lammers ever discuss his

team's steroid use with Mr. Theiro?"

"Not to my knowledge. Like I said, he was pretty clear about wanting me to take care of it myself."

"I see." Bloodworth looked at the clock at the back of the hearing room. "That's about all we have time for today. Are there any other questions for Mr. Ramella?" After a brief pause, he said. "Hearing none, the witness is excused. Thank you for your cooperation, Mr. Ramella."

"My pleasure," Ramella said. "Appreciate the change of scenery."

"Then you're welcome to come back tomorrow." Bloodworth looked over the remaining audience and said, "This committee will adjourn until tomorrow at ten A.M. At that time I'd like to recall Mr. Lammers in an effort to clear up some of the discrepancies between his testimony and that of the last witness."

Keaton pocketed his notebook and stood up.

Liz stood up with him and took his arm. "That Lammers is a first-class asshole. I'm glad you sicced Bloodworth on him. You did good, Lloyd."

Davy remained seated. "Coach knows that was a photo of my back on the screen. I'll be lucky to make the team next year, let alone play shortstop."

"Don't be silly," Keaton said. "There's not a chance in hell Lammers will be your coach next year. Bloodworth's already prepping him for a perjury charge. By the time this committee is finished with Lammers, he'll be lucky to stay out of jail."

"Then who will coach the team?" Davy asked.

"I'm not sure," Keaton said. "But I know an out-of-work ex-pitcher who would be perfect for the job."

Chapter Twenty-Five: To Rig the Vig

KEATON'S KORNER

While coach Stu Lammers and his lawyer grasped at straws before the Bloodworth Committee last week, they latched onto a particularly weak one when they argued that steroids were not likely to have led to the death of popular local athlete Buzz Fitzhugh. Their flimsy argument mirrored one put forward by O.J. Simpson's lawyers. To counter the prosecution's argument that Simpson's documented abuse of his wife made him a prime murder suspect, O.J.'s lawyers cited statistics showing that of roughly four million women battered annually, only one in 2,500 had been killed by their abusive husbands or boyfriends.

As Leonard Mlodinow points out in his book, *The Drunkard's Walk,* the relevant statistic is not the probability that a man who abuses his wife or girlfriend will go on to kill her, but rather the probability that a battered woman who has been murdered was killed by her abuser. Roughly ninety percent of the battered women murdered during the year preceding the Simpson trial were killed by their abusers, a fact that O.J.'s lawyers conveniently failed to mention. Stu Lammers and his lawyers cited statistics suggesting that fewer than one in 10,000 student athletes taking steroids go on to commit suicide, and therefore argued that steroids were not likely to have played a role in Buzz Fitzhugh's self-imposed death. This argument is not only slippery, it is irrelevant. The relevant statistics suggest that a high percentage of those student athletes who actually commit suicide have been steroid users.

> The Bloodworth Committee did not challenge Lammers's argument, but they left little doubt about their view of his overall veracity, and it looks as if the local coach will soon be facing a perjury indictment.

City editor Eddie Oliver leaned into Keaton's cubicle and waved a copy of the *New York Times.* "What do I see on the front page of this liberal rag this morning but a batch of photos attributed to our newspaper."

Keaton looked up from his computer. "I take it you're pleased with the recognition?"

"They spelled our name right. But they cribbed most of your story and didn't get around to crediting you until the last paragraph on page sixteen."

"Old news. We still scooped them."

"So how did they get the photos?"

"I'd given them to Bloodworth's committee. They must have passed them along to the *Times.*"

"And to the *Washington Post.* The photos make the story. Especially the ones of Aaron from the Hall of Fame."

"They were easy to get. The librarian at Cooperstown knew my dad."

"And the contemporary pictures. One was your boy Davy. How's he taking the exposure?"

"He doesn't know about the *Post* and *Times,* but his teammates recognized his back from the pictures we ran. He may forgive me before I'm under the ground."

"Give him time. You did the town a real service by exposing Lammers. Opened a lot of eyes." Oliver hooked one thumb under his red suspenders. "What are you working on now?"

"More on umpires."

The editor shook his head. "I don't know, Lloyd. That's getting pretty old. I mean, who really cares whether one umpire rings up fifteen strikeouts a game while another only logs eleven? Nobody but gamblers."

"Lots of gamblers out there."

"None in here, though, I hope."

Keaton raised both hands, palms outward. "I'm clean, boss. Haven't placed a bet since breakfast."

"It's not a joking matter, Lloyd."

"What do you want me to say, Eddie? I'm still in Gamblers Anonymous. And even if I weren't, my betting never affected my work."

"Wake up, Lloyd. It affected your whole life."

"The umpiring columns interest me. And we've gotten some good feedback from readers."

Oliver ran his thumb up under his suspender and let it snap back into place. "Well, I'd like you to shelve those columns for a little while. The majors are into their playoffs now. That's what local readers want to hear about."

"The Indians got knocked out in the first round. That sort of kills the local angle."

"But the Reds are still in it. They're just down the road, with the Giants coming in for three games. Why don't you drive on down, give our readers a taste of your caustic but insightful humor." Oliver checked his watch. "Lots of time before the first pitch. Drive on down, have a nice dinner on the *Herald,* and you should still be able to watch batting practice."

Keaton switched off his computer. "Since you put it that way, how can I refuse?"

Sitting in the press box at the Great American Ballpark in Cincinnati, Keaton wondered why he hadn't beaten down Eddie Oliver's door to insist on covering these games. It was the National League Championship Series, right here in Ohio, for Christ's sake, and the Reds hadn't been to the World Series since they upset the A's in 1990.

The Giants and the Reds had split the first two games of the best-of-seven series in San Francisco, with Jerry Neyer outdueling the Reds' fireballing youngster, Arturo Napoles, in the first game and the Reds landing on five Giants pitchers for ten runs in the second game.

Just before the National Anthem, the public address announcer listed the umpiring assignments for the game. Paul Cote, with his tight strike zone, was behind the plate, and Larry Bradshaw was umpiring at second.

Bradshaw's second-base assignment meant that he would be behind the plate for the fifth game of the series on Friday, two days from today. Keaton's mouth suddenly felt as if he'd been licking sandpaper. He stared at the screen of his laptop. The pitching matchup for the fifth game would be a repeat of the first, with Neyer going against the youngster. And Bradshaw would be calling balls and strikes.

It was exactly the kind of matchup that he and Dave Bowers had preyed on for over a year. The same matchup that had financed Bowers's new house. And the matchup that had done them both in less than two months ago. And left Bowers at the bottom of his own elevator shaft.

Someone was tugging at Keaton's shoulders. He looked up to see Bill Kiesling of the *Cincinnati Enquirer* jerking his head upward as a signal for Keaton to stand. The singer holding a hand microphone at home plate was already well into the National Anthem, climbing the scales on the rocket's red glare.

Keaton straightened his body and stood at attention, but his mind wasn't on the anthem. He looked down at Larry Bradshaw standing to the right of second base, facing the center field flag with his cap held over his heart. If Bradshaw were honest, his umpiring tendencies would make Friday the time to bet the farm on Neyer.

If the umpire was on the take, though, the game could go either way, depending on how the bets came across the counter in East Wheeling. Keaton felt like a player who'd just been dealt two kings in a game of Texas Hold-'Em but was beginning to suspect that the guy across the table was holding two aces. The sensible thing would be to fold his hand, but he'd never been able to bring himself to muck a pair of kings.

The anthem singer came down hard on "The home of the brave," and the plate umpire called "Play ball!" Keaton sat down. Why was he obsessing about gambling, anyhow? He shouldn't be sitting in on the deal, let alone worrying how to play his cards. He had no business gambling, even if he knew for sure whether Bradshaw was clean or dirty.

On the field, the game quickly turned into a seesaw contest. First the Reds went up by two runs, then the Giants were on top by one. Keaton was so busy trying to work out his betting options that he could barely concentrate on the back-and-forth lead changes. If Bradshaw was clean, there would be no questions about a betting strategy for game five. If he was dirty, though, a lot would depend on the size and direction of the bets handled by East Wheeling. The playoffs would attract a lot of money, so the payoff for rigging the game could be huge. Most of the money taken in by the East Wheeling book would probably be on Cincinnati, since the Reds were nearby and popular, and their games were broadcast throughout most of West Virginia.

In the game he was half watching, the Giants took a one-run lead into the bottom of the ninth, but lost when the Reds' second baseman homered with a runner on second. While the Reds mobbed their hero and the crowd was still celebrating, Keaton closed his laptop and stood up. He knew how to play his hand. He didn't have to fold it. Not just yet. First, he'd try to run a bluff.

On the way home from the game, Keaton called his friend Mike Brown in Las Vegas. It was still early in Vegas. It was always early in Vegas. At least, that was what the casino owners wanted you to think, and there were no clocks or windows in their gambling houses to suggest otherwise.

The first thing Brown asked was, "How's David?"

"Still comatose," Keaton said.

After an audible sigh, Brown said, "Tough. Still think it was the East Wheeling mob that did him in?"

"Can't be sure, but it looks that way. I'd like you to help me get back at them."

"Can I do it without experiencing a two-story drop?"

"I think so. Your sports book must handle at least ten times East Wheeling's take, right?"

"At least. And we're legit."

"So if you wanted to, you could lay off enough of your bets on one side or the other of a game to sink their operation, right?"

"Only if we were smart enough to lay off bets on the winning team. And only if they didn't limit their damage by laying some of our bets off on somebody else."

"I'm looking at Friday's Giants/Reds game."

"Neyer against Napoles."

"With Bradshaw behind the plate."

"Normally, that would give Neyer an edge. But you think East Wheeling has Bradshaw in their pocket?"

"I think it's possible. But I think I might be able to fix that."

"The line on Friday's game is pretty close to even. Let's see what we've taken in so far."

The phone went silent while Brown checked his computer. Keaton stopped for a traffic light and drummed his fingers on the steering wheel, waiting.

Brown's voice resurfaced on Keaton's speaker. "Bets here are running about two-to-one in favor of the Giants. But we're a lot closer to San Francisco than to Cincinnati."

"So it wouldn't hurt you to lay a few of those Giants bets off on somebody else?"

"Probably be a good idea."

"And what's a small trickle to you could flood out East Wheeling."

"Like I said, only if we win our laid-off bets. And only if they don't lay our bets off on somebody else."

"I don't think they'll lay them off. They haven't in the past."

"And they've won."

"In the past."

"You think because they've pocketed Bradshaw."

"But I think I can fix that."

"And if you can't?"

"You're not much worse off. You'd lose those bets anyhow. You'll just lose a little of the vig on the bets you lay off."

"But it's for a good cause."

"The best. If it works, you'll help to rid the Ohio Valley of the scourge of illegal gambling."

"And eliminate a competitor."

Keaton smiled. "There's that too, of course."

"We'd have to use several fronts so East Wheeling won't know where the money is coming from. But we've done that before."

"Then you're in?"

"You make it sound like our civic duty."

"Oh, it is. With a little dollop of revenge to spice things up."

"Payback's good too. Maybe even better than civic duty."

By the time Keaton arrived home, it was much too late to call Representative Bloodworth, so he phoned from home the first thing the next morning, and the congressman's secretary put his call through immediately.

"Well, Mr. Keaton," the congressman said, "If you're calling to solicit my appreciation for suggesting that I refocus my committee on steroid abuse at the amateur level, let me assure you that you've certainly earned it."

"Yes, I thought the hearings went quite well."

"And the press coverage was astonishing. There were your stories, of course, but the *New York Times* and *Washington Post* gave us front-page coverage. I have to say it was your before-and-after photos that made the story play nationally."

"I saw those stories."

"And the response has been equally astonishing. We've gotten requests from over eighty cities asking us to look into steroid use in their communities, and the letters are still coming in."

"So you'll have no problem keeping busy in the immediate future."

"That's true. But I have a feeling you didn't call to inquire about my future plans."

"No, Congressman. I need a favor."

"And would this favor be tied to your knowledge of certain thin circumstantial threads?"

"It could be. Or you could think of it as a 'thank you' for all the good press your most recent hearing generated."

"And just what is the favor?"

"I'd like you to make a public announcement of your committee's next target."

"I think my committee is likely to be quite busy in the foreseeable future responding to requests for local investigations into steroid abuse."

"I'm not suggesting you abandon those. I'd just like you to announce your next target. It's an easy job. All it requires is a timely press release."

"And what do you see as the committee's next target?"

"Gambling in professional baseball."

There was a brief silence on the other end of the line. Then the congressman said, "That's a pretty hot topic. Do you have evidence we should be pursuing right away?"

"Nothing that would stand up in court. In fact, I'm hoping that your announcement will discourage gambling in certain quarters."

"So this investigation I'm to announce may never happen?"

"Think of it as a campaign promise, Congressman."

"I know what I expect to get from my campaign promises. Can you be more specific about what you hope to gain from this announcement?"

"Not now, no."

"Eventually?"

"Maybe. Maybe not."

"I see. And when should this announcement appear?"

"Tomorrow morning's newspapers. No later."

"That doesn't give me much time."

"It doesn't have to be a long announcement. It would help, though, if you mention that you've gained access to some inside sources."

"And have I?"

"Just me, I'm afraid."

"I see." The line went silent again and Keaton could hear Bloodworth conversing in muffled tones with someone.

The congressman came back on the line. "I'll do it. But only because your last suggestion for my committee turned out so well. And Mr. Keaton . . ."

"Yes, Congressman?"

"Try not to make a habit of these calls. By my calculations, our account is about even."

Keaton couldn't wait to fill David Bowers in on the set-up. He stopped by his friend's house on his way to the newspaper. The daytime caregiver was late, and Judy had delayed her own trip to the office waiting for her.

He stood at the foot of Bowers's bed, making hand gestures that he knew his friend couldn't see to accompany words that he hoped could be heard.

"We've got the perfect set-up tomorrow night. Neyer against a young fireballer with Bradshaw behind the plate. I've got Las Vegas betting more money on the Giants than East Wheeling can handle. But if Little Bill runs true to form, East Wheeling won't lay anything off."

Keaton grabbed the rail at the foot of the bed and leaned over it. "The problem, of course, is Bradshaw. I still don't know for sure whether he's bent or not, but I've figured a way around that. I've got Congressman Bloodworth announcing a gambling probe, and I'll see Bradshaw after tonight's game to make sure he understands just what that could mean to him.

"If Bradshaw falls for my bluff and calls his normal game, the odds tilt in favor of the Giants, and a Giant win could sink East Wheeling. But even if the Reds win, we're not badly hurt. East Wheeling gets a big payday, and Las Vegas loses a little vig on the bets they laid off."

Keaton's excitement rattled the bed railing, but Bowers remained impassive. "I'm thinking Bradshaw will be too spooked to try anything funny, so the odds will favor the Giants. Makes me want to get a bet down myself."

"Why don't you put one down for me?" Judy had been standing behind him, listening.

Keaton turned. "I don't think you want to do that. Any money you give East Wheeling, they'll just take on account for that big bet David never covered."

"Then let me give you the money to bet in your name. You'll do that for me, won't you? We can settle up after you win."

"I'm not sure that's wise, Judy."

"Why not? You make it sound like a sure thing."

"There's no such thing as a sure thing. Bradshaw may not take the bluff. Or East Wheeling may have their hooks too deep into him. Or Neyer may just have an off day."

"But if East Wheeling loses they'll go down. It's payback for what they did to David."

"We're not sure they did anything to David. And if the Giants win, East Wheeling will go down whether or not we bet anything. That's the beauty of this deal. It's virtually risk-free."

"They must be the ones who hurt David. And I like the idea of being one of the straws that breaks their back."

Keaton shook his head. "I don't know. Right now we've got nothing at risk."

Judy nodded toward her husband's bed. "If David were awake, he'd bet. Wouldn't he?"

Keaton shrugged. "Of course."

"That settles it then. I'll get a cashier's check issued in your name. Say for fifty thousand dollars?"

"Fifty thousand is way too much. They'll know it's not coming from me."

"What's the most you ever bet with them?"

Keaton thought about the bet that had cost him his car and his marriage. "Twenty grand."

"Then twenty grand it is. What's the matter? Don't you want to rub their faces in it?"

"There are no guarantees here. A lot can go wrong."

"That's what makes it gambling. It's what David lived for. He had some Latin phrase for it. You must feel it too."

"*Alea ludo ergo sum.* I gamble, therefore I am."

"That's it. You'll do it then? Take my check. I know you want to. Think of it as David's money."

"All right." Keaton told himself he wasn't backsliding if it wasn't his money. "I'll do it, but we need to get the money quickly. I'll have to get to East Wheeling and back and still be in Cincinnati for tonight's first pitch."

Keaton was used to worrying and second-guessing himself on the two-hour drive to East Wheeling, but in the past it had been the betting itself that occupied his mind. This time his concern was different. Not more than two months ago, his life had been threatened, presumably by someone from East Wheeling. But that was when he'd been sniffing around OgrowSport's steroid supply. Now that OgrowSport's doors were closed, they'd have no reason to threaten him. Except maybe for revenge. But that didn't make sense. They couldn't be sure he'd helped to topple OgrowSport, and he'd come bearing gifts. Twenty thousand dollars' worth. Their best revenge would be to take his money.

Listen to him. His money. It wasn't his money. It was Judy's. And David's. But East Wheeling wouldn't know that. And it made him feel as if he had a piece of the action. He'd missed that feeling lately.

Keaton felt the same sense of anticipation and release he always felt as he crossed the Ohio River into West Virginia and saw the red brick warehouse that contained Little Bill's gambling operation. It didn't matter that he was more of a voyeur in this venture, watching someone else's bet. He wondered if alcoholics got the same jolt out of drinking near beer, or smokers from nicotine patches.

As Keaton climbed the stairs to the card rooms and sports books, the *chink-chink-chink* of the downstairs slot machines faded and was replaced by the sharp rasp of Little Bill Ellison's breathing. Ellison was in his usual spot, tied to a red oxygen canister and commanding two barstools in front of a tote board listing the odds on the day's baseball games. Bull Harding stood beside him.

When they saw Keaton approaching, Harding backed away

from Ellison like a gunfighter in a grade B western drawing fire away from his boss and clearing the path to his holster.

"Well, look who's here," Ellison said in his throaty rasp. "Fixin' to break me again?"

Keaton nodded. "Hope to."

"Didn't quite break me last time. Still, I imagine there's always hope."

"Guess that's what keeps me coming back," Keaton said without taking his eyes off Harding.

"And what keeps me in business," Ellison rasped. "Step aside, Bull, you're blocking this man's path to the cashier's window."

Keaton fumbled in his pocket and slid his cashier's check through the slot in the teller's window.

The teller's hand moved under his cash drawer and a light went on over his window. "I'm sorry, sir. I need to get approval for a wager this large."

Bull Harding appeared at Keaton's side and the teller handed him the check. Harding examined it and forced his lips into a tight smile. "Pretty big bet for you, isn't it, Scribe? I'd heard that the newspaper business had fallen on hard times."

When Keaton didn't answer, Harding laid the check on the teller's ledge and scribbled his initials on it. "Mr. Keaton's money is always good here."

Harding shoved the check back through the teller's window. "Let me guess. You're putting this down on the Giants tomorrow night, with Neyer pitching and that tight-ass umpire behind the plate. Didn't you learn your lesson last time out?"

"Always up for more education."

"Always glad to provide it. We've been getting a lot of play on that game. Most of it on the Giants. Pretty surprising, don't you think, what with Ohio just across the river?"

"It's differences in opinions that make for horse races." Keaton took his slip from the teller and nodded at the tote board. "And sports books."

"Ain't that just God's own truth, though," Ellison said.

As Keaton started to leave, Harding blocked his way. "Stay for a little poker, Scribe?"

"No thanks. Got to get to Cincy in time for tonight's game."

"Of course. Going to put a bet down on it?"

Keaton shook his head. "Hadn't planned to."

Harding opened his sport coat and tapped his wallet. "How about a little bet between friends. Give you a rooting interest tonight."

Keaton hesitated. Given the bet he'd just made, he could hardly use Gamblers Anonymous as an excuse.

Harding was still blocking his way. "Say ten dollars, even money, between friends. You pick the team."

Keaton glanced up at the tote board. The Reds were a slight favorite. "All right, you're on. I'll take the Reds."

"Good choice." Harding stepped aside to let Keaton leave. "Means I'll see you again. One way or the other."

Chapter Twenty-Six: Poking the Hornet's Next

KEATON'S KORNER

Sources tell me the Bloodworth Committee may eventually shift its focus from steroid abuse to gambling. I have to applaud this possibility. Gambling by players, managers, and officials has always been a greater threat to the integrity of the game than drug abuse. Of the forty-two individuals who have been banned from baseball since it was established as a professional sport, thirty have been banished for offenses related to gambling.

Baseball gambling neither started nor stopped with the Black Sox Scandal of 1919, the most memorable stain on the game. As early as 1877, four members of the Louisville Grays were banned for taking bribes to throw games. To show how seriously the commissioner's office views simple association with gamblers, Hall of Famers Mickey Mantle and Willie Mays were banned merely for taking post-retirement jobs as greeters at an Atlantic City casino. (They were eventually reinstated, but no longer greeted arriving gamblers.)

More recently, Pete Rose, baseball's all-time hit leader, was banned for life in 1989 for betting on Major League games when he was manager of the Cincinnati Reds. After denying his involvement with gamblers for fifteen years, he finally admitted that the charges were true in a 2004 autobiography, *My Prison Without Bars.* His banishment still stands, an indication that Major League Baseball justifiably views involvement with gamblers as a far more serious offense than involvement with steroid dealers, which carries a 50-day suspension for a first offense.

Even though he had a ten-dollar bet on the Reds, Keaton couldn't muster a rooting interest in the fourth game of the playoff series. It wasn't as if he'd wanted to make the bet, and, win or lose, the wager guaranteed a future meeting with Bull Harding.

He spent a portion of the game watching Larry Bradshaw umpiring at first base and scratching notes in the margins of his scorecard to remind himself of the points he wanted to make to Bradshaw later in the evening.

The Giants took an early two-to-nothing lead and added to it as the game wore on, winning four to one and tying the series at two games apiece. None of Bradshaw's calls at first base were the least bit controversial, and Keaton picked up his scorecard and laptop as soon as the final out was recorded so that he could beat the umpire back to the Netherland Plaza Hotel.

At the hotel, Keaton took a seat in the center of the lobby and pecked idly at his column, watching the hotel's revolving door over the screen of his laptop. From time to time he'd add a note to the margins of his scorecard. He'd come to think of himself as a master chef about to stir things up with Bradshaw, and his scorecard notes were the recipe for the bouillabaisse of bluff and truth he was preparing.

After Keaton spent forty-five minutes in the lobby, Bradshaw pushed his way through the revolving hotel doors and Keaton raised his hand to wave the umpire over. "Got a couple of minutes to talk?"

"Sure. How about the bar?" Bradshaw led the way to a booth in the same dimly lit corner of the hotel bar where Keaton had interviewed him three weeks earlier.

They both ordered draft beers, and Bradshaw said, "Here we are again, huh?"

Keaton nodded. He set the scorecard with his scribbled reminders on the corner of the table, but found he could barely make out his writing in the dim light.

The waitress came with their drinks and they clinked glasses. Bradshaw took a long pull on his beer. "I've been meaning to thank you for sending me those copies of your columns on umpires. For a while there, I was something of a celebrity. A couple of kids actually asked me for autographs."

Keaton managed a half-hearted laugh. He stared at the scorecard, hoping his eyes would adjust to the dim light.

"Something wrong?" Bradshaw asked.

Keaton took a sip of his beer. "No. Nothing." Forget the notes. He knew what he had to say.

"Need more material for your columns?"

"Not tonight, no. I'm glad you liked them, though, because I don't think you'll be as happy with what I'm going to tell you."

Bradshaw set his glass down carefully, as if he were afraid it might break. "What's that?"

"You know the Bloodworth Committee? They've been investigating baseball and steroids."

"Yeah. They just switched their sights from the majors to amateur ball."

"Well, they're about to switch again. They're going to look at gambling in baseball."

Bradshaw shifted his beer slowly to the side of the table. "I hadn't heard that."

"He'll be announcing it in a couple of days. As soon as he wrings all of the publicity out of his latest hearings."

"And why do you think I'd be unhappy to hear that? What's it got to do with me?"

"I'm coming to that. I told you I'm in Gamblers Anonymous. Bloodworth found out somehow."

"I thought that stuff was supposed to be secret and confidential."

"Welcome to the no-secrets millennium. Bloodworth evidently has the names of some GA members. I haven't exactly kept my membership secret. Anyhow, he summoned me to a private session on Tuesday. First thing he wanted to know was the names of other GA members with baseball connections."

"He's making a list." Bradshaw shrugged. "Or maybe he's just checking it twice."

"Sorry. I can't laugh about it."

"Did you give him any names?"

"You've got to understand. The guy's in a position to wreck my career."

"I don't understand how. Rule Twenty-One on misconduct applies to players, umpires, club officials, and employees. You're none of those."

"Baseball and Bloodworth define 'employee' broadly to include anyone with contacts that are likely to give them inside knowledge. That includes reporters and outside announcers. When ESPN was covering the Reds' first playoff game, their lead announcer quoted the pre-season odds on the team making the World Series at a hundred to one. But then one of his broadcast buddies jumped in to say that 'of course, their job wouldn't let them bet those odds one way or the other.' "

Bradshaw's finger traced the sweat mark his glass had left on the table. "I see. What names did you give Bloodworth?"

"I didn't have much to give. None of the guys in my local meetings have any baseball connections. I did give him two names, though. Guys I knew from other cities. Never mind who."

"And?"

"He didn't seem impressed. I got the feeling he already had the two names. That may be how he got my name."

"I still don't see how any of this affects me."

"I'm getting there. Bloodworth kept browbeating me, trying to get any information I had on baseball betting. He threatened to haul me before his committee publicly. Expose my past history of gambling."

"He can do that?"

"I tell you, he had stuff on me that even I had forgotten. Cancelled checks. Records of bets I'd made that eventually cost me my marriage. He threatened to make all of that public if I didn't give him some bigger fish to fry."

"Wait a minute. You gave him my name?"

"Not exactly."

"What then? Exactly?"

"I told him about those betting patterns we discussed. You know, all those games control pitchers won with you umpiring behind the plate."

Bradshaw raised both hands, palms outward, like a third-base coach holding up a runner. "We went over all that. There were at least two games that didn't fit that neat little pattern."

"That's part of the problem. I happen to know bookies in East Wheeling made killings on those two games."

"Are you saying I'm somehow connected with those killings?"

"I don't know. Hell, I don't want to know. Believe me, with my gambling history, I'm not in a position to criticize anyone."

"So you're not criticizing. But you gave my name to a congressional committee. That's like tossing me into a shark tank and chumming the water."

"I didn't give them your name, exactly. I just told them about the patterns I'd uncovered. And the way they matched up with East Wheeling wins."

"So you didn't throw chum in the tank. The sharks'll have to find their way all by themselves. Thanks a lot."

"You've got to understand. They already had me in the tank."

"Well now we're both there. Why are you telling me all this?"

"Call it a heads-up. You're behind the plate tomorrow. The

pattern is repeating itself. If I were you, I'd be extra careful with my calls."

"Extra careful?" Bradshaw slapped his open palm down on the table. "Is that some sort of code? Are you asking me to make sure the Giants win?"

"Far from it. I'm just telling you that you'd be well advised to call a straight game. If you're straight, that shouldn't be a problem."

"If I'm straight?" Bradshaw jumped to his feet, jarring the table and spilling his beer. Then he seemed to realize he was in public and lowered his voice. "*If* I'm straight? Who the fuck are you to ask if I'm straight? I can't believe this. I can't fucking believe you told Bloodworth your cockamamie theory."

The spilled beer spread across the table. Keaton tried to dam the flow with his scorecard and cocktail napkins. "I'm sorry. As things stand, I didn't think they could prove anything one way or another. Any evidence against you is purely circumstantial."

"Are you crazy? I've seen how those committees operate. They don't need evidence to ruin a guy. All they need to do is point their finger at him."

"I said I was sorry. I wouldn't have told you except, well, the pattern is repeating itself tomorrow, and I thought I owed it to you to tell you what I'd done."

"So you've told me. Thanks a lot. Every close call I make is guaranteed to get someone on the field pissed off at me. And tomorrow there'll be a nationwide TV hookup with stop-motion cameras so that every couch potato in the country can lord it over me if I miss one. Now you're telling me there's somebody in Washington looking over my shoulder as well. All because of your loose mouth. Well fuck you. And your loose mouth."

Bradshaw gave the table an angry shove that collapsed Keaton's napkin dam and stormed out of the bar. With the dam breached, the spilled beer drenched Keaton's lap. He looked up to see the bar patrons staring at him while the bartender studiously applied a towel to the inside of a cocktail glass.

A waitress appeared with a rag and mopped up the spilled beer. Then she asked, "Would you like another drink, sir?"

"No thanks. I'll just wear that last draft home."

The waitress disappeared and Keaton smoothed out the crinkling pages of his soaked scorecard. No point in crying over spilled beer. Except for the beer mess and the public shouting, though, his little scene hadn't gone too badly.

If Bradshaw is honest, Keaton thought, he'll just call his normal game and there's nothing lost here. If he's bent, though, he's got something to think about now. Will he call East Wheeling, or just hope that the Reds manage to win tomorrow without his help? If he does call East Wheeling, they could read tonight's scene as a bluff designed to protect our twenty-thousand-dollar bet. But Bloodworth's announcement of a gambling probe will go nationwide tomorrow. That should be enough to convince them. It may be a bluff, but it's a bluff with all the trimmings.

Keaton patted both sides of his damp scorecard with fresh paper napkins and stood up to leave. No, it didn't hurt to stir things up. It could only help. He held his laptop in front of his damp crotch as he made his way out of the bar. He no longer thought of himself as a master chef stirring up a broth of specific ingredients, though. No, he was more like a kid with a stick poking at a hornet's nest.

Chapter Twenty-Seven: The Numb Thumb

KEATON'S KORNER

My recent column on gambling in baseball generated a record number of reader responses on the subject of Pete Rose. For the most part, the correspondents felt strongly that Rose should be reinstated because (1) he only bet on his own team to win, (2) he has apologized publicly, and (3) he has been seeking help for his gambling addiction.

The fact that Rose only bet on his own team to win is hardly exculpatory. Baseball's Rule 21 forbidding gambling is posted on every clubhouse door, and players are reminded of the penalties every year when spring training begins. It doesn't matter what team a manager bets on. Nor should it. What sort of a message does it send to gamblers if a manager who always bets on his own team fails to place a bet on a particular day? Or when a particular pitcher is on the mound, which was evidently Rose's practice.

Worse, what if a player or manager loses so much to gamblers that they demand certain favors in return for debt forgiveness? This seems to be what happened to the NBA referee charged with rigging the outcome of games. Given baseball's rigid attitude toward betting, a gambling player need not lose heavily to find himself in thrall to gamblers. The threat of exposure, which would lead to banishment, should be sufficient.

As to Rose's apology, his exact words in his autobiography were, "I'm sorry it happened . . ." Just one step up from saying, "I'm sorry I got caught."

> In my view Pete Rose was aware of the penalties for his actions and has no beef with baseball over his banishment. The punishment had been meted out before, in 1943, to two Philadelphia Phillies owners who "only bet on their own team." Lest I seem to be coming down too hard on an addicted gambler, let me say that I myself am a member of Gamblers Anonymous and have up-close and personal experience with the havoc gambling can bring into one's life.

The next morning's newspaper carried a press release from Congressman Bloodworth's office announcing that the next target of his congressional committee would be gambling in baseball. The Congressman intimated that his committee had uncovered inside sources with firsthand knowledge of illegal gambling among professional players and officials. No timetable was set for the investigation, which would be initiated as soon as the committee completed its current hearings on the use of steroids in amateur sports.

It wasn't exactly front-page news, but the story was prominently displayed on the sports pages of the *Menckenburg Herald* and the *Cincinnati Enquirer.* The East Wheeling crowd probably got most of their news from the sports pages, so they weren't likely to miss it. And after last night's conversation, Larry Bradshaw would be looking for it. Bloodworth's announcement added just the right note of authenticity to the story Keaton had fed him.

If Bradshaw was dirty, and if he'd contacted East Wheeling about last night's conversation, the Bloodworth article might scare them into laying some of their Giants' bets off onto other bookmakers. He waited as long as he could and then called Mike Brown at 8:30 A.M. Las Vegas time. Mike reported that there was no indication that East Wheeling was laying off any of the Giants money he'd loaded onto them.

"At least they haven't come to us," Mike said, "and we've always been their first line of defense against an unbalanced betting line."

So they still think they have an edge, Keaton thought. And that edge most likely was the home-plate umpire. Maybe Bradshaw hadn't told them about last night's conversation. Would he still try to tilt the game to the Reds after their conversation and Bloodworth's announcement?

Keaton spent an hour polishing his next column and then took a break. He stared at his phone, wondering if he should call Vegas for an update, when it rang of its own accord. He picked up the receiver and heard Liz's voice.

"Lloyd, do you have a minute?"

She never announced her name. She never had to. Ever since their divorce, though, she always asked if he had time to talk, as if she might be intruding. She never was.

"I sat on the couch and watched last night's game with Davy," she said. "It was pretty exciting in the living room. It must have been even more exciting at the park."

"It was," he said, although his mind had been occupied by Bradshaw and tonight's game.

"Of course, it's too bad the Reds lost, but that just ties the series. You'll be there tonight, won't you?"

"Wouldn't miss it."

"Why don't you take Davy? He'd love to go, but he won't ask you to take him."

"I haven't been able to reach him since those steroid pictures showed up in the *Herald.*"

"This would be a good time to change that."

"Doesn't he have school? I need to leave pretty early."

"School's out at three, but he has study hall at two-fifteen. I'm sure he could get out of that if he mentioned he had a date with his dad in the press box."

"I don't know, Liz. The press box has been pretty full the last two games. It might be tough to fit a visitor in."

"He doesn't have to sit in the press box. Couldn't you get your hands on a comped ticket? I know he'd love to go."

"Worst case, I suppose I could come up with a scalped ticket."

There was a pause at the other end of the line. "Sounds like you might not want to take him."

"No. I've got a lot on my mind, is all. I might not be very good company."

"Is everything all right? I remember other times when you didn't want us at your games."

"No. It's nothing like that. I'd love to take Davy along. I'll pick him up at school. Can you arrange to have him sprung early?"

"I'll take care of it. I'm glad everything's all right. I know the two of you will enjoy the game. I had a lot of fun last night just watching Davy. Especially when the Giants had men in scoring position. He gets so involved. Like someone else I know."

Davy was ready at two-fifteen, and they drove in silence for a short time before he said, "Think the Reds'll win?"

Keaton smiled. "I know you'd like that, but my money's on the Giants."

"You mean you've got a bet down?"

"It's only an expression. I think Neyer will be tough tonight."

"What about Napoles?"

"He's just a little too wild for his own good. He'll be unbeatable when he learns to control all his pitches, but he's not there yet."

"So you'd bet on the Giants?"

"If I were to bet. But you know I can't do that." Time to steer the conversation away from betting. "How's school?"

"Okay. Now they're checking everybody on the football team for steroids. You really stirred up something."

"It needed stirring up. What about baseball? Heard anything about a replacement for Coach Lammers?"

"No. It's still a while before the season starts."

"What about Dale Loren?"

"As a coach? He's got the same problem as Coach Lammers. Steroids."

"What makes you say that?"

"He was up before the same committee as Lammers."

"But he was innocent."

"The guys figure there must have been some truth to the charges. He admitted he gave Sammy Tancredi something. And Sammy tested positive for steroids."

"But the Bloodworth Committee dropped all the charges against him."

"Wasn't that kind of like a plea bargain though?"

"No. That was more like correcting a mistake that should never have happened."

"I like Mr. Loren. And I know he's your friend. But when people think of him, they think of steroids. The way things are in school now, I just don't think they'll ever hire him."

"That's a shame."

They arrived at the Great American Ballpark two hours before game time. Fans were just beginning to queue up at the turnstiles and the scalpers were out in force. Keaton negotiated a seat for Davy along the first-base line at twice the face value of the ticket. As they passed through the turnstile, Keaton said, "We'll get you settled in your seat, and I'll come get you if there's room in the press box."

"That's okay, Dad. I'll be fine by myself."

"No. I'd like to watch the game with you. I just don't know how many seats will be claimed by other reporters." Actually, he knew that reporters from the *Cleveland Plain Dealer* and *Cincinnati Enquirer* had brought several guests to the press box the night before, and he hated to admit that the *Herald* was lower in the pecking order.

Lines hadn't yet formed at the concession stands, and the concessionaires were filling popcorn bags and heating hot dogs in anticipation of the coming crowds.

"How about a hot dog?" Keaton said.

"Great."

Keaton was pressing down on the mustard dispenser and watching Davy spoon relish onto a bun when he felt a hand squeezing his shoulder. He turned his head to see Bull Harding.

Harding kept the pressure on Keaton's shoulder. "Surprised to see you here in the stands. Sort of expected you'd be up in the press box."

"I'm on my way there."

Harding released his grip on Keaton's shoulder. "This must be your boy." He held out his hand to Davy. "So you're the young shortstop. I've heard good things about you."

After shaking Davy's hand, Harding turned to Keaton. "Glad I ran into you. About that bet on last night's game. Why don't we just let it ride tonight?"

Davy looked at his father. "Bet?"

"It was only ten dollars," Keaton said.

"Your dad had the Reds and lost." Harding shot the cuffs on his black pinstriped shirt so that maroon cuff links poked beyond the sleeves of his black blazer. "What do you say, Scribe? Let the bet ride? Double or nothing. Pick either team."

Harding's bulk pressed Keaton up against the condiment stand. He felt trapped. "What do you say, Davy?" Keaton asked. "Pick a team."

"Go with the Reds," Davy said.

Harding made a show of shaking hands with Keaton. "That

means you're a winner either way." He took a step backward, pulling Keaton with him. "Course, you're a loser either way, too. Except you've got a lot more to lose if the Reds win."

Harding finally released Keaton's hand. "See you later. To settle up."

"What did he mean, 'You've got a lot more to lose'?" Davy asked as Harding blended into the milling crowd. "Are you really betting again?"

"It's complicated."

"You are. You're betting again."

"I placed a bet for a friend. It wasn't my money."

"Why couldn't your friend place his own bet?"

"I told you, it's complicated. Trust me on this."

"Yeah, like you trusted me about steroids."

"Trust had nothing to do with it. We knew you were using steroids. We found them in your room."

"And it sure looks like you're gambling. Big time." Davy nodded toward Keaton's hot dog. "You got mustard all over your hand when that guy showed up."

Larry Bradshaw's call of "Play ball" rang out while the singer at home plate was still holding the final note of the National Anthem. Bradshaw dusted off home plate as the singer beat a retreat to the Reds' dugout and the spectators settled back into their seats.

From his seat in the press box, Keaton saw that one member of the crowd remained standing long after the anthem ended and everyone else was seated. A bulky figure in his black blazer, Bull Harding stood in the front row directly behind home plate, as much to be seen as to see.

Bradshaw finished dusting off the plate and put the whisk broom back in his pocket. The umpire gave no sign that he noticed Harding, but the gambler remained standing until

Bradshaw had turned his back and taken his position behind the squatting catcher to await the first pitch.

The first pitch from the Reds' young pitcher, Arturo Napoles, was a fastball that caught the outside corner of the plate. Bradshaw's right fist went up to signal a strike, and the hometown crowd chanted "Turo, Turo, Turo."

Napoles sent the Giants down one-two-three in the top of the first, striking out two batters. Keaton watched the overhead TV monitor to see if Bradshaw appeared to be calling more strikes than the pitcher was earning, but that didn't seem to be the case. Bradshaw did appear to be more deliberate with his calls than Keaton remembered from past games, often hesitating a beat before raising his right hand to indicate a strike.

Neyer duplicated Napoles's performance in the bottom of the first, retiring all three of the Reds hitters he faced. The Giants' pitcher worked both sides of the plate expertly, and Keaton was relieved to see that Bradshaw appeared to give him the benefit of the doubt on close calls, even if the umpire seemed a little slow to make up his mind.

Napoles walked the Giants' clean-up hitter to start the second inning, but left him stranded on first by shutting down the hitters behind him. Neyer continued to baffle the Reds, getting two ground-outs and a strikeout to end the inning.

Bradshaw's "Strike three" call to end the second inning came so late that a fan shouted, "Make up your mind, blue, you've only got two choices."

As the Reds took the field for the start of the third inning, Bill Kiesling of the *Cincinnati Enquirer,* who was sitting on Keaton's right, observed, "I don't remember Bradshaw being so slow with his calls."

Farther down the row, other reporters chimed in with comments: "Numb thumb" and "Playoff jitters."

"If he calls them any slower, he'll be one pitch behind,"

Keaton said.

It was probably a good sign that Bradshaw was working more slowly than usual, Keaton thought. Maybe the threat of a Bloodworth inquiry had struck fear into his heart. On the other hand, he seemed to be giving Napoles the same leeway on close calls he was giving Neyer, which would negate any advantage they'd hoped to get from the pitching matchup.

In the bottom of the fourth inning, the Reds' leadoff hitter blooped a broken-bat hit over the first baseman that landed on the foul line and spun crazily off toward the right-field stands. The batter wound up on second base with a double, was bunted to third, and came home on a sacrifice fly.

Keaton entered the run on his scorecard and shook his head. Down one to nothing on a fluke hit and a couple of sacrifices. Nothing Neyer or the umpire could do to control that. Just dumb luck. He wondered whether anyone could hope to control the outcome of a baseball game just by bribing one umpire. You probably needed to pay off at least half a team to be sure of an outcome. The way Rothstein did with the Black Sox in 1919. And even that fix had come close to unraveling.

The Giants tried to tie the score in the top of the fifth inning. Steve Brewer lined a clean double into the right-field gap and the next hitter singled sharply to left field, sending Brewer sprinting around third toward home plate. The left fielder caught the ball cleanly and threw it on one hop to the catcher, who was straddling home plate. Brewer slammed into the catcher and knocked him backward just as he took the throw and applied the tag.

When the TV announcer excitedly called Brewer safe, Keaton leapt to his feet and pumped his fist. But Bradshaw checked to see that the catcher had held onto the ball and belatedly raised his fist in an out call.

Keaton slumped back into his chair and "Shit," loudly enough to be heard throughout the press box.

"Who are you rooting for anyhow?" the *Enquirer*'s Kiesling asked. "That was a hometown call."

"There's no rooting in the press box," Keaton said.

"And there's no fucking in whorehouses," a *Plain Dealer* stringer answered.

The TV replays were far from conclusive, but it appeared that Bradshaw might have blown the call. The play was very close, but Brewer's foot seemed to land on home plate an instant before the catcher swung his glove into the runner's midsection.

"Bang-bang play," Kiesling said, watching the replay on the monitor. "Could have gone either way."

"Runner should have slid," the *Plain Dealer* stringer said. "He's safe if he slides."

No one watching the monitor suggested that Bradshaw had blown the call, and the play was so close that Keaton wouldn't ordinarily have faulted the umpire. But one of the replay angles showed Bull Harding smiling smugly in his seat behind home plate.

The inning ended with the Reds still ahead one to nothing. Keaton borrowed an extra press pass from the *Plain Dealer* stringer and went down into the stands to see Davy. He found his son shucking peanuts in his aisle seat down the first-base line and explained that he'd made arrangements for him to come up to the press box.

"You kidding, Dad? The Reds are up one-zip. Having my butt in this seat is lucky for them."

Keaton smiled. He knew the feeling. "Well, here's a press pass. Come up if the luck wears out."

The score stayed one to nothing until the top of the eighth, when the young Reds pitcher walked the Giants' lead-off hitter on four pitches that were just wide of the plate.

The kid seems to be losing a little of his command, Keaton

thought. Or maybe Bradshaw has reverted to form. He no longer seemed to be hesitating with his calls.

Napoles barely missed the plate with his first two pitches to the next hitter, Steve Brewer. The chants of "Turo, Turo, Turo" had stopped, replaced by a concerned murmuring.

Frustrated by his inability to get a strike call on the corners of the plate, the young pitcher threw a fastball that cut into the heart of the strike zone. Brewer turned on it, sending it deep into the center field bleachers and putting the Giants up two to one.

Keaton pounded the table so hard his laptop bounced, but the rest of the press box was as quiet as the crowd in the stands.

The Reds' manager trudged to the mound and took the ball from Napoles, who left the field to a standing ovation. By the time the left-handed relief pitcher had finished his warm-up tosses, Davy appeared at the door to the press room. "Guess my seat wasn't as lucky as I thought."

"Speaking for the *Enquirer,* you can only come in if you're rooting for the Reds," Kiesling said. "Your dad's already one more Giant sympathizer than we can tolerate here."

Davy grinned. "I qualify."

Kiesling made a ceremony of opening a folding chair. "Then, on behalf of the entire Ohio press corps, I welcome you."

The Cincinnati reliever shut down the Giants for the remainder of the half-inning, and the Giants' manager replaced Neyer with a reliever in the bottom of the eighth. With two new pitchers, all that was left of the starting combination Keaton had been counting on was Bradshaw, and he still wasn't sure that the umpire could be trusted to call a straight game. Still, the starting combination had resulted in a one-run Giants lead. Keaton hoped that the Giants' relief pitching could get six more outs before the Reds erased that lead.

The new Giants' pitcher gave Keaton several anxious moments in the bottom of the eighth, giving up a single and hitting a batter before getting a double-play grounder and striking out a batter for the third out.

It was Davy's turn to be anxious in the top of the ninth, as the Giants' lead-off hitter doubled and advanced to third on an infield out. Davy chewed on the end of a pencil and Kiesling drummed his fingers on his laptop while the Reds brought in a new relief pitcher. The new pitcher's first two offerings didn't come anywhere near the plate, but he recovered and ran the count to three and two.

The batter fouled off three consecutive three-and-two pitches, each of which threatened the life of the pencil in Davy's mouth, before striking out on a change-up.

As if he'd decided the previous hitter required too much work, the Reds' reliever struck out the next Giants' hitter on three straight pitches, stranding the runner on third and eliciting a mixture of sighs and applause from the press box.

Keaton thought the third strike Bradshaw called to end the inning had sailed wide of the plate, but the TV crew didn't risk distracting the cheering crowd with a replay that might have confirmed his judgment.

The Giants' closer had set the Reds down in order in the ninth inning on the previous night. Tonight, though, he dug himself a hole immediately, walking the first two batters he faced.

Oh, God, Keaton thought each time Bradshaw lifted his left hand to signal a ball. This is it. This is where the umpire gives the game away to the Reds. Just walk the runners around the bases. How could I have let Judy bet so much when I suspected Bradshaw might be bent?

The next batter sacrificed the runners to second and third on the first pitch he saw. Before the next Reds' hitter stepped into the batter's box, the Giants' manager strode to the pitcher's mound for a conference.

"They're deciding whether to walk York intentionally to set up the double play," Kiesling said.

Don't do it, Keaton thought. It's a bad play. Loading the bases will take away the pitcher's margin for error. And the way Bradshaw has been shrinking the strike zone and calling balls this inning, you're much more likely to get another walk that will tie the game than a double play to end the inning.

Bradshaw walked to the mound, broke up the conference, and then went back to his position behind the plate. As the Giants' manager returned to the dugout, he stopped on the foul line and held up four fingers, signaling for an intentional walk.

"No!" Keaton said. "No!" All the heads in the press box turned in his direction.

Davy kept his eyes on his father. "It's not a bad move, Dad."

"It is today." Keaton stood and turned his back on the diamond while the pitcher issued four perfunctory balls to York to load the bases. He couldn't watch. At least, he couldn't sit and watch. Instead of returning to his seat, he fidgeted behind Davy's chair as the next Reds' batter came to the plate.

Bradshaw called the Giant pitcher's first offering a ball. Just stand there with the bat on your shoulder, Keaton thought. The umpire will find a way to walk you.

Not being privy to Keaton's thoughts, the hitter lifted the bat from his shoulder, swung at the second pitch, and topped a slow roller down the third-base line.

The third baseman charged in, barehanded the ball, and threw it to the catcher just in time to force out the lead runner at home plate.

Davy's shoulders slumped as Bradshaw's thumb shot up to signal the out at home plate. No way to finagle that call, Keaton thought. The bases were still loaded, but now there were two outs.

One more out to go, but the Reds' clean-up hitter was at the plate. It doesn't really matter who's at the plate, Keaton thought. All he has to do is take the requisite number of balls and the score will be tied.

For the first two pitches, it appeared that at least one Reds' hitter agreed with Keaton's diagnosis. He watched the pitches go by with the bat on his shoulder, and Bradshaw called them both balls. Keaton thought the second pitch was close enough to have been a strike, but in his current frame of mind any close pitch was going to look like a strike to him, just as it would look like a ball to Davy.

The Reds' batter swung at the third pitch and lined a change-up into the stands in foul territory. The Giants' pitcher came back with another change-up that appeared to catch the outside corner of the plate. Bradshaw stared at the corner for a brief instant, and then raised his right hand to signal strike two.

First strike he's called this half inning, Keaton thought. Maybe there's hope for us after all.

The next pitch broke just a little farther outside and Bradshaw called it a ball. Three and two, two men out. The runners will be off with the pitch, Keaton thought, so a single will almost certainly bring in two runs to win the game. A walk will tie the score and leave the bases loaded.

The pitcher stepped off the mound, picked up the resin bag, juggled it, and wiped his pitching hand on his uniform pants. Keaton caught himself imitating the gesture, wiping his sweaty palms on his thighs.

The pitcher returned to the mound, bent over, got the signal from his catcher, and went into his stretch. The catcher shifted his weight and set his target on the outside corner of the plate.

The pitcher rocked back and strode forward, setting all three runners in motion. The ball sped toward the heart of the plate, then slanted away from the batter and thudded into the catcher's mitt at the exact point where he'd set his target.

The batter started to swing, but changed his mind at the last minute and looked back over his shoulder at Bradshaw. The umpire hesitated for a long second, then raised his right fist, thumb extended, and shouted, "You're out!"

Keaton mimicked Bradshaw's out signal with his upraised fist and yelled "Yeah!" Farther down the row of reporters, someone said "Shit!" just as loudly. The crowd outside the press box went silent.

Davy didn't move. "Sure looked like a ball to me." As Keaton reached around him to close his laptop, his son said, "Well, I guess at least one of us is happy."

Because he remembered what it felt like to be on the wrong end of a heartbreaking call, Keaton said, "Tell you what, we'll stop at Bannings for a sundae on the way home, and I promise to root for the Reds the next two games."

"By 'root for' you mean 'bet on' I guess."

"No. That won't be necessary. Not anymore."

The mention of betting caused Keaton to look down at the box seats behind home plate. Bull Harding was nowhere to be seen.

Chapter Twenty-Eight: Taking the Fall

KEATON'S KORNER

The paths of public opinion are strange indeed. A recent survey revealed that nearly thirty percent of U.S. citizens still believed that several white Duke lacrosse players were guilty of beating and raping an African American stripper at an off-campus party.

This after (1) all rape and felony charges were dismissed; (2) the accused players were officially exonerated and declared innocent (not just "not guilty," but *innocent*) by North Carolina's Attorney General; (3) the prosecutor who pursued the false charges for political gain was disgraced, disbarred, and sentenced to jail for lying to the court.

The press in this country has a history of printing accusations in bold headlines on page one and retractions in small print on page sixteen. We have a case in point right here in Menckenburg. Dale Loren, the ex-trainer of the Menckenburg Mammoths, has been formally cleared of all charges by the grand jury and publicly exonerated by James Bloodworth's congressional committee. Yet if you mention Loren's name to the average man on the street, the first word that comes to his lips is "steroids."

So today, more than a month after being cleared of all charges, Loren remains unemployed. It's not as if there are no vacancies that fit his considerable skills. His previous position with the Mammoths remains unfilled, and there is an ongoing search for a baseball coach to replace the disgraced Stu Lammers at Central High. Maybe it's time for the search committee to look closer to home.

On the drive home, Keaton filled Davy in on the betting action he'd managed through Las Vegas on the evening's game. "So, except for the ten-dollar bet you saw me make with Harding, I didn't have any of my own money at risk on the game," he said, keeping his eyes on the road ahead of him.

"But you think the bets you swung might break the back of the East Wheeling mob?"

"If they aren't broke, they're badly bent."

"Aren't you worried they'll try to get back at you?"

Keaton checked his rearview mirror. "They don't know I had anything to do with it."

"You placed a big bet in your name. And they know you were nosing around OgrowSport before the cops shut it down. That man in the ballpark was no dope. He knew I was your son and that I played shortstop before you ever introduced us. And it seemed like he knew a lot more than that. He didn't look like somebody you'd want to mess with."

"He isn't. But he plays percentages. And there's no percentage in coming after me. They're already circling the drain. Nothing they do to me can stop that."

"Get real, Dad. You watched *The Sopranos.* Those guys are into revenge big time."

"We're a long way from New Jersey, and *The Sopranos* is just a TV show. They've got no reason to think I did anything but place a bet on the Giants. They'll pay it off if they can, and that will be that."

"If you're right about the umpire being crooked, they'll know you contacted him."

Keaton checked his rearview mirror again. He'd been checking it regularly ever since they passed the outskirts of Cincinnati. He was sorry he'd told his son so much about the betting scheme. He'd only done it to convince Davy that he wasn't betting again. At least not with his own money. Now Davy was worried, and his worry magnified the concerns Keaton already had.

Raindrops started to pelt the windshield. Keaton turned on his wipers and started to leave the fast lane, nearly colliding with a red Camaro coming up on his right. The Camaro swerved, fishtailed, and regained the lane, speeding ahead with its horn blaring.

Davy stiffened his arms against the dash. "Jesus, Dad. Watch what you're doing."

Keaton put on his blinker and crossed to the far right lane, slowing to the speed limit. "Let's talk about something else. Wasn't it a hell of a game?"

"Yeah, but the wrong team won."

"Wrong team for you, maybe. Still, it was a hell of a game. I always enjoy watching baseball with you. You've become a real fan."

"I didn't start out that way. I remember the first game you took me to. You amazed me by standing and shouting, 'All right, everybody up.' "

"And the whole crowd stood up."

"Everybody in the stadium. I thought it was magic."

"It was magic for a couple of games."

"Then I learned about the seventh-inning stretch."

"You were sharper than me. It took me five games with your granddad ordering the crowd up before I figured out the trick."

"Took away the magic, didn't it?"

"The game's still magic. You just have to look harder for it."

Davy shifted in his seat and looked at his father. "Did my granddad bet?"

"Not on baseball. He played poker, though. That's where I learned. He loved all sorts of card games. Still does."

"I remember sitting on the stairs in my pajamas and watching him and grandma play bridge with you and Mom."

"Your granddad plays bridge the way he plays poker. He loves to bluff. Trouble is, he's just as likely to fool his partner as to mislead his opponents."

"What about your granddad? Did he bet?"

"He played the ponies. Don't know whether or not he bet on ball games. Wouldn't surprise me if he did. In his day, ballplayers and reporters bet on games pretty openly."

"But all that stopped with the Black Sox."

"Yeah. Granddad covered the series and their trial. I've still got the clippings." The rain stopped and Keaton turned off the windshield wipers. "Why all the questions about the family tree? You worried you might have the gambling bug in your blood?"

"Something like that."

"Well, there's a lot to heredity. If your parents don't have any children, there's a good chance you won't have any either." He paused, waiting for a laugh that didn't come. "But I don't think there's a gambling chromosome that gets passed from generation to generation."

"How can you be sure?"

Keaton slowed and turned into the cul-de-sac where he'd once lived with Davy and Liz. "Your grandfather and great-grandfather kept any gambling they did well under control. It never affected their jobs or their families."

He parked in front of his former home. The porch light was on, but the rest of the house was dark. "I'm the only rotten limb on the family tree. And if anything, my bad example should scare you away from gambling houses."

"That's for sure."

"Looks like your mom's asleep." Keaton took Davy's arm as he swung the door open. "There's no need to tell her about tonight's betting. Even though I wasn't risking my own money."

Davy leaned back into the car before he shut the passenger

door. "Why are you so worried about Mom? You ought to be more worried about the mob."

Keaton got up early the next morning and drove straight to the Bowers' house without stopping for breakfast. When no one answered his knock, he used the key Judy had given him, stepped inside, and called, "Judy. It's Lloyd Keaton." When there was still no answer, he hurried down the hallway and burst into David's converted bedroom, saying, "Did you hear about the game?"

He stopped short inside the doorway. Judy was nowhere to be seen. Instead, Bull Harding stood at David's bedside. In his left hand he held the cords that connected David to the bank of monitors and breathing apparatus. In his right, he held a shiny black automatic pistol.

"Of course I know about the game." Harding raised the pistol so it pointed at the ceiling and gestured for Keaton to come in. "I was there, remember?"

Keaton entered and closed the door behind him.

Harding lowered the pistol. "This is a pleasant surprise. I was expecting the lady of the house. Or maybe a caretaker."

"It's Saturday," Keaton said. "The lady of the house is the caretaker today."

"Then I suppose it's only a matter of time before she appears. Why don't we just wait for her?"

Keaton looked at the cords clutched in Harding's left hand. All the bedside equipment appeared to be working. The overhead screens blinked out a running account of David's heartbeat, a green light shone at the tip of the baby monitor's antenna, and the pulse oxymeter attached to David's index finger glowed red. The red finger pointed directly at the gun in Harding's right hand.

Harding saw Keaton looking at the monitor cords. "I haven't

unplugged anything, if that's what you're thinking. I will, though, if the lady of the house doesn't come up with the money she owes us."

Harding hefted the connections in his hand as if he were about to yank them loose. "Don't worry, though. We intend to be fair about it. We'll credit her account with your winnings from last night."

"That's big of you."

"You think we didn't know where that twenty-thousand-dollar bet of yours came from? I can give you the code of the bank transfer if you'd like. We knew you were betting some of the money we'd let her keep."

"I thought you'd decided to hold off on that collection until David recovered. After all, you were responsible for his coma."

"You haven't been paying attention. I told you once we had nothing to do with Bowers's accident. Why would we want him out of commission? It just made it more difficult for us to collect our winnings."

Harding shrugged, causing the monitors behind him to flicker. But the baby monitor still glowed green. Keep him talking, Keaton thought. Judy will hear and get some help.

"You must have taken quite a hit on last night's game," Keaton said. "What happened? Did you keep a lot of the Giants' bets on your books without laying them off?"

"We thought we had an edge. Turns out we were misinformed."

"Would that edge have been Larry Bradshaw?"

"You should know. You had a long talk with him Thursday night."

"I couldn't decide whether or not he was on the take."

"That's pretty funny. Neither could I. Little Bill thought he was, though. And that's all that matters."

"You're the guys with the bankroll. You must know whether

or not he was on your pad."

"We weren't paying him. It wasn't that simple. We had a few markers of his back when he was a Triple-A umpire. He did some betting with us in the off-season. Lost a bundle on his alma mater, Ohio State. He got in over his head and we forgave some of his debt. But we kept his markers. He wasn't supposed to be consorting with gamblers, so the markers could have ruined his umpiring career."

"Nice of you."

"We never pushed it, understand? After he made the bigs, we'd ask him to give a team the benefit of the doubt maybe once, twice a year."

"And did he?"

"Damned if I know. Before last night, we'd asked him to tilt five games our way. We won four of those. Lost one fifteen-to-three rout he couldn't do anything to stop. I tell you, though, I watched the games he was supposed to be tilting, and I couldn't see him shaving any calls."

"So you think the four wins were just luck?"

"I think so. But Little Bill was convinced Bradshaw was giving us an edge. So we went all out last night. Bet the farm on the Reds."

Harding shrugged again. "What the hell, it had worked for us four out of five times." The screens behind him blinked as he shrugged, but the baby monitor still glowed green. "You were there last night. You tell me. Did it look like Bradshaw was trying to throw the game?"

"I couldn't tell either. But that last call could have gone either way."

"Oh yeah. Fucking strike three. That last call cost us the farm. But Little Bill still thinks those old markers give us a hold on Bradshaw."

Harding nodded toward David Bowers. "Too bad your friend

here hasn't woke up. It'd make my collection job a lot easier. I don't much like using force on good customers."

"Didn't stop you with Sammy Tancredi."

"Sammy was a fool. Found out about our OgrowSport connection and tried to blackmail us. I mean, how dumb can you get?"

"How'd he find out?"

"Got a little too close to Sara Galardi. Or she got a little too close to him. She took care of it, though."

"Who took care of her?"

"What is this? True confessions? Sara's out of the picture. Part of our Witless Protection Program. Out of sight, out of mind."

Keep him talking, Keaton thought. "So, will you be able to survive last night's hit?"

"It's too close for comfort. What the hell, it's time to get out of the business anyhow. Time was, we had the gambling concession all to ourselves. Now we're competing with state lotteries, Indian tribes, and any fool who wants to open a website."

Harding turned his left wrist to look at his watch and the monitors behind him flickered. "Where is Mrs. Bowers anyhow? She shouldn't leave him alone for so long."

Keaton started for the door. "I'll go get her."

Harding leveled the gun at Keaton. "Stay right where you are."

"Let me call her then," Keaton said. "There's a phone in her bedroom."

"Okay. Go ahead. But I'll tell you exactly what to say."

Keaton took out his cell phone. "What do you want me to say?"

"Just tell her you're downstairs and that there's somebody here who wants to see her. Nothing else."

Keaton punched a number on his cell phone. When a voice

answered, "Officer Mayhew here," he said, "Judy, it's Keaton. I'm downstairs with David. There's somebody here who wants to see you."

Keaton dropped the cell phone to his side without snapping it completely shut. "Will you put that gun down, Bull? It's making me nervous."

Harding dropped the gun to his side without releasing it. "What did the lady say?"

"I got her voice mail. She must be taking a shower. Or maybe an early morning swim. In that case, she'll be coming through that glass door behind you."

Harding turned halfway so that he could see the sliding glass door. "Don't see any pool."

"It's behind that hedge row."

Harding nodded toward a windowed door in the side wall to his right. "Where's that door go?"

"To the garage." Keaton slipped his cell phone into his pocket, leaving the connection with Mayhew open.

"So the lady might be out?"

"I don't know, Bull. I came to talk with David."

Harding snapped his fingers twice next to David's ear. "Yeah. Like he can hear you. You got a little something going with the wife?"

The hall door opened and Judy came through it holding a nickel-plated .45 automatic. She pointed it at Harding and said, "Please drop those cables you're holding and step away from my husband's bed."

Harding hefted the cables. "Mrs. Bowers. There's no need for firearms."

Judy stepped closer to Keaton and waved the automatic. "Then put your gun down and come out from behind my husband's bed."

Harding shook his head, laid the cables down carefully along the side of David's bed, and patted them with his left hand. Then he glanced at the garage door and quickly raised his gun.

Two shots rang out, splintering glass. Keaton dove for the floor as five more shots sounded, one after the other. Then all was quiet.

Keaton rose to his knees. Judy stood trembling in the hall doorway, her gun at her side. Bru burst through the garage door, spreading shards of broken glass as he slammed it open. Harding lay crumpled across David's midsection, his gun on the floor beside the bed.

Keaton rushed to the bed and lifted Harding off the cables that linked David to the monitoring system. The pulse oxymeter clipped to David's finger still glowed red, and the overhead monitors still tracked his heartbeat. A bullet had pierced the pillow inches from his head.

"David's still connected and breathing normally," Keaton said. He felt for a pulse in Harding's neck, trying not to look at the gaping wound above his right ear. "That's more than I can say for Harding."

Judy still stood in the doorway, the .45 dangling limply from her right hand. "I told him not to pick up his gun."

"He only went for it when he saw Bru coming at him through the garage," Keaton said.

"He did go for his gun, though," Bru said. "You saw it. It was self-defense."

"Yes," Judy said. "We both saw it. It was self-defense. We'll tell that to the police."

"The police," Bru said. "I don't know if I want to stick around for that. This gun violates my parole."

"We'll say I shot him," Judy said.

"That won't wash." Keaton stepped away from Harding's body. "The bullets that killed Harding came from the side. From Bru's gun."

"We'll say I fired Bru's gun," Judy said.

"Then who fired yours?" Keaton asked.

"Man, I just can't stick around," Bru said.

"All right," Keaton said. "Give me your gun. We'll say I fired it."

"Yeah," Bru said. "That would work."

"Okay. So give me your gun." Keaton held out his hand. "Then walk me through what you did so I can get the story straight when we call the police."

Bru hesitated, then handed Keaton his gun. "We both heard you on the baby monitor, so I got together with Judy. I told her to go through the main door and be, like, a distraction, while I came in through the garage."

Keaton took Bru's gun to the garage door. "So you set him up."

"Yeah, man," Bru said. "And it worked. Slick as greased shit."

Keaton lifted Bru's automatic. "He caught sight of you through the garage window and went for his gun. That's when you fired."

"Yeah, man. You got that right."

"How many times?"

"I don't know. Three, maybe four times."

"And Harding shot once."

"Yeah, but he didn't hit nothing," Bru said. "Barely cleared his weapon before I dropped him."

"Judy," Keaton said. "How many shots did you fire?"

"Two."

"At Harding?"

"Of course."

"Did you hit anything?"

"I don't know. I don't think so."

Keaton stood in the garage door and pointed the barrel of Bru's automatic at Harding's body. Then he examined the curtains and glass wall behind the bed. "Okay. I think I get it."

"So I'll leave. And then you can call the cops." Bru started toward the door. "One more thing."

"What's that?" Keaton asked.

"You better fire my gun. Get that shit they check for on your hands."

Keaton turned the automatic over in his hands. "So the gun's still loaded? And the safety's off?"

"Yeah, man. Just pull the trigger."

Keaton leveled the automatic at Bru. "I think you better stick around, Bru. To make sure I've got the story straight."

"What you saying, man?"

"I'm saying I want you here when the cops come, and I'm prepared to shoot you if you move."

"You crazy, man?"

Judy moved from the hall doorway. "Lloyd. What are you doing?"

"I'm calling the cops." Keaton took his cell phone from his pocket. The line was still open, so he spoke into the mouthpiece. "Where the hell are you, Mayhew?"

"Stop it, Lloyd," Judy said. "Let Bru go."

Mayhew's voice came over the cell phone. "I'm trying to come in around the pool. Without upsetting anyone. Isn't that what you wanted?"

"Well, come faster," Keaton said. "Everything's under control here. For now."

Officer Mayhew appeared at the glass door leading to the pool area. Keaton backed toward the door and slid it open without lowering the automatic he had aimed at Bru.

Mayhew came through the door and gestured toward Harding's body with his own automatic. "Sweet Jesus. What happened here?"

"It was self-defense," Bru said.

Keaton kept his automatic pointed at Bru. "Here's the gun. There's the perp."

Bru shook his head. "Ain't no perp, man. It was self-defense."

"That so?" Mayhew asked.

"Something like it. You'll want to take him into custody anyhow." Keaton handed Bru's gun to Mayhew. "This gun of his is a parole violation. Might even have a slimy history."

"Chicken-shit charge, man." Bru addressed Mayhew. "I just saved this man's white ass. That dead dude had the drop on him with a gun."

Mayhew pointed at the gun on the floor beside David's bed. "That the gun? The one I heard you tell him to put down?"

"That's it," Keaton said. "He lowered it. He wasn't going to shoot me."

"He raised it again," Bru said.

"When you came at him with your gun," Keaton said.

"Then it wasn't self-defense?" Mayhew asked.

"It certainly was," Judy said.

Keaton shrugged. "It'll take some sorting out."

"Nothing to sort out, man," Bru said. "He went for his gun. We all saw it. And he's likely the man that shoved my brother-in-law down the elevator shaft."

"Anyhow," Keaton said. "There's more to sort out than whether this was self-defense."

Mayhew unclipped his phone from his belt. "Let's start sorting, then. Meanwhile, I'm going to call in our crime scene folks."

"While we're waiting, I've got a little story that might help with the sorting," Keaton said.

Mayhew covered the mouthpiece of his phone and said, "I'm listening."

"When I was about eight, there was an older couple living across the alley from us. They had a grandson, Brucie, about a year older than me, who came to visit them once or twice a year. During one of Brucie's visits, he and I went down the street to play with a friend of mine, Dickie Hager. Dickie wasn't in, but his mother let us come in and read his comics while we waited. Dickie kept all his comics in this little cubbyhole under the stairs that was just big enough for the two of us, and we waited for about a half hour. When Dickie didn't show up, we left. But Brucie took two of Dickie's comics with him. Just shoved them under his shirt and walked right past Dickie's mom."

"Man, what's this kiddy story got to do with that dead dude there?" Bru said.

"Just wait," Keaton said. "Brucie and I went back to my house and played with my toy soldiers. I had this one favorite soldier that I always chose first. A plastic soldier crawling on his belly with a hand grenade in one hand and a pistol in the other. We quit playing at dinnertime and Brucie went back to his grandparents' house.

"A couple of days later, when I went to play with my soldiers, I couldn't find my favorite one."

"No shit," Bru said.

"You know," Keaton said. "It wasn't until I was in college that I finally figured out what had happened to that soldier."

"So you're a little slow on the uptake," Bru said. "I still don't see what that's got to do with us here and now."

"I'm coming to that. The point is, I grew up in a fairly sheltered environment. Theft was something that happened on *Columbo* or in the Dick Tracy comic strip. It never occurred to me that Brucie took my soldier. But something a lot like that happened to me in college."

"What happened, man?" Bru said. "Somebody steal your freshman beanie?"

"No, but I had a good friend." Keaton nodded toward David Bowers's bed. "That friend right there, as a matter of fact, who was crippled for life in a drive-by shooting. Bad luck, we figured. Happened to be in the wrong place at the wrong time."

Keaton shrugged. "But, like I said, I grew up in a sheltered environment. I had no gut level experience with racial hatred. The Watts riots, the Detroit fires, those were just newspaper headlines. Other cities. Nowhere near our suburb.

"But then last month some research I was doing for my column got me thinking. I was reading about a key defense argument in the O.J. Simpson trial. His lawyers cited statistics that fewer than one in twenty-five hundred spouses who abuse their mates actually go on to kill them. But they had the argument backward. It's a common fallacy perpetuated by defense lawyers. If you've got an actual murder on your hands, and the victim has a previous history of spousal abuse, ninety percent of the time you don't have to look any farther than the abusive spouse to find the murderer. That's a statistic that O.J.'s defense team didn't cite."

"You whities," Bru said. "Always got a hard-on for O.J. Can't stand it that the brother was innocent. Let it go, man."

"Well, there were a few racial enclaves around South Bend when David and I were at Notre Dame. Polish Americans, African Americans. If you were to take any one of the blacks in the ghetto, the odds were pretty low that any one of them would be involved in a drive-by shooting."

Mayhew pocketed his cell phone. "What's your point, Lloyd?"

"If you look at it from the standpoint of the victim, though," Keaton nodded toward David Bowers, "my friend was dating a black girl whose older brother fairly seethed with racial hatred."

"Oh, man," Bru said. "You just stop right there."

"Lloyd, that's crazy," Judy said. "The police investigated Bru. He had an alibi."

"Air-tight alibi," Bru said. "Anyhow, the statute of limitations long since run out on that one."

"I'm not sure there is a statute of limitations on hate crimes," Keaton said. "They convicted Medgar Evers's killer thirty years after the fact."

"Police cleared me, man," Bru said. "That's all blood under the bridge."

"Maybe David's shooting was random. Maybe Brucie didn't steal my toy soldier. I don't want to argue about it."

"Damn well better not," Bru said.

"But the O.J. case started me thinking." Keaton nodded toward Bull Harding's body. "Harding there had a gun, but he didn't come to kill anyone. He just wanted to collect a debt. We were talking gambling, and he was pretty frank with me. I don't read a lot of crime fiction, but when the bad guy is holding a gun and spouting all his secrets, he usually doesn't bother to lie.

"Harding told me he had nothing to do with David's drop down the elevator shaft. This was after he all but admitted the East Wheeling mob did in Sammy Tancredi. So why would he lie about David?"

"He's a bookie, man," Bru said. "Those odds fuckers lie just to keep in practice."

"Maybe," Keaton said. "But the mob had nothing to gain by harming David. And his coma made it a lot harder for them to collect their winnings."

"So you think his statement was like a deathbed denial," Mayhew said. "But if the mob didn't shove your friend's wheelchair into that elevator shaft, who did?"

"Look at the cast of characters," Keaton said. "We've got brother Bru here, newly arrived on the scene, fresh out of the Indiana State Prison in Michigan City, with no more love for the white race than he ever had. And certainly no love for the white guy who married his sister."

Bru flew at Keaton, shouting, "What you saying, mother-fucker?"

Mayhew stepped between Bru and Keaton. "If I understand him, I think he's saying you shoved his friend down that elevator shaft."

"He sure as shit can't prove that," Bru said.

"Maybe not. But Bru was on the scene, and Bru knew about the elevator's defect. I'm guessing he heard Judy and David arguing about David's gambling loss and decided to do his sister a favor." Keaton turned to Judy. "You told me that you and David had been arguing."

Judy shook her head. "But Lloyd, Bru's been helping me nurse David."

"He's just been waiting for a chance to finish him off without arousing suspicions." Keaton pointed to David's pillow. "There's a bullet hole in that pillow right next to David's head. From Bru's gun. If Harding hadn't fallen across David, Bru might have fired again."

"Man, where you get this shit?" Bru said.

Judy shook her head and took a step toward her brother. "It's not true, is it Bru? Tell me it's not true."

"Course it's not true," Bru said.

"It is true, Judy," Keaton said. "You may not want to admit it, but you know it's true."

Judy spoke as if she were in a trance. "No. I don't believe it. He's been helping me with David."

Bru moved toward Judy. "You all right, sis?" He put out his left hand as if to steady her, then pulled her roughly to him and grabbed the automatic that still dangled from her right hand. Then he swung her around so that she shielded him from Mayhew.

Bru leveled Judy's gun at Mayhew. "All right, officer, just stand easy. I want you to take that gun of yours by the barrel and bring it to me nice and easy. Then do the same thing with the gun Keaton gave you."

The officer transferred his automatic to his left hand, holding it by the barrel.

"Don't do it, Mayhew," Keaton said. "Just stand right where you are."

"Who the fuck are you to be giving orders?" Bru said.

Keaton stepped between Mayhew and Bru's automatic. "I'm the guy you're going to have to shoot before you shoot the officer."

"It's all right," Mayhew said. "Let him go. He can't get far."

"It's not all right," Keaton said. "Keep your gun. You may have to use it. Bru's not going to use that one he's holding."

"What kind of crazy shit is this?" Bru said.

Keaton took a step toward Bru, backing him toward the one wall in the room that didn't have a door in it. "You're not going to shoot, Bru. You know it and I know it."

Bru pointed his gun barrel at Keaton and shook it. "Just stay where you are, motherfucker."

"You try shooting me and the officer will gun you down," Keaton took another step forward. "But you won't shoot me. Not while I'm looking you in the eye. You only shoot unsuspecting whites on street corners or shove them down elevator shafts from behind."

Bru took a step backward, dragging Judy with him. "Don't make no never mind to me whether you're looking me in the eye or mooning me with your white ass. You're so close I can't miss you."

"But you're not going to shoot, Bru," Keaton said. "You know you're not going to pull that trigger. You do and you'll sign your death warrant."

Bru took another step backward, pinning himself against the wall. "I ain't going back to stir. Not on some trumped-up charge. That thing with the elevator. That was an accident."

"Like David's drive-by shooting was an accident," Keaton said.

"I wasn't there, man."

Keaton took another step forward. "But you knew it was going down. Don't tell me you didn't."

Bru tightened his grip on Judy's neck. "Not another step, man. Another step and I shoot."

Keaton was almost close enough to touch Judy. He reached out. "Judy, give me your free hand."

Bru shook his gun in the direction of Keaton's outstretched hand as if he wanted to swat it. "Don't be messing with me, man. I'll shoot her too."

"Listen to me, Judy," Keaton said. "He's not going to shoot you. Now hold out your hand."

Judy reached out her hand. Keaton grabbed it and yanked as hard as he could. Judy stumbled forward, pulling Bru along until he released his hold on her.

The second he released his sister, Bru pulled the trigger. One shot sounded. Then a second and a third.

Keaton tumbled backward to the floor, pulling Judy down on top of him. Another shot rang out above them.

Keaton rolled free of Judy and got to his knees. Bru sat slumped against the wall, a red stain blossoming on his shirt front. He managed to say "shit" before red bubbles popped from his mouth and dribbled down his chin.

Mayhew kicked Bru's dropped automatic out of reach as he used his cell phone to request an ambulance. Then he turned to Keaton. "You all right?"

Keaton stood and helped Judy to her feet. "Think so."

Mayhew shook his head. "He shot you at point-blank range."

Keaton nodded toward the automatic Mayhew had just kicked aside. "His gun was loaded with blanks."

Judy knelt beside her brother and cradled his head in her

hands. "Oh, Bru. You bloody fool."

"How'd you know he was shooting blanks?" Mayhew asked.

"I'd just watched Judy fire twice at that solid wall of windows without harming any curtains or breaking any glass."

Mayhew looked at Bru. "Did he know he only had blanks?"

"He must have. He'd given Judy the gun in the first place."

Judy let Bru's head slip down onto her lap. A red trail smeared her white blouse. "It's the gun he gave me when we brought David home from the hospital. When we were ambushed."

"I'm pretty sure he staged that ambush," Keaton said. "I don't know whether he intended to have David killed to keep him quiet or whether he just wanted to divert suspicion from himself. I do know he gave you a gun loaded with blanks so you couldn't defend your husband."

Judy shook her head. "Bru. Oh, Bru."

"Anyhow," Keaton said. "The driving rain screwed up whatever plan he had. You couldn't see your hand in front of your face. The ambushers bailed. Maybe Bru's shots scared them. Or maybe it was all just a show to make Bru look good and innocent."

Mayhew scribbled something in his pocket notebook. "That's an awful lot of 'maybes' and guesswork."

"It's the only way it makes sense," Keaton said.

Mayhew pocketed the notebook. "So you didn't really know he was shooting blanks when you went after him."

"I was pretty sure. I had the house odds with me. Like I said, it's the only way it made sense."

"So you set him up," Mayhew said.

"He set himself up."

"He's my brother," Judy said. "You didn't have to shoot him."

"Judy, Judy," Keaton said. "He was threatening to shoot you."

"But you knew he didn't have any bullets in his gun. You

could have told the officer that."

"I wasn't sure about the blanks. If I'd been wrong, telling Mayhew could have gotten us all killed. He'd already tried to kill your husband. Probably more than once."

Sirens sounded and a flood of police and medical personnel inundated the room. Two paramedics loaded Bru onto a stretcher, and Judy asked if she could accompany him to the hospital. Mayhew nodded, then went off to confer with two photographers, gesturing to show them what he wanted recorded around Harding's body. When everyone seemed to be employed to his satisfaction, he returned to Keaton.

"I'll need a statement from you," he said. "Can you be in my office around one o'clock?"

"Okay."

"I guess it's all right for you to go, then."

"Somebody needs to stay and watch David."

"We'll have a slew of people here for at least three hours. If we're ready to leave before his wife returns, I'll give you a call."

Before he left, Keaton walked over to David's bedside. "Well, buddy," he said, squeezing his hand, "I'm not sure how much of that registered on you, but I think your survival odds just improved considerably."

EPILOGUE

KEATON'S KORNER

It's a couple of weeks before the Mammoths' season will officially begin, but local baseball junkies can get an immediate fix by coming to see the Central High Lancers open their season against St. Joes' Fighting Irish. The game starts at 3:00 p.m. on Menckenburg's sunken diamond.

The Lancers are defending municipal league champs, and it's a good time to welcome new coach Dale Loren and wish the team well in its bid for a repeat crown.

Keaton arrived late for Central High's first game. Two teenagers manning the old-fashioned scoreboard beyond the center-field fence were hanging a zero in the fourth inning column for the visiting team. The scoreboard summary had Davy's home team ahead four to nothing.

Keaton spotted Liz in the stands behind first base and went to join her. She was sitting beside a slim, attractive blonde woman whom he vaguely recognized, but whose name he couldn't place. He sat down next to his ex-wife and said, "How's it going?"

"We're up four-zip, and Davy knocked in two of the runs with a double in the first inning." Liz nodded toward the woman on her left. "Have you met Dale Loren's wife Robin?"

Keaton held out his hand. "Of course. I remember you from the hearings in Washington."

Robin leaned across Liz to shake Keaton's hand. "I want to thank you for everything you did to support Dale, both before and after the hearings."

Keaton nodded. "He deserved it."

"But he wasn't getting much help from anywhere else," Robin said. "So he really appreciated yours."

"Happy to do it."

"Why so late?" Liz asked.

"The Bowers deposition," Keaton said. "It ran into overtime. Damned lawyers kept picking at my story."

"I read about that case," Robin said. "A black man shot a white intruder in his sister's home on Peach Tree Court, and then was severely wounded by a white patrolman who arrived late on the scene. Right?"

"That's one version of the story," Keaton said.

"And the black man is suing the city," Robin said. "Isn't he paralyzed?"

"From the waist down," Keaton said. "It's the first glimmering of justice in the whole case."

"But wasn't the patrolman suspended?" Robin asked.

"For a short time. He's been reinstated. He did nothing wrong."

"So you think the black man's lawsuit wasn't justified?"

"I know it wasn't. I was there." Keaton bit his lip, then continued. "I'm sure he'll get everything he deserves. He has a criminal trial of his own coming up."

"Don't get Lloyd started on that case," Liz said. "We're here to enjoy the game."

"Oh, sorry," Robin said.

"That's okay." Keaton leaned back against the bleacher seat behind him and shielded his eyes against the sun. Somewhere along the line, the wheels of justice had come flying off. But he thought his deposition had gone well. Bru had little hope of winning his civil suit, and there was a pretty good chance he'd be nailed for shoving David down the elevator shaft. Not that either decision would bring David out of his coma.

On the field, Davy made a nifty backhanded catch deep in the hole to start a double play and end a scoring threat in the top of the fifth inning. Keaton leapt to his feet, cheering. Then he sat down and patted Liz's hand. "Nothing beats this," he said. "There's just no place on earth I'd rather be."

The visiting team scored a run on a walk, an error, and a single in the top of the sixth, narrowing the lead to four to one. Then, in the top half of the seventh inning, the Central High pitcher lost track of the plate. With one out, he walked a batter, gave up a single, and then walked two more batters to make the score four to two.

At that point, Dale Loren went to the mound, took the ball from his pitcher, a lanky left-hander with a face full of freckles, and waved in a relief pitcher. The departing pitcher ignored the obligatory pats on his butt as he left the field and took a seat alone at the far end of the dugout.

The relief pitcher struck out the first batter he faced, then gave up a double that plated two runs and tied the score. The freckle-faced pitcher who had put the tying run on base slumped forward on the bench.

Keaton watched Dale Loren walk to the end of the dugout, sit down, and put his arm around the dejected teenager.

"I'll bet Stu Lammers never put his arm around a player in all the fifteen years he coached," Keaton said.

"That boy on the bench is about the age our son would have been," Robin said.

Liz put her hand on Keaton's arm. "The Lorens lost a boy in a car accident."

"A drunk driver." Robin tightened her arms across her chest. "Nearly two years ago."

"I'm sorry," Keaton said. "I'd forgotten that."

The relief pitcher, who looked at least as shaken as the boy on the bench, walked the next batter on four straight pitches to load the bases. Loren left the dugout and went to the mound, where he put his hand on the pitcher's shoulder, said a few words, and patted him on the back before returning to the dugout.

"What'd he say to the boy?" Liz asked.

"Something deep, like 'Throw strikes,' " Keaton said. "It's not so much the words he's saying. He's hoping to steady the boy through the laying on of hands."

"How can this foolish game mean so much?" Robin said.

Keaton smiled. "It casts a spell."

The first pitch to the next batter was a strike, eliciting a smattering of applause from the stands. Part sarcasm, part encouragement, Keaton thought.

The hitter swung mightily at the next pitch and launched a towering pop-up behind the infield. Davy circled under the ball, waving his arms and shouting, "Mine. All mine."

Keaton stood up as soon as the ball reached the top of its arc and started downward.

The ball settled into Davy's glove for the third out, and he started to trot in to bat in the bottom of the seventh. He stopped short of the dugout when he caught sight of his father on his feet in the stands.

Keaton turned toward the spectators, looped his arm upward, and shouted, "All right, you fans. Everybody up!"

And the magic still worked.

Read ahead for an exciting preview of the next Lloyd Keaton Mystery

A PLAYER TO BE MAIMED LATER

Coming in 2013 from Five Star

Lloyd Keaton—who killed a successful sportswriting career with a gambling addiction—gets a second chance at the big time. Blaze Stender, a retired Major League superstar, asks his old friend to write his biography, and offers a good slice of the impressive publishing advance. Stender hopes the book will help him capture the only honor that has eluded him, election to baseball's Hall of Fame.

Keaton is barely on the job two weeks when Stender's pleasure boat crashes into a Lake Erie breakwall; the pitcher is missing and presumed dead. The accident triggers an outpouring of fan praise not only for the popular pitcher's on-field exploits but also his charity work, including the Tommy Fund, founded in memory of his only child.

With the help and encouragement of Stender's widow, Keaton continues his work on the biography. He soon discovers, however, that the facts of his old friend's life are at odds with his popular image, and that Stender was keeping some dark secrets, including blackmail payments that could be related to a mysterious death. Stender's widow tells him to stop; she doesn't want her husband's image tarnished by a tell-all biography. But Keaton can't stop following a story, even when it leads to another killing and the reporter himself becomes the target of an unknown assailant.

ABOUT THE AUTHOR

John Billheimer, a native West Virginian, lives in Portola Valley, California. He holds an engineering Ph.D. from Stanford University and is the author of the "funny, sometimes touching" Owen Allison mystery series set in Appalachia's coalfields. The *Drood Review* voted his first book, *The Contrary Blues,* one of the ten best mysteries of 1998. Four subsequent novels, *Highway Robbery, Dismal Mountain, Drybone Hollow,* and *Stonewall Jackson's Elbow,* explore road-building scandals, strip mining, phony insurance claims, and bank fraud in the Mountain State. He has also written *Baseball and the Blame Game,* a nonfiction look at scapegoating in the Major Leagues.

More information about the author can be found on his website, www.johnbillheimer.com.